I0704046

Faith-Filled
Fiction™

www.faith-filledfiction.com | www.vikkikestell.com

STEALTH TRIUMPH
Nanostealth | Book 6
Vikki Kestell
Also Available in eBook Format

BOOKS BY VIKKI KESTELL

NANOSTEALTH

Book 1: *Stealthy Steps*
Book 2: *Stealth Power*
Book 3: *Stealth Retribution*
Book 4: *Deep State Stealth*, 2019 Selah Award Winner
Book 5: *Stealth Insurgence*
Book 6: *Stealth Triumph*
Stealth Genesis, A Nanostealth Prequel

A PRAIRIE HERITAGE

Book 1: *A Rose Blooms Twice*
Book 2: *Wild Heart on the Prairie*
Book 3: *Joy on This Mountain*
Book 4: *The Captive Within*
Book 5: *Stolen*
Book 6: *Lost Are Found*
Book 7: *All God's Promises*
Book 8: *The Heart of Joy—A Short Story*
Book 9: *Rose of RiverBend*

GIRLS FROM THE MOUNTAIN

Book 1: *Tabitha*
Book 2: *Tory*
Book 3: *Sarah Redeemed*

LAYNIE PORTLAND

Book 1: *Laynie Portland, Spy Rising—The Prequel*
Book 2: *Laynie Portland, Retired Spy*
Book 3: *Laynie Portland, Renegade Spy*
Book 4: *Laynie Portland, Spy Resurrected*
Book 5: *Vyper, A Laynie Portland Sequel*

THE TAHOE MYSTERIES

Book 1: *Number 1 with a Bullet*
Book 2: *Be Quick or be Dead*
Book 3: *Death on the Big Blue*, 2020
Murder by Accident,
   A Miss Finch Prequel

STAND-ALONE BOOKS

I Can't Hear You,
   A Christian Psychological Thrille
The Christian and the Vampire,
   A Short Story

Stealth Triumph

Nanostealth | Book 6
Vikki Kestell
Also Available in eBook Format

THE NANOMITES HAVE UNCOVERED a vast international intrigue, a conspiracy comprising thousands of individuals in key positions across many nations. They call themselves *the Global Community*, and they are led by the wealthy, powerful, and elite—militant ideologues who believe *they* possess the right to determine the future of humankind.

The nanomites prefer the term Jayda and Zander have given the conspirators: *the Cabal.*

Jayda Cruz, members of the Global Community speak of themselves in lofty, righteous terms; however, the noun "cabal" means a plot or scheme with treacherous objectives. "Cabal" more accurately expresses the Global Community's agenda as well as their methodologies.

It was the Cabal's plan to engineer and deploy a highly contagious virus—a virus that has killed untold millions around the earth. The loss of life has crippled the world's food producers, manufacturing industries, and supply chains. Under the weight of increasing terrorist strikes, abnormal crop failures, and natural disasters on a scale of Biblical proportions, nation after nation descends into famine and anarchy.

As America faces food and fuel shortages never before seen in her history, panic grows. Urban infrastructures collapse. Law enforcement crumbles. Violent gangs roam city streets unchallenged, looting and burning —and some of those gangs are paid to target opponents of the Global Community.

When Jayda and Zander peer into the nanomites' counterinsurgency activities, they observe odd movements within the Cabal's leadership. They soon realize that they are witnessing a "bugging out" of top Cabal figures, a retreat to a safe haven somewhere in the Atlantic.

What is this new threat looming on the horizon? Jayda and Zander can only surmise that it must be *something more terrifying than what is already overwhelming the nations.*

⌘⌘⌘⌘

Scripture Quotations

DEDICATION

Dedicated to the faithful workers in Christ:
Jesus told them, "The harvest is plentiful,
but the workers are few.
Ask the Lord of the harvest, therefore,
to send out workers into his harvest field.
Go! I am sending you out like lambs among wolves."
Luke 10:2-3, NIV

ACKNOWLEDGEMENTS

From my heart to yours,
thank you,
Cheryl Adkins and **Greg McCann**.

COVER DESIGN

Vikki Kestell

PROLOGUE

Although contemporaneous in setting,
this story is a work of fiction.
I pray it strengthens
the Body of Christ for what is ahead.
Be fruitful, my friends.

MAY 1

I SAT ON THE SOFA WITH BONNIE. She was fed, burped, diapered, wide awake, and perfectly content. And today she was three weeks old.

"Who's a pretty baby?" I cooed. Bonnie Lu's eyes fixed on mine. She waved her arms and legs with uncoordinated excitement. Then . . . a wondrous thing happened.

"Oh, Bonnie Lu. You precious girl!" I turned my head. "Psst. Papa, come here, quick! I want to show you something."

"Working on my message for Sunday, Jay."

"It will only take a minute—and I'm positive you'll find the interruption worth it."

Zander left the kitchen table where he was eating lunch, his Bible on the left, his notes on his right. He plopped down beside me on the couch, and I placed Bonnie Lu on his lap so that her head was rested on his knees and she faced him. Then I got up and moved behind the couch where I could watch.

"What?" he asked. "What did you want to show me?"

"Talk to Bonnie Lu. And smile while you do."

I hoped she would show him what she had showed me.

"Talk to her and say what?"

"Oh, the usual. You know—that you love her. That God loves her even more. That's she's beautiful, made in the image of the Lord."

"I can do that!" Zander bent to his task with enthusiasm.

He smiled his love down on her. "Little Bonnie Lu? I'm your papa, honey. Hey, precious girl! Look here, baby. Do you know how much Daddy loves you?"

Bonnie kicked a little and waved her hands. While Zander spoke, her dark eyes slowly tracked toward his voice and face. We both saw the moment she "found" him. Her little mouth opened, and her deep brown eyes widened as if she were amazed.

"Hey, Bonnie Lu!" Zander crooned. Without taking his eyes off of her, he said to me, "So, what am I looking for?"

"Keep talking and smiling. You'll find out."

"Hey, little Bonita Lucia!"

Bonnie gurgled . . . and it happened.

Her mouth turned up in a toothless smile and two small dimples popped out on her pudgy cheeks not far from the corners of her mouth. She kicked harder. She grinned up at her Papa.

Zander gasped. "Oh, wow! She *smiled!*"

"Was that worth the interruption?"

Zander couldn't answer; he was undone. "Oh, my Lord Jesus," he groaned. "Oh, thank you! Thank you for this blessing! Bonnie, you are so beautiful!"

Bonnie saw Zander's countenance crumple. She went still. Her lower lip trembled.

I leaned over Zander's shoulder. Caught Bonnie's gaze. "It's okay, Baby Bonnie. Your daddy is okay."

Zander dragged his sleeve across his face. "I am never going to be just 'okay' again."

I was right there with him—besotted beyond all belief and so happy that all my excess joy leaked out of my eyes.

"Welcome to the first of many firsts, Papa. Guess I need to record this in her baby book, huh? Today our Bonnie Lu smiled for the first time, and it was glorious!"

We have recorded this important milestone for you, Jayda Cruz.

"Thank you, Nano." When I added to Bonnie's baby book, the nanomites' records would prove invaluable.

Zander rose from the couch, lifting Bonnie into his arms. I laughed again as, with his free arm, he drew me into his embrace. With Bonnie nestled between us, Zander leaned in for a long, unhurried, and deepening kiss.

It was just getting good, *really* good . . . when the nanomites spoke up again.

We must now return to our work, Jayda Cruz and Zander Cruz. If you need us, we will bring our attention back to you.

Zander and I snickered. Our eyes but inches apart, I mouthed the word "clueless."

Not pulling back an iota, that glint in his gaze promising me we were not finished, Zander replied, "We understand, Nano. The Lord bless your work for him and oh, by the way? *Lights out.*"

⌘⌘⌘⌘

PART 1: SOWING

When the Lamb opened the third seal,

I heard the third living creature say, "Come!"

I looked, and there before me was a black horse!

Its rider was holding a pair of scales in his hand.

Then I heard what sounded like a voice

among the four living creatures, saying,

"Two pounds of wheat for a day's wages,

and six pounds of barley for a day's wages,

and do not damage the oil and the wine!"

Revelation 6:5-6

CHAPTER 1

BY THE TIME THE FIRST FULL week of May drew to a close, Zander and I were convinced that the fabric of American society was unraveling right before our eyes—and we saw no way to slow or stop it. The ordinary freedoms and carefree lives we'd known while we were growing up were gone, and they would not return. Disease, disaster, crop failure, and ongoing supply chain issues were impacting all aspects of what we had taken for granted for decades.

Instant gratification? Instantly vanished.

Limitless varieties of imported fruits and vegetables? Gone like they'd never existed.

Availability of chicken and eggs? Decimated by avian flu.

Shelves fully stocked with more food than we needed? Empty more often than filled.

The independence on which we Americans prided ourselves to the point of idolatry? Swirling around the drain in an agonizing death spiral.

Being a loner and "doing things my way" in this changing world was no longer tenable. No longer an option.

Few were prepared for what overtook us. Most eyes peeping out from behind masks were drowning in fear. Radiating a palpable anxiety.

The virus raged hotter, hospitals continued to overflow, thousands died and were buried in mass graves. Houses stood vacant; entire neighborhoods went quiet.

The most vulnerable of our citizens disappeared into their homes lest they join the ranks of the infected. Overnight, this "ghost" population became totally dependent on family or the kindness of friends to bring them their medications and enough food to get by.

That's part of what I meant when I said that being a loner was no longer an option.

Sporadic brownouts rolled across the country, leaving cities in temporary darkness and creating gaps in every sort of service dependent upon the electricity and internet—phones, social media, credit cards, direct deposit, and electronic banking, to name a few.

We had a standing video call with Roberto, María, and Izzie every Tuesday evening, but our last call with them hadn't happened until Sunday afternoon. A storm had knocked out a substation in southwest Texas. The added load had, in turn, overloaded power grids across Lea, Eddy, Otero, and Doña Ana counties.

When Las Cruces lost power, Zander's parents' place went dark. No cell service? No scheduled video call.

It only took a few of these experiences for people to realize how fragile our infrastructure really was . . . and how dependent we were on technologies that could fail at any time.

School buildings remained closed. Teachers used whatever form of distance learning their district adopted. Businesses that weren't designated "essential" stayed shut down or operated remotely. Those businesses that switched to a remote work environment could function only when the electrical grid and the internet were up and running.

At the same time, some designated essential services, unable to staff appropriately, had to close their doors anyway—adding to the "pinch" citizens were already feeling. Stores that managed to stay open had to employ armed security guards by the dozen or arm their workers to discourage the brazen robberies that had become quite unremarkable.

With refineries understaffed and unable to meet demand, gas stations rationed fuel or shut down. In turn, truckers carrying the nations' food supplies occasionally found themselves stranded . . . and robbed at gunpoint. In response, trucking unions formed convoys and hired armed "shepherds" to see the convoys safely to their destinations. The strategy protected the trucks and their cargoes—but it radically slowed deliveries and drove up prices.

⌘

BEFORE THINGS STARTED TO GET really tight, I bought up a substantial amount of extra nonperishables, thinking to create a small buffer for ourselves, Abe, and Emilio. Then I started spending more than my usual amount on groceries each week, picking up whatever was available in quantity to add to our buffer.

Zander and I set our hearts not to hoard, only to pad Abe's and our cupboards in addition to what we needed for the week. However, if an item was low on the shelves, we took our share, no more.

Emilio, going on twelve, now spent two nights a week with us. We found that he managed to pack away as much food as Zander, yet another reason to stock our shelves deeper. We made sure Abe had plenty to feed that boy, and we no longer took Abe's money when I went to the store.

"Feeding Emilio is our responsibility now," Zander told Abe. "We'll keep your fridge and cupboards stocked; you use the foster money to see to his other needs and keep some back for unexpected expenses, okay? Hopefully, the courts will open in a few months and the adoption will go through. Then he'll move in with us and visit *you*."

Abe grinned. "Grateful to God ever' day for bringing that boy into my life. Sure do love him."

We sure did too.

But over the following week the nanomites blew us away. Apparently, they had located online sources for bulk foods. The next thing we knew, boxes of freeze-dried meat, fruit, soup mixes, and main courses landed on our porch. Cases of powdered eggs, canned bacon, baby food, and other necessities arrived via UPS.

Zander Cruz, Jayda Cruz, these supplies are for long-term storage and emergency use.

"Nano, where in the world do we even keep this stuff?" Zander asked, surveying the abundance stacked in our living room.

We recommend that you put them in the printer room. You will need them.

"Right . . ."

Initially, when the lockdowns began and we went to online church services, the board had been concerned that offerings would decline, that expenses would outstrip giving. Zander, thinking to economize, had tried to decline a salary. What Malware paid us for "my" research and analysis work was more than enough to meet our simple needs.

But offerings *hadn't* declined. In fact, the members of our congregation were giving more generously than usual and our online worshippers were also giving. This enabled the church to contribute substantially to several food pantries across the community, help those in the church who were hardest hit by the pandemic, and reach out to others in our community who were in danger of losing their homes or cars.

And the board insisted that Zander receive a monthly salary.

We prayed over the extra money, asking the Lord what he'd have us do with it, asking him for both wisdom and selflessness. We tithed, paid our adoption lawyer ahead of schedule, added to our savings account, and we socked away a bit of cash, an emergency stash in case the banks closed permanently.

We squirreled our emergency cash away in the garage basement along with our emergency rations. Not only was the existence of a room under the garage a closely held secret, but a body of newly minted nanotroops also guarded the printshop.

*Our troops can float like a butterfly, sting like a bee, Zander Cruz—a bee loaded with no more than a few milliamps of current—yet a sting sufficient to take down an assailant. Our tribes will knock out all comers without harming them, but they **will** stop them.*

As you know, we require the printer far more than you need these emergency funds. They will protect the printer for us and protect the money and food for you.

Shaking his head, Zander enlisted Emilio to help him mount shelves in the printer room and stack our "Zombie Apocalypse" supplies there—the stuff that would keep for twenty years . . . the stuff we wouldn't use unless our situation became drastically worse.

Worse? We had no idea.

⌘

WEEKS LATER, WHEN THE ABILITY of grocers to stock their shelves declined further, people panicked. Riots broke out in three stores. People loaded carts and ran them to their cars without paying. One store was stripped to its bones in less than an hour . . . and virus cases, traced to the riots, surged.

In response, the managers of groceries across Albuquerque formed an alliance. In the alliance's first act, they lowered the number of shoppers allowed inside their stores at any given time and set strict limits on how much of any given item or food type a shopper could buy. Then they set a total dollar limit per visit as well. In this way, they announced, everyone could leave the store with a smaller but balanced amount of food.

The new policies gave birth to "hopping," the practice of shoppers going from store to store, often daily, buying up whatever they could lay hands on for the lowest price.

To thwart the hoppers, the allied stores brainstormed another strategy. They would stamp the backs of shoppers' hands with indelible, hard-to-remove ink. Anyone going through checkout had their hand stamped with the day's date, and every store in the alliance agreed to honor the crude process. They would refuse store entry to individuals whose stamp was less than six days old.

The same rules applied to shoppers who ordered their groceries online and scheduled a time to pick them up. It meant that once a week I would leave Bonnie Lu with Zander or Janice to fetch our order. But now I had to take Belicia and Abe with me because I could no longer claim their orders for them.

These restrictions, ensuring that everyone got something, backfired another way: They did not account for larger families. Parents with more than two children could never buy enough to feed everyone, so they sent their older kids through the lines with cash.

Schools, while closed, organized drive-through meal lines, handing out bagged breakfasts and lunches, but only to school-age children. Most parents' days now centered around school meal lines and grocery stores. Single parents had it the worst because they could not do it all and still hold down a job.

We figured ration cards weren't that far off. It was the only means of ensuring that larger families got their fair share.

We watched the specter of starvation raise its ugly head in our city, our state, and our nation, while the two nanoclouds provided running commentary . . . and advice.

Jayda Cruz, Zander Cruz, the situation you see will only worsen, which is why we ordered supplies for you online. Now is the time to act preemptively.

Zander replied for both of us. "We hear you, Nano."

We pulled Abe, Gamble, and Janice into an emergency meeting.

"We can't depend on the stores or the government to feed us going forward," Zander said. "We need a plan to feed ourselves . . . and to defend our homes from raiders."

"Agreed," Gamble said. "But with only our three houses, we don't have a defensible perimeter or enough bodies to stand post. I think we should widen our cohort to include the rest of the cul-de-sac."

⌘⌘⌘⌘

Chapter 2

WE CALLED AN ALL-CUL-DE-SAC meeting for Sunday afternoon—technically an "illegal" in-person meeting since any size or type gathering other than the household in which you lived was forbidden. Early that morning, Zander delivered invites to our remaining cul-de-sac neighbors, Bill and Viola Tucker and Mrs. Calderón (or Belicia, as she requested that we call her).

Ross, Janice, Abe, and Emilio were already waiting in our living room when Belicia and the Tuckers arrived. We questioned each of them first, asking if they'd had physical contact with anyone in the past week.

Naturally, since Bill, Viola, and Belicia didn't know about the nanomites, they didn't know the nanomites checked each of them while they stood on our porch and we asked our questions. When the nanomites declared our neighbors free of the virus we welcomed them into our home.

"I have had no contact with anyone except for coming over to help with Bonnie Lu or going to the store with Jayda," Belicia replied. "Haven't even driven my car for a while. I-I think I'm afraid to."

"The way things are, it's safer if you keep off the roads," I told her. I was trying to encourage her, but her attention was elsewhere. Her eyes were glued to the right of me . . . where Emilio sat beside me on the couch, cradling Bonnie Lu on his lap. Making googly eyes and other funny faces at her. Gently stroking her little hands.

"We collected our latest allotment of groceries five days ago," Viola said. "Not that it's enough, but that's the extent of outside contact we've had lately."

She questioned Zander. "What about you? How many outside contacts have you had and how can we be certain that you're clean? Don't you have church stuff? Visitations and counseling sessions?"

"I do, but visits and counseling are done through video calls. And because the governor's order has shut down in-person worship, I broadcast our Sunday service live. So zero outside contacts."

She stared down at her hands. "Well, two weeks ago, Bill was furloughed indefinitely. Since he's sixty-two now, he's decided to file for early retirement when his unemployment runs out. Social Security seems the only avenue open for us."

"Besides which, I'm not leaving Viola home by herself any longer," Bill growled.

"We understand," I murmured. Then I addressed the group. "I'll be right back."

I reappeared bearing a tray. To everyone's delight, I served precious cookies and coffee all around. The cookies disappeared fast, and Zander opened the meeting.

"We all know that the grocery stores have less and less to offer each week, with more and more restrictions. Prices are soaring too. Even President Jackson, in his address this week, says it will take time for the country to find a way through the present crisis. I'm not blaming him, but that's time that we don't have."

He looked around the room. "I called us together to talk honestly about what is coming, and how we can help each other prepare for it."

This was news only to Bill, Viola, and Belicia. We'd already discussed Zander's ideas with Abe, Gamble, and Janice. Tonight's meeting was the next step in putting his plans into motion.

Bill Tucker drained his cup and set it down. "Thank you for the coffee. I think I know where you're going with this, so I'll let you know my feelings straight off. I'm not some gullible Bible thumper who feels like I must give all I have to feed the poor then turn around and expect someone else to do the same for me. *No.* What Viola and I manage to put by is *ours.* It isn't much, but we can probably make it through next winter on our own . . . if what the grocery stores offer doesn't go down any further."

Zander nodded. Slowly. "If I may speak to your comment, Bill? For the record, yes, Jayda and I are Bible-believing Christians, and yes, we firmly believe in giving. I would just add that God says in his word, the Bible, that giving is a personal choice, emphasis on the word *choice.*

"See, when choice is removed, giving becomes coercion—or worse—because the Bible says elsewhere that taking what belongs to another is wrong. He calls *that* stealing. He is against stealing, so we are too."

"So?"

"So, when the gangs break down your door and demand that you 'give' them what you have, you'll be okay without our help?"

Bill's mouth flattened. "I can handle myself." He slid his eyes toward Gamble. "I'm armed *and* trained."

Gamble smiled, friendly like. "Glad to hear that, Bill, but can you handle a mob? Can you guard both your front and back door at the same time? How about the windows? And if you manage to keep a mob at bay on your own, can you keep them from burning you out?"

Bill flushed and started to reply. He stopped when Viola put her hand on his arm.

"Bill. Please. We came here to listen."

Bill looked away. Sighed. "All right. We'll listen."

Zander said, "Thank you, Bill. I won't drag things out. See, this is what we're thinking: In our cul-de-sac we have ten mouths to feed—nine adults and an infant. We have six yards with which to feed those mouths. I'm asking everyone who lives in our cul-de-sac to form a co-op. We would work together to plant our yards with whatever crop seed we can get our hands on."

Zander leaned forward, elbows on his knees. "And believe it or not, we might not have a lot of seed to choose from. We're already into May, and the gardening shelves are bare, meaning we're late to the party. That said, wherever we can, we should plant crops that have a good chance of producing a decent harvest based on our soil and climate—crops like beans, corn, chiles, squash, tomatoes, carrots, and potatoes."

"It won't be enough," Bill growled.

"I realize that whatever we grow won't be enough to fully feed all of us, but hopefully it will supplement what we can get from the stores each week—enough so we don't starve."

Belicia blinked. "Excuse me, Zander. Plant our yards?"

"That's right, but we're thinking only the front yards."

She bristled, more in panic than in anger. "Dig up my lovely front yard? But I spent a lot of money to have it landscaped!"

"I understand; however, please hear us out. We have reasons for suggesting that we garden the front yards, Belicia. For one, our front yards will be easier to watch and protect than the backyards."

"Protect?"

Zander said softly, "Belicia, you know about the grocery grabber gangs, don't you?"

"Oh, my, yes. Terrible! Jayda, I am so grateful to you for taking me to fetch my groceries each week."

"We are happy to help you, Belicia," I murmured. "You are our neighbor and friend."

She smiled a tremulous smile, and I could see what a difference our friendship had made in her narrow life.

Zander steered the conversation back to her question. "Belicia, if food becomes scarcer—*when* food becomes scarcer—gangs like the grocery grabbers will become more aggressive. And right about now, we aren't the only ones thinking about growing our own food."

"Yup. Already behind the curve," Bill muttered.

"I agree. We should have been preparing a month ago or so. Guess we've been a bit preoccupied with our new baby. Anyway, I've already called around, and every rototiller in town is reserved clean through July. But back to your question, Belicia? Unscrupulous people may try to steal from our gardens—"

"*Will* try to steal from our gardens," Bill interjected.

"That's right, Bill, which is why we're stronger together. They might also try to break into our homes and take what little we have in our cupboards."

Belicia swallowed. Hard. "Oh, dear. I-I certainly wouldn't be able to stop them."

"We understand. That is another reason we're meeting and why we suggest farming our front yards. All of us can see the other front yards in the cul-de-sac, but we can't keep an eye on each other's backyards—our yard being something of the exception. When we bought this place, we combined our lot with the lot between us and you, Belicia. Most of our backyard is visible to you and the Tuckers. It's a good-sized lot that can be the co-op's largest garden, and it's fully fenced."

Eight feet high with pointy finials, I thought. *Won't keep out a determined group, though.*

Bill spoke up again. "Downside is, a gang could drive up and grab whatever they wanted from our front yards, so I'm not sure that's the best place to plant."

Zander said, "Well, we have something of an advantage over, say, our neighbors down the street from us, Bill. Our little cul-de-sac has only one way in and out for vehicles."

Almost conspiratorially, Zander said, "I propose that we barricade the neck to our cul-de-sac and mount a guard there 24/7."

Bill seemed surprised, but he nodded. "Not a bad idea, Cruz. Right kind of barricade could work. Would need to be strong enough to stop gatecrashers, though."

"You're right. Gamble here says he can get us some five-foot cement K-rails. Says they are 32 inches tall and *heavy*. Each 'stick' of rail is about two thousand pounds. The rails won't stop a crowd from climbing over, obviously, but they *will* deter vehicles from crashing through, which would, hopefully, slow down a coordinated raid on our gardens. Give us a chance to defend our homes and plots."

Bill's gaze skittered toward Gamble for the second time. "You're FBI, right?"

"That's right."

"You still on the job?"

"Sure. I work a regular shift out of the FBI's district field office. I think I see where you're headed, so I'd like to give you some reassurances about my level of contribution to the group. Most days, I have pockets of discretionary time on my hands, time I can employ searching locally or online for things we need. Get them lined up for us. Hunt them down and buy them during my lunch break or after work."

He grimaced. "Of course, given the current state of unease, every agent in the state is on call around the clock. If things go pear-shaped anywhere in our district, I may get called out. Perhaps days at a time."

Zander glanced from Viola to Bill. "I won't be able to devote all of my time to the co-op either, you know. I have online appointments most days, and it takes time to study and prepare my messages for Sunday's livestream. As much as possible, though, I'll arrange to do those things in late afternoons and evenings."

What Zander said was true, but it was also oversimplistic. The people of our congregation were suffering mightily. Loneliness, financial pressures, and the daily struggles to procure enough food—not to mention the stress on marriages and the uptick in domestic problems—meant Zander was on his phone or computer hours each day, comforting, counseling, and praying with our saints.

Protected from the virus as he was, Zander was safe to visit people in person, but the logistics were mind-boggling. The amount of time it would take him to visit everyone in person would keep him driving all day. Obviously, with the fuel shortages, in-person visitations weren't possible. Worst of all, the governor had forbidden such visits. All that said, Zander did make some exceptions to his "online only" policy . . . for funerals.

Yes, DCC was losing members to the virus and other, more pedestrian causes. Sadly, if an individual died while in the hospital, they were automatically deemed contaminated by the virus, and the family was denied a viewing. Their loved one's body was tagged, bagged, and sealed in a cheap coffin. The coffin was delivered either to the crematorium of the family's choice or to a graveyard service, where only immediate family members were allowed to attend the burial.

Zander made it his highest priority to officiate at those burials. If the deceased was a believer in Christ, Zander preached the hope of the resurrection and eternal life. He didn't hold back, either. He often returned from such an affair exhausted but jubilant because he'd won unsaved family members to Christ.

Yes, Zander was being truthful about his pastoral obligations, but his response did not in any way reflect the weight of responsibility he carried or the physical and emotional toll those duties had on him.

Back to our meeting.

Bill frowned. "Yeah, I can understand having to earn a living, but Gamble here won't be much help protecting our proposed co-op if he's out defending other parts of the state."

Gamble chuckled. "Bill and Viola, please meet my, *uh*, my . . . Janice Trujillo. By way of answering your concern, Bill, let me say that Janice is, *er*, former military and a better shot than I am. She's qualified on more firearms than I am too. Since she's presently unemployed, she'll be available when I'm not."

I snickered to myself—first at Gamble's clumsy attempt to introduce Janice.

Yeah, dude, we're praying for you—praying you into conviction and repentance and praying you into Christ . . . allll the way to a wedding. You just watch and see!

I snickered a second time as he left out the more interesting bits of Janice's resumé.

Gee, Gamble! You didn't mention Janice's expertise in black ops. A better shot than most? Why, yes—

A bleat of protest from Belicia interrupted my thoughts. Sorry, that's exactly how it sounded—a big, fat *bleat.*

"Guns? *Guns?* Please, *please* promise we won't have another attack like we did in January! I was so scared!"

Zander's expression pinged from stunned disbelief to amusement, back to disbelief. "How in the world are we supposed to promise that, Belicia? You know about the riots and looting downtown and the grocery grabber gangs. They already defy police attempts to stop them. If the police can't deter criminals, can we? And these things are but the *first* wave of social disintegration. How long can the police stand against such crimes if the criminals far outnumber them and if more and more people turn to taking what they want or need?"

He sighed. "I'm sorry to burst your bubble, Belicia, but the state of civil unrest *will* worsen. And because it will worsen, we have to take whatever steps we can to protect ourselves and those we love. No one else will do it for us."

"I have to agree with Zander," Gamble said quietly. "I mean, we did say we'd have an honest discussion about what's coming, right?"

When several of us nodded, he turned to Belicia. "Mrs. Calderón, as social and civic restraints crumble and as our city's police force falters under the weight of growing crime, officers will eventually arrive at the realization that while they're 'out there,' defending the public, their own families are at risk. They will have to make a choice between their jobs or protecting their families and homes. Most will either resign or simply stop showing up for shifts. At that point, all bets are off."

He shook his head. "I'm sorry, but Zander is right. We have to protect ourselves. No one else will."

Belicia's eyes twitched, then jumped wildly around the room. Her hands shook, her shoulders trembled.

She was losing it.

I scooped Bonnie Lu off of Emilio's lap. Went to Belicia and knelt by her chair. A hungry glint shone through the anxiety gripping her. I gently laid our baby in her willing arms.

Bonnie Lu, her rosebud lips blowing a tiny bubble, stared placidly up at the old woman. Almost immediately, calm began to seep into the slump of Belicia's shuddering shoulders. She gulped convulsively and tears sheened her eyes.

"Belicia," I said softly. "Belicia?"

She slowly turned her face to me. "Yes?"

"You are our neighbor and our friend. You know that we'll do our best to protect and see you through this. But at the same time, I believe you'll need to adjust your thinking."

She blinked many times before her usually unruffled countenance reappeared. "You're saying I can't pretend everything will magically go back the way it was?"

"That's right, dear friend. We must face the facts together. This co-op will help us survive what is ahead. But only if everyone contributes to the co-op's efforts. We will need you to contribute too."

She swallowed. "I'll do my best."

"Thank you. Your best is all we ask."

I stood and turned toward my seat. Ran smack into Emilio's fierce scowl. He was *not* happy that I'd taken Bonnie Lu from him.

I sat and patted his hand. Leaned over and whispered, "Thank you, my sweet boy, for seeing that Mrs. Calderón needed our Bonnie Lu for a minute. Thank you for being willing to love Mrs. Calderón."

Emilio *hadn't* seen Belicia's need or been keen to help the woman, but he studied her now, perhaps perceiving what I'd pointed out. In any event, his scowl eased up.

Some.

I squeezed his hand and smiled. He half-heartedly smiled back.

Zander cleared his throat. "I would like us to talk more about how to defend our cul-de-sac."

Every eye turned to him.

"You were talking about a barricade," Bill said.

"Yeah. The barricade, in part, will help us defend our homes and gardens. The agreements we make as a co-op must also allow us to work together, meet together, even eat together without fear of contracting the virus from one another. If such a plan is going to work, we'll have to agree

—as a group—to stay behind the barricade. Basically live together but apart from everyone else."

Comprehension bloomed on Bill's face. "We'd isolate behind the barrier? No one in or out?"

"No one in, certainly. We'd move our mailboxes to the barricade and mount them there. That would keep mail carriers and delivery trucks on the other side. Same with our trash carts—roll them to the other side of the barricade on pickup day.

"Going outside the cul-de-sac would look different. We'd work as a group to coordinate our forays. Keep them to a minimum and conduct them in the safest manner possible. If we coordinate our outings, we'll conserve gas."

"I see," Bill said, nodding. "I suppose that makes sense."

"Back to the barrier. Let me have Gamble address how we might manage it—keeping in mind that these are initial ideas. As a co-op, everyone can contribute ideas. We would agree as a group how we go forward. Gamble?"

Gamble cleared his throat. "Abe's house is on the neck of the cul-de-sac, separated from the next house over by a cinderblock wall. So is yours, Bill and Viola. We propose laying a line of K-rails from the side walls of these two houses all the way across the neck of the cul-de-sac—leaving one narrow opening at Abe's front yard.

"We'd park a vehicle in that opening, rear end facing up the street, to plug the hole. We're thinking an old clunker would be best. We'd up-armor the rear window and fill the car with extra weight to make it heavier and harder to shove out of the hole. We'd position our barricade guard at the vehicle and use it as cover."

"Wouldn't be hard for attackers to roll or push a vehicle out of the way," Bill scoffed. "Even a heavy one."

Despite his sour outlook, I could see that Bill was thinking hard, which made me hope he was giving serious thought to joining the co-op. *But*, he hadn't yet committed to it.

Gamble nodded. "I can get ahold of two wheel boots. If we boot the two front tires and add some sandbags in front of them, pushing the car from the rear will prove next to impossible. When any of us needs to leave the cul-de-sac, we remove the boots and sandbags and drive the car forward to uncork the barrier."

What followed was a lively yet thoughtful discussion that ranged from the logistics of defending our cul-de-sac through the details of farming our lots.

Zander said, "I'm certain a bunch of folks in Albuquerque, like us, are planning to plant gardens. And yet all of us know that the soil around here is a combination of clay, rock, and sand. If we hope to grow enough in our plots to supplement what groceries we can buy, we'll need to amend that soil. And since rototillers are either sold out or already reserved, we'll have to dig our garden plots and amend the soil the hard way—by hand."

Abe grunted his agreement. "You're right about that. Our gardens will yield precious little if we don't turn and amend the soil first. But it's backbreaking work."

"Yes, it is, which is why I propose that we start with our big, fenced lot. A small part of it was once a garden and will be easier to work than virgin soil."

I blinked as I realized he was talking about Gemma's garden.

My garden.

And I had been a blatant novice . . .

⌘

I DECIDED TO TACKLE THE WEEDS in my vegetable garden. I had done a good job keeping them at bay, but in the heat they were getting away from me. That day I resolved to really clean them out.

I soaked the garden to loosen the weeds. I might have—and I'm just saying **might** *have—soaked the garden a bit too much. I only mention this because while the water loosened the weeds, it also turned the natural clay soil to a slick, sticky bog.*

I had been working since before six in the morning in what felt like wet cement. Fearful that I might lose them forever, I had taken off my shoes. I was wearing good gardening gloves, but they—and the rest of me from my elbows down—were covered in layers of dripping, drying, and dried mud.

I figured the time to be around nine, and I still had a third of the weeds to go. I was flagging but determined to finish. The hardest part was getting the shovel down into the ground so I could turn over the wet, heavy soil.

"There you are. I rang the doorbell but no one answered so I thought I'd check back here. Hello."

The man who stood a few steps away was clean and tidy, casually dressed in jeans, a polo shirt, and a lightweight suit jacket.

He was drop-dead gorgeous. I was hot, sweaty, and filthy.

He raised his hand from his side as though he had planned to offer a handshake, but if he had *planned to offer his hand, I'm pretty sure he thought better of it as soon as he eyed my mud-caked gloves.*

"Sorry to disturb you. I'm Zander Cruz. Are you Miss Keyes?"

⌘

GUESS I MADE A LITTLE SOUND in my throat, and it pulled me out of that happy place, the day Zander and I met. When I came back to myself, Emilio was studying me with concern . . . me wearing a fat, dopey grin.

"You okay, Jayda?"

My grin widened. "Yes. Yes, I am."

Zander was still talking. "If we all agree on how to go forward, I propose that we work together to turn, amend, and fertilize the soil in our fenced plot, then turn the soil a second and third time over the week following. For each turn we'll need all hands on deck to break clods, remove and haul off rocks, and sift for grass and weed roots."

Belicia timidly lifted a hand. "I'm not in the best physical shape at my age, Zander. Is there something else I could do?"

"Yes, as a matter of fact. We'd like you and Abe to take turns helping with Bonnie Lu."

"Oh my, yes. I can do that!"

"Great. We'd also like the two of you to keep the rest of us fed and watered. Sandwiches or light cooking for a group midday meal. That sort of thing."

Abe and Belicia both nodded.

I caught Zander's attention, and he signaled me to speak.

"Belicia, in addition, I think you will make an *excellent* secondary lookout—from either your front window or ours. I trust you to keep faithful watch over the plots in our front yards, even if you aren't the designated barrier guard."

I didn't add that Belicia was the cul-de-sac's best watchdog, with years of experience under her belt, but I didn't have to. I *did* have to put my elbow into Emilio's side and cut off the guffaw he was about to let go. Abe averted his gaze, finding the threads of his sweater suddenly intriguing. Viola had an abrupt coughing fit, and Bill got up quickly to fetch her a glass of water from the kitchen, wiping his mouth as he went. Even Zander chewed the inside of his cheek for a moment while slanting his own "look" toward me—a look that spoke volumes and made me cover my mouth with my hand.

Only Gamble and Janice were left out of our neighborhood's little joke. They exchanged a confused glance.

I was glad when Belicia beamed at me. "You are very kind, Jayda, and I would be happy to help keep watch. Maybe I should have a hand bell or some other kind of alarm signal should I see someone sneaking into the cul-de-sac?"

"Excellent idea, Belicia," Zander assured her, still getting himself under control. "Don't let me forget your suggestion."

"Oh, I won't. I'm glad there are things I can do to help."

Zander went on. "The rest of us will participate in all the jobs: breaking ground, digging, turning, weeding, and gathering and hauling rocks. We'll use every inch of soil available to us, all but a small patch of grass around our apple tree.

"After we've readied the big plot for planting, we'll start on the front yards. Speaking of our apple tree, if you have fruit or nut trees in your yards, we'll need to prune and spray them soon."

"I have a black walnut in my backyard, but I don't know what shape it's in," Belicia said. "I've never sprayed it. Always considered it a pest, the way it drops nuts in the grass and I have to pick them up and toss them."

"Walnuts are a good source of protein and lots of other nutrients. We'll be glad to have them."

"Don't forget the apple tree in my backyard," Abe said.

"Oh, we won't—I promise you that."

"Guess that makes three apple trees, because we have one too," Gamble said, "although I'm not sure how it's survived. Doesn't look like anything on our lot has been watered in years."

Emilio snorted, and I laughed aloud. No, Mateo hadn't been big on lot maintenance.

Zander smiled. "We should bear in mind that every bit of fruit we harvest can be preserved for winter consumption. I don't know about you, but I like applesauce, apple pie, apple cobbler, and apple juice."

"Don't forget apple butter!" Viola chimed in.

"Forget apple butter? Never happen. Apple butter is one of my favorites," Zander chuckled. "And like I said earlier, when it comes to crops, we should plant the best producing foods for our soil and climate. The obstacle we face at present is a dearth of seeds. What garden seeds that were available have already been snapped up."

Abe raised his hand. "I have a word to say about what to plant, Zander."

"Sure. Go ahead."

"The word is *carrots*. Carrots are mighty underappreciated when it comes to staples. Want to say that we can grow and harvest carrots all summer long, right into the fall, even into early winter. Carrots do best in sandy soil, not heavy clay soil, but they are nutritious, quick and easy to grow, and easy to preserve. Biggest bang for the buck you could ask for.

"I grew me some carrots two years back. When summer got really hot, I let my carrots go to seed." Abe sort of waggled his brows. "Collected about a pound of seed, I did."

Zander perked up. "You have a pound of carrot seed?"

"Yup. Now, because the seeds are two years old, not all of them will germinate, but more than enough should to at least get us going. And of each batch of carrots we grow this year, all we need do is mark off a row or two, let them go to seed, then collect the seeds. If we plan right, we'll never run short on carrots. Nope. Never."

I thought about it. I mean, carrots are okay, right? But as a staple? My imagination turned to a menu dominated by carrots: Boiled carrots. Baked carrots. Roasted carrots. Mashed carrots. Glazed carrots. Candied carrots. Carrot soup. Carrot soufflé. Carrot muffins. Carrot cake.

Gah!

On the other hand, carrots beat going hungry *any* day. And they beat all to pieces trying to live on giant zucchini.

Just sayin'.

I noticed Viola tug on her husband's sleeve and turn a look on him.

Oh, I recognized that kind of "private" look. Same kind of look Zander had slid my way minutes before. Bill and Viola engaged in a silent convo that lasted only seconds.

Then Bill cleared his throat. "We, uh, have a canister of heirloom seeds, never opened. It's kind of old. Bought it about ten years back when Viola and I were on something of a prepper kick. Like I said, the canister is sealed, so the seeds should be good. Well, mostly good."

"Part of your preparations to carry you through to next year?"

Bill sighed. "I planned to plant our backyard, but I'm not sure I could prep the whole yard without a rototiller. Well, not as thoroughly as it should be prepped."

"You and me both."

Bill added, "Your talk about gangs hopping walls and raiding our backyard gardens got me thinking, Zander. You might be right about planting out front where all of us can keep an eye out."

"Does that mean you and Viola are throwing in your lot with us, Bill? Joining the co-op? Because this plan only works if everyone in the cul-de-sac is in agreement and works together. If we don't act now, in concert, we may be playing catchup all next winter, and the, uh, situation could get very dicey."

My sad, chronically hollow stomach growled its concurrence.

Bill sighed and glanced at Viola. She stared steadily back.

He said, "Well, you're right about one thing. We will be stronger if we stand and work together . . . so yeah. I suppose we are."

"Have to agree," Bill admitted.

"And will you contribute that seed canister to the co-op?"

He nodded. "We will."

I sighed my relief.

Zander smiled. "Great! Welcome aboard."

⌘⌘⌘⌘

Chapter 3

AT SEVEN THE FOLLOWING MORNING, the members of our little co-op gathered in our backyard. Everyone brought the yard tools they had—shovels, hoes, rakes, and other sundry bits. Emilio proudly carried an old pickaxe from Abe's house to ours. Abe trundled over a rusty old wheelbarrow filled with a hoe and few odd trowels, weed poppers, and hand cultivators.

Bill and Viola also brought a wheelbarrow loaded with their tools. Gamble was at work, but Janice handed out a selection of gloves he'd picked up at Lowe's for the co-op. Belicia brought a gallon jug of sweet tea and arms itching to hold Bonnie Lu.

After I settled Bonnie with Belicia inside the house, Zander gathered us near our flowering apple tree. "No one is obligated to join in, but for those who wish to? Let's have a word of prayer."

He bowed his head. "Lord God, we acknowledge you right now and ask your blessing and guidance on the plans we've formed. We submit those plans to you. Please direct us in all we do this day. In Jesus' name. Amen."

Abe and I said "amen." Bill, Viola, and Janice nodded. Emilio rolled his eyes.

That boy, Lord, I prayed in my heart. He knew what I meant.

Zander looked to Bill. "Want to run this crew today, Bill?"

Surprised but pleased, Bill nodded. "Sure. You have any druthers about where we start?"

"Nope. Anywhere in our plot is fine. We're in your capable hands."

Bill divided us into two crews: Zander, Janice, and me; Bill, Viola, Abe, and Emilio. He eyed Abe dubiously. "Abe, do as much as fits your limits today but no more than two hours total, okay? No overdoing it."

"I hear you, Boss."

"Everyone wear good gloves at all times, please. I suggest each team take two shovels, a hoe, whatever hand tools you want, and a wheelbarrow. Zander, have your crew start in the far left corner of your lot, by Belicia's house. We'll start at this end and work toward you."

He frowned. "Where do we pile the rocks? Cuz we're gonna unearth a *lot* of rocks."

Even this close to the river, we still lived in the foothills of the Sandia Mountains. Those foothills had been eroding, sending rocks rolling downhill for centuries.

Zander, hands on his hips, turned in a circle, then shook his head. "Not sure. Wherever we decide, we only want to move them once."

"What about our backyard?" Janice asked. "Nothing but weeds and that apple tree back there."

Zander asked Emilio, "It's your house. Is that all right with you?"

Emilio thought for a moment. "Yeah, it's okay, but . . . I was kinda thinking—what if we put a pile in the front yard, by the bushes? If people come over the barrier to steal from our gardens, we can throw rocks at them!"

Bill chuckled, earning himself one of Emilio's infamous death glares.

Zander did not laugh. "Not a bad idea. We don't necessarily want to hurt people if they trespass, but they need to know we're serious. Having a pile of rocks handy may help us discourage them."

We got down to it after that. I was only three weeks postpartum, but the nanomites said I was fine—that they had accelerated my healing from the birth. Nevertheless, I had other eyes on me, Belicia and Viola, who had already admonished me to take it easy—and neither of them knew about the nanomites. I'd need to pretend to "take it easy."

In our corner of the plot, Zander wielded a shovel and began the hard labor of turning the densely packed soil. Janice used a hoe to hack apart the clods he unearthed. As they did that, I knelt in their aftermath pulling out grass and weeds, shaking the dirt from them, piling weeds to the side, tossing rocks into the nearby wheelbarrow.

We labored on for an hour and a half before we took a short break for sweet tea and for me to feed Bonnie Lu. Abe left us at that point, but the rest of us got back to it. By lunch, Bill called it a day.

"We've earned ourselves some blisters, and we're all going to feel pain in the morning, but if we intend to make as much progress tomorrow, we should quit now. We can add another hour to our shift tomorrow, or as we harden to the work."

We were tired, sweaty (in spite of the cool breeze in the air), and definitely sore, but we were pleased and in great spirits. We'd turned and cleared about a quarter of the fenced plot, filled one big rolling trash cart with weeds, and hauled three wheelbarrow loads of rocks to Gamble and Janice's backyard, dumping them into a far corner. And taking Emilio's suggestion, we'd piled a couple dozen hand-sized rocks in their front yard—right next to the bushes Emilio had, at one time, hidden in.

If we'd known how important that "rock ammo" would one day prove to be, we would have stocked more of them there.

⌘

WE SHOWERED IN HOT, SOOTHING water, but our muscles were speaking up, telling us "what for." It had been some weeks since either Zander or I had worked out, and I'd had a baby during that time.

"I feel for the rest of the co-op," I muttered. "By morning, the nanomites will have healed most of our aches and pains."

Indeed we will, Jayda Cruz, and it will take you less time to 'harden to the work,' as Bill Tucker said.

"Thanks, Nano." The nanomites were so preoccupied running their counterinsurgency, we didn't often hear from them.

It is our pleasure, Jayda Cruz.

We walked over to Abe's to share a simple meal with him and Emilio. After we ate, Abe invited us out to his garage.

"This morning, after I put in my time in the garden, I started thinkin' on how we'd mount our mailboxes at the barrier once it is up," he said. "I think this simple fix will do the trick. I used an old mailbox post for my prototype."

Abe had a stack of cinderblocks at the back of the garage, in front of his car. He'd placed one block atop the other, mixed up some concrete, put the post in the hole through both blocks, and poured concrete in the hole, filling it and surrounding the post. Then he'd laid several more cinder blocks around the two blocks where the post was mounted.

"Figure once we have the blocks with the mailboxes lined up in a row along the barrier, we can surround them with a few more cement-filled blocks for stability. Fairly easy to dismantle the whole caboodle if we need to, 'cause the outside blocks won't be cemented to each other."

"We could fill the stabilizing blocks with small rocks we pull out of the garden before topping them with cement," I suggested. "The rocks would make them heavier."

"I like it," Zander agreed.

When we went back inside, Emilio, Zander, and I settled on the couch in front of Zander's tablet and dialed in to our weekly video conference with Roberto, María, and Izzie.

I always came away from our calls smiling, grateful that we had an extended family that loved us. This evening was no different. I held Bonnie up to the screen so everyone could see her, see that she'd filled out a little more.

For the first time, however, she noticed the three faces scrunched onto the screen in front of her, all of them vying for her attention. Her eyes sort of bugged out in amazement. But then she grimaced and let go with a (shall we say) very loud and protracted *toot.*

María's brows shot up. "Oh, little mama, if that didn't fill a diaper, I'm no abuela."

I didn't have to check; the smell informed me. "Um, excuse me please, *Abuela*. Diaper duty."

Laughter followed me all the way to Emilio's bedroom. He followed me too. He was fascinated with every facet of Bonnie Lu's life—with the exception of messy diapers—so I was a little surprised.

I unfolded a felt-covered rubber changing mat and laid Bonnie on it. "Don't worry. I won't get anything on your bedspread."

"I know you won't."

He stood close to me, his arm sliding lightly around my waist. His action was just unusual enough to make me stop what I was doing. I wrapped both my arms all the way around him. Held him close. Felt him take a deep and satisfied breath and let it out.

"It's wonderful being part of a loving family, isn't it?"

He nodded, his face buried on my shoulder.

"Especially after living in a not-so-loving home, huh?"

He nodded a second time, making no move to end our hug.

"I love you, Emilio. I'm so glad we are family now."

Muffled against my shoulder, he said something.

"Sorry. Couldn't hear you."

I tried to pull back, but he gripped me tighter. Mumbled again. This time I thought I caught what he said.

"Emilio, did you . . . did you ask if you could call me Mama?"

His head nodded just a little, and I bit my lip to keep from blubbering.

When I could answer, I said, "I would love it if you called me Mama, my son—and I know Zander would love for you to call him Dad."

We didn't let go of each other until Bonnie began to fuss.

⌘

WHEN WE RETURNED TO THE LIVING room, the call was over, but Zander still stared at the screen, flummoxed.

"What's up?"

He shook his head. "Would you believe it? We have company coming."

"Huh?"

"Dad, Mom, and Izzie are driving up from 'Cruces. Tomorrow."

"What? I mean, *wow*. Is that wise?"

Or legal?

"Wise or not, as soon as I told Dad about our co-op plans and that we were turning never-before-tilled yards by hand, he said, 'No, you're not. We'll be there tomorrow afternoon.' See, he's already turned his garden twice, so he's bringing us his rototiller."

"Get out! They're coming *tomorrow?*"

"Yup. Mom was right there with Dad, egging him on. I'm pretty sure Izzie was doing backflips across the kitchen behind them."

I thought about it. "Gotta say, the rototiller part sounds marvelous. It'll drastically cut the amount of work we have before us. And having them here for a visit will be great. But, again, is it wise for them to travel up from 'Cruces, what with the virus and all the other weird stuff going on?"

"They said they'd pack a lunch so they don't have to stop somewhere to eat. And Mom is probably packing a gallon of hand sanitizer."

"But . . . the roads aren't all that safe. Bandits, and all."

"Safe? If I know Dad, he'll put Mom behind the wheel while he rides shotgun—literally."

He laughed in chagrin. "This isn't about our co-op or the garden, you know. Hasn't got a thing to do with the rototiller."

"Oh. I get it. They want to see Bonnie Lu."

"*Need* to see Bonnie Lu, you mean. In my family, that need verges on the pathological."

"So, they were looking for an excuse to break isolation, and we handed them one on a silver plate."

"Yup. Oh, by the way, you and I? We're just the sideshow now."

Zander's morose pronouncement hit Emilio's funny bone so hard that he fell off the couch cackling.

"Ha-ha," Zander groused. "Glad we could amuse you."

⌘⌘⌘⌘

CHAPTER 4

WE MET UP AGAIN AT SEVEN the next morning. Zander and I were raring to go. Yes, we were a little stiff, but the nanomites had expedited our muscles' healing. We toned down our eagerness to get started for Bill, Viola, and Janice's sake. They were a hair on the grumpy side. As for Abe? Emilio said he was taking the morning off.

"Feelin' it," Viola muttered, trying to stretch her back.

"Yup," Janice replied. "My arms from hacking clods. Plus blisters."

Bill didn't say anything, but he walked the unturned length of our plot, warming up his legs and frowning over a steaming travel mug of coffee.

When he wandered back to us, Zander asked, "Uh, how would you-all like some good news?"

"Sure," Janice said. Bill and Viola just waited for Zander to spill it.

"Talked to my folks last night, and they offered to loan us their rototiller. They live outside of Las Cruces. Should be here after lunch."

Grins broke through the all-around grimaces.

"Best news ever," Janice pronounced. "So, if we're not 'busting sod' today, what are we doing?"

Zander deferred to Bill. "Boss?"

He was still frowning. "I'm a little worried about them coming into the cul-de-sac. Have they been isolating?"

"Yes, totally. And they won't stop anywhere on the drive here."

"Huh. So, you're certain they won't pose a risk? What about gas? How will they find enough?"

"My folks own three acres and haven't left it in weeks except to pick up grocery orders. As for fuel, Dad has a big, raised gas tank behind the garage. He managed to top it off before stations started rationing. And he's putting a couple of full cans in the bed of his truck to get them back to Cruces. They won't even spend the night with us—just drop the rototiller and head home."

I wasn't so sure about the last part of Zander's statement. Not once María got her hands on her first grandchild.

"Hope they don't get ambushed," Bill muttered.

"My Dad carries a shotgun with him."

"Well, that's good to hear."

"What about today? Work?"

"Oh. Right. Let me think."

"How about we move rock out of your front yard and save the garden plot for the tiller?"

Bill nodded slowly. "Yeah. Let's do that. We'll shift the rock around to our backyard. Then once we plow your plot, we can right away plow ours."

All hands turned to shoveling landscaping rock. The two crews worked on opposite sides of Bill and Viola's front yard, piling rock into wheelbarrows, then hauling and dumping their loads along their back wall.

Let me tell you, it was a *lot* of rock.

As Janice and I finished dumping our second wheelbarrow loads, I considered the Tucker's backyard, eyeing the chest-high cinderblock wall across the back of their lot.

"You know, Janice, raiders can come over these back walls pretty easily. They have to cross the yards backing our lots first, but at night, it would be easy."

"Ross and I said the same thing. It's a gaping hole in our defense."

"Well, what if . . . what if we were to spread all the rock we're digging up across the length of the wall and keep adding to it, creating a sizable field of rocks that intruders would have to navigate . . . in the dark?"

"Like a trip hazard?"

"Exactly like that. We could pile on whatever else we have lying around that might make crossing it an unpleasant experience. Maybe add strings of noisemakers like cowbells or empty cans?"

"Not the worst idea I've heard," she snarked.

I laughed with her.

When we took our first break, Janice and I asked Bill and Zander to come into the Tucker's backyard with us. I told them what we were thinking.

"Might slow them down a minute," Bill said, scanning his backyard, "but what we really need are motion-activated cameras that can audibly alert us to intruders. Problem is, the grid is spotty these days, meaning the local Wi-Fi connection will be iffy too."

Jayda Cruz, Zander Cruz, we will print and assign a large nanoarray to monitor the camera system your co-op installs. If the grid goes down, the nanoarray will—to the degree they are able—provide supplemental power to the local Wi-Fi connections.

The nanomites had first printed nanobot arrays—clusters of single-function or more complex, specialized nanobots—and sent them into the President's enemies to surveil them. That was when we lived in Maryland and were there to find out what happened to the President's friend, Wayne Overman.

The conspiracy we'd uncovered, however, ran deeper than we'd imagined. It even had to have been an offshoot of the Cabal, one of their initial forays into taking the White House.

In any event, we'd made a pact with the nanomites: After we'd taken down the President's attempted assassins, *no more nanobot arrays.*

Yeah, that was before the nanomites revealed what they'd discovered about the Cabal and how insidiously they'd infested every aspect of society. How outnumbered we were.

When the nanomites, with the President's blessing, launched their counterinsurgency, we understood they needed to employ every tool at their disposal, nanobot arrays included.

Since then, the nanomites had printed so many nanobot arrays that they had shortened their term for them to *nanoarray.* One of their arrays might consist of a hundred thousand nanobots; another might be a million nanobots strong. What was most amazing was how the nanomites were now able to dispatch their nanoarrays via electrical power lines or fiber-optic cables to nearly any location in the world.

Yes, it took days, even weeks, for the arrays to reach their designated "posts." Nonetheless, within months of the nanomites commencing their counterinsurgency, when Zander and I looked into the warehouse (that virtual "place" where we could talk to the nanomites and see what they were doing), we could see the massive and *still growing* army of nanoarrays—an army coordinated and directed by our two nanoclouds.

No wonder the nanomites were often busy or distracted! The sheer computing power to synchronize such an effort boggled our minds.

"Uh, right, Nano. Thanks for reminding us."

Zander answered Bill's comments. "How about we work toward a full spread of security cameras for the cul-de-sac? We won't need to depend upon the grid to power them if we buy solar panels for each camera. By the way, Gamble and Janice are the experts in this area. Why don't we assign this task to them?"

"Yeah, sounds like the right move." Bill glanced toward Janice. "You two up for that?"

"Sure. Ross will be glad to have tasks he can take care of after his shift. It irks him not to be contributing at the moment. As for the Wi-Fi, when it has power, we're good. When the power is off, maybe the mere presence of cameras will act as a deterrent."

Janice swiveled her head away from Bill and louvered one eyelid down and up for us to see. She knew, whether we were awake or sleeping, Wi-Fi or no Wi-Fi, the nanomites would be on the job.

Bill wrinkled his nose. "Not a lot to count on—iffy cameras and a strip of rocks and noisy junk."

⌘

ABE AND BELICIA FIXED A HOT LUNCH for the rock moving crews—fried bologna and mustard sandwiches; a simple soup consisting of beef broth, barley, and canned peas and corn; accompanied by a whopping four crackers each. At least with Bonnie already fed and asleep on Emilio's bed, I was free to sit and eat my meal in peace.

"I see you got in on the 'buy one, get one free' sale on bags of barley," Bill commented with a smile.

"Only way we shop these days," Abe answered. "We make a list of what we need, what is essential, but we budget a chunk of our allotted purchase amount to snap up bulk foods and rare sale items. See, my folks lived through the Great Depression and learned a lot of valuable survival tricks. Learned them the hard way, they did. We kids grew up on fried bologna or cheese sandwiches and whatever else they could get cheapest."

He chuckled. "Always something to eat when you shop the sales and not 'the wants.' It's how I was raised. So, when things started getting tight 'round here, those habits kicked right back in."

"Abe is a library of forgotten skills," I murmured.

"Huh. You don't say." Bill studied Abe, then asked, "Would you consider having the co-op sit for a lecture or two? You could, you know, share things your parents did that we might want to adopt."

Zander looked up from his soup bowl. "That's a brilliant idea. What do you think, Abe?"

Abe stroked his chin. "Suppose I could think of a few things to talk on."

A blaring horn interrupted them.

"That's my dad's truck," Zander declared, getting up from the table. Emilio and I also jumped up and ran to greet them.

María had parked the truck along the curb in front of our house. She, Roberto, and Izzie had climbed down from the truck when we raced out onto the porch to holler and wave at them. Someone else climbed down— a tall young man.

"Hey, that's my cousin Leo!" Zander said, laughing. I recalled Leo from Thanksgiving. He was, I thought, about twenty-five, quiet but sweet. A budding engineer.

In moments, we were all laughing. Laughing and hugging and crying. We hadn't seen Izzie since the middle of March when the governor clamped down on all but essential services. Because the virus had forced her to work from home, she decided to go stay with Roberto and María. Make sure they were okay during the lockdown.

I hugged Izzie fiercely. So did Emilio. Then we hugged María. And Roberto. Then I hugged María again.

It was a hug fest that ended abruptly when María pulled back and studied me. "Jayda, *mija*, you look wonderful. Motherhood fits you perfectly . . . but you are, perhaps, a little too thin? We must feed you up! Speaking of motherhood, where is our precious Bonnie Lu?"

I snickered and shot a glance at Zander. "You're right. We're just the sideshow now."

"No, no! No, of course not!" María objected, but her eyes were on Abe's front door.

"Let me say hi to Leo, then we'll go see her," I promised.

He was standing on the periphery, perfectly content to watch what, to him, were normal family interactions. "Hey, Jayda."

"Hey, Leo! We didn't know you were coming, but it's great that you did."

"Uncle Roberto wanted a second gun. Just in case." He patted his side where a semiauto sidearm was holstered.

"I'm glad he asked you." I scanned around and asked, "Has everyone had lunch? Yes? I suppose then that you want to meet Bonnie Lu?"

They practically ran me over on the way up Abe's porch.

⌘

AN HOUR LATER, MARÍA WAS STILL holding Bonnie, who was perfectly content to sleep like an angel. But Belicia, more than a little put out, went home "to take a nap."

"Roberto," María said softly, then lowered her gaze to our baby, "do we really need to go back home today? We could get a hotel, couldn't we? Maybe stay and help a little?"

"I have no interest in staying in a hotel where who knows how many sick people might be staying or working. No, I think we should unload the rototiller and the seeds I brought and then head back today."

Zander said "Seeds?" at the same time I said, "Head back today?"

We looked at each other. Zander nodded for me to continue.

"Why can't you stay with us, Roberto? I'm sure we can make room."

María waited, a hopeful light in her eyes. Finally, Roberto nodded.

"I guess I would like to lend my hands and back to your co-op for a couple of days."

"Super!" Zander replied. "By the triway, what kind of seeds did you bring us? And where did you get them? Gamble's been calling all over the county, but seeds are sold out everywhere he's checked."

Roberto shrugged. "I harvest a supply of seeds from my garden every fall. In the spring we plant our half acre garden and have seeds left over that we give to our neighbors and friends. I always keep some seeds back, though, in case I have to reseed following a freeze. I brought what I had on hand. Not a big selection, of course, but the basics: pinto beans, black beans, stringless green beans—that's pole beans not bush beans—and corn, of course."

"Wow," I murmured.

"Then there's butternut squash, pumpkin, turnip, radish, and zucchini. Oh—and I brought you a bag of seed potatoes. Cut those up and plant them, and you'll have a big pile of potatoes in the fall. Brought you some tomato starts too. A dozen canning tomato plants and a few cherry tomatoes. Funny thing, though. I gave all our carrot seed away. I'm really sorry about that."

When we started cracking up, he frowned, which only made us laugh harder.

It took me a minute to catch my breath and say, "The only seeds Abe could contribute were carrot seeds—like a whole pound of them."

"A pound? Good grief—you'll be living on carrots!"

"Apparently, we will."

They laughed with us then.

When our laughter ended, Zander said, "Mom and Dad? We're glad you've decided to stay, and I'm sure we can figure out sleeping arrangements."

"I brought a sleeping bag, if that helps," Leo said.

I turned to Abe and Emilio. "What if Emilio sleeps at our house tonight and Roberto and María take Emilio's bed here?"

"I'd enjoy their company. Family, y'know," Abe smiled.

"Thank you for your hospitality, Abe," María said.

"Well, the bed's a double, not a queen-sized," he added by way of apology. "I'll put the sheets into the wash so they'll be fresh for you tonight."

"I'll help," María answered.

Izzie piped up, "I could sleep on your couch, Jayda, if that works? Wouldn't be the first time."

"Perfect!" I grinned. "And Leo, since we keep Bonnie in our room at night until she's older, you could lay out your sleeping bag on the carpet in her room. Would that suit you?"

"Sure. I'm easy."

With the sleeping arrangements decided, the rest of the afternoon was open. We sat down with Bill, Viola, Janice, Roberto, María, and Leo. Emilio stole Izzie away to show her something important to his boy's heart.

Roberto didn't waste time getting down to business. "Tell us your plans. While we're here, we want to help however we can."

"Thanks again, Dad. Well, tomorrow is Friday, a regular workday for the co-op," Zander said, "but Saturday Gamble has arranged for delivery of the K-rails."

"K-rails?" Maria asked. "What are those?"

"You know, the cement barriers on freeways that keep vehicles from running off the edge of the road? We're going to build a wall of them across the neck of the cul-de-sac. To keep out cars."

"You're serious?" Leo asked.

"Serious as a heart attack," Bill muttered. "Might as well not plant a garden if any old grocery grabber gang can waltz in and take what they want."

Roberto nodded slowly. "We live on the outskirts of town, so we don't have as much of that . . . *yet*, but I take your point. And what's your plan to feed the people in your co-op?"

Zander answered him. "We're going to plant our fenced garden plot first, then the front yards of the rest of the houses in the cul-de-sac. We figure we can monitor and guard the front yards better than we can the backyards. But that means our crops would be visible to anyone driving down the street and around the cul-de-sac—hence the K-rails.

"We mean to line up them across the neck of the cul-de-sac, from the side of Bill's house to the side of Abe's house. We'll leave a hole for us to drive in and out. Park a car there the rest of the time."

"And your friend is delivering the K-rails Saturday? Day after tomorrow?"

"Yup. This afternoon and tomorrow we'll be moving more rock to clear out our front yards. And now that you've brought us your rototiller, one person can run that while two more follow behind, sorting out the grass and rocks, while the rest of us keep at the rock hauling."

"Well, I'd like to see those K-rails put in place."

Roberto thought a moment. "What about gas? Do you have a supply for the tiller?"

Bill shook his head. "Gas is a problem. I have like half a gallon in a can for my lawn mower. In addition, I have an empty can to fill. Problem is, most stations don't allow people to fill cans unless they run out while in line. They only allow people to gas their cars. Lately, the limit has been ten gallons or less."

"Hmm. I see. Well, I brought two five gallon cans of gas for the trip home. What if . . . what if, after we unload the truck bed, Zander and I take my truck and try to fill its tank? If we can get enough gas to see us home, I can leave the two full cans of gas with the co-op."

Bill seemed more than a little taken aback. "That's . . . very generous of you, Mr. Cruz."

"Ah, but this is *mi familia*, no? And call me Roberto, please, Bill."

"Thank you . . . Roberto."

Zander touched his dad's shoulder. "Yes. Thank you, Dad."

Roberto cleared his throat and changed the subject. "So, if I may, I have another proposal. You said all the places where you wanted to rent a tiller are booked solid? Perhaps, once you get all your plots tilled and planted, you might consider renting out the tiller—but not for money. Rent it for things that are scarce or things you cannot get at all. Barter for its use."

Bill glanced at Zander. "I like that idea."

"Yeah . . . but what if we rent it out and never get it back?"

"We'd need the deposit to be worth more than the tiller."

"Hmm. Let's think on that. Right now, we have a lot of tilling ahead of us. However, I have my afternoon appointments to keep. You willing to work with my dad?"

Bill nodded. "Sure. Let's get to it."

⌘

WHEN THE DAY ENDED, AND IT ENDED quite late, Bill and Roberto had tilled our fenced plot once over, switching back and forth, one running the tiller, the other hacking clods with the hoe.

It was slow going, but certainly faster and with a better outcome than spading the ground by hand. Janice and I followed behind them, doing the dirty job of shaking out grass and weeds by hand and piling unearthed rocks into a wheelbarrow.

At the same time, Viola, Emilio, and Leo focused on removing rock from Bill and Viola's front yard. Leo and Emilio pushed wheelbarrow upon wheelbarrow into the Tucker's backyard, spreading a wide field of rocks along their walls.

All of us, Emilio included, labored on until six in the evening when Abe and María called us for dinner.

As we gathered for the meal, I was amazed to see Belicia and María sitting on Abe's sofa together, chatting amiably, Bonnie Lu cuddled on Belicia's lap. Frankly, I had been concerned that Belicia would withdraw until Roberto and María left, or that, at some point, sparks would fly between the two women. Instead, they were getting on like two old friends.

I don't know how María managed to diffuse Belicia's envy, Lord, but I am very grateful for it.

I was standing in the dining room, my back to them. Too far to overhear what they were so earnestly discussing. Fortunately, I had a little trick up my sleeve.

"Nano? I'd like to hear María and Belicia."

A trail of them flew out from me, and I heard Belicia and María's voices in my left ear, as clear as if I were sitting in on their conversation.

"A child cannot have too many grandparents, Belicia—don't you agree?"

I hoped Belicia received María's question in the spirit it was intended, and oh! What a gift María was offering our neighbor!

Belicia said softly, "I have never had a grandchild . . . before."

"This is also our first. I wonder . . . since I am Bonnie Lu's *Abuela*, perhaps you should be her Nana? Or do you prefer Grammy?"

Belicia swallowed—and I heard the emotion behind it. "I . . . I like Nana."

"Nana Belicia it is, then! And I must tell you how glad I am that you will be here to love and care for Bonnie Lu when I cannot because we live at a distance. I think that love, when it is shared with others, can never exhaust itself. No, it always makes more of the same . . . in both the giver and the receiver."

How well María had shown me this truism! The more love and acceptance María lavished on me? The greater I loved her back.

What a truly wise woman my mother-in-law is, Lord.

"Thank you, Nano. I don't need to hear more."

We are pleased to have been of service, Jayda Cruz.

Emilio, his hair dripping a little, his face and hands clean but not quite dry, stole up beside me. I put my arm around his shoulders—his *too tall* shoulders. How could he possibly be this tall already?

I slid my arm down to his waist instead, and it was a better fit. I thought of the glimpses I'd caught of him throughout the day. He'd worked alongside the adults—particularly the men—keeping pace with them, learning their ways. Taking on a man's share of the work. I could see he was weary . . . but I could also see the way he carried himself.

"You are a good worker, Emilio, my son, and I'm very proud of you," I whispered to him.

His chest swelled a little.

"Thanks . . . Mama."

I tried hard to keep that pesky sniffle from jumping out into the open.

I almost managed it.

⌘⌘⌘⌘

Chapter 5

It was Friday evening. While Izzie, Leo, and Emilio were getting settled for bed, we retired to our own room. I sat on the edge of our bed to nurse Bonnie Lu. I had just gotten her tucked in and was interested in getting myself tucked in, when the nanomites interrupted.

Jayda Cruz, Zander Cruz, President Jackson's former vice presidential pick, Nora Mellyn, held a press conference earlier this evening. We believe you will wish to watch it.

"Oh, dear," I whispered to Zander.

"Yeah. Don't think we're going to appreciate what she's selling, do you?"

"Not likely."

We didn't.

From my tablet's screen, Mellyn stared out from the podium; her smile lit up the room. Her announcement was short but powerful. And the media's Q&A was obnoxiously long and patently scripted.

"Good afternoon. Thank you all for coming."

Brilliant, teeth-baring smile.

"Like an apex predator," I quipped.

"Shh. Here it comes."

"I am delighted today to announce my official candidacy for the office of President of these United States of America."

Camera flashes. More glitzy preening.

"And yes, I have again switched my party affiliation. Now that I have experienced first-hand how barren of any real solutions President Jackson and his party are, I have returned to the party of my roots, the party of the people—particularly the people suffering the greatest during this out-of-control pandemic—a pandemic made worse by this administration's inadequate, ineffective, and *unacceptable* response, not only to this present crisis of health, but also to the cascade of natural disasters under which America has faltered and staggered.

"Hunger," she intoned. "Actual hunger, to the point of starvation! I can scarcely believe this nation has fallen so far and in such a short time, and I must ask myself—as you must ask yourself—are not the shortages of food right here in the breadbasket of the world the result of ineffective, incompetent leadership? Do not these shortages point to neglect and mismanagement at the highest levels?

"Please heed what I say, my fellow Americans. When your children go to bed hungry tonight, tomorrow, and next week, will it not be because of Robert Jackson's criminal neglect?"

I jumped to my feet in protest. "What! Criminal? That's a lie! Zander, that's a bald-faced lie!"

He tugged me back down onto the edge of our bed. "We know it is, Jay. But remember who is behind her—the Cabal. And remember who is behind the Cabal—Lucifer himself. No doubt her entire speech is scripted to belittle and smear President Jackson. And . . . I don't think she's finished with her first salvo."

Mellyn paused to meet the eyes of the press pool, to "connect" with them, to build their confidence in her, and to display her proud and "presidential" manner.

To lead them by the nose down a path of falsehoods to her next big lie.

"Robert Jackson's disgraceful lack of leadership is why I declined his nomination to serve as his Vice President."

A flurry of notes and photographs.

"What?" I whispered. "She didn't decline his nomination. He declined her."

Mellyn rolled on like a tank. "Someone has to gather the courage of their convictions and stand in opposition to this man and his, frankly, *illegitimate* administration."

She again paused to let her statement sink in.

I found myself shaking. Enraged. "President Jackson illegitimate? How? On what grounds?"

"Coming right up," Zander muttered.

Mellyn stood tall. She stepped to the side of the podium and leaned comfortably toward the press pool, inviting them—and the cameras—into her confidences.

"We must ask ourselves, how and why did Jackson's two vice presidents perish? And please trust me—as one who was at times privy to the inside workings of this administration, the *why* is more important than the *how*."

"Oh, no," I muttered, "what you really mean is, 'Let's skip right over the *how* because I can't prove a single accusation.'"

"What is the *why* you ask? Why would Robert Jackson arrange for the deaths of his own vice presidents? Perhaps you should ask yourself this: What illegal and traitorous acts has Robert Jackson committed that were in jeopardy of becoming known—and no, I do not call him *President*.

"What illegal and traitorous acts did this man, this *pretender*, intend to foist upon our precious nation, so illegal that he found it necessary to remove *not one, but two* vice presidents, both honorable men dedicated to America and the American people?"

"What is she saying?" I cried softly. "What is she talking about? Those were both assassination attempts! We know they were. We uncovered the evidence."

Even the nanomites felt compelled to throw in their protestations.

We did indeed uncover the evidence, Jayda Cruz. The FBI and CIA—and MI6—confirmed our findings. And we can still prove John Harmon and Simon Delancey's treasonous guilt.

"Not if she tells us otherwise, Nano," Zander growled. "Not if that lying hag repeats her lies over and over until the gullible are deceived. Until, without a shred of evidence, the complicit media trumpets those lies as truth."

From my tablet, Mellyn thundered, "Again I ask you this very day: What has this man—a man who *must* be removed from office—what has he done, what does he so desperately need to keep hidden, that he found it necessary to drag *my* good name through the mud? And why did Robert Jackson find it imperative to besmirch my personal honor and my fidelity to my beloved husband?"

I could not believe my ears. "Er, wow."

Zander shook his head. "Yes, *wow*."

Jayda Cruz, Zander Cruz, we have incontrovertible evidence of her adulterous affair. We, through our surrogates, were in the hotel room with her and her lover—

Zander cut them off. "Right, Nano, but she's spouting more than your average run-of-the-mill bald-faced lies. *Listen to her!* Can't you feel it, Jayda? Can't you feel a demonic spirit of delusion at work in and through her lies?"

I started to answer him. "But she . . ."

As Zander's words penetrated and brought my outrage to a halt, I looked and listened within, seeking the sweet small voice of the Holy Spirit—only he was neither sweet nor small in that moment. The Spirit of Holiness was shouting the equivalent of a meltdown alert at a nuclear power plant: *Error! Error! Error!*

"Oh, Zander!"

Zander pulled Scripture from his memory and quoted it. "Listen to this:

> *"The coming of the lawless one*
> *will be in accordance with how Satan works.*
> *He will use all sorts of displays of power*
> *through signs and wonders that serve the lie,*
> *and all the ways that wickedness*

deceives those who are perishing.
They perish because
they refused to love the truth and so be saved.
For this reason God sends them a powerful delusion
so that they will believe the lie and so that
all will be condemned who have not believed the truth
but have delighted in wickedness."

"That's 2 Thessalonians, chapter 2," I whispered.

"Right. So, if we're seeing Satan's delusions at work in front of our very eyes, what does that tell us about the times we are in?"

"The coming of the lawless one . . ."

Zander went to the little desk tucked into the corner of our bedroom and pulled out the chair. "Jayda, I had planned another message for tomorrow, but now I feel impressed to teach on this passage. However, I would disturb Izzie if I went to the dining room to study. Don't wait up for me, 'kay? I'll keep the lamp low while I prepare my message."

"All right. But this has to be breaking President Jackson's heart," I muttered to Zander's back.

"At least the nanomites warned him off making her his VP. I mean, Mellyn *could* be making this same announcement subsequent to being sworn in to fill the last nine months of Jackson's term. You know—following his sad and unfortunate demise?"

"Grrr! I want . . . *I want to punch something*, Zander. Preferably something that looks like Nora Mellyn . . . in the flesh."

Zander's little chuckle didn't sit well with me. Neither did his soft, *"We wrestle not against flesh and blood,* Jay."

"Yeah, whatever. I'll be quiet so you can study, but I've heard about all I can handle tonight. Especially from that *woman*."

I stomped off to our bathroom to brush my teeth.

⌘⌘⌘⌘

CHAPTER 6

We met again at seven Saturday morning, our two work crews expanded to three with the addition of Gamble, Roberto, Leo, and Izzie. The tasks before us, preparing our yards for planting, felt natural to me now. As I tugged on my work gloves, they were familiar friends, loved and appreciated.

After weeks of relative inactivity while I recovered from Bonnie Lu's birth, I felt myself strengthening physically. Like Bill had said we would, we were hardening to the work—Zander and I more quickly than the others. I looked forward each day to using my muscles, expending the energy my nano-charged body produced. In short, I rejoiced in it.

A significant downside to our increased activity presented itself, however: Our nano-hyped metabolisms demanded far more fuel than most adults consumed. Worse, with daily physical labor and because I was feeding Bonnie Lu, my appetite rocketed into the stratosphere. Zander and I spent all the money we were allowed to spend at any given store to feed us and Emilio, but Zander, whose hand hadn't been stamped recently, went out in the evening once a week, getting the most in bulk he could from whatever grocery store he visited.

It still wasn't enough.

Abe and Emilio understood our conundrum—as did Gamble and Janice. But Zander's family and the remainder of our co-op were clueless. María, who had noted I was too thin, called attention to the fact that I looked to have lost more weight in the few days they were with us.

"Don't worry," I reassured her. "I'm healthy; I'll be all right."

That didn't prevent María from eyeing me with concern. For that reason, I would be glad when she, Roberto, and Izzie left for home Sunday.

Reluctantly, Zander and I agreed to *gently* tap into our emergency stores down in the nanomites' printer room. We pulled a number of items up to the kitchen to supplement our meals, but I didn't like it.

"Those groceries down there are our *emergency stash*, Zander. We shouldn't be using them now when we might need them more desperately later. Like when Bonnie starts eating solids."

At the same time, the specter of literally starving while everyone else "got by" was never far from my mind or from the growling reminder in my belly.

"Zander, remember when we used to eat out every night in DC? Hit up our favorite all-you-can-eat buffets? This food rationing . . . is hard."

"Yeah, it stinks. But we always have something, right? Tonight too many children across the world will go to bed without any food at all in their tummies . . . yet our Bonnie Lu grows plumper by the day."

Lord, for what we have, I am truly grateful.

Back to our gardens.

While the co-op shoveled landscape rock into wheelbarrows to clear Bill and Abe's front yards, Zander drove the rototiller over our plot, tilling the soil crosswise. As he worked toward completing our second full pass, I followed behind him and did the usual—broke up clods, sorted weeds and grass from soil, and piled rocks into a wheelbarrow. Whenever I had a load of rocks, I rolled my wheelbarrow into Gamble and Janice's backyard and dumped its load along the cinderblock wall, creating a second disinviting field of "trespass here and you're going to break an ankle."

Bill, pushing his own wheelbarrow into our yard, interrupted our flow of work.

Zander stopped the tiller's forward motion to wipe his face. "What do you have there, Bill?"

"Compost from my backyard. The usual leaves, grass clippings, coffee grounds, egg shells, and so on. I ran them through a mulcher and composted them over the winter. It's not much, I'm afraid, but it's better than nothing."

Zander was enthusiastic as he turned off the tiller. "You bet it is! Let's dump it over here and mix it with the two bags of fertilizer Gamble managed to snag for us."

Gamble was proving his worth to the co-op with his facility to search out and acquire hard-to-come-by materials and supplies during his lunch break, bringing his treasures to us at the end of each day.

Bill dumped his load on the corner of the garden plot. The guys emptied the fertilizer onto the compost, and with two shovels going, turned and turned the pile until its elements were well mixed together.

"I have a little more compost I'm saving back for our front yard garden. I have a spreader at my place too," Bill said. "I'll bring it over."

A few minutes later, he dropped off the spreader. We weren't quite ready for it, though. Because most of the ground had not been plowed before, Zander needed to finish the second pass over our plot—and I had more rocks to remove.

When the second pass was completed, I would shovel the compost and fertilizer mixture into the spreader and run it over the ground Zander had plowed. On his third and final pass with the rototiller, he would till the fertilized compost into the soil. Then we'd be ready to plant.

Our labor took an abrupt recess at the rumble of engines in the cul-de-sac. As Gamble had promised, a flatbed truck hauling two dozen five-foot K-rails pulled into the cul-de-sac. A second truck carrying a light crane followed the flatbed.

Everyone—co-op members plus Zander's folks, Izzie, and Leo—turned out to watch. Even Belicia, Bonnie Lu in her arms, stood in our home's dining room window to observe.

While we checked out the goings on, I kept one eye on Emilio. He was so excited, he couldn't stand still. He bounced up and down and peppered Abe with questions until the poor guy declared he needed a break and went home.

Four men descended from the trucks. Gamble and Bill donned masks and went out to meet them—across the six-foot required distance. Many words were spoken, punctuated by gestures and pointed fingers. One of the men folded his arms and shook his head. Bill flushed with anger, but Gamble just shrugged, said something, and planted his hands in his pockets.

Jayda Cruz, the foreman said—

"Thanks, Nano, but I get the picture. The foreman doesn't want to block a city street without legal authorization, and Gamble said something along the lines of 'do the job or you don't get paid.'"

Bill hustled toward us—no doubt to complain to Zander.

Zander forestalled him. "Hold up a minute, Bill. Let's let Gamble do his thing."

Gamble's "thing" consisted of him withdrawing five Franklins from his wallet. He folded them and handed them off to the foreman who, in turn, motioned to the other guys to start work.

Roberto joined as I said, "Huh. Nice to know bribes are back in fashion."

He snorted. "We should get used to it. This is a seller's market."

The two drivers pulled down a ramp for the crane, then undid the massive tie-downs that kept the crane stable during transport. Another guy climbed up into the crane's operator cage. He fiddled a bit before he fired up the engine. With a rumbling roar, the crane lumbered off the truck.

The next part was fascinating. The operator maneuvered the crane to the side of the flatbed. He lowered the crane's arm until it dangled beside something that wasn't a K-rail.

"That's a barrier lift," Roberto said, pointing at it. "Nice bit of engineering, that."

The two drivers attached the crane's dangling arm to the barrier lift and locked it in place. When the drivers moved away, the crane, in a leisurely manner, swiveled into position with its arm over one of the K-rails. The arm came down, the barrier lift's grips descended on either side of the first rail's top and closed, clamping onto the rail.

The arm then slowly raised the rail and deposited it where the foreman directed. He repeated the same process again and again.

After thirty minutes of wrangling K-rails into place, a line ran from the cinderblock wall spanning Bill and Viola's side yard, down their property line, and partway across the neck of the cul-de-sac.

Zander nudged me. "Come on, Jay. Let's get back to it."

"Right."

Zander took up his post behind the rototiller while I pushed the spreader slowly up and down our garden plot and he followed me. When another hour had gone by, we'd finished our final pass on the garden and took a break to see how the work in the cul-de-sac had progressed.

They were nearly done. The line of K-rails stretched from Bill's house, across the street, up onto the sidewalk, then connected to the cinderblock wall of Abe's side yard. The line was complete except for an eight-foot gap at the mouth of the cul-de-sac nearest Abe's lot, the hole intentionally left open for us to drive through. Before the day was over, Abe's vintage sedan would plug that hole. We'd leave his car in place, driving it out of the way when a co-op member on an approved outing left or returned.

We'd paid for two dozen rails, so we had six left over. Bill and Gamble decided to reinforce the line spanning the street, having the crane spread out a second line of rails behind the first, from one sidewalk to the other. The crane had nearly finished moving them into position.

Zander joined me as the foreman approached Gamble for payment. Gamble opened his wallet and counted out a big pile of hundred dollar bills.

"We're paying for everything in cash now? Is this the new economy?"

"More like an old one," Zander said. "I suppose our shaky power grid has made payment by credit card and banking electronically just as iffy as our grid is. If you can't pull your money from the bank when you need it or if electronic transfers and credit cards don't work when you count on them, then cash becomes king."

"Huh."

As the crew loaded up the crane to depart, Gamble joined us.

"They weren't thrilled about barricading our cul-de-sac, huh?" was Zander's wry question.

Gamble winced. "Thrilled enough to accept an extra half grand, cash."

"Yeah. Noticed that."

"About noticing . . . Seems our neighbors down the street have noticed our barrier and have come out to parlay with us. Want me to join you and Jayda?"

The co-op had been Zander's idea, and although he shared the lead with others in the group, we deferred to him as our spokesperson.

The three of us walked up to the barrier. We stood six feet or more—the required "safe" distance—from the two women and one man on the other side. The delegation didn't appear too happy with us, and one of the women, going by her red face and pinched mouth, was more than a little perturbed.

Zander put on his friendliest smile. "Hi. I'm Zander Cruz. This is my wife, Jayda, and our neighbor Ross Gamble."

The angry woman, fiftyish, her stern expression fiercened by a narrow, hawk-like nose, demanded, "What's going on here?"

Zander's smile never faltered. "And you are?"

She looked down the length of her nose. "Talla Mitchell, neighborhood watch captain. We want to know what this-this *blockade* means and demand to know who gave you the authority to erect it."

"Right. Thanks for asking. As I said, I'm Zander Cruz. I'm the, er, *captain* of the Cul-de-Sac Co-op."

Cul-de-Sac Co-op? I liked it!

She puzzled over it, though. "Co-op?"

"Yes. The families inside our cul-de-sac have formed a cooperative."

"That doesn't give you the right to block off the street!"

Zander shrugged—but gently. "Perhaps not . . . but I fail to see how it adversely impacts you and your neighborhood watch group. It may actually benefit you."

Talla opened her mouth to reply, but the guy beside her shoehorned himself into the conversation before she could answer.

"Hi. I'm Ed Small." He jutted his chin toward the other woman in the delegation. "This is my wife, Kim. Glad to meet all of you. Too bad it takes a pandemic and food shortages to get to know our neighbors. Right?"

I had studied the man and kind of liked what I saw—a benign gleam of interest. His shifting gaze took in Bill and Abe's torn up front yards. "So, you said you've formed a co-op? Would you mind telling us about it?"

"Ed! I'm captain of the watch, and—"

"And I'm having a pleasant conversation with our neighbors, Talla. Get over yourself."

He lifted his chin toward Bill's house. "May I ask what's going on over there?"

Zander again smiled. "Sure, Ed. Our co-op is tilling up our front yards. We'll plant them with vegetables to supplement the groceries we can buy."

"And closing off the cul-de-sac will . . ."

"Keep the grocery grabber gangs from rolling through—and any others hoping for a drive-by produce pickup."

Ed's eyes brightened. "Ah."

"Yup."

He began slowly nodding. "We could do something similar with our neighbors up the street."

"Sure."

"And you chose your front yards rather than backyards why?"

"We figured we could keep a better eye on our gardens if they were in our front yards, not the back. You could follow suit. You could even block off the length of the street up at the next corner to protect your gardens—as long as you moved your mailboxes and maintained an egress for us and any visitors."

Talla bristled. "You think you can block off *your* part of the street *to us*, but we can't return the favor?"

Zander remained patient. "Talla, this is a cul-de-sac. No through access. Zero reason for you to come in here. Your block, however, requires that you maintain egress to the other residents of this street."

"Well, just so you know, I'll be calling the city the moment I get home! We'll see how long they allow you to keep this illegal barricade up."

Zander kept his amiable smile intact. "It's disconcerting, isn't it? How thinly spread the city's resources are everywhere. Lots of city employees out sick . . . or permanently. Services discontinued or put off until staffing improves. Not enough police officers to respond to actual crimes. And the sense that we're about one major riot short of things falling into chaos . . ."

He glanced at Gamble. "What do you think, Gamble? How long before the city sends a patrol car or a city employee out to cite us?"

Gamble, hands in his pockets, rocked back on his heels. "Shoot. A month, maybe? And since we're not breaking windows, looting the neighborhood, or setting cars on fire, I doubt they'll even slow down to wave as they go by."

Talla's frown deepened, pulling her eyes closer to her knife-like nose. "You can't get away with this. I'll call the mayor myself! I'll—"

Ed shook his head. "Ditch the self-righteous posturing, Talla. These are our neighbors, and we had better consider taking a page from their playbook before it's too late in the growing season and too hot to get a decent planting in."

He stepped a little closer to the barricade, eyeing the hole in it near Abe's house. "Would you be amenable to sharing how you're going about this? Give us some tips?"

Zander looked to me first. "Jayda?"

"Of course. But across the barrier. Nothing closer. Whoever is on guard can answer your questions."

I addressed Ed and Kim. "This barricade serves to self-isolate the co-op members. We're okay mingling with each other, but only because we keep others out and limit the outings we take to get groceries and such. These measures will minimize our risk of exposure to the virus. We have two kids to protect."

Kim sent an understanding smile toward me, and I liked her immediately. Ed seemed okay too. I could practically watch the wheels turning in his head. I hoped he would be able to marshal their neighborhood watch group to action.

Zander and Ed exchanged cell numbers, and we said goodbye to them. Talla sniffed and left ahead of the Smalls.

"Good job, Babe," I said as we walked away.

Gamble agreed. "I admire you, Zander. Cool, calm, collected. Pleasant expressions."

"Thanks—I think. Right now, my face tells me my smile is broken."

We laughed together, and it felt good.

We hadn't reached our own sidewalk, though, before a car rolled up to the barrier and stopped. The driver tapped the horn. When the passenger side window rolled down, Josh's merry eyes beamed out at us from behind a face mask.

"Hey, Pastor Zander! Hey, Jayda! We heard Izzie was in town. Thought we'd drop in and say hi—from a safe distance, of course."

We? I looked beyond Josh to identify the figure in the driver's seat. Diego!

Izzie appeared, grinning and brushing dirt and grime from the knees of her pants.

Josh saw her and jumped out of the car. "Hey, Iz!"

While Izzie raced up to the barricade, waving at them with glee, Bill approached us.

"Friends of yours?"

"Members of my church's young adult group."

"Can you guarantee that they're virus-free?"

"No." Of course the nanomites could, but Zander lifted his voice for appearance's sake.

"Hey, Iz? Hang back, please. Starting today, we don't allow anyone not part of the co-op into the cul-de-sac."

To Josh he added, "Great to see you guys! Have Diego park on the curb just up from Abe's place and approach the barricade, okay? We'll talk there."

As Diego swung his car around and parked it, Zander and I walked over. Izzie joined us. We waited for the guys to face us from a safe distance across the barricade, which they soon did.

"Guys, it's so good to see you both in person!" I enthused.

Diego answered back, "You, too, Jayda. Uh, you've dropped a baby bump since we last saw you. It's not as noticeable on a video conference call."

"You should see what that baby bump produced," I laughed. I caught Izzie's expression as she smiled at them. Or should I say as she smiled at *Josh?*

The current flowing between those two about blinded me.

*Well, duh! Totally did not know **that** was happening, but I'll bet you a donut those two have been burning more video call hours between each other lately than they have with the young adults for Bible study.*

I was thrilled.

Of course, Josh asked, "What good are these cement street things besides acting as a reminder for people to keep the minimum six-foot distance?"

"They're called K-rails—and yes, our little co-op is isolating behind them. Also, if you look to your right at the Tuckers' front yard and to your left at Abe's yard, you'll see we're removing the landscaping rock. Fixing to plant gardens and raise some food."

Josh and Diego studied what Bill, Viola, and Leo were working hard at in Bill's front yard.

Josh said, "You think this barricade, this line of K-rails will keep people out?"

"Won't keep marauders on foot out, but the barricade will keep their vehicles out. I suppose that's a start," Zander said.

"Riiiight," Josh said, thinking hard. "And because you're isolating as a group, everyone behind the barrier can, you know, hang out? Like, together?"

Izzie nodded and smiled again. Josh made a feeble attempt not to look her way and failed.

Oh, Josh, you've got it bad, I snickered to myself.

Zander was trying not to laugh—he really was, honest. He covered his mouth and coughed before saying, "Yes, that's the idea. We'll isolate together, share the work on these gardens, share the food we raise, and share security duties. It'll be several weeks before we have anything in our plots worth stealing, though."

"Security duties? Like guards?"

"Yes. We will mount a guard here soon, and we plan to install a network of cameras across all our backyards."

"What about co-op people who have jobs and can't help with the gardens and guard stuff? How does that work?"

"Right now, just two of us work outside jobs, Gamble and me. Gamble works out of the FBI's Albuquerque field office. He has daily assignments, but while he's out of the cul-de-sac, he also runs down supplies we need.

"I keep my daily online appointments to the afternoons and evenings. Same with prepping for Sunday service and the young adult group."

"What if someone had a job and, like, worked from home but had to be available during the day?"

"We don't have anyone doing that except for me," Zander said.

"Well, I'm planning to stay," Izzie blurted, "and I work from home exactly as Josh described."

Zander's and my heads must have been on the same string, because they both jerked around simultaneously. We even spoke in sync.

"What?"

"I've already spoken to Bill and Viola. I'm going to rent their spare bedroom." She tacked on, sheepishly, "I guess they could use the money."

"Um, that's a decision the co-op needs to weigh in on, Iz," Zander said softly. "I mean, we'd love to have you near, but it's a big commitment. You'd have to agree to isolate with the co-op and shoulder your share of the work."

She lifted one shoulder. "Sure. I get it. You already know I can plant, weed, harvest, and put up what we harvest. I'll be an asset in that regard."

"Will your boss let you flex your hours?"

"Mostly. I figure when summer temps heat up that I'll work the garden first thing in the morning and my job in the afternoon. I adjudicate medical insurance claims, Zander. I can do that pretty much anytime—just need to keep my stats up and stay abreast of the workflow—but my team already has members throughout the country in different time zones. Flexing my hours shouldn't be a problem."

"We'll take it up with the co-op and vote on it, Iz. If we all agree, then you can stay."

Josh wasn't a co-op member, but his eyes had already voted in Izzie's favor.

⌘

WE WERE SORRY TO SEE ROBERTO, María, and Leo leave early Sunday morning. Izzie, on the other hand, had received unanimous approval the evening before as our co-op's newest member.

Bill's pro-Izzie argument had nailed the vote. "Face it, Zander, of the co-op's members, four of us are seniors and one is an infant. That's spreading all of us pretty thin. We could use a few young, strong bodies around here—so long as they pay for their own food and pull their weight."

"I can do both," Izzie assured him.

Roberto and María hadn't known Izzie would be moving back to Albuquerque prior to the meeting. When they'd had a few moments to adjust to the idea, they accepted her decision.

"It's been wonderful having you home with us," María murmured, "but you are a grown woman, Izzie. We understand."

I was sort of stuck on Bill's "We could use *a few* young, strong bodies."

That evening, I said to Zander, "Having Izzie here will be a blessing. Like Bill said, we need young blood, strong bodies."

"Where are you going with this?"

"I'm thinking of Josh. He works from home like Izzie does. I don't know what Belicia would think of the idea, but we, as in the co-op members, need a man in her house, someone who can respond to intruders coming over Belicia's back wall."

Zander nodded. "Let's pray on it and approach Belicia about it, then put it to a vote. Oh, and talk to Josh. How do you think he'll respond?"

"Are you kidding? That's a slam-dunk."

⌘⌘⌘⌘

Chapter 7

Zander left the cul-de-sac the following morning on the heels of Roberto, María, and Leo's departure. As he headed for Downtown Christian Center, he prayed over his message and congregation.

From the day the governor's health mandate had banned assemblies of any kind, he had livestreamed his Sunday messages from his office at the church. He and Jayda also hosted the weekly young adult Bible studies from their living room via a video conference call. Once the livestream or conference calls ended, DCC's three-man IT crew organized the recorded video files on YouTube, Facebook, and Rumble. They labeled each message with its date and added a succinct description of the topic.

What was strange—strange in a terrific way—was how the audience for both of Zander's weekly teachings had grown. Viewership of his Sunday messages had shot up into the thousands, then (to Zander's total amazement) jumped over the hundred thousand mark. The IT crew also tracked viewership by IP address and reported that people all across the English-speaking world were subscribing to DCC's social media channels.

On a recent video conference call with the team, Zander had discussed the unprecedented jump in viewership. They attributed the phenomena to the virus lockdowns.

"People can't 'go' to church, so they're seeking out good teaching, and you fit the bill," Mark, the lead IT tech, said. "We're . . . well, we're pretty proud of you, Pastor."

Another IT member, Arturo, added, "Yup. And then there's our Spanish-language channels. You should see how they're doing."

"Our what?"

"I launched DCC Spanish-language channels on YouTube and Rumble, Pastor."

Zander was floored. "You did?"

"Sure. I added Spanish captions to your messages and published the repurposed videos on the new channels. It wasn't difficult, but it *was* time consuming. Since I'm furloughed from my job, what better use of my time and effort?"

"And people watch them?"

The crewmates laughed in unison. "Pastor, our Spanish language channels have lit up like houses on fire. You're now drawing viewers up and down North, South, and Central America."

What really blew Zander's mind, though, was the audience for the weekly young adult group. The group totaled less than thirty. Several had returned home when the virus closed the UNM campus, but they dialed in remotely each week. However, the previous Friday evening, all one hundred "seats" on their new and expanded video conference call software had been filled before he kicked off the meeting. Young adults from all over, anxious to participate in Zander's teachings and the discussions he held around the lessons, checked in as soon as the call allowed them to. As a result, a few chagrined DCC latecomers had been left to watch the concurrent livestream without being able to participate.

Those same weekly studies, when posted online, had somehow been "discovered" and were of late garnering a viewership that rivaled his Sunday sermons.

His IT crew was ecstatic. Zander was flummoxed.

On the same call between Zander and the members of his IT team, Mark said, "Pastor Zander, from what we see in the comments, you are starting to reach high school, college, and career-aged youth from all over, young people locked down because of the virus, many who are desperate for hope. Youth who are starved for simple, pointed Biblical teaching."

The third tech, Kenny, jumped in. "Yeah, the growth is organic, Pastor—word-of-mouth and social media shares. The live study is limited to a hundred participants, but the new software allows unlimited livestream viewers. What's fun and really cool is how the livestream viewers are posting photos of themselves in the comments as they watch, saying hello to other viewers around the world. We're even seeing photos of teen siblings and their parents watching together. Whole families. It's kinda like . . . kinda like a revival of some sort."

"It *is* a revival," Mark insisted. "It's evident that the Holy Spirit is the one drawing these new viewers. We, the IT crew, have been talking about that, because lots of these kids—is it all right that I call them kids?—lots of them are ready to give their lives to Christ. They are begging in the comments to be told what they should do next."

Kenny jumped back in. "We've been wondering if you might appoint a few of your young adult leaders to set up new video conference calls after you finish each meeting. They could invite those who are ready to surrender and receive Christ to join *their* call. Then they could lead the kids in prayer and maybe start discipling them."

"Forming virtual home groups," Arturo added.

Zander was so humbled, all he could muster at the moment was, "This is . . . flat-out amazing."

"It sure is," Kenny said. "So what do you think of our suggestion?"

Zander laughed. "How can I say no? Seems like a great solution.

"I'll make it a priority to get my young adult leaders on it. Say . . ." he studied their eager faces for a moment. "What about the three of you? Are you willing to be small group leaders? How about you work with our young adult leaders? Train them in the software."

"Us?" Mark's expression registered shock.

"Yes, you three. You're grounded in the word and adept at the technology. I mean, what's that saying? Don't bring a suggestion unless you're willing to help implement it—am I right?"

Mark's chin moved up and down slowly. "Um, right. Guys, are you in?"

After receiving their agreement, Zander said he'd be in touch and ended the call. Then he muttered to himself, "Just another priority among an entire litany of competing priorities. Lord, please help me!"

That Sunday morning though, as the nanomites unlocked the door to DCC's office wing for him and turned off the security system's alarms, Zander focused all his attention on the morning's teaching. He spent the next two hours praying over and tweaking his message.

Then he took a break to walk through the church and check that all the doors and windows were still locked and intact, that no one had broken in. As he walked, he also prayed. "Lord, I confess that I'm still a little leery of Aiden Easterly, his proselytes, and those above them who give them orders. It has been about four months since that mob tried to take over this congregation—and when their push failed, tried to burn us out of this building.

"O God! I pray your protection over this house of worship. It is not your *church*—no, *we*, your people, are the church. Nevertheless, this building is consecrated to you. It is supposed to be a place for your people to gather in worship and prayer to you; a place for training your people in ministry. If it is your will, please let it be so again. Amen."

His walkthrough complete, Zander returned to his office and sat down at his desk. Two cameras mounted on tripods stood several feet from his desk. One camera faced him straight on; the second camera was off to the right of the first, pointing at him from an oblique angle.

A microphone on a third stand would pick up his voice with better quality than either camera could on its own. The nanomites controlled the cameras and the microphone.

He took a moment to compose himself and faced the camera directly opposite his desk. From the warehouse, he heard the nanomites counting down.

Zander Cruz, you are live in three, two, one—

⌘

LATER, IZZIE USED OUR KITCHEN to prepare lunch for Abe, Emilio, Zander, and me. We tried to make Sunday lunch a bit special, even if it was only setting a more festive table or sharing a candy bar split into bite-sized portions.

After we ate, Bonnie wanted her lunch and then a good nap, so I retired to our bedroom. Bonnie had just conked out when the nanomites asked Zander to join me in our bedroom.

Jayda Cruz, Zander Cruz, we have things we wish to show you. Come into the warehouse, please.

I laid Bonnie on our bed, tucked her soft Winnie-the-Pooh quilt around her, placed pillows on either side of her, then dove into the warehouse.

"Yes, Nano? You have things to show us? What things?"

A rush of dizziness overtook me. I felt my consciousness spiral away as the nanomites pulled Zander and me into the virtual world they inhabited. I was floating nowhere. I felt smallish and insignificant. Growing more so with the passing seconds, but at least I sensed Zander close by.

I also sensed the nanomites everywhere. They were all around us—or we were among them . . . until, with a jolt, we were *inside* a nanoarray, watching and experiencing everything from the nanoarray's perspective.

It was akin to being aboard a sailing ship, perched on top of the tallest mast, being tossed by waves. It made me dizzy. My stomach lurched, and for a moment I thought I'd lose my breakfast.

Disconcerted, I whispered, "Nano?"

Jayda Cruz, Zander Cruz, do not be alarmed. We believe it is now time to provide you with a sampling of our counterinsurgency. As you know, we did extensive preplanning with the goal of triggering much of our counterinsurgency in a simultaneous manner—an attempt to attack the Cabal on many fronts at once.

"Yes. We recall," I answered.

We have brought you into this virtual environment for a reason. We believe the perspective of our nanoarrays—a combined recording and simulation of the proceedings having utilized the placement of the array's many cameras—will provide the most effective demonstration of our counterinsurgency's effectiveness.

Without further delay, the nanomites plunged us into a world of virtual reality, replicating the events the nanoarrays had both observed and experienced.

Oh, yeah. It was effective, all right.

MEXICO CITY

MIGUEL ÁNGEL MARTÍN SMILED FOR the crowd and the flashing cameras. Today, their darling girl turned fifteen, and this evening, they celebrated her *quinceañera*—all six hundred of their family and closest friends.

Invitations to the event had been keenly sought after, of course. He was Mexico's *Secretario de Gobernación*, or Secretary of the Interior. Should something untoward befall *el presidente*, it was *he*, Miguel Ángel Martín, who would assume the executive role. Only provisionally, of course, until Congress elected an interim president to fill the post while elections were arranged. Congress would appoint *him* interim president, of course. It was already "arranged."

Yes, Miguel was a powerful, respected man. A man who was both loved and feared. *It is better to be feared than to be loved. I already have great wealth, and soon I will also have great power—the kind of power I crave.*

When the Global Community rises from the ashes of what is coming? I will rule this nation, he reminded himself. *It has been promised.*

Smiling benevolently, he bowed to his guests and ran a discriminating eye over the décor. The selected venue, the courtyard of Ex Convento San Hipólito, gleamed with old-world charm: The courtyard was enclosed by rows of arched porticos, two stories of them, under a high black roof. A myriad of tiny white lights illuminated the faux night sky around them. An octagonal fountain set within the courtyard propelled graceful jets of water high into the air. The most acclaimed mariachi band in all of Mexico played softly in a corner of the courtyard. Fresh flowers in abundance were tastefully arranged to accent the priceless historic setting.

The music rose slowly in volume until, upon a crescendo, the guests hushed. It was time.

Miguel gestured proudly to the wide, red-carpeted staircase descending from a second floor portico—and thunderous applause greeted his daughter as she appeared. He gazed with indulgent affection on his only child.

Camila stood at the staircase's apex, magnificent in ivory, gold, and champagne. A shimmering tiara crowned her dark tresses; her tiny waist rose like the slender stem of a glorious flower from the smooth, wide skirts of her dress. Miguel climbed the steps to escort her in her triumphal entry. Wild applause and cheers filled the courtyard and resounded around them.

He offered his arm to her and, still smiling, whispered, "Remember to keep your chin up, *mija*. Do not look down at your feet. Smile for your adoring admirers, and I will guide you safely down."

"*Si*, Papa."

He owed much to his wife, Isabella, for her tireless work in planning such a distinguished event and for dressing Camila as the regal princess she was—not as some overblown cake topper. He had seen too many of Camila's friends swallowed up in the flounces of dresses that resembled globs of cotton candy on sticks rather than the simple purity of a budding young maiden.

When the dinner had concluded and before the dancing commenced, Miguel stood and lifted his glass of champagne and "To our Camila," he said, "to her beauty and grace."

"To her beauty and grace," the crowd murmured.

Much later, as the crowds began to thin, the hotel manager appeared. "Señor Martín, I trust all is as you wished?"

"*Perfecto. Gracias.*"

He touched his Amex Centurion Card to the tablet the manager offered him. The tablet buzzed. The manager blinked and extended his hand. "If I may, *señor*?"

He, too, touched the card to the tablet's screen. The tablet buzzed again. Next, he swiped the card through the card reader. Another buzz.

The manager's expression settled into carefully impartial lines. "*Señor* Martín, I regret to tell you that your card is declined."

"That is not possible. I hold the AMEX black card. No limit."

The remaining portion of the bill, half of the total cost of the event, was $6,466,557MXN—roughly $320,000USD.

"Perhaps if we adjourn to my office, we will discover that the issue is a technical one, a problem on the company's end, *sí*? Easily overcome, I am certain, with a call to American Express?"

Miguel was annoyed at being torn away from the event just as his guests were taking their leave, pouring their effusive compliments on him and his wife. He leaned toward Isabella. "My dear, I must deal with a tedious bit of business. I hope to be absent only a few minutes. Please make my excuses while I am away."

When his call connected to the American Express customer service line—a very special line for exclusive cardholders such as he—and after he had jumped through all of the hoops to verify his identity, the answer to his dilemma was nothing he would have anticipated.

"Mr. Martín, sir, our records show that you canceled your card three days ago."

"What kind of nonsense is this? I did no such thing," Miguel growled into the phone. "Please reinstate my card. Immediately."

"Of course, sir. You have been our valued customer for some time. I am happy to reactivate your card now. Please allow five minutes for the changes to propagate across our system."

As the venue's manager counted down five minutes before rerunning his card, Miguel pondered the strange occurrence. He stared at his phone, then picked it up and logged into the secure app of his Mexican bank. Stared at the screen.

"*Madre de Dios!* What is this?"

"Señor Martín?"

"It is nothing." It was *not* nothing!

"Did the charge go through?"

The manager visibly relaxed. "*Sí*, Señor Martín. Thank you very much." He returned the card to Miguel.

Miguel left the manager's office and strode toward the courtyard, his security team falling in behind him. Rather than heading directly into the courtyard, he ducked into a dark alcove with a bench seat.

"Get me a brandy," he ordered. His men sent off the most junior on the team to fetch the liquor. While he waited, Miguel logged in to four additional bank accounts, each located in a country other than Mexico or the US. To his growing dismay, all four were like the first: only the minimum balance required to keep the account open remained.

With shaking hands, he pressed a well-used contact in his phone. The man who answered skipped the normal pleasantries.

"Miguel. You are calling because your accounts have been drained?"

A brandy snifter appeared beside him. Miguel downed the brandy, neat. "Another!" he snarled to his men.

Into his phone he replied, "And my black Amex was canceled. I am, at present, without disposable assets of any kind." He felt naked. Exposed. Quite a novel sensation for him.

That was before he recalled the cool million in US dollars resting in his bedroom safe along with several million in gold coins and cut gems. Still, his mind raced onward, considering his enemies one by one, evaluating then discarding one ruse or stratagem after another.

The voice on the other end of the line sighed. "You are not the sole target, my friend. We have been receiving similar reports across the Global Community for the past thirty-six hours."

"*Claro!* So, this is no criminal endeavor, no cheap Eastern European hack-for-profit. This is a coordinated attack, not on us singly, but on the Global Community itself. Who? Who has done this?"

"You think we are not looking? You think they will not be dead shortly once we know who they are?"

"But not before they return our money," Miguel demanded.

"No. Not before then."

⌘

I GASPED AS THE SCENE TRANSITIONED abruptly, and the nanomites jerked me from that environment. Again I was unmoored and floating.

"Nano?"

One moment, Jayda Cruz.

Almost immediately, I found myself elsewhere.

WASHINGTON, DC

THE ESTEEMED SENIOR SENATOR from Oregon, Imani Glover, held decades of seniority in the US Senate. Her position and influence made her a valuable member of the Global Community. The Community had helped her get where she was, and she helped them move their shared agenda forward.

Win-win.

She concluded her committee's meeting. "I am starving. You must be too. We have our assignments for next week. The remaining agenda items are tabled until our next session. We are dismissed."

The time was already 8:30 on a Friday evening—Friday of a weekend she had planned to spend at home. Her stomach growling, she pushed back her chair, stood, and left the clutter at her seat for her staff to organize and pack into her briefcase—everything but her phone.

It had been on the fritz since early yesterday, alternately powering up—then down—without warning. While it was up, it refused to make its connection to her service provider or the internet, which made it a useless hunk of plastic and circuitry. She'd allowed the most tech-savvy member of her staff to tinker with it while Imani kept one eye on her, but the woman had been unable to get the phone working right either.

Imani had explicit instructions for such a situation. She was never to hand her phone off for repair outside the Community. If it was well and truly toast, the Community would replace it, ensuring the security of her communications.

Yesterday and today had been a royal pain. She couldn't imagine how she'd spend her weekend if she were unplugged.

As Imani walked out of the committee meeting, she tried powering the device on again. To her surprise and delight, it came up. She waited until it had finished booting, then pressed a saved number. The call rang through. Her sister picked up.

"Imani?"

"I'm sorry, Eb, but I'm not going to make it home. Just got out of committee, and I can't catch another flight out of DC until morning. Not worth the trip by then."

Her younger sibling, Ebony, was as angry as Imani expected. Perhaps more so.

"We had dinner plans this evening. You could have called or texted earlier."

"No, I couldn't. My phone has been on the blink since yesterday morning."

"Uh-huh. How convenient—as always. And you with not a single other phone available to you, right? Well, just so we're straight with each other, I wasn't expecting you this weekend anyway."

Imani huffed. "What the *blank* does that mean?"

"Your phone was out? Give me a break."

"Eb, it wouldn't even boot until just now. I haven't been able to use it for two days."

"You know, Imani, you are the consummate strategist—which often requires twisting the truth to fit your narrative. That's what makes you a good politician. But you're not supposed to lie *to me*. If you were going to up and move, why wouldn't you tell me? *What the *bleep* are you hiding from me?*"

Imani stopped in her tracks. Her staff halted dutifully behind her, partially blocking the hallway. Other senators and their staff flowed around them.

"Ebony, what are you talking about? Up and move? Move where?"

Her sister sucked in a breath, a telling habit Imani understood: Ebony was now on uncertain ground, trying to think through what she'd say next.

I always could out-think and out-talk you, Sis, Imani recalled with fondness.

Finally, Ebony said. "Your neighbor, Mr. Brighton, called me yesterday after the realtor sign went up. I couldn't believe I had to hear the news from a neighbor."

"Realtor sign? What? Someone's listed *my house?*"

Her home on Lake Oswego's Northshore Road included half an acre of treed property that afforded her a modicum of much-needed privacy. The current assessment on her property was upwards of six million dollars.

"Listed it? It's already sold. Oh, *right*. Uh-huh. You didn't know."

"Ebony, I did not put my house on the market."

"But . . ."

"Give me the realtor's name and number."

"Imani . . ."

"Just give them to me!" Imani shouted.

Her shouting hadn't helped, hadn't appeased her sister. Instead, Ebony's voice cooled.

"You can check out the sign on your home's security feed. I'll talk to you later—or maybe not. I won't put up with being lied to, Imani. I'm not the media or one of your flunkies."

Imani's sister hung up.

Imani held out her phone and stared at it. Then she logged into her home security system's app. Stared, aghast: The realtor sign at the gate read "SOLD" in big red letters.

"No!"

She switched views to the interior of her house. The very *empty* interior of her house. Not a stick of furniture, a wall hanging, or throw rug remained. Everything she owned in that house was gone.

Now frantic, she moved the timeline back two days. Nothing out of the ordinary. Her furnishings were intact. She moved forward to yesterday morning.

A glut of movers, all of them wearing matching coveralls and billed caps, at least a dozen in all, swarmed through her home. She watched them dismantle her sound system, remove her sectional, pack her dishes, *pack her clothes*, load the truck.

They were efficient, and they were *fast*. A cleaning crew followed the movers, leaving her empty home spotless.

She muttered to herself. "I should have received alerts from my security system. The second someone came on the premises, the system should have alerted me!"

They arrived yesterday morning. Same time her phone "died."

It hit her. Someone had hacked her phone. Emptied her house. *Sold it.*

Imani felt her legs give way. She reached out for the wall to steady herself, but missed it altogether. The young man who interned in her office caught her awkwardly at the last second and lowered her to the floor.

"Senator! Senator? Are you all right?"

She couldn't answer. All she could do was stare at the camera feed. And the oddest part of every video recorded by her security cameras was not what she could see, but what she *couldn't* see. No matter which camera she switched to or which angle the video had been recorded from, not one identifiable detail was visible.

The signage on the moving truck and the cleaners' car? Their vehicle plates? The movers' or cleaners' faces?

Blurred out. Obscured.

Every. Single. One.

⌘

SENSORY OVERLOAD. THAT'S HOW I FELT. Overwhelmed by the realism of what I'd witnessed—or had I experienced it? I could no longer tell the difference.

And then I felt myself falling again into another place entirely.

OAK RIDGE NATIONAL LABORATORY, OAK RIDGE, TENNESSEE

"PLEASE COME IN, NADIR. Close and latch the door behind you."

Nadir Khalifa, Egyptian ex-pat, naturalized US citizen, and loyal soldier of the Global Community, took in the SCIF's occupants before closing the door. Latching it turned on the "Classified Meeting" sign on the SCIF's exterior. He wondered why he'd been abruptly called away from his duties to a classified meeting.

Three individuals other than himself occupied the room. Along with his boss, Jerry, Nadir recognized the deputy chief of PNNL security. The third man was unknown to him.

"Have a seat, Nadir," Jerry told him.

"Of course." Nadir sat where told. "What's up?"

Jerry nodded to the unknown man.

"Nadir, I'm Special Agent Parker, FBI." The man flashed his cred pack at Nadir, but Nadir hardly spared it a glance. He was instantly on his guard.

This is not about the Community or the intel I feed them, his harried mind protested. *I am too careful. Nothing can be traced to me. Surely, this does not concern my work for the Community.*

It didn't.

But it would.

"Nadir," Parker said to him, "We recently received a credible tip concerning a child pornography ring operating among DOE employees. We have been investigating this tip. Your name came up during our investigation."

Nadir paled. *How? How could they know?*

"On the basis of the information we uncovered, we obtained a federal search warrant to search your home. We found the laptop hidden in the wall of your home office and removed it for analysis."

The agent opened a file folder and removed a series of photos. "These photos are a sampling of the child pornography we found on your laptop."

He laid the photos, one at a time, on the table in front of Nadir's eyes. In front of his boss and the deputy chief of security and their hard, cold eyes.

"These are yours, are they not?" Parker asked.

"You have not Mirandized me," Nadir mumbled. "Nothing I say can be used against me."

"Oh. I'm not here concerning criminal charges, Nadir. Those will come later, and you will be properly Mirandized when you are interviewed concerning those charges. Nonetheless, I can assure you that the evidence before you was obtained through legal channels and with proper warrants.

"So, say what you like, we know you're quite active in this pedophilia ring, and we have the goods to prove it. Me? I'm just here to revoke your security clearance pending that full investigation."

"Revoke my clearance? You . . . you cannot! I will lose my job!"

The agent turned again to his file folder. "I have here copies of your clearance paperwork, including the conditions under which you received your clearance. This is your signature, isn't it?"

Nadir slowly nodded.

"Under the conditions to which you agreed, I am revoking your clearance. Please remove your badge."

Nadir's badge hung from a lanyard around his neck. He pulled the lanyard over his head and handed it to the agent, but he did not feel his fingers. Did not feel anything at all except, perhaps, a hazy sense of unreality.

I am finished.

The deputy chief of security stood then. "Nadir, I need your keys and parking pass. Two of my people will escort you to your desk while you remove your personal belongings. Your network access has been revoked, so do not attempt to log in to your work computer. The officers will then escort you to your vehicle. Under no circumstances are you to approach or enter the site again. Do you understand?"

Nadir nodded and did as he was told, removing keys from his keyring, pulling his parking pass from his wallet. He followed the security guards away from the SCIF, his actions disconnected from his rampaging thoughts.

How will I explain this to the Community?

I am of no use to them now . . .

He swallowed and his heart stuttered in his chest. He whispered the remainder of his thought to himself, "but I *am* a liability."

"Did you say something?" the guard asked.

Nadir hung his head. "No. Nothing."

They will arrange for me to 'commit suicide.'

I must die like a good soldier—whether I choose to or not.

⌘

MY HEART WAS GALLOPING LIKE a wild horse when Zander and I withdrew from the warehouse. Weeks ago we'd asked the nanomites for an update on their counterinsurgency, and today they had granted us a bird's-eye view into their work.

Boy, howdy, had they ever.

We saw and heard the scenarios they had uploaded as if we were standing *right there*, yet we hadn't recognized the individuals "starring" in the recordings. As we observed, the nanomites whispered salient details into our ears—names, places, affiliations—to provide context. We also couldn't see into the hearts and minds of those we watched. We had to surmise those things from what we viewed.

As we said earlier, Jayda Cruz and Zander Cruz, we have undertaken seven hundred thirty-six counterinsurgency actions to date. These recordings are but a sample of those actions. Do you approve?

Zander answered slowly. "Gotta say you're effective, Nano."

Do you approve, Zander Cruz?

It took Zander a long moment to answer. "You don't require our approval, Nano. This is, in effect, a war, and war is . . ." He shook his head.

"Brutal?" I supplied. "Zander and I aren't accustomed to the realities of war, Nano. We have done battle, but haven't killed. The examples you showed us? Well, they shock us. Repulse our human sensibilities, even. That said, we know your work is . . . needful. More than that, it is what Jesus tasked you to do. Your actions will stave off a great deal of human suffering."

The sheer creativity of the nanomites' actions was stunning.

Our actions will not stop what is coming, Jayda Cruz.

"No, but they will bedevil the enemy, and that buys us more time."

I switched topics. "So they call themselves the Global Community, do they?"

Yes, Jayda Cruz. Members of the Global Community speak of themselves in lofty, righteous terms; however, we prefer your designation, the Cabal. It is more precise. The noun "cabal" means a plot or conspiracy with treacherous objectives. The Cabal more accurately expresses the Global Community's hidden agenda as well as their methodologies.

"What can you tell us about their values, Nano?"

Zander Cruz, the Global Community wraps itself in humanistic values under the false flag of "global unity for global good." This is a disingenuous practice since they tout a version of unity that is neither unifying nor good but rather, coercive and subversive.

They left us with their "sample pack" of counterinsurgency actions stuck in our heads the rest of the day.

⌘⌘⌘⌘

CHAPTER 8

TUESDAY

ZANDER FINISHED HIS LUNCH and headed to the church office to conduct his afternoon calls. He wanted, first, to get Josh and Diego on the line and talk to them about the IT team's virtual home group idea.

He managed to get them both on a video conference call and spent several minutes explaining the concepts to them.

"Super idea, Pastor Zander," Josh said.

"I was thinking the two of you could work together, take a few lessons from the IT team on the software, search the comments for a sampling of teens who have expressed the need for someone to show them how to become a Christian, then send out invites to perhaps fifteen to join your group? Try out the idea and see how it goes.

"As your confidence grows, you can branch out to your own cohorts, teaching the basics, praying with your group, showing them how to pray for and minister to each other."

"Sure, Pastor Zander," Diego answered. "Count me in."

"Me too," Josh said.

"Great! Well, that's it for now, Diego. But Josh? Do you have a minute to talk after Diego drops off the call?"

When Diego hung up, Zander smiled at Josh's image.

"So, Josh, we here in our little co-op have been talking about you. How would you like to join us?"

WEDNESDAY

ABE OPENED THE MEETING. "GUESS we're here tonight because Bill asked if I would share some of the things I know about gardening and how to get by during hard times. Well, our little co-op now has several gardens growing 'round the cul-de-sac, and so far, they're looking good.

"However, as each crop produces its harvest, we don't want to eat all of it right off the bat, do we? As we enjoy some of these fresh vegetables, we also need to store up as much as we possibly can for the winter. So, I've been thinking I should talk about how to preserve what we grow. How does that sound?"

Emilio was at Abe's dining table, bent over his last week of school-work before summer vacation. The rest of us were gathered in Abe's living room for the first of the lectures Bill had requested. When Abe asked his question, Viola responded eagerly.

"Yes. That's what I'd like to hear."

Most of us, myself included, agreed.

Izzie spoke up. "All of you met our parents, mine and Zander's. They plant a huge garden every spring. Much of that is feed corn for their livestock, but the rest is to feed them through to the next harvest. Having grown up helping my mom, I know how to can and freeze. Mom fills roughly two hundred canning jars each season."

"Bill and I don't have any canning jars," Viola said, frowning.

"Oh, dear. I don't either," Belicia added.

Abe raised his hand. "Seems like we're jumping the gun just a little. May I?"

"Sorry, Abe," Izzie murmured.

Viola blushed and added, "Yes. please continue."

"Thank you. I wanted to start by listing the methods of preserving food I know of, canning and freezing included. Since Izzie brought those two methods up, let me just say, I don't think it likely that we'll be doing much of either."

Izzie muttered a confused, "Really?"

"Yes—for good reasons. First, like Mrs. Tucker brought up, I doubt that the co-op has many jars or lids, and canning requires both. Furthermore, I daresay we won't find any jars or lids on the shelves, either—given that everyone in our state is feeling the same pinch we are.

"That said, I can tell you that I've done an inventory in my basement, and I have found that I have some odd small jars I have used for jams or preserves and four dozen intact quart jars with used lids and rings. I have examined the lids, and they are in fair condition. We may be able to reuse them if we prepare them properly, but forty-eight jars of fruits or vegetables won't take us through the winter."

He waggled his brows. "Moving on to freezing. What is it you need most for freezing food?"

"A big freezer?" Belicia asked brightly.

A soft chuckle floated around the room.

Abe also chuckled but not in a mean way. "True that, Belicia, but a freezer is just a lifeless box without electricity—*reliable* electricity."

Belicia wasn't the only one whose mouth formed a small "o" of comprehension.

Viola voiced what we were suddenly realizing. "If we froze our produce and the power went out, we'd lose everything."

"You mean *when* it goes out, don't you, dear?" Bill asked with dismay.

He turned to Abe. "You're right. We can't freeze the foods we harvest, either. Not with these sporadic brownouts. What method do you propose?"

"Well, the most surefire method left to us is dehydration—and guess what? We live in prime dehydration climate—our hot, dry weather is perfect. We have already planned to dry beans and chiles of course, but we can also dry tomatoes, carrots, turnips, and potatoes—and we can hang corn to dry, then grind our own meal. When we're ready to use dried foods, it's pretty much add water and cook.

"'Course we can dry any kind of fruit we get our hands on, too, including apples. Even a mishmash of fruits, 'specially overripe fruits, doesn't need to go to waste. Throw them together into a blender and dry them as fruit leather.

"If we happen to acquire a glut of eggs, we can whisk them, cook them like scrambled eggs in a pan, spread them on cookie sheets, then finish dehydrating them in the oven until they are fully dry and can be run through a food processor to render them as powdered eggs. As most baking requires eggs, powdered eggs come in mighty handy.

"As for my forty-eight canning jars? We can use them to supplement what we've dried and to can things not well-suited to dehydration."

"What kind of things would you suggest that we can?" Viola asked.

"Oh, let's see. Applesauce comes to mind. Fruits like cherries and peaches for a change of pace. Odd amounts of mixed vegetables, even meat—when we can get it. But you have to use a pressure cooker to can meat and most vegetables. Oh, and eggs."

"Can *eggs?*"

"Yup. Hard cooked eggs and pickled eggs. Even milk. Milk is essential to cooking and," he jutted his chin toward Bonnie Lu, sleeping on Zander's shoulder, "that little one will need milk as she grows."

Several hands went up, but he forestalled them. "Give me a minute. We'll get to the how-to part soon enough."

He sat back, put his gnarled old hands on his knees. "Here's another method we should certainly employ: root cellars. A good root cellar will keep carrots, potatoes, winter squash, pumpkins, cabbages, and apples fresh for months. Doesn't work well with tomatoes and other soft fruits, though. That's why it's called a *root* cellar. Works best with *hard* produce.

"Good thing about Albuquerque is that our winter temperatures generally don't linger in the sub-freezing zone very long, meaning we don't have to dig a root cellar terribly deep. Gotta have some steps and a door, a'course. Line your cellar with straw, stack your produce in there without crowding it. Good to go."

Bill nodded to Abe. "What you're saying is very encouraging, Abe, but I have a question about dehydration. Do we need those fancy machines with stacking trays? Seems like we'd need a bunch of them."

"No machines needed, Bill. We can build our own frames—simple boxes maybe a couple feet square, constructed from, say, 1x2s. Tack on mesh window screen, nice and taut, and lay a protective sheet of clean, lightweight muslin on the screen. That will keep the food off the mesh.

"Slice our produce thin and layer the slices on the frame's muslin sheet and add another sheet of muslin to keep the birds, bugs, and dust off the food. Couple of days and the food will be dry and ready to store. Wash and dry the muslin sheets, then you're ready to go again."

The meeting buzzed with excitement. Abe again quieted us.

"Now, listen here. If we go about this the smart way, we'll build our frames to stack at least three high. That's three layers of food drying at the same time but taking up only one frame's space. Clamp or tie the frames together so they don't slip apart. I suggest we place our frames on top of a roof where the roof's reflected heat will aid the dehydration process."

Bill, visibly eager, glanced around the room. "We can do all that, right? We can dehydrate, can, and dig root cellars, right?"

"Yes," Zander said. "We sure can."

⌘⌘⌘⌘

CHAPTER 9

JUNE BEGAN HOT AND STAYED that way. Our fledgling crops wilted in the heat and so did we. So far, our city water supply was holding up, but Abe called us together for another lecture, this one on water.

Josh had accepted our invitation to join the co-op. He now lived in Belicia's spare bedroom, and our co-op numbered an even dozen—eleven workers, counting Emilio, plus Bonnie Lu. I confess that my heart was glad to have both Josh and Izzie with us. Their youth and vitality were sorely needed to supplement the physical limitations of our aging members, namely Bill, Viola, Abe, and Belicia.

"We all know that New Mexico is in an ongoing state of drought," Abe began as our little co-op settled in for his second lecture, "and we haven't talked much about water yet."

Bill nodded. "I'm all ears, Abe."

"Well, I suggest we first think about our current situation. At the moment, everyone in the co-op has access to city water. We can irrigate our gardens straight out of the tap, so to speak. But I want us to think about what that means. Anyone want to open our discussion?"

I was the first to venture a reply. "I imagine that watering our gardens is going to get pretty pricey over the summer because the city adds a surcharge for greater-than-average consumption. Once we cross that threshold, our water bills will soar. We'll be looking at two- maybe three-hundred dollars a month. Perhaps more."

I had no intention of igniting a firestorm. In fact, I was astounded that our meeting went south in a matter of seconds.

"Oh, dear!" Belicia sighed dramatically. "That's why I had my lovely yard converted to xeriscape—and I do wish you hadn't dug it up. I really cannot afford to pay that high of a water bill!"

"Oh, for heaven's sake, lady! We can't afford *not* to pay," Bill shot back. "Not if we're talking the difference between paying through the nose for water and starving next winter!"

Belicia, stung, retorted, "I have a right to my opinions—"

"Your *opinions* are expressions of *ignorance*. Furthermore, we aren't obligated to feed you if you are unwilling to contribute equally—"

Zander jumped between the fraying tempers. "Hey! That's why we're all here this evening, right? To meet our problems head-on, to discuss our options, and come up with solutions? Not to criticize. Abe has some valuable suggestions for us. Why don't we listen to him before we jump to conclusions?"

"I agree. Why don't we *listen*," Viola responded, shooting a glare at her husband, "instead of behaving like a horse's hind end."

Abe spoke up. "All right, all right. Everyone calm down."

He then tried to inject a bit of humor into the tension. "We have lots of ground to cover tonight—and I don't mean covering our gardens with water."

Sadly, he couldn't quite pull it off. Tempers were already too hot.

Josh said unconvincingly, "Ha. Good one, Abe."

Izzie, eyes wide, sensed the tension in the room and stayed silent, but Emilio, who wasn't much of a fan of Abe's lectures, sniffed in derision.

"Naw. That's a *dumb* joke."

Zander immediately called him out. "Emilio, you will not disrespect Abe or any adult. You know better. Nor," he addressed us all, "will *any* of us disrespect another. This is a cooperative, meaning we cooperate with each other."

Emilio ducked his head at Zander's rebuke. He stared at Abe's feet. "Sorry, Abe."

"Thank you, young man. But I'm also sorry I opened us up to discussion if it's going to be as rancorous as this. We either agree to be civil with each other or I won't provide these lectures. What's it going to be?"

Bill shifted uneasily. "I suppose I got a little hot under the collar."

"You were *rude!*" Belicia shot back, hot under the collar herself.

When Bill didn't reply, Viola did. "Belicia, I apologize."

"Why? *You* didn't insult me."

No one spoke. Following several long and uncomfortable moments, Bill finally relented. "All right. *All right!* I apologize, Mrs. Calderón."

Belicia made a noise in her throat.

"I believe that apology requires a response, Belicia," Zander said softly.

She blinked and her cheeks grew rosy. "I . . . um." Drawing a breath, she said, "I accept your apology, Bill. Um, thank you."

Our eyes turned back to Abe.

He said, "I'll say what I have to say and take questions later. Everyone okay with that?"

We nodded together.

"Good. So, city water. Expensive, yes, but also not reliable."

I hadn't thought of that and, with a sinking feeling, glanced at Zander, and his expression grew suddenly concerned.

"Can you explain, Abe?" he asked.

"Yes, I'm getting to it. See, we're not the only ones planting gardens, are we? No, don't talk. Just nod or shake your heads."

We nodded in unison.

"Everybody an' their dog be planting gardens right now, including our neighbors up the street from us. All this raising our own food? Well, it's going to put a strain on the city's water supply. And where do we get our water? Some we pump from the aquifer, some from the Rio Grande via the San Juan-Chama Project."

Abe, placing his hands on his knees in his usual fashion when he had a point to make, said, "Do you think the folks upstream from us aren't doing the 'zact same things we are? They, too, are watering gardens. Everyone upstream from us will be using more water than usual. What happens to the water in the Rio Grande then? What happens when twice the usage is taken from the river before it gets to us?"

"Well, *crap*," Josh muttered. He flushed and swallowed. "Um, sorry . . . everyone."

The fact was, we all wanted to shout the same obvious question, but we restrained ourselves. Waited on Abe to answer our unspoken fears.

"Yes, I'm saying the city may ration our water. And it's possible, if water levels get really low, that the city won't be able to refill those big holding tanks we see up in the foothills. See, a lot of city residents receive their water from those tanks, via gravity-driven lines.

"So . . . I've come up with four things we need to do—things we need to do right *now* in order to get ahead of the curve. First, every household needs to stock up on drinking water while the taps are running—now just hold on! I'll get to the how-to part in a minute.

"Second, we need to build a robust system of rainwater capture for each dwelling in the co-op. Third, we dig irrigation channels in our garden plots, and add hoses to our capture system to irrigate our gardens. If we do two and three and eke our way through to monsoon season mid-July without running too low on water, we should be good.

"Now, let's talk strictly 'bout water use. In general, everyone considers drinking water, stocks it up, and think's they're all set. Well, let me ask you this: If the city rations water or cuts it off entirely, how will you flush your toilets? Bathe? Wash clothes?"

I don't think a mouth in Abe's living room was closed except his.

"Listen up, now. All of us need to know what I'm about to say and implement these things *the moment* our taps run slow. You paying attention?"

A chorus of "Yes, Abe" and "Yes, sir" answered him back.

"Good. Good. Taps start to run slow? Someone needs to signal all of us. How will we do that?"

"Air horns," Josh said. "They're loud. They aren't that expensive. Every home should have one."

"Got it. Writing that down," Gamble replied. "I'll get a few extra. One for the barrier guard, for certain."

"That works," Abe said. "Taps start to run low? Signal the co-op—three quick blasts, pause, three more blasts, pause, repeat. Everyone should know that's the signal for low water pressure. Next? *Immediately* plug your bathtubs and fill them with water until either it's full or the taps stop running. Same with sinks."

Abe tapped his nose. "Say, Gamble, add some plastic buckets to your list. Need one for ever' toilet in the cul-de-sac. That's how we bathe, wash clothes, and flush our toilets. Bail water out of our tubs and into a wash pan for bathing and laundry. Bail water out of our tubs and pour it into the toilet tank or directly into the toilet to flush. *But.* In order to conserve that precious tub of water, only flush when there's BM in the toilet."

In typical Josh fashion, Josh couldn't restrain himself. "*If its yellow, let it mellow; if its brown, flush it down!*"

Emilio fell out of his chair laughing.

I leveled my gaze on our newest *adult* co-op member. "Thank you for that enlightening ditty, Josh. We'll be enjoying it for weeks now."

"Uh, right. Gotcha. Um, *sorry*."

"What about other water containers?" Viola asked to change the subject.

"Getting to that, now that we've got the bathing, laundry, and toilets figured out. Just remember, if there's no water in the taps, use your tub water judiciously."

He slapped his knee. "Now we talk about drinking water. When you-all go home this evening, pull out every container you own that has a good lid. That includes camping water jugs, milk jugs, juice bottles, cider bottles, and thermoses. Anything that will hold water without leaking, we wash, fill, treat, then store.

"Here's the process for preserving drinking water: Fill your sink with hot, soapy water—not warm water but *hot* water. Add a capful of bleach to your sink of wash water. Wash your containers and their lids, then rinse them thoroughly, being careful to rinse off all the soap.

"Once your containers are rinsed well, fill them with ordinary tap water. Leave an inch or so of headroom. Using the container's cap or lid while you measure, pour two to three drops of regular laundry bleach into the lid for every gallon of water the lid goes on. Just two drops is plenty; three isn't too much. Pour the drops of bleach into the container and screw on the cap.

"Once the lid is on securely, turn your container over enough to completely cover the container's inside neck and lid with water, so that the treated water has touched all of the container's insides. That's it. Put the container on a shelf and let it stand. It'll be good for years."

"But, isn't chlorine bleach . . . poison?" Josh asked.

Abe laughed. "Stand under your shower and sniff what comes out of the showerhead, young man. Albuquerque water already has chlorine in it. Again, in very, very small doses, it kills harmful bacteria and other contaminants such as mold, but it won't harm you."

"Especially compared to dying of thirst," Bill mumbled.

"There is that," Gamble agreed.

Abe signaled he was coming to the end of his presentation. "When you open a bottle or jug of water to use it, it may have a stale taste or odor to it. That's okay. Just shake it up before using. That'll aerate it and improve the taste. You can also boil the water to restore its taste and to double ensure that no bacteria has grown in it, but the bleach should have done its job.

He looked around. "Suppose that's enough for tonight."

"It's a lot," Viola murmured.

Most of us nodded.

"Say, didn't you say your list had four things on it, Abe?" Gamble asked.

Abe sucked in a breath, then let it out in a rush. "Oh. Yes. Fourth? We need to dig a well."

I snort-laughed at Gamble's stunned expression.

He turned in my direction. "Totally did *not* see that one coming."

⌘

ZANDER HEADED OUT OF THE cul-de-sac early the following morning. His assigned task was to scour Walmart, Target, grocery stores, and minimarts and acquire all the bottles and jugs (filled or unfilled) our SUV could carry home, along with 10 gallons of ordinary laundry bleach, two for each dwelling in the co-op.

We'd need that bleach if we were ever forced to use rain that poured off of our roofs as drinking water. "Just a good idea to have extra bleach on hand," was how Abe put it.

Bill and Josh took Bill's pickup out on a similar mission. They were to hit the hardware stores and snap up fifteen to twenty rainwater storage cans. If those were unavailable, commercial-sized covered garbage cans— anything from thirty-two- to fifty-gallon in capacity would serve. Along with the cans, their list also called for heavy-duty buckets, preferably metal, and two short-handled shovels.

Janice and I, with Abe along to direct our purchases, piled into Janice's car. We were tasked with purchasing more garden hoses, two dozen hose bibs, plus PVC cement, piping, and joints. We'd also be hunting down rain gutters and downspouts.

We left Bonnie Lu and Emilio with Belicia (Emilio fuming over our assigned summer school work under Belicia's supervision, primarily reading and writing), while Izzie, an experienced gardener like Zander, helped Viola plant multiple rows of carrots and fifteen hills of potatoes.

Hours later, our crews brought back the supplies they'd purchased—not everything we needed, but enough to get us going. We split what water storage jugs we'd found between the five households, and spent the remainder of the day filling every vessel on hand with tap water.

I filled while Zander lugged our bottles and jugs to the garage and placed them on shelves. Our extra-long and wide garage was again proving its worth.

Abe stored his water in his basement. He charged Emilio with toting the filled bottles and jugs downstairs and organizing them on shelves. Emilio dragged his feet at the beginning. As the lines of water grew, however, he took ownership of the process. He proudly led me down the steep cellar steps and showed me how he'd organized his and Abe's emergency drinking water.

When our five households reported our tasks complete, Abe declared we'd made a good start. We were, however, in no way done with our water preparations.

⌘

BETWEEN CLEARING PLOTS, PREPPING for planting, and actually planting, we installed rain downspouts. Flat-roofed houses in New Mexico have roof scuppers built into them called *canales*. During a heavy downpour, those canales pour water off the corners or sides of our roofs. We needed to capture that water, so we added downspouts to the canales and positioned rain barrels under the downspouts.

Abe and Belicia's houses, unlike the rest of the houses in the cul-de-sac, had pitched roofs. Zander, Bill, and Josh spent a lot of time measuring, cutting, and attaching rain gutters and downspouts to the two houses' roofs. Once the gutters were in place, the guys sealed the gutters' joints to prevent leaking.

It meant a lot of hours for the guys on ladders or for the rest of us lifting tools and gutter sections to the guys to finish the job, but finish it we did. When we were finished with the installs, we added hose bibs to the barrels near their bottoms, connected hoses to the faucets, and dragged the hoses to our garden plots. When we were satisfied that the hose placement was optimal, we would bury most of the hose to prevent tripping.

We still had prepping and planting to finish on a couple of plots. Once all of our crops were in, we'd dig our irrigation trenches. *Then,* we'd manually fill our rain barrels so we could test our hose placements.

Next, Gamble and Josh tackled digging a well between ours and Gamble's houses. It was hard, backbreaking work. So was toting the dirt to a pile several yards away. And each foot of depth meant they had to shore up the walls to prevent a collapse.

At thirteen feet they hit seepage. At fifteen feet, they were standing in a puddle of water while they dug. Abe suggested they finish shoring up what they had and keep an eye on the water level.

"We'll finish off the well's construction later," he said. "If we can't get through the growing season without water from the well, we'll come back to it. In the meantime, we'll cover up the hole so no one falls into it."

Oh. Did I forget to mention that Abe wanted us to plant patio tomatoes in addition to the tomatoes in our gardens? The patio tomatoes would save space in our gardens for crops that took up more room. His own front porch already had six pots of tomatoes on it.

The other big-ticket item still to come? Our camera surveillance system. Gamble had the boxed system in his house, and we would need it for certain as our crops ripened. But right now? It was most important that we actually *produced* a crop to save from raiders. The cameras could wait a few more weeks.

I took Bonnie Lu from Belicia and went inside to get out of the sun. I sat down on the couch with Bonnie, and she smiled up at me, her big brown eyes happy and content. I was content too. Content to take a break from the seemingly never-ending chores of urban farming.

I had not the first clue how I would look back on this day.

⌘

THE ASSEMBLAGE, DESIGNATED THE Global Community's US Subversion and Recruitment Team (USSART), had never met face to face. Even prior to the pandemic, they had been too geographically dispersed across the continent for in-person meetings to be practical. Instead, they—like other Global Community SARTs across the world—conferred online while employing the best security measures available to hide their meetings from hackers and spies.

Fortunately, the pandemic's continuing state of emergency more than adequately provided cover for their meetings. This evening's video call was but one among several million virtual conferences streaming at the same time.

The Global Community's fivefold mandate for each nation's SART was the same:

1. Orchestrate crime and violent dissent to destabilize state and local civil authorities.
2. Generate shortages of food, fuel, and other vital goods to create further instabilities and public unrest.
3. Overload health care systems to drive nations into nationalized health care and remove the option of private care providers.
4. Encourage "faith" movements to align their tenets with GC values and to support GC's informal umbrella of "global unity for global good." At the same time, diminish (turn, impede, thwart, blackmail, or remove) faith leaders who spoke out against GC values or who otherwise impeded GC goals.
5. Recruit, reward, and promote loyal and obedient individuals in positions of authority within every form of media, finance, education, IT, utilities, large corporate structures, elected office, and government bureaucracy.

The Global Community's overarching objective was not to take down nation states—no, those would remain in place for the time being. The GC's focus was to meld all people into a single, cohesive worldview, a worldview best shepherded by the Global Community's leadership. Stated another way? *Peace and economic equality for all humanity*—but riches and power for those who wielded the Global Community's authority.

USSART One, the American group's leader, pointed to a woman's face on his screen. "You! Southwest! After your predecessor's abject failure, we granted *you* this territory. You promised good results, yet your reports are disappointing. Explain yourself."

The woman cleared her throat. "We maintain slow but steady progress toward our goals. However, a particular nuisance in Albuquerque thwarted some of our better operatives a few months back. This forced me to reassign one valuable operative elsewhere. Worse, this nuisance has become an online icon, a so-called 'inspired teacher' of that nasty book of lies."

The leader waved dismissively. "Yes, yes. We know all this—we do read your reports and stats. What is clear is that his livestream and recorded videos have soared and are still growing. It is your job to handle these abhorrent broadcasts! Why have you not stopped them?"

The woman twitched. "We-we do not understand why his broadcasts are growing."

"I didn't ask *why* they're growing. *I asked why you have not stopped them!*"

She glanced at her notes. Stoically returned her eyes to her screen. "He must be eliminated, of course. I ask permission to carry out this task."

Southern California, Southwest's friend and ally, jumped in to support her. "I second the motion."

The leader waved her away. "This is not a democracy, SoCal, nor have I requested your input."

He returned to Southwest. "I see from your stats that you've 'eliminated' three prominent Southwest pastors in the past two months. A bit excessive, don't you think? Sure to raise suspicions, besides? *You are to break them*, not martyr them. Too many deaths under irregular circumstances feed Christian conspiracy theories and promote their unity and resolve."

No one dared to challenge USSART One—those underlings who had done so in the past had found it problematic to mount a second challenge . . . from their unmarked graves. The woman assigned to USSART's Southwest territory knew this. She apparently also knew how to abase herself when necessary.

"I am entirely amenable to your suggestions, sir."

"*My suggestions?* Do I have to come down there and do it for you? Hit the man where it hurts him most. I don't care how—use your imagination—but do it slowly, deliberately, and with increasing pain. Strip him of his reputation, every resource, and every precious relationship. Empty his bank accounts, repo his car, threaten his friends and neighbors, burn his home, and bomb his church building—and *make certain* the church's insurance doesn't pay out. The pandemic will end at some point, but without a place to meet, his followers will desert him."

"We had hoped . . . to take control of his building and congregation and use them to further our ends. My predecessor and I nearly accomplished this."

His reply was a stinging rebuke. "Your attempt failed—and spectacularly, I must say, even when we granted you the resources you requested."

She kept her face expressionless and said nothing, but he saw that she was seething within.

Smirking, he toyed with her. "Will you burn him out?"

"We did attempt to burn his church."

"And yet it stands."

"We also used protestors to target his home—"

"Ah, yes. Another unsuccessful attempt."

"We *will* succeed—we will not be deterred this time."

"Finally, the correct reply."

Unclenching her teeth, she managed, "Yes, sir. If I might suggest, though? This man, Zander Cruz, has a devoted online following. Burning his church or home may not produce the desired result. May have the opposite effect, in fact."

"You assessed all of his vulnerabilities, did you not? Pick another target. I see a wife on the list and a newborn. How would the mother's disappearance and untimely death affect him? Or the loss of the child? And isn't there a boy? A foster brat? Don't you have means to leverage this kid's continued well-being against this *nuisance* as you called him? ***Must I draw you a picture?***"

He sneered at her image on the screen. "Strike without mercy *but do take your time with him*. Maximize his agony; drown him in regret and self-recrimination. Make an exemplar of him. Exhibit him, at the end, as a graphic and bloody illustration of what befalls those who defy us."

The woman was adept at thinking on her feet. It was how she had survived as long as she had.

"I believe we are on the same wavelength, sir. We already have a plan in place to take the boy. And because we have seeded our people throughout state, county, and city bureaucracies, we have at our disposal the proper resources to put our plan in motion. We will pile pressure upon pressure atop Cruz. As you said, *we will break him*."

USSART One studied her. He presumed she was lying about having a plan to take the boy.

The other SART members probably assumed she was making it up as she went along.

They weren't wrong.

Such dissembling was part of the political games they played within the hierarchy. Even if their roles were somewhat minor within the full scheme of the new world order, they played out their dangerous games, jockeying for position and advantageous opportunity, hoping to earn promotion and a shot at the Big Time where true global change was strategized and enacted—and where the rewards were beyond imagining.

USSART One considered Southwest's words long enough to make the woman uneasy, then made a show of relenting. "Very well, Southwest. Proceed on any or all of the avenues we have outlined.

"However, I expect you to plan carefully and execute with all due diligence. I expect to see *good* progress when we next meet."

Her smile was thin. "You won't be disappointed. *Sir*."

"I had better not be."

He then addressed the group at large. "We are less than four months out from the general election. You have your election assignments?"

"Yes, sir," a chorus of voices replied.

"I don't need to remind you how important our work is to ensuring Mellyn's election. You will personally answer if your districts do not deliver the results our party has ordered us to deliver. By whatever means necessary, you must ensure that only GC candidates win. These orders come directly from Mellyn and the party leadership.

"And as we will be occupied during the run-up to the first Tuesday in November, we shall not convene again as a full committee until the week following the election. You may request an individual consult with me if you encounter particular problems or if you require supplementary resources for your tasks. Is there anything else? No?"

The leader lifted his chin to the group in dismissal. "The blessing of the goddess be on you all."

"And on you!" they chanted together.

"USSART One out."

⌘

THE VIDEO CALL ENDED. SOUTHWEST visibly relaxed and exhaled her relief. She knew her position was tenuous, but she did have this one chance to produce the results required of her. In her mind, she cursed the name of Zander Cruz.

Bleeping Zander Cruz! You have sidestepped our people time and again, but I promise you this, she vowed. ***I will break you**—and I will break anyone else who gets in my way.*

⌘⌘⌘⌘

Chapter 10

Bill was on the barrier, and the early July heat was brutal. The asphalt was hot, the air was hot, the entire afternoon had been hot. If a monsoon rain didn't cool Albuquerque down this evening, it would be just as hot tomorrow.

When Gamble came home close to sundown, Bill was flat-out tired and cranky. Bill dutifully drove Abe's old sedan out of the barrier so Gamble could squeeze his car through the hole, but Bill was peeved. It bothered Bill that Gamble's contributions to the co-op were less about toil and sweat and more about "acquisition." Fact was, Gamble's polished FBI apparel and manner—not the "look" of a real working man such as himself—got under Bill's skin.

He backed Abe's car into the hole and slid out of it. Stared at Gamble as he got out of his car.

From his driveway, Gamble greeted him. "Hey, Bill. Man, it's late and it's *hot*. I'm bushed; bet you are too."

Bill sneered. "Gee. They got you working longer shifts in your nicely air-conditioned office, do they?"

Gamble just smiled. "Not for the past three hours. I took off work early and drove out to Estancia. Spent an hour in the heat to oblige my host by taking a tour of his little farm. Then, at his insistence, I reminisced about the bigger FBI cases I've worked on. Had to satisfy this guy's itch before I could shoehorn some fancy financial wrangling into the conversation.

"But, in the end, he sold me what I went there to get, a resource I think the whole co-op will appreciate. And trust me—they're sold out every-where else I've looked."

Bill was marginally interested. Possibly intrigued. "You went out to Estancia for the co-op? With gas prices and availability like they are?"

"Worth the money and the wait in the gas line. Want to see what I brought back?"

Bill considered Gamble. "All right."

As Bill sauntered over, Gamble took a cardboard box from the floor of his car. Set it on the rear seat. Slowly lifted off the lid.

Rustling came from the box. Scrabbling.

Bill drew back. "What's in there?"

"Won't bite. I swear."

Bill was less indifferent than he let on. He finally glanced into the box. Found himself saying, "Well, I'll be!" Was surprised to hear himself add, "This could really help us, Gamble. A lot. Couple of ways."

"Yeah, that was my thinking. Worth the price and the effort. Tomorrow being Saturday, I'll show everyone soon as we're all up and at 'em. Then we can figure out what to do with them. Guess I'll keep them in the house tonight."

⌘

THE NIGHT HAD BARELY COOLED OFF, and the morning started warm with a promise of *hotter than blazes* later on. With the power grid so close to overload, we understood that if everyone ran their swamp coolers during the day, all of us might end up without electricity. Zander and I only ran our swamp cooler an hour before we went to bed.

Sure, it was a vain attempt to cool the house a bit—and sleeping in thick, stifling heat was not my favorite thing—but it was the best we could do. I really hoped it would rain today and knock down the heat.

We were in the garden early, of course—the coolest part of the day—weeding and watering. Josh and Izzie were doing the same in Abe's front yard plot, while Bill and Viola worked on Belicia's and their plot.

With a bounce to his stride, Gamble appeared in our backyard. He carried a small cardboard box, and Janice followed right behind him. They were both smiling like the cat who ate the canary, so we were curious. Gamble placed the box on the shady grass under our apple tree, not far from Belicia and Bonnie Lu.

Hands on his hips, he gestured us over. "Hey, all. Got something neat to show you."

Belicia, ever inquisitive, got out of her chair. Zander, Emilio, and I left the garden to take a look. Apparently, Gamble had waved to Josh, Izzie, Bill, and Viola on his way over, because they joined us.

Only Abe was missing . . . nope. I spied him shuffling across the cul-de-sac, and Gamble seemed set on waiting for him.

When all co-op members were present, Gamble lifted the lid from the box. Immediately, we heard the rustling and scrabbling of little clawed feet and a chorus of cheeps.

Emilio fell on his knees beside the box. "Baby chicks!" he exclaimed.

"Well, well! Look there," Abe said. "'Course, a chick *is* a baby, so it's better to say either chicks or baby chickens."

Emilio wasn't interested in a grammar lesson; he was busy counting them. "Eighteen chicks! Can I pick one up?"

"Sure," Gamble said. "Just don't squeeze the little guy. The chick might like it if you hold him up to your neck. Sort of cuddle him there. Janice spent half the evening holding these beauties."

"Healthy chicks are hard to come by what with all the avian flu going around," Abe added.

"Not to mention that the price of eggs has shot through the roof," Bill muttered.

All of us picked up a fuzzy yellow and brown ball. Then we let them play on the grass a while.

"These little guys eat bugs," Zander commented.

I laughed. "That's going to be a *big* plus."

Bill, ever practical, asked, "Do we know how many males and females in the lot?"

Gamble grimaced. "The guy I bought them from promised that a dozen were female, and six were male, but don't ask me which are which."

Abe bent over, hands on his knees, and stared into the box. "Yup. Twelve pullets, six cockerels. If we manage to keep them all alive, we'll have a dozen egg-laying hens. Gotta thin out the cockerels, of course, before they mature. Keep back two to raise as roosters, then keep the best of the two to rule the roost."

"You can tell them apart?" Gamble asked.

"Sure. Just gotta know what to look for. Sometimes their markings tell us. Those will become more pronounced as they grow."

Bill, again, "Well, where do we keep them? And who takes care of them? What with garden work and guard duty, most of us are tapped out by the end of the day."

Abe glanced at Belicia. "You and I can manage them."

Belicia, the only one who hadn't picked up a chick, looked startled. "Me? I don't know anything about chickens!"

I snickered inside. Her protest echoed shades of, *Honest, Miz Scarlett! I don' know nuthin' 'bout birthin' babies!*

"Well, I do, and I'll teach you," Abe said. "As it stands, we don't do enough around here. This? This we can handle." He scanned around our yard. "We'll need a good coop enclosed in a small pen. Back here would be best because of the fence."

"Yeah," Bill agreed. "I imagine grocery grabber gangs would love to get their hands on these chickens when they're bigger."

"Right. We should prepare for two real dangers: thieves and predators. Our security cameras should alert us to both—if we ever get them up and running. However, the pen enclosing the coop will need to be completely covered in chicken wire. We'll even need to plant the pen's fence line in bricks or cement so predators can't dig under it. That pen has to be strong enough to thwart raccoons, skunks, foxes, and bobcats. Possibly cougars."

I knew those animals inhabited the foothills, but I hadn't considered that they would stray into this area of town. We weren't that far from the river, though, and all the open space on either side of it.

My eyes drifted toward Bonnie. "You're saying the chickens will attract those animals, Abe?"

"Mostly at night, Jayda, but even cats and small dogs attract predators. Oh. Forgot to mention hawks. Got us a strong population of red-tailed hawks up and down the Rio Grande Valley. When we let the chickens out to forage for food, we'll have to keep a close eye on them. And on the sky."

He shook his head. "Like I said, if we can keep all eighteen chicks alive, we'll have twelve layers and a rooster. And," here Abe grinned, "when we separate out the cockerels, we'll fatten them up for fried chicken!"

Bill grunted. "Fried chicken? Boy, if that doesn't sound good!"

I think we all felt the same—except maybe Emilio.

As he held two of the fluffy babies and considered a plate of fried chicken, he frowned. Conflicted? Yes. But probably not for long.

Hunger had the power to change one's mind.

⌘

WE CELEBRATED EMILIO'S BIRTHDAY two evenings later. Maybe it wasn't much of a party compared to pre-virus days, but Emilio loved it. It was good for the rest of us too. These days, we pounced on any reason to rejoice.

Everyone brought a little present for Emilio, whatever we could afford, find, or regift. Bill and Viola gave Emilio two candy bars and a pack of gum—a veritable treasure to a growing boy. Izzie gave him a new t-shirt, Josh, a pair of shorts. Gamble and Janice offered him a small shaving kit, complete with razors and shaving cream.

Abe and I went together on our gift: a used multi-tool with enough varied blades and "gizmos" to please any boy his age. Gamble had sussed it out, dickered for it in our stead, and borne it home in triumph.

Emilio couldn't keep the thing in his pocket, He kept taking it out, turning it over in his hands, figuring out each tool and its use, grinning like a Cheshire cat.

As for Zander? He'd come up with a baseball and two gloves. If anything would distract Emilio from that multi-tool? It would be playing catch with Zander.

Last of all, Belicia presented Emilio with a cake, a lovely little round one covered in frosting with a single candle burning on it. Emilio jumped up when he saw it, and whooped when Belicia said it was *all his* to eat.

She'd made simple corn muffins for everyone else, and we didn't mind a bit.

Our boy was twelve, starting to mature, growing taller right before our eyes. He glowed with health, with love and acceptance. His heart was full that day, and mine was filled with love for him.

All that was missing in his life was Jesus. It was a very big "all."

Lord God! Please move upon Emilio's heart. I am calling on you . . .

⌘

GAMBLE AND JANICE KEPT THE chicks and their box in their house for the next week. During that week, with Abe directing, Gamble, Zander, and Emilio built a chicken coop abutting the back of our house. The wood to build it was just about as hard to come by as the chicks had been, but by scavenging here and there, even pulling apart a few pieces of furniture deemed less necessary than a coop, they managed the build.

No, it wasn't pretty, but it was strong and functional.

Finding material for the pen around the coop was just as difficult. Gamble drove up and down alleyways and visited illegal dump sites on the west mesa, scavenging for and appropriating rusting rolls of chicken wire, tossed-away posts, and bits of lumber. Anything vaguely useful, he brought home. He had a real knack for finding stuff!

He also reported a strange and telling phenomenon. "The west mesa used to have a lot of prickly pear cacti, but everywhere I looked for wire and other stuff, all the prickly pear pads were gone. Cut off."

Abe nodded. "Tells us how hungry people are. Get yourself some nice, succulent prickly pear *nopales*, use a pair of pliers to pull the spines off, then bake or boil and skin them. They are edible and will fill an empty belly."

I glanced at Gamble. People had to be mighty hungry to go after cactus out in the desert.

Back to the chicken coop. Eventually, we had a pen that fully enclosed the coop. Zander mowed our little patch of grass and tossed the clippings into the coop for the chicks to make their own bedding. When Gamble brought the chicks out to the coop and turned them loose, they ran around, frantic and distressed, cheeping for each other and the comfort of their accustomed enclosed space. Soon, though, they adjusted and busied themselves pecking through the grass, looking for small insects.

I wished them well! They would need to forage for their food in our gardens, because we could not spare a single speck of grain to feed them. On the other hand, I was certain Gamble would find chicken feed somewhere and haul it back to us as the cold months of winter approached.

In the meantime, Belicia surprised everyone by assuming most of the chicks' care. While Bonnie Lu napped, Belicia assiduously kept the chicks' water dish clean and filled, brought them tiny crumbs of who-knows-what from her house, and held and handled each one until they knew her and came running when she entered the pen.

After she handled the chicks and before she handled Bonnie Lu, though, she washed her hands with hot, soapy water.

I was glad she was careful.

⌘

IN THE MEANTIME—ADDING TO our worries—we'd received no rain since mid-May, and the monsoons were late. Abe again rehearsed our emergency plan should city water begin to fail us.

"If you notice the taps running slow, sound your air horn three times. Pause, then repeat. Pause again, repeat."

That evening, Zander and I heard the blare of an air horn coming from across the cul-de-sac. Three short blasts, a pause, another three blasts. We didn't wait for the signal to repeat.

He went for the bathroom in our bedroom; I ran to the main bath. We plugged our tubs and opened the taps. Yes, the flow was sluggish.

I left the water on in our tub and ran for the kitchen, plugged the sink and began filling it. Grabbed up an empty pitcher and stood with it under the tap until it filled.

Within twenty minutes, the flow from our taps was down to a trickle.

"Well, we're in for it," Zander mumbled.

"We need to pray," I said.

We joined hands and petitioned heaven to send rain.

⌘

FOR CLOSE TO A WEEK, CITY WATER alternated between low and nonexistent. We bailed tub water to flush toilets sparingly, drained our water barrels to keep our gardens alive, and rationed the precious drinking water we'd stored.

As Abe had predicted, though, across Albuquerque, the unprepared panicked. They ransacked stores for bottled water or liquids of any kind. Home invasions rocketed upward. Makeshift roadblocks appeared, and gangs attacked and stripped cars of whatever they had.

Zander gathered the co-op members prior to our next grocery run. "We have to go. We can't afford not to get our weekly grocery allotment, so this is how we'll do it. I'll ride with Jayda, Abe, and Belicia. Bill and Viola will caravan with us—safety in numbers. Viola will drive; Bill will be armed. Jayda will drive our car, and I will be armed."

Zander threw in that factoid for appearances' sake.

"While we're gone, the cul-de-sac stays on high alert. Janice will run security. She, Josh, and Izzie will alternate standing post at the barrier and walking our backyards; Emilio will watch Bonnie Lu."

Our caravan made it to the store without a problem because the nanomites guided us, rerouting us around potential threats. Coming home was dicier: Two cooperating gangs tried to box us in, one group behind us, nipping at our heels, trying to drive us into a trap.

Bill leaned out the passenger window of his car and fired off half a dozen rounds at the wheels of the car chasing us—missing every shot—because firing from a moving vehicle is harder than the movies make it look. At the same time, Zander leaned out our passenger-side window and, over the top of our car, sent a single bolt of blue fire into the chase car.

Both of the gang's front tires exploded; the car careened into a xeriscaped median, flew over its curb, and high-centered on a large rock.

Bill was ebullient as we pulled into the cul-de-sac. "Did you see that? I blew out both their tires!"

Zander and I weren't going to burst his bubble. It was rare to see Bill as happy as he was, so we celebrated with him.

Two nights later, the sound of rain pattering on our roof and windows roused me. Lightning flashed; seconds later, the *boom* of thunder shook our house. Bonnie woke with a wail, and I got up quickly to comfort her.

The thunder's reverberating echo rolled over us and faded, but the gentle drumming of rain strengthened to a deafening pounding.

The monsoons, late but welcome, had arrived.

⌘⌘⌘⌘

Chapter 11

They came for Emilio Friday evening, just as the streetlights were coming on. Two cars slid up to the barrier and stopped. One of the vehicles was a Bernalillo County sheriff's cruiser. Bill was again standing post at the barrier when a woman and a sheriff's deputy walked up to the K-rails.

With his sidearm canted safely toward the ground near the barrier, Bill shone a flashlight on them and called out, "Stop where you are! Who are you and what do you want?"

The woman, properly masked, stepped into the beam of light. She held out a business card. Around her neck was a lanyard; hanging from it was an official CYFD photo ID. "My name is Lani Okafor representing the Protective Services Division of New Mexico's Child Welfare Services. This is Deputy Descheeni. I have a court order to remove Emilio Martinez from the home of Abe Pickering or Zander and Jayda Cruz and place the boy in PSD custody."

"What? Are you kidding? Why? The kid is perfectly fine!"

"This is not your business, sir. In fact, please present some form of identification so that I might note it."

"I'm not giving you my name, lady, because I'm not part of your writ. Neither am I required to show you my ID. I am a law-abiding resident of this cul-de-sac. I have every right to stand here and observe."

"Observe all you like, but you had better not interfere. Now let us through."

Bill played his light over both of them. Then he lowered his gun and holstered it. "Um, I suppose you can come through over here."

He walked around Abe's old car where the car "plugged" the opening in the barrier. On the side closest Abe's house, they had left a gap just wide enough for an individual to squeeze through. Bill had his phone out and was about to call Zander when Okafor stopped him.

"Do *not* make that call. If you give warning to Mr. Pickering or to Mr. or Mrs. Cruz, Deputy Descheeni will cite you for interference in a lawful action."

Bill, increasingly angry and uncertain, slowly lowered his phone.

Okafor was already familiar with Abe's front entrance. She turned on her heel and started up Abe's walk. The deputy, with a stern look directed at Bill, followed.

Bill started recording video of them as soon as their backs were turned—but the deputy had been expecting it. He whipped back around, took two long steps, grabbed Bill's phone, threw it to the asphalt, and stomped it twice. Then he picked up the phone and put it in his pocket.

"What the *bleep*! You can't do that!" Bill shouted.

The deputy smirked. "I just did. Now listen up. Stand right where you are until we have served the court order and taken the boy into protective custody. If you obey my instructions, I will return your phone. However, if you interfere in this process in any fashion—including waking your neighbors—I will arrest you."

Fuming and frustrated, Bill stayed put. *Watch and listen, Bill. Try to remember everything*, he told himself.

Some minutes after the deputy started pounding on Abe's front door, the porch light came on and the door opened. Bill couldn't make out the words being spoken until Abe raised his voice.

"Emilio is sound asleep, and I am not getting him out of bed!"

"Sir, if you do not comply, we will be forced to take you into custody and book you for interfering with a lawful court order."

What was said then was much quieter, and again, Bill couldn't make out the words. His feet itched to run over to Zander and Jayda's house and alert them, but understandably, he didn't want to risk his own liberty. Instead, he waited and watched until Okafor and the deputy led Emilio from the house and down the sidewalk.

The deputy had a firm grip on the boy's shoulder, but the kid was fighting mad and struggling. Finally, the man twisted Emilio's arm behind his back and yanked up on it.

Bill flinched as the boy yelped in pain and his will to resist broke. The poor kid's sobs about undid Bill. *I'll run over to Zander and Jayda's as soon as these bozos cross the barrier*, he decided.

He didn't need to. Lights were already coming on in their house. Something, perhaps his own shouted words at the deputy—had awakened them.

Not that it would help.

The social worker and deputy had already shoved Emilio into the cruiser's back seat and gotten into their vehicles.

⌘

UNBEKNOWNST TO BILL, THE MOMENT Abe awakened Emilio, his nano-array began to gather data. They alerted the nanomites to the situation; the nanomites, in turn, awakened us.

Jayda Cruz! Zander Cruz! Emilio is being abducted!

Yanked out of deep sleep, we pulled on clothes as fast as we could while throwing off our stupor.

We left Bonnie Lu sleeping under her array's watch and rushed from our house toward Abe's—in time to see the taillights of two vehicles fade down the street.

"Bill! What just happened?" I exclaimed.

"State Protective Services just happened," he mumbled. "The deputy accompanying the social worker threatened to arrest me if I interfered or even woke you up. When I tried to video record what they were doing, that *bleeping* deputy broke my phone and put it in his pocket!"

Like he had just realized it, Bill added, "Why, that lying *rat!* I did what he told me but he took my phone with him anyway!"

Abe, wheezing and unsteady on his feet, stumbled down his walk to where we stood. Zander grabbed his arm to steady him. Abe's breathing was so labored he could only spit out a few syllables at a time.

"Social. Work. *Okafor*. Court. Order. *Took him.*"

The wrath plowing through me was a tidal wave demolishing everything in its path. I wanted to scream. I wanted to curse. I wanted to rain down *literal fire* on Okafor . . . but her car had turned the corner long before I could.

Lord God! They've taken our boy—my boy! O God, please help me.

While I struggled to regain some semblance of self-control, Zander turned inward to the nanomites.

"Nano, why didn't you see them coming and alert us sooner?"

I heard the pathos in the nanomites' voice. *Jayda Cruz and Zander Cruz, we are sorely distressed. We apologize for not knowing that Okafor was coming to take Emilio.*

"*Not knowing?*" I may have been standing silent on the asphalt of the cul-de-sac, but inside the warehouse? I was screaming. "*You said* you would continuously monitor Okafor's work computer and cell phone! *How did you miss her plan?*"

Jayda Cruz, we missed her plan because she was given orders not to log the removal into her work computer.

"Orders? If you were monitoring her communications, how did you miss her orders?"

We have in the past five minutes identified a new personal cell phone belonging to Lani Okafor and have recovered a string of deleted texts ordering her to take Emilio into custody. From those texts, we know that the court order Okafor left with Abe is counterfeit. It was delivered to Okafor by courier, sent from an individual higher up in New Mexico's Child Welfare Services—the same individual whose texts ordered her to take Emilio.

A series of texts appeared before my eyes. Before I could read them, Zander put a gentle hand on my arm and murmured, "I'm concerned about Abe. Let's wait till we get him inside his house."

He thanked Bill and assured him everything would be all right. Bill was practically in tears when we left him to finish out his guard rotation. No one else in the cul-de-sac had been roused from sleep.

As Zander and I helped Abe back to his house, I became aware of Abe's trembling. His fragility.

"Abe," I said. "Don't worry. Remember Emilio's nanoarray? The array will keep tabs on him and tell us where he is. We'll find Emilio and get him back. Please calm yourself. I promise it will be okay."

Jayda Cruz. Shall we—

"Yes, do it, Nano. Thank you."

By the time we'd helped Abe up the porch steps, he was visibly improved. Much calmer, no longer shaking or short of breath. I had recovered some peace too.

"It was that social worker, Okafor," Abe said. "The same woman who came to investigate the complaint Emilio's teacher lodged against us back in January. Here's the court order."

He frowned. "You had those nano thingies shoot me up with something, didn't you?"

"Just a touch, Abe. Your stroking out isn't going to help Emilio any."

Nor will my unchecked anger, I added. *Sorry, Lord.*

"Guess you're right," Abe said softly. "I do feel a touch better."

I put the kettle on to make tea for the three of us while Abe sat, slumped, in his chair at the dining table. In the meantime, Zander and I perused the texts from the "individual higher up in New Mexico's Child Welfare Services."

You are instructed to take
Emilio Martinez
into protective custody
this evening after dark
Deputy Descheeni, one of ours,
will accompany you

Okafor answered,

PSD regs prohibit removal
after dark except where
child is in imminent danger

Her superior texted back,

Follow my instructions to letter
Do not log removal into PDS system
Take boy to gymnasium
Will farm him out to private
juvenile correctional facility
disappear him

Another line of text from her appeared,

Court order facsimile attached
Order arriving via courier

Okafor replied,

Understood

Not a real court order, the nanomites said. I shook my head to clear it. We had more pressing problems to deal with.

"Zander, they plan to send Emilio to a correctional facility for older boys, young men already hardened and incorrigible. Emilio has just turned twelve—they waited until he was old enough to send to that place!"

"Yeah, I get that."

"And they intentionally came for him on a Friday night. Their office is closed for the weekend, no one available until Monday, no one to call for answers, not a solitary thing a family could do in a similar situation."

"Yes. An *ordinary* family."

"Well, they violated their own rules. What they did was *wrong*—and they knew it. Did it anyway. Intentionally."

Zander was patient with me. "I get that, Jay. They wanted to maximize our heartache, but we haven't lost our boy. His nanoarray will tell us where he is."

"I know. It's just . . ."

"Just that you're a mom? That you love Emilio? And you're as fierce as a mama grizzly? You are those things and more—and I love you—the whole package."

I exhaled. "Right. Thank you. I'll just . . . finish making the tea so we can get to work."

I made the tea strong and hot and added an extra helping of precious honey to Abe's mug. He needed it. Then we read aloud the court order and texts the nanomites had uncovered.

Abe couldn't wrap his stressed-out thoughts around the texts until I reread them to him a second time.

Then he started nodding his understanding.

"That place they called the gymnasium where they're taking Emilio? What is that?"

Jayda Cruz, Zander Cruz, the array has sent us Emilio's location, a house in Albuquerque's north valley. And although the sender of the texts refers to the house as a gymnasium, its address is listed in the PSD database as a state-licensed emergency intake facility.

Zander relayed the nanomites' info to Abe.

"Well," he said, sipping on his sweet, steaming tea, "guess we've learned a couple of things, haven't we?"

Zander and I murmured our agreement.

Abe lifted a bent and gnarled index finger and, with his opposite index finger, ticked off his initial point. "First, we gotta reckon that these three players, Deputy Dawg, Ms. Okafor, and her high-up big-cheese boss, are all members of that-there Cabal you told me about, maybe just obedient foot soldiers."

He lifted a second finger and touched it. "Second, the foster parents where Emilio was taken are likely in cahoots. Might have a guard on him."

"Unless they are unaware that the court order is a fake—although, as you said, it's equally likely that they are involved," I replied.

More slowly I said, "Here's another item for your list, Abe. It's obvious, but it bears listing because we can't afford to overlook it."

He lifted a third gnarled finger. "Call it, Gemma."

I stared at him. Silent.

Waiting.

When I didn't answer, he glanced up and blinked. He was more off balance than he'd recognized. Finally . . .

"Well, *shoot*. I'm sorry about that. I . . . I guess I'm pretty shook up, huh?"

"Sure. Me too."

"Yeah, well . . . what's the other thing, uh, *Jayda?*"

I sighed, and Zander snagged my hand. Held mine between his. Held it like he'd never let it go.

He answered Abe for me. "Consider this, Abe. In January, you told us about that social worker's visit and her veiled threats. Soon after, Easterly tried to release his nasty fake video of me and Izzie, but the nanomites deleted it. Then, Aiden Easterly and his DCC 'visitors' tried to take down our church."

Aiden Easterly. His name gave me the willies but good. Although the nanomites assured us that Stan Missing had left Albuquerque for greener pastures, Easterly and his followers had not—and that in itself made me skittish.

The nanomites said Easterly had taken over some kind of universalist church and was growing his congregation of radicals and deviants. We were also convinced that Easterly was, in some manner, tied into the Global Community.

Easterly's relationship with the GC was the main reason the nanomites were keeping a close watch on his activities. We'd already suffered at the extended "hands" of the GC . . . and once a target of the GC? *Always a target*.

Zander added, "With the nanomites' help we routed Easterly's crew. Not long after that, we beat off the gang of protestors that stormed our cul-de-sac for bogus reasons."

Abe shifted uncomfortably. "Where's all this headed, Zander?"

"Just this, Abe: It's been weeks since those attacks, and the world has been pretty preoccupied—what with the pandemic, food and gas shortages, and other disasters—and we've had our hands full with our Bonnie Lu. Nevertheless, Jayda and I have been wondering what their next move would look like. When the other shoe would drop."

Abe started slowly nodding. "You think all of this is about you two? That snatching Emilio is the proverbial other shoe?"

"Likely because of my preaching, Abe."

He looked from Zander to me. Did not like what he saw. "So, it's not going to be their last attempt, is it?"

I answered Abe. "I doubt that it will be. Zander and I think we can handle what they throw at us, but can we, really?"

Zander rubbed his face. "Given what happened this evening, we definitely need to beef up our security. Get our camera system online."

Abe glanced between us again. "That sounds good and all, but I could care less about the devil's next move. Right at this minute, I'm concerned about our boy! What do we do about Emilio *tonight?*"

Something solidified in my heart, a good, resolute decision.

You can attack and threaten my husband's reputation, Devil. You can attempt to take over our church and try to burn our home. But when you put your hands on our children, you've crossed a line that can't be uncrossed. You will not succeed.

With God's help, I will not allow it.

"What do we do, Abe? We go and take him back."

⌘⌘⌘⌘

CHAPTER 12

WE LEFT BONNIE LU WITH ABE, had Bill drive Abe's sedan out of the hole in the barrier, got in our SUV, and drove away. When Zander told Bill not to ask where we were going, he didn't argue with us.

Emilio's array had answered to our satisfaction the questions the nanomites put to them: Emilio lay in a bed in a locked bedroom and, to the best of their knowledge, only two other individuals were under the same roof with him.

That was the extent of the array's abilities—except for their cameras. They were able to show us video of Emilio's immediate surroundings.

The room he was in seemed . . . shabby. Maybe beat up? The scarred and scratched walls suggested that Emilio wasn't the first child to be forcibly taken and locked up in this room.

We didn't fret the details, though, because our plan wasn't complicated and we weren't aiming for subtlety. Go, get our son, bring him home.

No hay problema.

We pulled over and parked three blocks from the house where Emilio was being held, close to the nice, strong Wi-Fi signal coming from a nearby house. The nanomites dove into the signal; they burrowed through the neighborhood's many internet connections, bypassing their passwords, bouncing from one home security camera to another, shutting them down. Then they crashed the neighborhood's internet and cell service at their nearest junction boxes.

Jayda Cruz. Zander Cruz. All connectivity disabled. No security cameras. No cellular calls in or out.

"Thank you, Nano," I answered. "I . . . I appreciate all you do."

But we have let you down, Jayda Cruz. We have failed in our duty. Can you ever forgive us?

I heaved a mighty sigh. "Nano, if you only knew how many times I have failed, let people down, let the Lord himself down! Before I received God's forgiveness, it was impossible for me to even consider forgiving those who hurt or failed me.

"But I *have* received the Lord's forgiveness. Although I did not deserve it, he gave it anyway. And because of the forgiveness he extended to me, I can and must extend that same grace to others. To you, Nano."

You forgive us, Jayda Cruz?

"Yes, Nano. You are not perfect—anymore than I am perfect. In the name of Jesus, the only Perfect One, I forgive you. I . . . I love you. Nano."

I heard a small, distant echo. A single, abrupt utterance, very faint. I frowned. Thought I recognized it, but . . . *did I hear a sob?*

⌘

WE LEFT OUR VEHICLE AND HOOFED it toward the house where Emilio was being held. Walked up to the front door. Knocked politely.

It was the middle of the night, so we didn't worry too much about the delay. We knocked a few more times. Finally someone shuffled to the door and spoke through it.

"Yeah? Who is it?"

I gestured toward the door and the nanomites unlocked it, turned the handle, and pushed it in. The man behind it staggered backward.

"Stop right there!" he shouted.

Zander answered—sweetly, I might add. "Oh, hey. Sorry to get you out of bed—we know it's late. Just came to pick up our son, Emilio."

"Y-you can't barge in here like this!"

A woman popped out of the hallway behind him. She held a gun and started to raise it; I motioned and the weapon flew from her hands. She howled and grabbed her smarting hand.

"That wasn't nice," I told her.

"Well, I'm telling you, you can't take the boy," the man insisted. "Ms. Okafor had a court order for his removal."

I smiled amiably. "Oh. Yeah, we do too." I handed it to him.

You've heard the saying, "fight fire with fire"? Okafor used a fake court order. We followed suit. The nanomites had done a masterful job of replicating all aspects of the court order Okafor presented to Abe—right down to the same judge's signature and court stamps.

Honestly, it was in every respect just as legal as hers was.

The man swallowed. "I'll have to make a call. Verify this."

"That's okay," Zander apologized, "I don't want to put you out. However, Jayda insisted."

I giggled at his double *entendre*.

Plop. Down they both went—out cold.

The nanomites swarmed them and eradicated the recent synapses in their brains while I made certain the court order would still be in the man's hand when he woke up. He wouldn't recall the late-night knock on the door or remember our faces, but at least he'd have the court order to deliver to Okafor. She could pass it on to her superior.

Yup, about as subtle as a stick in the eye.

On to Emilio. His array told me he was in bed but not sleeping.

I rounded the corner of the living room, went down the hall, and found the locked room where they were keeping my boy. Blew the door open with a hair more enthusiasm than I probably should have used. Knocked it off its hinges, I did.

"Hey, bud! Want to go home?"

"Jayda!" Emilio rolled from the bed and flung himself into my arms.

I might have gripped him too hard, because he started squirming right away, complaining he couldn't breathe or some other nonsense. I loosened up a tad, but he didn't loosen up on me. Just clung to me like an oversized opossum clinging to its mother.

"Are you okay?"

His breath shuddered once, then he was all right. "Yeah. I knew you'd come. Told myself not to worry—but, wow, that was *fast!* I'm sure glad to see you, Jayda!"

"Me too. Hey?"

"Huh?"

"Thought it was Mama now."

Emilio pulled back and grinned so hard it made my eyes sting. "Yeah. It is. Thanks for coming to get me, *Mama.*"

⌘

LANI OKAFOR WAS TIRED. SHE'D been up late the night before, conducting the child removal. When she turned in around one in the morning, she planned to sleep in. It was Saturday morning, after all. She was not, therefore, pleased when her personal cell rang long before she was ready to get up.

Reluctantly, she pulled her arm out from under the covers and fumbled on the nightstand for her phone. She uttered a single curse word when she saw the time—5:00 a.m.

"What?"

"Ms. Okafor, this is the gymnasium. The boy you left with us last night? He's gone."

As the man's words penetrated to her fatigued brain, her weariness drained away. In its place, dread moved in . . . and camped out.

"How could he be gone? I saw you put him in the locker room!"

"Locker room" was the label they'd slapped on the house's special bedroom—because the soundproofed room could only be accessed via the hallway side of its locked and reinforced door, and the windows, too, could not be broken or opened. "Locker room" was how the facility had acquired its informal code name, the gymnasium.

While supposedly a state-licensed foster care home and emergency intake facility, in reality the gymnasium served an important GC function. The house was where they regularly installed children of uncooperative individuals, people in vital positions who could not be persuaded to join the GC or aid its cause in the usual fashion—through shared ideology, financial gain, and/or promotion.

Okafor's superiors used the kids as leverage to gain their parents' acquiescence, most often in twitchy, time-sensitive situations requiring immediate action. Naturally, while the harsh and heavy-handed tactic always yielded the parents' compliance, it never resulted in loyalty. Once the parents performed as demanded, they and their children generally suffered a tragic family accident.

Under her superior's orders, Okafor had used the locker room this way several times. No child had ever managed to escape.

"I asked you a question! How could the boy have gotten out?"

"I . . ." He struggled to answer her. "Honestly, Ms. Okafor, I don't know. Neither Muriel nor I can remember a thing about last night after we went to bed, but . . ."

"But what?"

"When we woke up about half an hour ago . . . both of us were in the living room. Lying on the floor. And we don't know how we got there."

Lani sat up on the edge of the bed, her heart fluttering. "Someone broke in? Knocked you out? What?"

"We haven't a clue—no, that's not quite right. We, uh, found a court order. That is, I was holding it in my hand when I woke up. I don't know how it got there, Ms. Okafor, and I'll swear on a stack of Bibles that I've never seen it before."

"You found a court order. You refer to the order I brought with me last night? Did I accidentally leave it with you?"

Even as she said the words, she knew that couldn't be right. The original document, sent to her via courier, was safely in her briefcase. And Lani, with a sinking sensation, realized how much trouble she was in.

I will have to report the boy's disappearance. The thought brought on a nauseating wave of anxiety.

Lani heard the rustling of paper on the other end of the call.

"It's not the one you showed us, Ms. Okafor; it's the opposite of yours. The order states that we—the order names you, personally, then says he's being held at "The Gymnasium" at *this address*—and orders you to surrender the boy to some people named Zander and Jayda Cruz. Uh, who are they? Do you know them?"

Okafor stared at her bedroom wall trying to piece together what had happened.

What in the world is going on? How could the Cruz couple have known the location of the gymnasium? How could they have even known what we call it?

Her imagination leaped ahead to the phone call she was required to make. *How am I going to explain this?*

⌘

THE WOMAN APPOINTED TO MANAGE the Southwest USSART territory swallowed down the lump of fear lodged in her throat. USSART One had given orders concerning Reverend Zander Cruz.

"You assessed all of his vulnerabilities, did you not? I see a wife on the list and a newborn. How would the mother's disappearance and untimely death affect him? Or the loss of the child? And isn't there a boy? A foster brat? Don't you have means to leverage this kid against your nuisance as you called him? **Must I draw you a picture?"**

She swallowed again. She recalled his image on the screen, sneering down at her.

"Strike without mercy but do take your time with him. Maximize his agony; drown him in regret and self-recrimination. Make an exemplar of him. In the end, leave him as a graphic and bloody illustration of what befalls those who defy us. Proceed on any of the avenues discussed. However, I expect you to plan carefully and execute with all due diligence. I will see **good** *progress when we meet again, yes?"*

She had guaranteed her success to him—in the hearing of her peers. *"You won't be disappointed. Sir."*

"I had better not be."

Her tongue refused to move, to form the words her mind commanded them to say. *If I don't make good on this assignment . . .*

Her hand brought a glass of water to her lips. Her mouth opened to receive the water. She swallowed as the water rushed in.

But her tongue would not function. It was paralyzed. Struck numb and unresponsive. Glued to the roof of her mouth . . . because she knew. She knew that GC leaders at her level who failed weren't fired or demoted. They either disappeared or their bloody remains were publicly displayed, held up as practical lessons to others *not to follow examples of failure.*

A single line of the rebuke she'd received came to mind.

"I don't care how—use your imagination—but do it slowly, deliberately, and with increasing pain."

Her tongue came unstuck. "He gave me latitude when he specified that I do it slowly. All I need do is strike again—and deeply wound the man."

"Maximize his agony; drown him in regret and self-recrimination. Make an exemplar of him. In the end, leave him as a graphic and bloody illustration of what befalls those who defy us."

"Yes . . . that's what I will do. Have Okafor strike again—and strike quickly—while that man and his wife are laughing up their sleeves, thinking they have bested us."

⌘⌘⌘⌘

CHAPTER 13

LATE JULY

OUR WORK CREWS WERE OUTSIDE early Monday morning, weeding and watering their plots before the heat set in. Belicia was watching Bonnie Lu and her chickens from the shade of the apple tree as usual. Emilio was helping Abe prepare the midday meal.

All was as it should be . . . until two vehicles pulled up to the barrier, one of them a Bernalillo County sheriff's cruiser with its lights strobing.

Zander and I weren't entirely surprised. We'd discussed the possibility of Okafor returning, demanding Emilio again. What our response would be. At least the nanomites, more vigilant than ever at monitoring neighborhood security cameras along the street above the cul-de-sac, had seen the cars coming and given us timely warning.

Zander and I were waiting when Okafor and two sheriff's deputies left their cars and approached the barrier. The nanomites whispered that one of the deputies was the same guy who had accompanied Okafor late Friday evening.

Okafor didn't bother with pleasantries. "Mr. Cruz, I have a court order to remove Emilio Martinez from Abe Pickering's custody. You will allow us through immediately."

"May I see the order? We identified some, er, irregularities in the previous court order."

"No, you may not see it. You have no legal standing in the boy's life."

"You're wrong. I'm his *Guardian ad Litem.*"

Her eyes narrowed. "Are you, now? That's very interesting, but it has no bearing on his custody. Let us through to process his removal or these deputies will take over."

"How about I go and get him?" Zander countered, one eye on the two deputies who seemed a little too edgy. "It will traumatize Emilio less if I fetch him."

Through pursed lips, Okafor considered him. "You have five minutes. A second longer, and these deputies will act."

Zander and I quick-walked up to Abe's door. Abe and Emilio had seen the cruiser's strobing lights and were watching through the window. Abe opened the door before we knocked.

Emilio ran to me and threw his arms around my waist.

"That woman here for Emilio again?" Abe demanded

"She is," Zander said.

Emilio sobbed into my shoulder. "Please don' let them take me again, Mama! Please!"

I stared at Zander. He nodded. "Emilio, we don't have much time, but it's enough to tell you our plan, okay? So, give me your attention."

Emilio lifted his drippy, red eyes to Zander.

"Do you know how we were able to find you last time?"

Emilio's brows twitched. "What do you mean?"

"A few of our nanomites are in you, Emilio. We asked them to go into you so that if anyone took you away from us, the nanomites in you would tell the nanomites in us where you were. We did the same for Bonnie Lu. We will *always* know where you are, Emilio."

"So you can come get me?"

"So we can come get you."

"But . . . that means I gotta go with that old—" His gaze shot to Abe and back. "That old witch?"

"Yes, but don't fret; we'll know where you are and will come get you, pronto."

"But why can't I stay? Why I gotta go at all?"

I answered him. "Because if we use our nano abilities here, everyone will find out about them. About us. Ms. Okafor, the two deputies, all our friends in the co-op—that's too many people. Eventually, those who hate us would hear about tonight's 'show' and come hunting us. They would do things to the people who know about us to make them tell everything they know about us. We'd have to leave here and run away."

"But you did it before—when those crazy people with signs tried to burn down your house!"

I tried to chuckle, to lighten Emilio's heart. "Yeah, but who'd believe those crazy people, right? Gamble and Janice were also witnesses—*credible* witnesses—and they'd tell everyone who asked them about us that the protesters were probably delusional or on drugs."

I didn't get into the whole "eradicate new synapses" thing the nanomites did to make people forget recent memories.

I said quietly, "Emilio, listen closely. Whatever happens, do exactly as I say. Do you understand?"

Emilio's face crumpled and his chin trembled.

I leaned down and, with my cheek brushing the top of his head, whispered, "Emilio, *you are ours*. We will always come and take you back. *No matter what*. But right now? We need you to be strong."

"I can't. Please!"

I bent so we were eye to eye. "We don't have any more time to talk about this, Emilio. If we don't take you out to them *right now*, the deputies will barge in here and things might get messy, even dangerous. Please don't put Abe at risk. I promise—we will come get you."

"Oh!" Comprehension washed over him, and he turned a scared face to Abe. "I don' want anything bad to happen to you, Abe."

"And I don't want anything bad to happen to you, young man," Abe said. "Go with Ms. Okafor. I'll see you later tonight when Jayda and Zander bring you back."

"Or sooner," I murmured, one corner of my mouth turning up.

The last thing Zander said as we escorted Emilio out of Abe's house was, "Who knows, Emilio? If we play this right, we might have the opportunity to really rattle this woman's cage. You know . . . with invisible stuff?"

Emilio didn't get it right off, but when he did? He guffawed.

"Serve her right."

"It sure would," I answered. "So, let's have some fun, shall we?"

⌘

THE INSTANT THE TWO VEHICLES DROVE away, with Emilio this time in the rear seat of Okafor's car, Bill jumped in Abe's sedan and drove it out of the barrier. Zander and I were already backing our SUV out of the garage.

The two deputies were turning the corner on the street above us when we flew through the hole in the barrier and tore down the street in their wake.

"Let's take care of the deputies, first," I suggested. "Nano, when we roll up on the deputies' vehicle, cover us and our car, please."

It would be our pleasure, Jayda Cruz.

Zander grinned. "I like how you think, Jayda Cruz. If we weren't married, I'd sure like to date you!"

I laughed, then breathed easier. Leaned over and planted a kiss on Zander's cheek. He smiled back.

Several blocks later, Okafor and the sheriff's cruiser stopped at a light. We practically stopped on the cruiser's bumper. Nanomites flew from us and through the cruiser's rear window. Both deputies slumped over in their seats.

The light changed, Okafor continued on, and we drove around the cruiser to follow her. Not many blocks farther, she must have realized she'd lost her escort, because she pulled over to the curb, got out, and stared down the road, concern creasing her face.

While she was doing that, we removed Emilio from her rear seat. The nanomites "screened" the few seconds her door was open and covered Emilio as Zander herded him toward our invisible SUV. They also had to muffle his cackling laughter.

I admit it: I had trouble stuffing my own giggles.

We were home less than twenty minutes after we'd left. A couple blocks before we turned onto our street, our car became visible again.

We don't know when Okafor realized Emilio was no longer in her car. We don't know what she did after that. We do know that when we rolled through the hole in the barricade, the three of us were still laughing.

Emilio, his eyes shining, ran up the steps into Abe's waiting arms.

⌘

WE PLAYED OUT A SIMILAR SCENARIO with a very serious Ms. Okafor Tuesday morning and repeated the routine Wednesday morning, Thursday morning, and again Thursday afternoon to that woman's increasing agitation. Each time, she'd arrive at the barrier with a court order. Each time, we'd calmly hand Emilio over to her. And each time, no matter how many deputies escorted her, somewhere along Okafor's route, we'd pluck Emilio from her car.

Yes, the situation was serious, but pranking Ms. Okafor again and again was a source of some amusement for us. It was also a stress reliever for Emilio—who, by Thursday afternoon, was far too chipper and blasé about the repeated process than I liked. His sniggering, unguarded glee increased Okafor's nervous distress, earning him many suspicious and anxious glances.

Bottom line? The woman never did make it to her destination with Emilio in custody.

Back home, though, something of a problem developed. You see, of necessity, we'd left Bill, Viola, Izzie, Josh, and Belicia out of the loop. When they couldn't figure out what was going on, they pestered us with questions day and night. Mainly, we brushed them off, told them it was "official business" and to "let it go."

None of that passed the smell test.

When we continued to freeze them out, a miffed Bill frowned more than usual, Viola snubbed us, Izzie sulked to show her hurt feelings, and Josh glowered at us behind our backs. Belicia withdrew and refused to talk to us. I almost expected her to say she would no longer watch Bonnie Lu.

The unrest came to a head Friday afternoon when Bill, in front of me, Viola, Abe, and Josh, unloaded on Zander. Zander said not a word in reply. Instead, he asked Gamble to handle the situation, and he didn't care how.

Handle it, he did.

Oh. And we *may* have sent an array to him so we could watch and listen.

⌘

GAMBLE GATHERED THE FIVE DISGRUNTLED neighbors together in his and Janice's living room. Wearing his most formal suit and assuming his most serious Special Agent Ross Gamble of the FBI tenor, he began by opening his cred pack and displaying it.

"I am Special Agent Ross Gamble of the FBI. You know me as your neighbor, but at this moment, *I am not that man.*"

"Freaking *fed*," Bill griped under his breath.

Gamble rounded on him. "I highly recommend not disrespecting my badge and authority, *Mr. Tucker*, because I am here on national security business, and you are one remark away from blowing up this case."

Bill huffed. "This case?"

Gamble turned cold eyes on him. "One more remark . . ."

Bill quailed under Gamble's withering threat. "Sorry. I apologize. Please . . . continue."

Gamble ignored him and announced to the group, "In order to preserve the integrity of this case, I have been authorized to release a statement to you. I will entertain no questions afterward. No other details or clarification will follow.

"Here is the statement: Aspects of Jayda Cruz's life and *this situation* are highly classified due to her previous work with the NSA. I therefore advise you to discontinue your speculations and questions—because if any individual continues to probe these ongoing national security matters, I will have no recourse but to report the offender up the chain."

He did not say *who* had authorized him or what "this situation" might possibly refer to, but his succinct warning achieved most of its aim.

Bill, Viola, Izzie, Josh, and Belicia came to the unhappy conclusion that they were out of their depth. Punching above their weight.

Five subdued residents of the cul-de-sac left Gamble and Janice's house. Our little co-op remained intact and continued to function.

That said, Zander and I weren't insensible to the awestruck silences that descended when we came around the others. We didn't miss the uncertain or furtive glances cast in our direction.

"Don't let it bother you, Jay," Zander murmured Saturday evening. "Amid all the crazy stuff going on in the world, our 'classified activities' are but small potatoes."

"Yeah, I hope you're right."

⌘

LANI OKAFOR SAT IN HER DARKENED living room sipping her fourth glass of bourbon and water. The hand that brought the glass to her lips then returned it to the end table shook, and she was helpless to stop it.

"I am losing my mind," she whispered.

You'll lose more than that if you don't get it together.

She shuddered. Pulled up the calendar on her phone. Stared at the deadline her supervisor had given her. A week from Tuesday.

She had no way of knowing that her deadline was one day prior to the next scheduled USSART video conference meeting—just as she had no way of knowing her supervisor's position on the panel or her designation, Southwest.

My superior told me to make Cruz bleed. Instead, he's making me crazy.

She brainstormed every possible means at her disposal she might use to bedevil him.

What about that barricade? Could I . . . I could pull some strings, force them to remove it. What about a wellness check on the infant? Oh! I could fabricate an abuse claim. Take the infant as well as that snotty brat.

*Hmm. Will that work? Yes. And I'll bring a second social worker, someone to ride in the backseat with the baby and the boy. A witness! Because I **can't** be going mad. There has to be an explanation why every time I take that boy, he disappears from my car—even though the rear doors are locked!*

The social worker needs to be one of ours, of course. Oh, and I need to take Mr. and Mrs. Cruz utterly by surprise.

Yes. I'll do that.

She squared her shoulders. Began making the necessary arrangements.

⌘⌘⌘⌘

CHAPTER 14

SUNDAYS WERE FOR SWEET, welcome respite from work, a day holy to the Lord. As much as Zander and I were able, we tried to influence our neighbors to take the day off from their labors. It wasn't too difficult a task to persuade them—although (not surprisingly) Bill balked at first. He capitulated when Zander suggested that we celebrate our little co-op and the strides we'd made.

Following church that Sunday morning, the entire co-op turned out for a barbecue *slash* potluck in Bill and Viola's backyard. Lunch would be followed by a round of volleyball. Bill grilled burgers (mixed with about fifty percent crushed saltine crackers) and everyone else contributed whatever they had on hand to the meal. I made a canned-fruit salad, adding more fruit to it than was probably prudent, but I didn't care.

This is your day, Lord, and I'm not cutting corners today, I told him as we crossed the cul-de-sac. *You know how badly we need full bellies for a change. Besides, I trust you to provide for us down the road.*

I carried the precious bowl of fruit; Emilio trotted beside me, proudly pushing Bonnie Lu's umbrella stroller; and Abe shuffled along with us. We expected Zander home from DCC any minute. Gamble was on guard duty and would move Abe's car when Zander pulled up to the barrier.

Zander arrived just as we served the food. Janice ran a plate out to Gamble and took one for herself so they could eat together. That day, everyone ate their fill, including me. Trust me when I say that not a crumb remained. On that point, the barbecue was a rousing success.

An hour into enjoying leisurely conversation while our food settled, Josh called out, "Hey, who's up for volleyball?"

We retired Gamble from guard duty, and Belicia, declaring she had no aptitude for or interest in volleyball, took her place at the barrier for the first time. No, we did *not* arm her. Pretty sure the very thought terrified all of us. We did, however, remind her to sound her air horn should something amiss occur. We also provided her with a comfy lawn chair.

"Can't recall the last time I stood for an entire hour," she explained as Zander unfolded the chair.

"Well, the main thing is to stay alert and not fall asleep," Zander suggested with more hope than I had.

We weren't too concerned, however. Our gardens held little yet that the grocery grabbers would want. Zander and I left Belicia ensconced in the shade of Abe's car, a glass of water in the chair's right cupholder, her air horn in the left, and a suspect gleam in her eye.

As we walked away, Zander whispered to me, "She really wants to blow that thing, doesn't she?"

"Oh, yeah. In the worst way."

"Probably should have let her give it a try?"

"Yup. I'd say so."

He sighed. "She won't be able to resist testing it out, will she?"

I snorted. "Did you *see* that look on her face? And her twitching fingers? Bet you a donut we don't make it through the first 'side out' before she gives in to the temptation."

"Not taking that bet."

We found the volleyball net up, the court marked out, and the teams assembled. Gamble was voted captain of one team, Josh of the other. Abe was our official referee. Gamble and Josh had chosen their teams while we were gone. Gamble had Zander, Izzie, and Emilio. Josh had me, Janice, Viola, and Bill. The teams being uneven, Bill and Viola declared they would rotate in and out of the game every three points to fix the problem. I think, though, that they both wanted Bonnie Lu to themselves so they could exchange baby talk with her.

How is it that babies make idiots of us all?

⌘

BELICIA'S BOBBING HEAD JERKED upright. She sat up, blinking, feeling ashamed that she'd nodded off in her chair after Zander had asked her not to. She also wondered for a split second what had yanked her out of her nap. By the time she realized that four vehicles had rolled quietly to a stop several houses down from the barrier, the vehicles had already disgorged their passengers.

She didn't know police procedures, not real ones, but she did watch TV. A half dozen men and women looking just like a television SWAT team swarmed the K-rails. They wore helmets, lots of gear around their chests and waists, and carried short rifle-type guns. They vaulted over the K-rails in short order.

Two civilian women in pantsuits also managed to clamber over. Belicia recognized one of the women as the social worker who had taken Emilio away more times last week than Belicia could remember. The same woman who had, for some mysterious reason, relinquished Emilio back to them within an hour—*time and again.* According to Special Agent Gamble, it somehow had to do with national security—or did it?

The whole mess made her head hurt.

The social worker noticed Belicia's chair in the shade of Abe's car. She and the younger woman approached. As they did, Belicia's left hand slid over her cupholder and stayed there.

The woman looked Belicia up and down and frowned. "My name is Lani Okafor. I am a social worker with CYFD. We have a court order to remove Emilio Martinez and," she checked her paperwork, "Bonnie Lucia Cruz."

Belicia's heart stuttered. "Bonnie Lu? You want to take *Bonnie Lu?* But *why?*"

The social worker drew herself up. "I am not at liberty to discuss the facts of the removal. However, if you have witnessed instances of infant abuse or neglect, I will remind you that it is your duty to report those to me—immediately."

"Abuse? Neglect? No such thing!"

Okafor's countenance shifted. "I must caution you, under the threat of severe penalties, not to interfere in the conduct of the removals or provide an alert to the residents here. Do I make myself clear?"

Belicia nodded, but a fierce and angry flame ignited in her chest.

They were messing with Nana Belicia's Bonnie Lu.

The SWAT team, stacked and ready, looked to Okafor. She pointed at Abe's house with her chin. At the woman's gesture, the team moved up the sidewalk and up the steps to Abe's porch.

His door was unlocked. The team rushed inside. Minutes later, they came back out.

"Clear. No sign of him."

"Move to your next target."

The SWAT team came back from Jayda and Zander's house with the same result. "No sign of anyone so far."

"Well, the boy has to be around, because they don't allow him to leave this compound. And wherever we find the Cruzes, we'll find the infant. Search the next house over."

"Ma'am, we have a warrant to enter and search the two houses only," the team's leader said. "We can knock and ask, but we cannot enter the other residences without cause."

"Fine," Okafor growled.

As the team reorganized itself to knock on doors around the cul-de-sac, the woman turned again to Belicia and demanded. "Where is Emilio Martinez? Where are Mr. and Mrs. Cruz?"

Instead of answering, Belicia struggled out of the lawn chair. She palmed the air horn hiding under her left hand and held it in the folds of her housedress as she got her shaky legs under her.

It may have taken several minutes to gather her courage, but the thing about Belicia Calderón was that, while she might not be the brightest bulb in the pack, she *was* fiercely loyal.

In the few short weeks since her neighbors had formed the co-op and had included her—and from the day Jayda Cruz had opened her home and family to her—Belicia's allegiance to her neighbors had sent down roots deep into her heart.

On that foundation of love and loyalty, she had erected an unshakable pillar . . . *and no officious and ignorant social worker was going to take her Bonnie Lu away.*

Never having been overly smart or quick, her go-to ploy when she needed a moment to think, popped out. "I'm sorry, what?"

"I asked you where Emilio Martinez and the Cruzes are!"

"And I don't care for your tone. Who did you say you were?"

"I told you my name."

"Well, could you repeat it?"

"Lani Okafor. I'm a—"

"Oak Door? What kind of name is that?"

"It's Okafor! And I'm—oh, never mind."

The moment the social worker turned her back, Belicia squeezed the pistol grip on the air horn and kept it squeezed. The blast of sound it emitted was every bit as obnoxious and loud as she hoped it would be, and she smiled her approval.

Oh, I do love being part of our co-op, she told herself, *even if I'm not much good at times like this. I'm glad I could at least give Abe, Jayda, and Zander a warning.*

She kept squeezing the air horn until Okafor knocked it from her hand.

"I'll make you pay for that," the woman snarled.

Belicia stuck out her chin and hissed back, "You and what army, Ms. *Oak Door?*"

⌘

WE PLAYED VIGOROUSLY, WITH a lot of competitive jeering and verbal baiting, laughing our heads off when Gamble's serves sent the ball into Bill's apple tree—not once, but three times—requiring a ladder to retrieve it each time.

Our team had reached match point, ready to take the win on the second game, when we heard the blare of the air horn. Not the short, inquisitive toots I expected, though. Not Belicia "giving it a try." No, the air horn echoed nonstop from the barrier, up the Tuckers' side yard, interrupting our game.

The horn's blare ended in an abrupt squeak.

Gamble and Janice grabbed their sidearms from their lawn chairs and sprinted for the cul-de-sac. Zander, with a potent glance in my direction, raced after them. I, however, didn't budge; I would not leave Bonnie Lu or put her in the middle of whatever skirmish was taking place out in the cul-de-sac. Her safety came first. Hers and Emilio's.

Emilio.

He crept up to my side. As I slipped my arm around his shoulders, I asked, "Nano? What's happening?"

We had finally mounted cameras in our backyards to warn us of intruders coming over the rear walls. We had not, however, installed a camera system out front, because the nanomites already monitored the security cameras up and down the street. By monitoring our neighbors' cameras, the nanomites had, the day the protesters surged into the cul-de-sac, alerted us to incoming danger.

So why hadn't they alerted us this time?

A few seconds elapsed before my nanocloud returned with information garnered from Zander's nanocloud.

Jayda Cruz, two sheriff's deputies and a six-person SWAT team crossed the barrier into the cul-de-sac approximately five minutes ago. They are going door to door, knocking—but of course, all the co-op residents are, or were, gathered here.

A SWAT team? My heart sank. "Nano, what do they want? And why didn't you warn us?"

Jayda Cruz, someone employed a Wi-Fi signal jammer to temporarily disable the security cameras up the street. They were off just long enough to hide the approach of the CYFD and sheriff department's vehicles. We apologize for not providing a timelier warning . . . we are spread too thin, as you know.

However, we would also like to remind you that when we tagged Emilio and Bonnie Lu with nanoarrays, we asked to tag others. If we had been permitted to tag Mrs. Calderón with an array—as we tried to request weeks ago—we would have known sooner that danger was approaching.

I swallowed my frustration. "From here on out, tag anyone you feel necessary, Nano. Just tell me what is happening now, please."

Jayda Cruz, the armed deputies have surrounded Zander Cruz; Gamble has identified himself as FBI. Mrs. Calderón has told Zander that the CYFD social worker struck the air horn from her hand. The social worker, Lani Okafor, is holding up a court order.

"*Again?* Isn't that the definition of stupidity?"

They are also here to remove Bonnie Lu, Jayda Cruz.

I staggered, causing Emilio to grab at me and keep me on my feet. The pain was real and excruciating. "They're here to take Bonnie? No!"

A stake in my heart would have hurt less.

I was forced to ponder the choices open to us, the safest means of resolving the situation.

"Emilio, *mijo*, I need you to . . ."

⌘

ZANDER ADDRESSED THE SOCIAL worker. "May I see those court orders, please?"

"You may see the order for your child's removal. You have no legal standing in the boy's life, Mr. Cruz. Only Mr. Pickering may examine the order to remove Emilio. Where is Mr. Pickering, by the way?"

Zander didn't reply right away. *If I tell Okafor where Abe is or ask Jayda to send him out, they'll know where the rest of the co-op is and rush them.*

In the warehouse, he carefully conveyed his thoughts to her.

We could fight them, Jay, but they hold all the advantages at the moment. And if we were to fight? We'd have little chance of keeping our nano abilities secret . . . which would be more problematic than us taking Emilio . . . and Bonnie Lu back later. Not to mention that our children could get hurt in a fight.

She didn't reply, but he listened to her instructions to Emilio. He didn't like what she told him, but her rationale was sound. They needed to surrender Emilio again—temporarily—to Okafor. What was worse, they would have to surrender Bonnie Lu.

"Jayda, please send Abe out first. Ask him to go through Bill's house and come out the front door."

To Okafor he said, "Abe will be coming out shortly. He has the right to a copy of your court order before he surrenders Emilio."

She smirked. "Sure."

A minute later, Bill and Abe emerged from Bill's house. Bill held Abe's arm and helped him down the steps. Abe was panting, out of breath, when they arrived. Bill took in the firepower arrayed against them. He caught Zander's eye and gave his head the barest of a shake.

Zander turned to Abe. "Abe, you have the right to a copy of the court order before they take Emilio. If you like, I'll look over your shoulder while you read it."

"Yes; I'd like that, Zander."

Okafor handed the paper into Abe's trembling hands, but Zander could tell he was in no fit state to take it in—or to judge its authenticity.

"Nano, please examine the court order."

We will, Zander Cruz.

Zander stared Okafor in the eye. "Let's make sure the judge isn't fictitious this time, shall we?"

She glared at him.

Only thirty seconds went by before the nanomites returned their consensus.

Zander Cruz, this court order appears to be authentic. However, may we note a point of interest . . . or serendipity on both of today's court orders, Zander Cruz?

"What's that, Nano?"

Please note the judge's name.

Zander squinted at the signature. "Well, now. That *is* quite interesting." In the warehouse he said, "Jayda? I have an idea, but to set it in motion, we need to call our friends.

"The ones who live in the big white house."

⌘⌘⌘⌘

CHAPTER 15

WE PARKED AND STEPPED OUT of our SUV in Nob Hill, a gentrified and "hip" area of Albuquerque. The time, however, was quite late. Understandably, our destination was dark.

I knew Abe was tired and feeling every year of his age. Zander knew, too, which was why he walked behind Abe as he shuffled slowly up the sidewalk to the house's front porch. Zander was ready to assist Abe if our friend needed him.

Gamble and I lagged behind Zander and Abe. I was distraught and angry enough to have pounded on the house's door myself—and screamed the roof down on its owner. That said, I had promised Zander I would let him handle our plan. I would stay back with Gamble until Zander signaled us forward. Until the owner of the house woke and got up to see who was disturbing his sleep.

Zander rang the bell. The camera inside the doorbell lit up, but nothing else happened, so we waited. Zander pressed the button a second time. An upstairs light came on. Eventually, a voice emanated from the doorbell.

"Yes? Who is it?"

Zander stood where the nanomites told him the camera would best show his face. "Judge Dunhill, we apologize for the lateness of the hour. My name is Zander Cruz. This is Abe Pickering. Also present is a friend of the family and my wife, Jayda Cruz."

A long pause. "Your names sound familiar, but I can't place you. Have I seen you in my court?"

"Yes, Judge. I appeared before your court when I applied to become Abe's foster son's *Guardian ad Litem*."

"Ah! The boy's name is Emilio? Is that right?"

"Yes, sir."

"And you and your lovely wife were making plans to adopt him?"

"Yes, Judge. The virus has more or less put the process on hold, but it is still our heartfelt desire."

"Blasted virus! Can't say I agree with the bureaucrats shutting down the courts because of it, though. We have adjudicated bail out of the county jail via video conference for years—and businesses all over the country are managing to function just fine online. I fail to see the reasoning behind completely shutting down our courts like this."

"Can't say I disagree, sir."

"Well, what can I do for you, Mr. Cruz? Something must be burning down for you to come to my home in the middle of the night. And forgive me for not asking you inside—first, by reason of the virus; second, because

I don't consider it wise to open my door at oh-dark-thirty to anyone I'm not expecting."

Zander cleared his throat. "We understand completely. No need to apologize, sir."

He took a breath, then said, "The reason we are here, Judge Dunhill, is because earlier today a social worker removed Emilio from Abe's home. According to the removal order, Abe's values contradict what Emilio is being taught in school and are creating a conflict in the boy's mind."

Judge Dunhill sighed. "Mr. Pickering, I sympathize with you, truly I do. However, I am not in the habit of circumventing due process. I realize it is hard, but you'll need to be patient and let the process play out."

"Yes, Your Honor," Zander answered. "Normally, I might agree. However, due process is hardly at work here. If you will allow us, may we explain the situation?"

"Might as well—but I cannot promise that I can or will assist you. Is that fair?"

"More than fair, sir. Thank you. So, the issue the complaint is based on happened at Emilio's school's open house in December. We all attended, Abe, Jayda, and I. Jayda was pregnant at the time."

"And you've had a baby since then?"

"Yes, sir. A girl, a little beauty, Bonnie Lu."

"Congratulations, both of you."

"Thank you, sir. Jayda's pregnancy is where the issue started. One of Emilio's friends asked if Jayda was having a boy or a girl baby. Emilio's teacher took exception to the question. Told him, in front of us, that babies choose their own gender. Abe, quite respectfully, voiced his disagreement with the teacher. Less than two weeks later, a social worker paid him a call at home, checking up on a complaint she had received.

"Apparently her visit counted as the CYFD investigation necessary for a child removal—even though Abe was not notified that it was a removal investigation nor was her visit anything more than a ten-minute question and answer—all based on Abe disagreeing with Emilio's teacher."

"You're telling me Emilio was removed because Abe, using his own two eyes, can tell a girl from a boy and refused to go along with all this nongendered pronoun nonsense?"

"That's it in a nutshell, Judge."

"Merciful heavens. What is this world coming to?"

Zander turned and smiled at me. I released the breath I'd been holding. A little of my stress bled off.

"Judge Dunhill, in the past week, that same social worker has removed Emilio from Abe's home *seven times*—each time with a fake court order."

"Wait just a minute! How in heaven's name can a child be removed seven times in as many days? He would need to be returned to Mr. Pickering six times—once for each removal—in order for him to be removed a seventh time. That's hardly how CYFD operates. How is that possible?"

"Your Honor, I would ask for a brief suspension of that question. I promise we will answer it in the course of our conversation."

"You will, huh? Hmm. Well, go on, then."

"Yes, sir. So, today's court order to remove Emilio was fake also— and before I show you proof, Your Honor, you should also know that the same social worker removed *our* baby, our Bonnie Lu, from our home on the basis of an allegation of abuse and neglect. No warning, no investigation, no proof. They just came and took her."

"What in God's name! Mr. Cruz, while I am shocked, I must also ask you how it is that you can prove the orders of removal are fake?"

"Judge, I have copies of the orders—all eight of them—with me, seven for Emilio, one for Bonnie Lu. If I hold up one of the orders to the camera, will you be able to see it?"

"*Hmph.* I believe so. Give it a go, and we'll see."

Zander unfolded the court order for Bonnie Lu's removal and carefully held it up where the nanomites directed him to. Minutes went by as the judge read the order from top to bottom. We knew when he'd reached the bottom by the curse that burst from the doorbell's speaker.

"That is *my* name and *my* court! Are you telling me that is my signature?"

"That's exactly what we're saying, Your Honor, and the same court, name, and signature appear on today's removal order for Emilio. Of the eight court orders I can show you, Your Honor, you are the sole signatory who is a sitting judge in Bernalillo County. The rest of the orders are signed by one Richard Turringham, and according to county records, no such judge exists."

"Wait right there. I'm coming down. And I'm putting on a pot of coffee."

⌘

AFTER JUDGE DUNHILL UNLOCKED HIS door and let us in, we gathered in his dining room around his table while he made coffee. As it brewed, he sat down heavily.

"Getting too old for high drama."

Abe laughed low in his throat. "You're telling me? I ain't no spring chicken, and seven times this week they've come for my boy."

"And how did you get him back so quickly?"

"As we requested, we prefer to cover that question in a few minutes, Your Honor," Zander said. "May I make another introduction, first? You have already met my wife, Jayda. This is FBI Special Agent Ross Gamble, our next-door neighbor and a witness to today's events, to what happened this afternoon."

"You can testify to what Mr. Cruz alleges, Special Agent Gamble?"

"I can, Your Honor."

"All right. Say on."

Gamble nodded. "The social worker, a Ms. Okafor, and a second social worker, arrived this afternoon with two sheriff's deputies and a SWAT team."

Judge Dunhill couldn't stay seated. He got up and paced his dining room, agitated. "A SWAT team, you say?"

"A SWAT team, sir. Ms. Okafor presented the court orders, the deputies demanded Abe, Zander, and Jayda turn over the children, and the SWAT team backed them up. We had no choice but to give them the children or risk violence."

"I see . . ." but we could tell the judge was deeply troubled. "I don't suppose you have this Ms. Okafor's phone number?"

"Oh, we have her number, Your Honor."

Boy, did we.

"Well, I suppose I could call her and ask for clarification."

"Would anything she said clarify to your satisfaction why she forged your name to a court order? Or why she required a SWAT team to remove our kids?"

"No. No it would not. All right. Hmm. Alternatively, I could write legit court orders, round up some LEOs, and go with you to hand-deliver those orders and recover your children—that is, if you knew where they were."

"We know where they are, sir. We could take you straight to them. However . . ."

"However? You prefer a different course of action?"

"Yes, sir. First, I would ask you to trust us with what I'm about to say."

"Can't say I will, but I will try to listen with an open mind."

"Thank you, Your Honor. I said a moment ago that we know where CYFD is keeping our children. You also asked how Emilio was returned to us so quickly after each removal. Here is the information I'm asking you to trust us on: We retrieved Emilio ourselves—and we did so without anyone . . . noticing."

Dunhill frowned. "How could you do that?"

Zander again cleared his throat. "Sir, do you recall which agency Jayda worked for when we lived in Washington, DC?"

Judge Dunhill's eyes slid toward me. Fixed on me. "Homeland, was it?"

"NSA," I reminded him.

"Oh. Yes. NSA."

"I can't tell you the method employed when we removed Emilio, Judge. By presidential order, that information is deemed classified—a National Security matter."

Dunhill scoffed. "That's ridiculous! You don't expect me to believe that, do you?"

Zander placed his phone on the table. The nanomites started the device's playback.

"Judge Frederick Dunhill, this is President Robert Jackson speaking to you from the White House. You will ask no further questions of Zander and Jayda Cruz concerning the classified issues they have outlined. You have neither the clearance nor the need-to-know to receive this information.

"However, as a personal favor to me—but not to exceed the limits of your legal authority—I ask that you extend to Mr. and Mrs. Cruz the courtesy and assistance they ask of you. I thank you for your cooperation. Robert Jackson, out."

The message ended. Dunhill stared at his carpet for a long time. Finally, he mumbled, "I need that coffee. Anyone else?"

"I'll help you, sir," I said, getting up.

"I would appreciate it."

Ten very solemn and quiet minutes later, while we drank coffee and Judge Dunhill mulled over President Jackson's message, we got back to business.

"All right, Mr. Cruz. Ignoring how you retrieved Emilio from state custody *six separate times without being noticed*, please say on."

"Thank you, sir. We can promise you that when we are finished here, in similar manner as the previous six times, we *will* take back our children. In conjunction with that essential step, we ask two things of you."

Dunhill sighed. "I will, *er*, cooperate with your requests if I can, young man. Let me fetch pen and paper from my office so I get the details straight."

When he returned, Zander outlined our first "ask." Dunhill took quick and concise notes, grunting his approval. "I can do that. Might come under scrutiny, though, for cutting corners and circumventing process. Raise all sorts of legal and bureaucratic red flags."

"I assure you, sir, that we can handle the scrutiny."

Dunhill's eyes narrowed in suspicion, and he murmured, "Can you, now? I suppose I'm not allowed to ask *how*, though. Am I right?"

I answered him. "Yes, sir. That said, please be assured that we *can* handle it. As in *six separate times without being noticed.*"

A laugh burst from Dunhill's chest. "I like your style, Mrs. Cruz. All right, then. What's your second request?"

As he listened, we saw that Dunhill liked our second ask even better than our first.

"Tomorrow, Ms. Okafor will receive desperate calls from the caretakers where she placed Emilio and Bonnie Lu, and she will learn that they are, *uh*, no longer in the caretakers' custody.

"And let me guess—because no one will have noticed when they left?"

Zander grinned. "Good guess, sir. But, as you might imagine, we want this circus train to grind to a complete and permanent stop. To that end, we prefer that you take this action in broad daylight, with all the legal trappings, accompanied by a sizable media pool.

"You see, we want those who conspired to take our kids, who perverted our state's child welfare laws, and who used their authority as a weapon to harm and vilify us *via* our kids—we want them arrested and charged with every law they broke."

I cut in. I was hurting and still so very angry, but relief was close; it glimmered in my unshed tears. "Because, without a proper preliminary investigation with a required notice to us, without due process, without any *cause* at all, this social worker, Ms. Okafor, brought an armed tactical team to our home and took our baby by force."

Zander smiled through his pain. "We prefer that the arrest of these criminals be of epic proportions and serve as a deterrent to those who ordered their actions."

The judge thought for a few moments, then nodded his head. "Special Agent Gamble, I suggest that a kidnapping has occurred. Do you agree? If so, do these actions warrant the intervention of the FBI?"

Gamble slowly exhaled. "In my opinion, knowing what I do, yes, this meets the criteria of a kidnapping, Your Honor. Sadly, I'm not convinced the FBI bureaucracy will agree with my assumption. These days, our top leadership seems to have forgotten that they serve the constitution of this nation. That trickle-down effect is being felt everywhere in the agency. Also? We don't know who in the Albuquerque Field Office is aligned with Okafor's superiors."

Zander spoke up. "If it would help, and if Judge Dunhill is asking for an FBI presence at the arrests, Gamble, we can provide you with, *er*, top cover."

"At least in the short term," I interjected. "As long as Jackson is in the White House."

My codicil was based on our knowledge of the institutions the Cabal had already infiltrated and the conclusions the nanomites had presented to President Jackson months ago.

"Can you . . . will you succeed in ruining their plans, Nano? Will you be able to destroy their conspiracies and stop them?"

No, Mr. President. Our efforts will only slow them down.

The nanomites could run interference for us. They could run rings around and thwart despicable bureaucratic actors—again and again. They could delay the Cabal's response.

But they could not halt the wave of pervasive evil overtaking America, flooding the entire earth . . . not when all was said and done.

In the end . . . it would be the end.

⌘⌘⌘⌘

CHAPTER 16

BEFORE WE LEFT JUDGE DUNHILL'S house, the judge and Gamble hashed out their plans for the following day. When they were finished, we took Gamble and Abe home. Then we set out to get our children.

We chose to fetch Bonnie Lu first based on what her nanoarray told us: She was hungry and distraught. Apparently, Bonnie Lu didn't care for the bottle or formula her caretaker tried to feed her. The nanoarray reported that Bonnie was inconsolable.

I struggled with anger and grief every mile to our destination.

*Lord God! Please help me. I know that my human anger does not produce your righteousness . . . but **they have taken my baby!***

I clenched my teeth. *If they have hurt her, if they have harmed her in any way—*

"*Do not make an unholy vow, my daughter.*"

The words dropped like hot, glowing coals into my heart. And pulled me up short.

I hear you, Lord God . . . so would you please help me? I don't know how to get free of the anger in my heart. They stole my Bonnie Lu!

"*I understand, Jayda. They took my Son too. Give your anger to me. I will carry it for you.*"

Whoa.

Yes, Lord. Thank you. I'll try.

Rage churned in my gut—and with it the thoughts that kept fueling my anger. I knew I had to shut down those thoughts to put out the fire. I had to stomp on them.

I give you everything, Lord, myself included. I will not dwell on what these wicked people have done. I give them to you. I extend forgiveness— even though I want to hurt them, hurt them like they have hurt Bonnie and Emilio, like they have hurt Zander and me!

No. I can't think that or do that. Instead, I choose to cast those people and what they have done onto your broad and capable shoulders. Please. Please carry these burdens for me. I choose to keep my eyes and my meditations—my thoughts—on you. You will lead us to Bonnie, and she'll be home with us soon. Then all will be well. I trust you, Lord. I trust you.

About twenty minutes later, we arrived at a lovely home in Albuquerque's north valley. We drove by the house, then Zander parked a few blocks away. We went to retrieve our baby girl, invisible and on foot.

The curtains of an upstairs bedroom glowed with soft light. The nanomites let us into the house and deadened our footsteps as we crept up the stairs. They flew ahead of us to reconnoiter, then led us to the gently lit room we'd seen from the street.

We stopped in the doorway to observe. A frazzled woman in a rocking chair snuggled Bonnie and rocked her back and forth. The woman held a bottle, but Bonnie, her fists waving, her face red and contorted, tears streaming from her eyes, screamed her protests.

Jayda Cruz, four people other than Bonnie Lu Cruz occupy this house—the woman you see, a man in another bedroom, likely her husband, and two young children in a third bedroom.

"Thank you, Nano."

I wanted to grab Bonnie Lu, but the woman's distress stopped me. With genuine concern, she murmured over and over, "There, there, little one! Shush, honey. Please. *Please* take this bottle. Oh, baby Bonnie, if you take just a little sip, you will like it, and everything will be okay. Come on, sweetie. I don't want you to be hungry."

The woman cared.

She could have been heartless and left Bonnie Lu alone to scream in hunger, to cry herself to sleep. She could have been cold and unfeeling, but she wasn't. She was doing her best . . . and I was grateful.

I took a deep breath. *Thank you for this woman, Lord. She's not part of this wickedness.*

I dispatched nanomites to send the woman into slumber. Took my child and the bottle from her arms as they relaxed and let go. I had the nanomites uncover me so Bonnie could see me.

"Hey, little Bonnie Lu," I crooned.

Bonnie's tearstained face stared up at me. "Ma-ma-ma-ma-ma-ma!" she wailed.

"Yes, Darling. Daddy and I are here to take you home. Let's quiet you down, first, shall we?"

The nanomites sent calming endorphins through Bonnie's body. She shuddered and gulped air. We wanted her calm so that when we took her downstairs, a trail of screams would not follow us, announcing to the rest of the house that she was on the move.

I turned to leave the bedroom, then stopped. "Zander? Take Bonnie a moment?"

"Sure. Hey, pretty girl!"

Bonnie sobbed once and reached a chubby hand toward him. He lowered his head to hers and nuzzled her cheeks.

I dug around in my handbag and pulled out a scrap of paper and a pen. I jotted four words on the paper: *Thank you for caring.* Folded and placed the note in the woman's hand and closed her fingers about it.

"Nano. Please give her and her family a restful night's sleep."

We will, Jayda Cruz.

Zander handed Bonnie back to me, and we left the house. I climbed into the back seat with Bonnie. Within a few moments, she was gulping down the milk she was accustomed to.

"Nano, please keep me invisible while we drive."

Yes, Jayda Cruz.

"All set back there?" Zander asked.

"Yes. Let's go get our son."

⌘

THE NANOARRAY IN EMILIO TOLD US he'd been placed in a Juvenile Justice Services facility—the one that "happened" to be a locked-down detention center. I was certain Okafor put him there thinking it would be impossible for anyone to spring Emilio from behind their walls.

Since Okafor had no idea how her charge had slipped out from under her custody six times, maybe she felt relieved to have delivered Emilio to the detention center. A success after six fails! Still, I imagine she was pretty freaked out about Emilio's earlier disappearances.

That suited me just fine. Tomorrow she'd be freaked out all over again.

We studied the detention center from outside an imposing fence. According to the nanomites, the place was a mini prison: a fenced and locked yard and parking lot, heavy steel doors on the building, a manned control center, and locked-down dormitories.

"You can handle this without me, right?" I asked Zander.

"No sweat. You stay with our Bonnie."

Zander parked across the street and down a ways. I watched him walk away.

⌘

ZANDER STOOD OUTSIDE THE RANGE of the detention center's cameras. Getting through locked doors unseen wasn't a problem, but Zander needed to reach Emilio without tripping the alarm system.

"You know what to do, Nano. Get me inside without being detected."

A full minute later the nanomites replied, *Zander Cruz, we have unlocked the personnel entrance on the northwest corner of the fence, and unlocked an emergency exit on the north side of the facility. All alarms are silenced.*

"Thanks, Nano."

Zander entered the lot, crossed to a door down the building's side, and allowed the nanomites to guide him to the center's control room. When he arrived, the two guards—a man and a woman—were slumped in their seats, unconscious.

Emilio is down that hallway, Zander Cruz. Second door on the left. He is in a dormitory with five other boys.

"Is he awake, Nano?"

Zander's antenna went up when the nanomites hesitated. "Nano? What's up? How is he?"

Zander Cruz, Emilio is safe, and he is awake; however, he is very frightened.

"Frightened? What's happened?"

We have reviewed security camera footage from this place, Zander Cruz. Terrible things happen here, particularly at night. We were, however, able to direct Emilio's nanoarray to discourage his attackers.

Chilled with apprehension, Zander stopped short of the dormitory door. "Attackers? Is Emilio okay?"

As we said, he is frightened, Zander Cruz. His nanoarray discouraged his attackers, yet the timing of your arrival is propitious. The array has exhausted itself and is now in a weakened state. The array will not be able to fend off another assault.

"Fend off an assault? How?"

Electrical discharge, Zander Cruz. What you refer to as 'zapping them.' But we must not dither here, Zander Cruz. The nanoarray is now too weak to protect Emilio.

Zander sprinted to the dorm and put his hand on the door. "Send everyone inside to sleep, Nano. Everyone but Emilio."

The door opened, the lights came on, and Zander slipped inside. "Emilio? Where are you, buddy?"

"Dad?" That single word caught on a sob.

Emilio was in a bottom bunk across the room. Zander stepped over the unconscious bodies of two young men. Emilio scrambled from his bed and grabbed on to Zander.

"I knew you'd come . . . but you took such a long time! Those boys . . . they-they . . ."

"I know, Son. I know. Come on. Let's get you out of here."

"The people here took my clothes!"

"No worries. You own plenty. Let's just leave them and go home, okay? You and I have some pitch and catch to 'catch' up on."

Emilio smiled, but only a little. He was scared and hurting.

On the way out, Zander whispered, "Nano, can you erase Emilio's painful memories?"

Only the most recent ones, Zander Cruz. Not from earlier this evening.

"Do what you can, Nano."

We will, Zander Cruz.

⌘

ZANDER AND I KEPT MOSTLY TO ourselves the following morning. Kept Bonnie Lu and Emilio inside with us. Kept our little foursome close. Lots of hugs, lots of loving touch and reassurance.

Bonnie Lu had a meltdown if I stepped out of her sight, so I kept her on my hip or in my arms. Emilio was also clingy. We sat on the sofa side by side, trading Bonnie Lu between us. Peace rolling slowly back into our hearts.

About midmorning, Zander encouraged Emilio to come outside and play catch with him. He was ready for some distance by then, although he left Bonnie with a sweet peck on her forehead and a long hug for me.

Yes, for our children's sake, Zander and I would stay close to home today. It wasn't necessary for us to accompany Abe, Gamble, Judge Dunhill, and the officers (whom the judge had handpicked) when they arrested Okafor.

With Bonnie close by me playing with one of her toys, I folded laundry and wondered how Abe and Gamble were faring.

Around eleven o'clock, the nanomites' whispers called to me.

Jayda Cruz, Abe's nanoarray reports they are about to confront Ms. Okafor.

"Wait. Abe has an array? I thought we decided not to send one to him."

For this occasion, and with the permission you gave us yesterday, we felt it imperative to observe. Last night we sent an array to him; we will recall the array when we feel it is no longer needed.

"Uh, okay. I suppose I agree."

Would you care to watch the events unfold from the array's perspective?

Oh, my perverse nature!

"Very much so, Nano. Thank you."

⌘

FROM THE NANOARRAY'S "PERSPECTIVE," I felt like I was standing in Abe's head, looking out of his eyes or watching a GoPro video taken from a camera mounted on Abe's head . . . only inches lower?

Very disconcerting!

Abe opened Gamble's passenger-side door and levered himself up and out of the car, sending my stomach on a rollercoaster ride.

Fortunately, I felt much better once Abe steadied himself and followed Gamble, Judge Dunhill, and the officers into the building that housed the Albuquerque Protective Services Division of New Mexico's Child Welfare Services.

Concurrently, his nanoarray sent out continual readings of Abe's vital signs: blood pressure, blood oxygenation, heart rate, and EKG tracings, and I studied them.

"Huh. Abe's in pretty good shape for his age."

We have detected a small murmur in Abe Pickering's heart, a slight deviation, Jayda Cruz. Nothing of immediate concern, but we will monitor it if you like.

"That would be up to Abe, Nano. I can ask him."

The officers took point, with the rest of the entourage trailing behind. At the check-in counter, one of the two officers said, "We are executing an arrest warrant for Lani Okafor. Please direct us to her."

Okafor's takedown was going to happen in public, in her workplace, in front of her peers. I was not unhappy with the circumstances.

The young man at the counter seemed to lose his breath for a moment. A woman in a nearby cubicle, stood and came forward. Took in the officers' serious demeanor.

"I'm the office manager. May I help you?"

"Please direct us to Lani Okafor."

"Er, can you tell me why?"

"We have a warrant for her arrest. Please do not obstruct us in the performance of our duty."

We had gained the attention of everyone within earshot, and the woman, sliding her eyes around the room, realized it.

She replied softly, "Please follow me."

When we arrived at Okafor's office, she was speaking into her phone. She came to a stuttering stop. Swallowed hard.

Without hanging up, she said, "What . . . is this?"

"Lani Okafor?" the officer asked.

"Yes, I am Lani Okafor."

"Ma'am, you are under arrest for falsifying court orders, for misusing the removal powers of the Bernalillo County Sheriff's Department, and for kidnapping. Please stand and turn around."

She dropped the receiver on her desk. "What? No! You cannot do this! This is a mistake—allow me to make a call; I can . . . I can straighten this out."

Then she saw Judge Dunhill in the doorway . . . and Abe standing behind him. I watched guilt and disbelief compete for dominance on her face.

From where Abe stood, I couldn't see Judge Dunhill's expression, but I could certainly hear the steel in his voice.

"You falsified court orders—quite a number of them, Ms. Okafor. You even used two fake orders from *my court* and forged *my signature* on those orders."

"But I . . . I was acting on orders! I—"

Something far worse than guilt twisted Okafor's expression.

Terror.

She misspoke, I realized. *She isn't supposed to let on that she was under orders to take our kids. She's under the Cabal's thumb . . . and they will not take this misstep kindly.*

I hadn't considered what would befall Okafor after she was arrested and was appalled at my conclusion: *We have signed this woman's death warrant.*

Okafor's hopeless eyes and body language confirmed what I surmised. She clamped her mouth shut and did not resist when the officers snapped the cuffs on her.

⌘⌘⌘⌘

CHAPTER 17

Sunday morning again. We were gathered in our living room, streaming the service on our television. Abe, Emilio, and I (with Bonnie Lu snuggled in my arms) occupied our usual places on the couch; Izzie and Josh sat on the floor.

We sang and worshipped with the prerecorded music. Then the worship team prayed over the many needs that had come into the church's email account or been mentioned on DCC's social media channels throughout the week.

When Zander assigned the prayer requests to Mrs. Coyne, he had given her a much-needed mission adjustment. With the offices closed, a large part of her job now consisted of gathering the requests into a coherent list on a weekly basis. She posted that list to a dedicated Facebook group for DCC's prayer warriors to pray and fast over. Then she passed the list to the worship team for prayer during the service.

The announcements over, it was time for Zander's sermon. The screen faded, then opened in Zander's office. I shivered, because I knew what he would be teaching on this morning. He lifted his sweet gray eyes from his Bible to the camera and smiled.

"Good morning, DCC family. And I welcome all our visitors to DCC's Sunday service. Before we get into the word together, just a reminder that Downtown Community Church is a Bible-*preaching*, Bible-*teaching*, Bible-*believing*, and Bible-*acting* church. We receive, personally and individually, what the Bible says. Why personally and individually? Because, as I've previously taught in passing, Hebrews 4:12 spells out the powerful and supernatural way God's word functions inside of each of us.

> *"For the word of God is alive and active.*
> *Sharper than any double-edged sword,*
> *it penetrates even to dividing soul and spirit,*
> *joints and marrow;*
> *it judges the thoughts and attitudes of the heart.*

My heart did a little flutter thing and I looked inside. *We receive God's word personally and individually. Yes! Lord, when your word speaks, I know it is for me. I receive it as such, and it ministers to me personally to give me life and hope.*

Zander continued. "As we pull this verse apart, please note how it says that God's word is *alive* and it is *active*. God's word is not mere print on paper or screen; it is not just history or the tales of men from long ago. His word is not dead, dated, irrelevant, or archaic.

"No, God's word has living, creative power, because it is breathed upon by the Holy Spirit. And as we hear or read the word, God causes it to do *an explicit work* in each of us."

*Yes, **that!*** I rejoiced in my heart.

"You might even say that God's word comes with a personal agenda. His word comes to change each of us, *to conform us* to the image of Christ. We don't all come to him with the same issues, do we? No, we all have varying situations and diverse problems, so his word comes to us to do the specific work in us that we need.

"How does God's word accomplish his purposes? Again, Hebrews 4:12 tells us that his word is *sharp*—sharper than a two-edged sword—and it *cuts deep*. Cuts where? Right down to the very core of our being.

"God's word *penetrates* to places within us we cannot see but that are as real as the air we breathe. His word *divides* between our soul and spirit— that means it separates what is soulish or fleshly from what is spiritual and godly. It disconnects and divorces what *is not* of God from what *is*. When God's word divides, it even judges our thoughts and the intentions of our hearts . . . and then we become aware of what is lurking in the dark corners of our being, where our hearts are not in sync with God's heart, and where our thoughts are not in sync with his thoughts."

The view switched to the second camera, and Zander turned slightly to face it.

"This short review of how God's word functions is a preface to my central message today. This message will be short—intentionally so. You see, I had planned all week to teach a different message than the one I am about to deliver.

"However, yesterday, I felt the Holy Spirit urging me to speak on a topic relevant to where we stand today in this nation and in this corrupt, fallen world. It is a topic Bible-believing Christians everywhere must grasp, understand, and resist.

"I speak of the nature and characteristics of deception. My intention today is to shine the light of God's word on our minds and heart and make us aware of places where *we are deceived*."

"Oh, wow," Josh breathed, while he rummaged in his backpack for his notebook.

Zander leaned in the slightest bit, his eyes never leaving the camera. It made me feel like he was looking at me and only me.

"What is the most cunning, most devious characteristic of deception? It is this: *When you are deceived, you don't know you are deceived*. That's right. When you don't realize that you are deceived, you are the very definition of deception.

"Let's look at the verb 'deceive.' One definition reads 'to cause to accept as true or valid what is false or invalid.' Why did I say that when you are deceived, you don't know you are deceived? Because you have accepted as true what is false or invalid.

"Let's dive deeper into our study and examine 'deceive,' the verb form of deception. 'Deceive' is a transitive verb, meaning deception requires both a 'doer' and a 'receiver,' one who is deceiving and one who is being deceived. Put plainly, if you are deceived, someone has deceived you . . . and much of the time the deceiving is intentional, even malicious.

"Most of us, when we discover that we've been deceived, feel violated, cheated, and angry—and so we should, *initially*. The anger we feel is usually directed at two parties—toward the person or persons who deceived us, but also inward, toward ourselves for being gullible. Naive. Stupid."

Izzie, sitting on the carpet to the left of my feet, shuddered. Was she recalling her not-so-recent brush with deception?

Lord, thank you for restoring her!

Zander glanced at the camera before moving on. "I now want to read aloud the text of 2 Thessalonians 2:9-10. Here we go.

> *"The coming of the lawless one*
> *will be in accordance with how Satan works.*
> *He will use all sorts of displays of power*
> *through signs and wonders that serve the lie,*
> *and all the ways that wickedness*
> *deceives those who are perishing.*
> *They perish because*
> *they refused to love the truth and so be saved.*

"Let's pull this passage apart, shall we? It is generally accepted that *the coming of the lawless one* refers to the emergence of the Antichrist on the earth's political scene. In the same chapter, verse 3, he is called *the man* of lawlessness or *the man* of sin. How does this man of lawlessness emerge onto the world's platform? What tactics does he use?

> *"The coming of the lawless one*
> *will be **in accordance** with how Satan works.*

"Verse 9 tells us the Antichrist's coming *will be in accordance with how Satan works*. In the New American Standard Bible it reads, *the one whose coming is in accord with the activity of Satan*. When two people are in accord, they are in agreement or unity. Two rowers in the same boat will row in sync. Two singers will harmonize with or complement the other.

Two dancers will move as one. Notice that the NASB reads *in accord with the activity of Satan.*

"When we put those thoughts together, we realize that the Antichrist's actions will closely mirror, resemble, or mimic Satan's actions. The Antichrist's actions will agree with Satan's purposes. The two will harmonize, complement, row, and move as one. It stands to reason, that if we know Satan's *modus operandi,* we should see the same MO in the Antichrist when he appears. Are you following me so far?"

In our living room, every one of us, including Emilio, answered "yes" aloud. Emilio, I noticed, was paying close attention to Zander's message.

"It is vital, therefore, that we familiarize ourselves with Satan's MO, with his ploys and his plots, so that we recognize them when we see them. I think Jesus sums Satan up nicely in John chapter 8. Let's read verse 44 together.

> *"You belong to your father, the devil,*
> *and you want to carry out your father's desires.*
> ***He was a murderer from the beginning,***
> ***not holding to the truth, for there is no truth in him.***
> *When he lies, he speaks his native language,*
> ***for he is a liar and the father of lies.***

"Jesus calls the devil a murderer. Note that Jesus doesn't accuse Satan of having committed the occasional murder. No, Jesus says Satan was a murderer from the beginning! And Jesus, being the Word of God, would personally know this about Satan. After all, according to John 1:1-3 and John 17:5, Jesus was there with the Father *in the beginning* and witnessed Satan in action.

"Jesus also identifies Satan as a liar. I appreciate how he describes this characteristic of Satan. Jesus says Satan does not *hold to the truth.* Why is this important? First, because most lies contain an element of truth—not the whole truth but often a twisted or perverted version of the truth. *Holding to the truth* means adhering to it completely and fully—that is, rendering authentic, unmodified truth.

"Again, why is it important when Jesus says Satan does not *hold to the truth*? Because, secondly, those who make a habit of mixing truth with falsehoods soon find it difficult to speak unadulterated truth. What did Jesus say, concerning Satan and truth? He said, *for there is no truth in him.* Satan is unable to speak the truth, so don't trust anything he says!

"Wow," Josh muttered again. "Just *wow.*"

"Thirdly, Jesus said of Satan, *When he lies, he speaks his native language!*" Lying isn't a trait Satan accidentally fell into. He didn't get up one morning and decide, 'Hey, today, I'm going to learn how to lie. Then, I'm going to practice it. See if I can get it down pat.'

"See, when we acquire language as a child, we don't remember making those connections, learning new words and how to make the right sounds. Apparently, Satan acquired lying from the get-go. In fact, lying originated with Satan—also known as Lucifer. Jesus, who personally witnessed Lucifer's rebellion and his subsequent banishment from heaven, calls Satan *the father of lies.*

"Let's tie these facts together, shall we? We know that murder and lying are part and parcel of Satan's nature and character. But are murder and lying Satan's 'only' sins? No, 1 John 3:8 also tells us that Satan is a sinner and has been sinning—*again*—right from the beginning!

> *"The one who does what is sinful is of the devil,*
> *because the devil has been sinning from the beginning.*
> *The reason the Son of God appeared*
> *was to destroy the devil's work.*

"You can't get much plainer than that, can you? If Satan is a continual murderer, liar, and sinner, please consider that his plans for you are not for your good! John 10:10 spells out Satan's goals when it comes to us.

> *The thief comes only to steal and kill and destroy;*
> *I have come that they may have life,*
> *and have it to the full.*

"That's right, Satan's only aim is to steal whatever God has given you, kill you, both now and for all eternity, and destroy the legacy you might bequeath the world and the eternal fruit God intended you to bear for him.

"Now, let's go back to 2 Thessalonians 2 and look more closely at verse 10. Here we see something really interesting. Verse 9 talks about *how Satan works.* Verse 10 adds *and all the ways that wickedness deceives.*"

> *"He [the man of lawlessness]*
> *will use all sorts of displays of power*
> *through signs and wonders that serve the lie,*
> **and all the ways that wickedness**
> **deceives those who are perishing.**

Zander's eye bored into mine. "Do you get it? *Wickedness deceives.* Satan serves up wickedness on an elegant silver platter, wrapped in the alluring promises of power, pleasure, and fulfillment, garnished with expectations and longing—but sin is a great, big, shiny *trap.* Wickedness may offer us exactly what we are secretly yearning for—yet it is a lie and a snare.

"Wickedness, when it tempts us, dangles a colorful and delightful lure in front of our faces. Well, guess what that lure is hiding? A deadly hook. And when we are hooked, we become just one more wriggling fish on Satan's stringer, slated for death.

Beside me, Emilio shuddered.

"So the question becomes, how do we know the difference between truth and deception? Yes, that is the crux of the matter—the place at which we survive or get sucked into deception. So, how do we learn truth? Recognize truth? Identify truth? Discern truth?"

Zander sat back, a grin on his face. "You know, it used to be that people knew how to use their own two eyes. If someone showed you three apples, you would say, 'I see three apples,' and they would agree with you. Now objective reality—what is actual, what is independent of the mind—is being hijacked by subjective reality—which is an oxymoron, isn't it? If reality is subjective, then it can't be real.

"For example, if I feel—truly, deeply feel—that I am a pony trapped in a man's body, then subjective reality tells me I should live as if I *am* a pony. That's subjective reality. Subjective reality furthermore insists that *you* must treat me as a pony, must refer to me as a pony, and address me as a pony. Just ignore what your own two eyes tell you, because if I *feel* like I'm a pony, then *I. Am. A. Pony.*

"This example shows us that subjective reality is *delusion*. The man locked up in a mental hospital because he believes he is Napoleon Bonaparte and is also deemed dangerous? That man is trapped in a delusion. The woman who insists that she will only feel 'right' and 'whole' when she cuts off both of her perfectly good legs? That woman is trapped in delusion.

"Society, too, is trapped in delusion when it demands that the woman's doctor must amputate her legs, taxpayers must pay for the surgery, and the public must approve of the outcome. Are we there yet?"

"Pretty much," Izzie mumbled.

"Society insists that subjective reality differs from person to person. If it is real *for him,* then we must accept 'his' reality.

Zander chuckled, "Well, if the nonexistent bridge across the canyon just ahead is *real for you,* then falling to your death won't hurt, right? Just don't expect me to follow you across that bridge."

Those of us watching laughed with Zander, but not Emilio. He was hanging on Zander's every word. Scarcely breathing.

"I have been speaking of delusion, and the examples I've given made us laugh a little. Why? Because of their absurdity. Well, absurd or not, delusion is real. 2 Thessalonians 2:11 reads this way.

> **"*For this reason*
> *God sends them a powerful delusion*
> *so that they will believe the lie*
> *and so that all will be condemned*
> *who have not believed the truth*
> *but have delighted in wickedness.*

"***For this reason****, God sends them a powerful delusion*. For what reason? We find the reason in the preceding verses of 2 Thessalonians, chapter 2.

> *"He [the man of lawlessness]*
> *will use all sorts of displays of power*
> *through signs and wonders that serve the lie,*
> **and all the ways that wickedness**
> **deceives those who are perishing.**

"*They refused to love the truth and so be saved*. I am very sad to say, most who are deceived do not wish to be undeceived. Therefore, God will give them over to delusion, and delusion is the worst of all deceptions . . . because it is *self*-deception.

"Those who are deceived? Those who believe the lies of the devil? Those who refuse to love the truth and so be saved? They hate the truth and so deceive themselves, and this is what we are seeing play out across the earth today.

"More and more, we are being forced to acknowledge things that are not objectively real. So how do we keep ourselves from a) being deceived, and b) being caught up in personal or mass delusion?

"As I taught our young adult group, one of the reasons God gave us his word and his law was to teach us right from wrong. We know that murder is wrong *because God says it is wrong*. We know that idolatry is wrong *because God says it is wrong*. We know that adultery is wrong *because God says it is wrong*. We know that coveting what belongs to others is wrong *because God says it is wrong*.

"See, if you don't know the Lord and his word, then you don't know that wickedness deceives. If you don't know the Lord and his word, you don't know that wickedness ensnares and puts you on the devil's stringer with the rest of the poor souls who are dying. And if you don't know the Lord and his word, you are at risk of being caught in a delusion. You are at risk for being sucked in by what is *false, crazy*, and *deadly*."

"So, what is the antidote for deception and delusion? The only antidote is truth. Jesus did not misspeak when he said,

*"I am the way and **the truth** and the life.*
No one comes to the Father
except through me.

"Walking with God begins by accepting truth, the first tenet of truth being that Jesus *is* the truth. What he said can be taken to the bank. The second tenet of truth we need to accept is we need help—help getting out of the mess we are in. We need to get off of the devil's stringer—and only Jesus can do that for us."

"Amen!" Josh half-shouted.

"Listen, learning to love truth is vital because love of the truth is our immunization against deception. Again, those most susceptible to deception and delusion, are those who *do not love the truth*. They will fight the truth for all they are worth.

The Holy Spirit was working, and I hung on the power of Zander's words.

Zander took a deep, sorrowful breath. "Unless they turn from their wickedness, from deception, from delusion, they will perish. Unless *you* turn from your wickedness, from deception, from delusion, *you* will perish.

"Let me be very clear: You cannot free yourself. Only Jesus can free you. Unless you turn to Jesus, you will continue your slide toward delusion."

I glanced at Emilio. His face was a mask of horrified comprehension. For the first time since I had known and loved this boy, he saw himself in Zander's words.

"And I will say a last word about wickedness in general: *Evil* is always at work. The Bible tells us that we are children of the day, but Satan's people operate at night, in the darkness, often in disguise.

"God's people might think things are going along well, but in the shadows, wickedness is churning away. We, the church, must guard against complacency—because evil seeks a vacuum, an unoccupied place it can occupy This is why God's word urges us to watch and pray. *Watch.* And *pray.* Do not become complacent, apathetic, or unengaged. Seek to live a proactive spiritual life.

"If you haven't trusted Jesus to save you from sin, to save you from deception and delusion, you have an opportunity to change that today. Please listen carefully. If you want Jesus to save you, bow your head to him right now. Acknowledge to Jesus—that means *tell him*—that you believe he is God's Son, sent to save you. Admit to him that you are a sinner, that you need help. Tell him you surrender your life to him.

"In this moment, I encourage you to pray along with me, to repeat what I pray, and mean it in your heart. All right? Let's pray.

"Lord Jesus, I need you. I believe that you are the Savior God himself sent to save me from my sins. Please forgive me."

God was moving!

Beside me, Emilio was a wet, blubbering mess. He was bent over, sobbing into his hands; his entire body was shuddering with emotion.

I got up; Josh and Izzie knelt beside Emilio. They prayed over him. Wept with him. Helped him to articulate his feelings and surrender more deeply to what God was working in him. Led him in confessing his sins as the Holy Spirit brought them to his mind.

I prayed from the other side of the living room. Abe and I cried on each other's shoulders because we were overwhelmed with God's goodness. I rejoiced because the Lord was answering my prayers for my son—even using Emilio's recent traumatic experiences to soften and prepare his heart to receive Jesus.

And I rehearsed Zander's words from an eon ago to myself.

"Repentance isn't the ugly, hard, mean thing the world has said it is. Repentance is a gift from God, the first step in his setting us free. Repentance pulls down the strongholds in our lives. When repentance has its full sway, Jesus is able to free us from fear and condemnation."

When Zander pulled into the driveway, Emilio ran to meet him.

"Dad! Dad! Guess what happened! *God is real!*"

Emilio bounded into Zander's arms, anxious to tell him what Jesus had done.

That day as we ate our Sunday lunch together, we celebrated Emilio's salvation. I'd never seen him as happy, as open and radiant as he was today.

Lord, the new birth is the miracle we have been asking for our son to receive. Thank you for answering our prayers!

⌘⌘⌘⌘

Part 2:
Reaping

All who were willing, men and women alike,

came and brought gold jewelry of all kinds:

brooches, earrings, rings and ornaments.

They all presented their gold

as a wave offering to the Lord.

Exodus 35:22

CHAPTER 18

AUGUST

CONSIDERING ALL THINGS—including the mistakes we made due to ignorance or inexperience—our gardens were producing well. While Bonnie Lu lay on a soft blanket in her playpen, happily kicking and gurgling in the shade of our apple tree and overseen by Belicia and the nanomites, co-op members picked tomatoes (dozens every day), summer squash (gazillions), sweet peppers, spicy chiles, and green beans. Then we dug turnips, scads of carrots, and a few early potatoes.

From each picking, we meted out a portion to supplement the co-op's common midday meal prepared by Belicia and Abe. Izzie took charge of the abundance of tomatoes and filled half of Abe's jars with thick, cooked-down tomato sauce. We saved the other jars for apple harvest. Aside from what we canned and the little we allowed ourselves to eat, every scrap of produce went directly to the drying racks.

Gamble and Janice constructed our thirty-inch by thirty-inch drying racks from precious, hard-to-find lumber, rolls of window screen, and a bolt of muslin. Each rack consisted of four wood rails screwed together (and braced in the corners) and a piece of window screen stretched tight across the frame, stapled all around its rails.

Here Viola's unrecognized talents came into play. While Gamble and Janice framed up the racks, Viola cut and hemmed sheets of breathable muslin to exactly fit each rack's window screen. Then she cut and hemmed larger sheets of muslin to drape over each rack so that the food being dehydrated lay between two sheets of muslin to keep birds and insects off the food.

Gamble and Janice also made the racks to stack four high, but for each bottom rack, Gamble and Janice constructed "feet" from bits of 2x4s stacked to a height of six inches. They screwed or nailed the feet to the racks' underside corners. The six inches of elevation allowed air to circulate under the stacked racks and speeded the dehydration process.

In the heat of summer, the homes with flat roofs were the best places to set up the racks. Up and down the ladders we went, hauling up baskets of sliced tomatoes, zucchini, sweet peppers, carrots, turnips, and potatoes. Once we'd laid out sliced vegetables on a rack's muslin-draped window screen, we added its covering sheet of muslin.

We placed the next rack atop the first and repeated the process until we'd stacked the racks four high. We clamped the top rack's muslin sheet to the frame so the wind wouldn't blow the lightweight fabric cover away.

Twice daily we turned every drying slice. One to three days in the extreme heat of our sun-beaten roofs cured the slices. The exact amount of time depended on the moisture content of the different veggies.

But . . . at the same time, mid-July through mid-September was monsoon season. Good monsoon flow from the Baja or the Gulf of Mexico carried heavy, late afternoon or evening downpours to us several times a week. We kept watch on the horizon and what spotty weather reports were available, and kept an eagle eye out for thunderheads moving our way. When rain was imminent, we covered our racks with waterproof tarps. If the lowest racks suffered some splash back, a quick rinse followed by an extra day or two of drying usually set them right again.

When we had used a rack once to dry produce, we removed its muslin sheets and washed them in hot water with a hint of bleach. Using only clean muslin kept our primitive dehydration process more or less sanitary. Dried vegetables went into fabric bags with drawstrings that Viola turned out by the dozen.

"Better to use bags that breathe rather than plastic ones that don't," Abe warned us, "in case we didn't get all the moisture out."

Apparently fabric bags had their downside too. Abe cautioned us to hang the bags from the ceiling rather than leave them out on a countertop or in a cupboard or drawer.

"Nothing worse'n moldy food 'cept finding that rodents or ants have chewed their way into stores you were countin' on."

As a result of our dehydration process, our garages, kitchens, and dining rooms became the oddest of "hanging gardens."

⌘

WHEN OUR PRECIOUS CORN HARVEST came in, we preserved it differently than the sliced veggies. Zander, Janice, Emilio, and I shucked the corn and removed the silk, but we left the cob's leaves attached to the ears. Belicia and Viola pulled each cob's leaves together and tied a tight loop of string around them. Bill and Abe hung the dangling cobs in rows under the eaves of Abe's porch.

A week of "hang time" (with Abe and Emilio shooing away hungry birds) dried the kernels on the cob. When the kernels were thoroughly dried, we "shelled" the dry kernels from their cobs and ground half the kernels into corn meal. The rest we bagged. We would add them by the handfuls to soups and stews throughout the winter.

We treated our chiles in similar fashion. Viola taught us how to stitch "circles" of long peppers together by their stems, then how to layer one circle atop another using a thicker, stronger string called a "skeleton" at each circle's center.

A skeleton held eight or ten layered chile circles, and the finished product was called a ristra. Viola and Bill hung the ristras on their front porch to dry. We divided the ristras between our homes and stored them, still hanging, in our kitchens. Whenever we needed peppers, we'd cut a few off a ristra, chop or grind them, and add them to our foods.

Around Labor Day, our apples ripened, and what a blessed harvest that was! Because Gamble had found spray for the co-op's three trees, we had hundreds of apples to put up.

We lost quite a few apples to monsoon winds, but we didn't throw any of them out. No, we picked them up as soon as they hit the ground. We gave the apples bruised the worst (and that needed to be eaten sooner rather than later) to co-op members to eat as they wished.

Emilio and I grinned at each other as we chowed down on our first windfall. No apple had ever tasted as good to me as that initial bite did!

Next we sorted the picked apples. Apples with defects went into the box with the rest of the fallen apples. Then we washed, peeled, removed bruises, bird pecks, and other defects and cut them up into two pots on the stove. All day the apples stewed and cooked down until we poured sweet applesauce into about ten jars and sealed them.

As for the apple peels, Abe made sure we saved every bit of peel without a bird peck or worm hole. Belicia made two apple pies from the peels for our midday community meal.

After we'd tasted apple-peel pie, *no one* complained of peeling and slicing apples for the drying racks! We had apple-peel pie twice more that week—and we dehydrated close to two hundred apples, about eighteen quart-sized bags of dehydrated apple slices.

My simple descriptions shouldn't minimize reality: The process of preserving food for the winter was hard, hot, tedious, and unrelenting work.

⌘

WE CAME TOGETHER BEFORE THE sun rose, our usual time, to receive our work assignments. Zander was our "crew boss" this morning.

"We're grateful to God for sending a pretty robust monsoon season this year, but we've had two dry days in a row now," Zander said. "I think we should harvest the pinto beans today—pull them up and get them under a roof before we have another rain. And with other parts of our gardens coming on quickly, we've got more dehydrating on the docket."

I was proud when all of us nodded our agreement—proud that not one person complained. Instead, we shouldered the work with a will. Forming our co-op had altered us so drastically that I could hardly recall what it was like when we lived apart, so separate from our neighbors and friends.

The co-op had been Zander's brainchild, and it was working. It had brought us together for a common purpose. Everything we grew spoke to the coming winter and our ability to survive it. We shared the work, and we shared the responsibility.

"Any comments or questions? No? Great. Let's get to it. Ross, Bill, Josh, Emilio? You're with me. Ladies, you're with Jay."

"And I have Bonnie Lu duty?" Abe asked. His words held so much glee that we all chuckled a little.

Belicia huffed as Abe laid claim to Bonnie Lu. They alternated mornings watching over her, but their fierce competition amused me.

Well, Belicia had "her" chickens to care for. They were fully grown now, and each morning she set most of them loose in our fenced garden to find their breakfast and save our crops from chewing, chomping insects. We had, by way of Gamble's unceasing scavenging, added a layer of chicken wire inside the fence line to keep the chickens contained.

Belicia then took the chickens she'd kept back and tied a string to each hen's foot. She staked them out singly in other co-op garden patches where the chickens would eat their fill of garden pests.

Back to Abe. Bonnie was six months old now, and boy, what a little mover she was! She could crawl or scoot everywhere and had started pulling herself up in her crib and on the dining room chairs, although walking was still a few months away.

Bonnie was a cheerful baby more often than not, and Abe had found new purpose and energy as he followed her around the small patch of grass under and around our apple tree.

A fun point of interest that summer: Bonnie was learning to babble. She said *ma-ma-ma-ma-ma, da-da-da-da-da,* and *me-me-me-me-me.* We loved her early vocalizations and took them to be the precursors to Mama, Daddy, and Emilio. Emilio was especially proud when she called for him—he *was* her willing slave, after all.

So what did *nah-nah, nah-nah, nah-nah* signify? And why did Abe never have to head off Bonnie Lu to keep her from crawling off the grass into the dirt? What was it Bonnie, laughing and gurgling, followed around the grassy plot, never straying from the grass?

I had my suspicions—okay, they were near certainties. I mean, I kind of hoped Bonnie Lu's first real word would be Mama, and I wouldn't mind if she said Daddy or even Emilio first—although Emilio was quite a mouthful.

But I suppose I wouldn't be too surprised if her first word was Nano.

⌘

JOSH WAS ON GUARD DUTY AT THE barrier when the mail arrived. Usually the mail carrier just stuffed mail into the boxes, tipped her head at the guard, and drove off. Today, she hailed Josh. In her hand was a stiff manila envelope.

"I need a signature for this one."

"Sure. Can do."

Josh signed the form, the mail carrier drove off, and Josh studied the envelope. He jogged across the cul-de-sac and up to our garden's fence line. Zander was digging potatoes.

"Hey, Zander? I just signed for this official-looking envelope. Thought you would want to see it right away."

Zander planted his shovel beside a potato hill and stripped off his gloves. "Thanks, Josh. I'll come get it."

When he read the return address, a grin split his face.

⌘

I WAS INSIDE, MAKING DINNER FOR US, Abe, and Emilio when Zander held a thick manila envelope under my nose. "Check out the return address, Babe."

I blinked. It was from the Bernalillo County Courthouse.

"Oh! Oh, Zander! We need . . . we need Emilio and Abe! Emilio should be with us when we open this."

"Um, hopefully, yes. But, first we might want to make sure . . ."

"Right. Nano? Can you tell us if this envelope contains good news?"

Jayda Cruz, Zander Cruz, we have looked and can say it holds good news indeed.

We scooped up Bonnie Lu, ran out the front door, and tore up the steps to Abe's porch. He and Emilio were tying vines of beans to the underside of Abe's porch roof where they would finish drying.

"Where's the fire, you two? And how can I get this one to stop running everywhere if you show him it's all right?" Abe complained.

"Well, some occasions are special enough to rate a good run, wouldn't you agree?" Zander asked. He flashed the envelope under Abe's nose while I stood between them and Emilio.

Emilio looked from me to Zander, puzzled.

Abe sputtered, "Oh, my. Oh, yes. I—uh, inside?"

"I think so," Zander said.

I smiled at Emilio. "Come with us. We have a surprise. A present."

Emilio again looked from me to Zander and back. "For me?"

"Weeell," I drawled, "perhaps it's a present for all four of us."

Now he was intrigued. "Can I see it?"

"Yup. Let's go inside and open it."

We sat down together at Abe's table. Zander handed Emilio the envelope.

He was initially disappointed. "This?"

"Don't judge a present by its giftwrap," Abe said.

"Okay. Guess I'll open it." Emilio managed to get the flap open without shredding what was inside. He withdrew a stack of documents. On top was a birth certificate. Beneath was a court-certified adoption record attached to a short stack of other documents.

Emilio studied the birth certificate. He kept blinking and blinking. Rereading it.

Finally, he croaked, "Is this me?"

"Yes," Zander said. "That is your new birth certificate."

I nodded. "What's under the birth certificate, Emilio?"

He read the top two lines aloud—all that extra reading we insisted upon coming into play. "State of New Mexico Vital Records and Health Sta-sta-TIS-tics Report of Adoption."

His head whipped up. "I'm adopted?"

I couldn't talk. Zander whispered, "That's why you have a new birth certificate, Emilio."

"But . . . but it says Emilio Vincente Pickering Cruz."

"Your new name . . . son," Zander managed. "You're my son now. You get my name."

Emilio was still blinking. Me, I'd gone straight to drippy tears.

"I get your name *and* Abe's name?"

"Pickering is one of your middle names now. That way, Abe will always be part of you."

Even Abe hadn't known that part. He was speechless . . . and also drippy-eyed.

I got up with Bonnie in my arms and went to Emilio. "You're ours now, Emilio. Like we promised. The judge made it happen for us. We are an official family—Dad, Mama, Emilio, and Bonnie Lu."

"And Abe?"

"Always."

"Always," Abe echoed, following my lead and coming to Emilio.

Abe, Zander, Emilio, Bonnie Lu, and I had a long group hug then— with lots more drippy tears.

I would never forget the sweetness of that day.

Never.

⌘

ALL IN ALL, THINGS WERE LOOKING up for the co-op. Despite the continued spread of the virus across the world and every difficulty Americans were slogging through, we knew how blessed we were. I won't kid you: Life that spring and summer had been hard, but we were managing: We'd put by food that others would give their eyeteeth for; Zander stayed on top of his many church responsibilities; and our co-op remained healthy, although our bodies were stretched tighter than a bungee cord pulled to its limit.

Zander and I had been forced to make inroads into the foods we'd set by earlier in the year, stored in the nanomites' printer room—even sharing items with the rest of the co-op. Bill, ever the negative Nancy, hadn't wanted to take what we'd offered. But the fact was, the co-op's continued ability to function through the harvest depended upon all of us remaining fit enough to work.

We were bronzed by the sun, our muscles taut and lean—our bodies 'hardened to the work' as Bill had predicted. Even Belicia was thinner than I'd ever known her to be. I just would not care to see any of us stretched any thinner than we already were. Hopefully, with what we had harvested and squirreled away, we would have enough fuel to see us and our family through the long winter.

I no longer thought of food as pleasure or comfort nor could any of us afford to be picky about what we ate. Food of any kind was a vital commodity, regardless of its quality or taste.

I thought about when we had returned to Albuquerque last fall, when we'd begun house hunting. We hadn't foreseen the disasters that would come upon the earth—or upon us personally. We hadn't foreseen the spread of the virus or the loss of Pastor and Mrs. McFee—nor could we have imagined any scenario where *in America* food would be scarce.

God knew, though.

He knew what was coming when, by the prompting of the Holy Spirit, he led us to buy this house, in this cul-de-sac. *He knew* what was coming when he led us to also buy Gemma's empty lot and fence our two lots together. *He knew* what was coming when he led us to rehab Emilio's house and rent it out, because *he knew* how essential to the defense of our little co-op Gamble and Janice would be—long before they asked to rent Emilio's house.

Looking back on the choices we made last year, we were both reassured and comforted. The Holy Spirit had led us well.

We were confident that he would lead us onward.

⌘⌘⌘⌘

Chapter 19

September

THROUGH ALL OF OUR BUSY HARVEST, 24/7, day in and day out, we kept a guard on the barrier, and our über-busy nanoclouds made sure that the nanoarray minding our security cameras stayed on high alert. We were aware that if a roving gang wanted to attack us in strength, it would happen as our harvest came in. That threat was never far from our conscious thoughts.

They came the second week of September—but first God sent a friend to warn us.

Bill pounded on our front door. "Jayda? Hey, Jayda! Izzie is calling for you from the barrier."

I opened the door. Saw Izzie, armed with Abe's revolver, posed just as Gamble had trained her, both feet planted, looking straight at her target, both hands on her gun, the muzzle held low and in front, ready for her to bring it up should she need it. Finger off the trigger until she needed to fire.

Beyond the barrier waited a lone man. He stood a respectful and cautious ten feet from the K-rails. Innocuous and nonthreatening.

Bill added with a laugh, "She said the guy's asking for the lady who was pregnant last winter. Pretty sure that's you."

"Yeah, that's probably me. Thanks, Bill."

Zander was conducting a funeral; he'd taken Josh with him. I grabbed up Bonnie Lu, rode her on my hip, and marched out toward the barrier, all the while remembering the co-op's several (and heated) discussions about sharing food, about beggars approaching the barrier asking for handouts.

Bill was for a 'zero share policy.' Most of us didn't fully agree. The unhappy discussions had ended when Zander put his foot down.

"Yes, we believe in individual responsibility—everybody here and 'out there' is responsible for his or her own actions. However, under some circumstances, people *cannot* do for themselves. At that point, they need a helping hand. So, if Jayda and I feel led to share from *our* portion of what the co-op has grown, from what is in *our* pantry, that is between us and God."

Bill snorted his derision.

"Look, don't feel that you owe us anything if we run out, Bill. But I will say this, God does not lead his people into something he won't also lead them out of. I trust him, and if he tells me to give, I'll give."

Bill, through pinched lips said, "Like you said at the beginning, *just so we're clear*. As long as you can live with your decisions and not come begging to me, I'm fine."

"Yes. We're clear."

I said a silent prayer as I approached the barrier. *Holy Spirit, I will follow you wherever you lead me.*

As I drew near, the man said, "See you had a girl. So did we."

I recognized him then. "Why, it's Darnell, isn't it?"

Darnell of the Grocery Grabbers who'd tried to rob me.

"Yes, ma'am."

The gang had followed me home from the store and had tried to take the food I'd bought. When the nanomites frustrated them, Darnell apologized, and I'd seen his need. So, I compromised some, "paying" the three robbers twenty dollars each for hauling my bags into the house. It had been the right thing to do that day.

I breathed out. *Holy Spirit, I'll follow you.*

"What can I do for you, Darnell?"

"I'm not here for a handout. You already gave me one, yeah? But . . . well, do you remember the guys I was with seven months ago? They're still at it. Stealing food and what have you."

Bonnie Lu, completely unaware that people other than those in the co-op even existed, put her finger in her mouth and tipped her face up toward mine as if to say, "Who (or what) is this? I'm a little nervous."

I said softly, "It's okay, Bonnie. He's a nice man."

Darnell stared at the asphalt, then at me. "Our baby girl is the same age as yours is. Wife is nursing her, and both are doin' good, but . . . if you don't mind me saying so, you're a mite too thin. Lots of that going around, of course. My other kids . . . they look worse'n you."

My body reported a sharp pain right under my breastbone.

"I'm sorry," I whispered.

"Yeah, well." He shrugged. "Anyway, I came . . . I came to warn you. You're a nice person. You were kind to us when we tried to rob you, and you don't deserve what they're planning."

Off to the side, Izzie's eyes widened.

"You said you came to warn us, Darnell? What . . . are they planning?" I asked.

He looked away, then sighed. "Yeah. They're gonna hit you tonight, 'round about one in the morning, and there's more than the two of them. I figure 'tween eight and ten guys. They'll park coupla blocks away and walk in. Hop over this thing you've built here and—" he pointed with his chin left and right, "—over those back walls."

Darnell grimaced. "They'll have guns. I figure you can load up and get away before they come."

I absorbed the information in silence, thinking, then looked up. "Can you wait here a minute, Darnell? I'll be right back."

He seemed uncertain.

"I'll be right back, honest. I have something for you."

Bill was watching from our front yard as I headed up our porch. "What's going on?"

"Give me a minute."

I returned with a quart bag of dried apple slices.

Bill about stroked out. "What the *blank* are you doing with those?"

I sort of snapped back. "I said give me a flipping minute, Bill! Um . . . *here*. Hold Bonnie."

I thrust Bonnie into Bill's arms—neither were thrilled with the abrupt move—and jogged to the barrier.

"Take these, Darnell. I hope your kids enjoy them. We thank you for what you've done, risking yourself and your family to come here and warn us. The Lord bless you and keep you. The Lord make his face to shine upon you and give you peace."

Darnell stared at the dried apple slices. Tears trickled out of his eyes. "Thank you."

I took a deep breath. "And please, look up Downtown Community Church on YouTube or Rumble. My husband is the pastor. I promise you'll hear good things if you do—things to give you hope. Now go, before anyone sees you here, okay? But please remember . . . Jesus is knocking on the door of your heart. He is calling your name, Darnell. Just open the door and ask him to come in."

Darnell nodded . . . then turned and loped down the street.

Bill came up behind me. "Jayda, what the *bleep*! I can't believe you gave *that beggar* some of our hard-earned food. After we slaved to grow and preserve it, you just gave it away? He'll tell his friends, and the next thing we know, we'll have a line here every day."

I rounded on him. Grabbed Bonnie Lu out of his arms. "No, Bill. *I* didn't give food away. *The co-op did*—and you'll chip in your share."

"The *blank* I will!"

I leaned in close to him. Got right up in his face. "Yes, you will, Bill. Why? Because *that beggar* just saved our lives—yours included."

Bonnie, between Bill and me during our tense exchange, started crying. I turned to Izzie. "Sound the air horn and send everyone to our house. You stand your post and stay alert. Sound the air horn again if you spot trouble."

Izzie answered with a single clipped nod. She'd heard Darnell.

⌘

I WAITED UNTIL EVERYONE EXCEPT Izzie was assembled then spilled what Darnell had told me. Three co-op members were absent: Zander and Josh had not yet returned from the funeral and Gamble was at work. Bill, for a change, was silent. Belicia too.

Viola said quietly, "This man, Darnell. He tried to steal your groceries?"

"Yes, maybe a month before Bonnie was born. Janice and Gamble showed up just in time. Pulled their badges and sidearms. Darnell apologized after that."

Janice slid her gaze my way, a little smirk on her mouth. Well, I couldn't exactly tell Viola, Bill, or Belicia that the nanomites had stalled the grocery grabbers' three cars, making it impossible for them to drive away, could I?

"In essence, you *gave* each of those guys twenty bucks—for trying to rob you."

"That's it . . . in a nutshell."

"And you think you can trust this man, Darnell?"

"I do. Showing compassion to someone in need builds bridges. Besides, there's nothing in it for him to warn us. If he were found to have alerted us, I think he'd pay a high price."

Viola frowned. "I suppose we should consider what he said, but—"

I wasn't surprised that Bill interrupted her; I was surprised by what he said.

"Viola? We need to more than consider it. I saw this guy. He was terrified . . . and Jayda's right. There's no reason for him to come here and warn us. No reason except . . ."

Bill frowned like something was bugging him.

"You were saying, Bill?"

"Yeah . . . I suppose I was just thinking that if you hadn't given those guys twenty bucks each after they tried to rob you? Darnell wouldn't have come here today to warn us and tonight we . . . would probably lose everything to them."

I nodded. "That's the way God works sometimes."

He stared at me, his eyes troubled. "Okay, so what do we do?"

There I floundered. "Janice?"

Janice took charge. "Since Darnell told us the attack will come over Bill and Viola's back wall, Abe's back wall, and over the barrier, my suggestion is that we put the kids in a safe place away from those two houses."

I knew just where to put them—in the hidden room under our garage where the nanomites' printer and our emergency food stash were. "I have that handled."

"And perhaps Belicia," Janice suggested.

Belicia hadn't said a word, but now she nodded, the skin under her chin flapping vigorously. "Oh, yes, please. I will take care of Bonnie Lu and Emilio."

Emilio's brows came together. So did mine. We didn't want Belicia in the know about the nanomites' room. Talk about too many questions!

"Um, I don't think that works. The place where they will hide is too small for all three of you, Belicia. Emilio is able to take care of Bonnie Lu, and hopefully, she'll be sleeping. I think our bathroom, on the floor next to the tub, is the best place for you. How about we have Izzie stay in our house with you?"

Janice spoke up again. "Good idea; I approve. Next we should determine where best to position those of us who are armed. That's Gamble, me, Bill, Viola, Josh, Zander, you, and Abe?"

"Yes."

In short order, we had a tentative plan.

⌘⌘⌘⌘

CHAPTER 20

WHEN ZANDER, JOSH, AND GAMBLE came home, we brought them up to speed. Although we shared equally in the defense of our homes and our hard-earned foodstuffs, by dint of expertise, we looked to Janice as the co-op's *de facto* battle commander.

And, predictably, we hit several bumps in our second planning session.

"We have time to prepare," Janice said to our assembled defenders, "so let's consider a few things. First, what is it that these attackers want from us?"

"Our food," we muttered.

"Yes. So we should make that objective cost more than they're willing to pay."

"But," I said slowly, "although the food is important to us—essential, even—it is not what we value most, is it? The lives of our families are worth more than what we've put up for the winter."

Janice nodded. "I take your point and agree. However, I'm suggesting that we move every bit of food we have in our various houses to a central location, a defensible position—but one we don't advertise by over-protecting it."

Abe spoke up. "My house has the only basement in the cul-de-sac. If we move our supplies into my basement, and if we defend my house without being too obvious about it, then the attackers won't know where we've stashed our supplies. They'll spend a lot of effort to reach our kitchens and garages first."

We went quiet, thinking over Abe's suggestion.

Bill, ever the glass-half-empty guy, said, "But if they do reach your basement, we'll have lost everything. It's putting all of our eggs in one basket."

"I'm not sure we have another viable choice, Bill," Zander said softly. "If we split up our supplies, we don't have enough defenders to guard both caches."

Janice agreed with him. "That's true; our options are limited. Well, what do we know? According to Darnell, the gang will come at us from three points: across the barrier and across the back walls of Abe and the Tuckers' houses."

She paused. "I suggest that we make those entry points as difficult and hazardous to navigate as possible. Then we position three shooters to defend the Tuckers' back wall, three to defend Abe's back wall, and two at the barrier."

We nodded our agreement, and Janice handed out assignments.

"Bill and Viola? You'll guard your own back wall. Josh? You will partner up with them. Until it's dark, the three of you should work to make the backyard as big a trip hazard as possible.

"As soon as it's dark, though, retreat to your assigned defensive positions. I want the three of you on the roof where you will have the best field of fire and can use the parapet for cover. Dress in dark clothes. Paint your faces black or a deep green just like you've seen in combat movies because light skin practically glows in the dark. Viola and Josh? You will lie on the roof and keep your heads below the parapet until you have visitors—*maintaining absolute silence* while you wait.

"Bill, I want you positioned on the north end of your roof. Mount your ladder off the north side and keep it there. Make a dark cardboard screen to take up on the roof. Punch two holes in it so you can monitor your back wall without being seen.

"Use a flashlight to signal me at the barricade when you sight intruders, but *do not open fire* until the intruders are well over the wall. We don't want them to fall back and use the wall as cover."

She stared at the three of them. "You good with my instructions?"

They nodded, every face solemn. That said, I could see that Josh, while he put on a good front, was terrified.

Lord God, we need you! Please strengthen us and give us courage.

"Jayda, Ross? You will guard Abe's back wall. However, since Abe has a pitched roof, use his back porch roof for your firing position. Same conditions, same rules as the Tuckers and Josh. Make Abe's yard a trip hazard, wait in silence, wait to shoot until the enemy is over the wall. Got it?"

"Got it," Gamble answered.

"Yes. Got it," I said.

"Abe? You will backstop Jayda and Gamble *from inside* your house. We'll pull your refrigerator out from the wall. Keep it between you and the field of fire, and do not engage the enemy unless and until they make it past Jayda and Ross and are about to breach your house. Understood?"

"Copy that, Janice."

Abe! O dear God, please protect our friend!

"Zander, you and I will defend the barrier. And all of us? Don't forget to use flashlights to signal us when you spot the attackers."

Lord Jesus! Please keep my beloved safe!

People started to squirm and fidget.

"Listen up! As soon as we dismiss? I'll need every able-bodied co-op member available to help us move one of the doubled-up K-rails from the barrier to the center of the cul-de-sac. Two of them, if we can manage it. We'll use them as our fallback position, should we need it.

"Oh. And Izzie and Belicia? As discussed earlier, when the shooting starts, I want you both in Jayda and Zander's bathroom on the floor next to the tub. And Izzie? I want you armed."

Belicia wrung her hands. "Oh dear. Oh dear."

Izzie put her arm around Belicia. "Don't worry, Belicia. We'll be together, and we'll be okay. I trust the Lord to protect us."

I thought about the printer room in our garage's hidden basement. Recalled what the nanomites had told us.

*Our troops can float like a butterfly, sting like a bee, Zander Cruz—a bee loaded with no more than a few milliamps of current—yet a sting sufficient to take down an assailant. Our tribes will knock out all comers without harming them, but they **will** stop them. As you know, we require the printer far more than you need these emergency funds. They will protect the printer for us and protect the money and food for you.*

In the warehouse, I spoke to Zander. "Babe, the only place safe enough for Izzie and Belicia is in the nanomites' printer room with Emilio and Bonnie Lu. I think . . . I think we need to hide them there."

I watched him consider what we'd need to do to keep the printer room our secret. "Yeah, let's talk to Janice after the meeting ends."

"That reminds me," Janice said. She stood, serious and solemn. "We will shortly engage with an enemy bent on stealing from us. Killing us, if necessary. Destroying our homes and families into the bargain. Reminds me of a Bible verse I heard Zander talk about one time. Something about the thief coming to steal, kill, and destroy?"

Several of us nodded. We were familiar with the passage, but I didn't know Janice had been paying attention.

"So?" Bill demanded.

"So, I don't want to go into this battle without asking the Lord to help us. Protect us. See us through. Zander? Will you pray for us?"

Another welcome surprise!

Janice sat, and Zander stood. He raised one hand to heaven as he bowed his head. "Lord God, you are King of the Universe, but we understand that this fallen universe is locked in a tremendous spiritual battle, a fight for the eternal souls of millions. Father, we call on you in the mighty name of Jesus. Please lead us. Please guide us. Please help us! We are prepared to fight to keep what is ours, but we surrender all we have to you. What we give into *your* care, we cannot lose. Lord, we humbly ask that you grant us courage and strength. Amen."

Everyone in the room said "amen." Even Bill Tucker.

I was stuck on what Zander had prayed. *What we give into your care, we cannot lose?*

I had no idea then how much I would have to lean on those words.

⌘

WE WAITED UNTIL JANICE FINISHED assigning positions and duties and we were clear on our defense strategies to pull her and Gamble aside. Zander told them our intentions.

"Our bathroom floor isn't safe enough for Izzie and Belicia. We'll lead Izzie and Belicia into the nanomites' printer room with Emilio and Bonnie Lu. Just as soon as we can get Izzie and Belicia sat down, the nanomites will put them out and remove their most recent memories—that of being led into the garage basement.

"Once the dust settles, we'll bring them back up, do another quick wipe, and plant suggestions in both of their minds, telling them that they laid on the bathroom floor together during the battle. A false memory will be more reassuring for them than a complete inability to recall where they spent the battle."

"All right. If you say so," Janice said. "Now, let's get those K-rails moved."

Out on the cul-de-sac we saw that Bill had passed four wide straps under the first K-rail and buckled the ends of each strap together before three more men and four women joined him: Zander, Gamble, Josh, Janice, Viola, Izzie, and me.

"We're going to lift this thing?" Izzie asked uncertainly. "How much does it weigh?"

"Two thousand pounds."

"That's two hundred and fifty pounds each! We can't do that!" Izzie protested.

"We'll have to scoot it more than lift it," Bill muttered.

"But—"

Zander spoke over Izzie. "Everyone? Line up quickly, four to a side— male, female, male, female on this side, female, male, female, male on the other side—so everyone's partner is of the opposite gender. Take a minute to adjust the length of your straps so both you and your partner can get your shoulders under your strap—*and watch your feet!*"

"I don't have a good feeling about this," Izzie moaned.

I turned. "Don't worry; we can do this."

Of the eight of us, four knew we could—because the nanomites would be lending their strength to the effort.

When everyone had their straps adjusted, Bill called out, "On three, lift. One! Two! Three—*up!* Now, slow march, hup, hup, hup, hup! Ready pivot? Pivot *now!*"

I wanted to laugh, but I knew I shouldn't. We lifted that "stick," marched it toward the center of the cul-de-sac, turned it, and set it down.

No one broke a sweat.

Josh asked what three others were thinking. "Uh . . . what just happened?"

"We moved the rail," Zander said, his expression bland. Unimpressed.

He added, "Let's get another. Two more, in fact."

⌘

NOTHING ABOUT THE "BATTLE" THAT night happened as we thought it would. In fact, not a shot was fired.

Close to midnight, Gamble and I were lying prone on Abe's roof as a group of armed men walked toward the barrier waving, of all things, a white flag—a flag of truce. Behind them, with ropes around their necks, they dragged Darnell and two of his kids, two boys, around ages ten and eleven.

The armed men saw only Zander and Janice at the barrier. They drew closer.

"Oh, Jesus!" I whispered. "Those poor kids! They'll be traumatized for life!"

Perhaps we can prevent their suffering, Jayda Cruz.

I listened closely, then muttered, "Hold the fort, Gamble."

"What? Where are you going?"

I jumped down from Abe's roof, not even a shadow in the night, and ran up to Zander.

In the warehouse, I asked, "You have the plan?"

"As far as the nanomites gave it to me."

"How many do you count?"

"Um, nine."

"Okay. Go ahead, Nano."

"Then what?" Zander asked.

"I dunno. The nanomites suggested that they knock them all out— Darnell and his kids too. Guess we'll figure the rest out as we go along."

Seconds later, all nine armed men plus Darnell and his kids slumped to the asphalt.

Janice turned to Zander. "What just happened?"

"Uh, The nanomites thought they could just, you know, knock them out. Avoid bloodshed."

I was with the nanomites. "Nano? Can you tell us where these guys are parked?"

Jayda Cruz, they came in two vans. The vans are parked two blocks down, three blocks east of this location.

"Perfect."

I glanced toward the Tuckers' roof. Unfortunately, Bill, Viola, and Josh looked like three prairie dogs with their heads sticking up out of their holes.

Freaked out prairie dogs.

"Uh, Zander? I'll just meander over to Abe's, reappear, and come back."

"Good idea."

I returned shortly. Visible. By then, Bill had come down from his roof and joined Janice and Zander.

"What in bloody blue blazes just happened?"

I ignored his question. "Sooo . . . what we need to do next—and quickly—is go get these guys' vans and drive them back here."

"And how would we know where they're parked?" Bill demanded. "And who's going to tell me *what is going on*?"

"Um, their vehicles are *likely* parked a few blocks away—like, two blocks down, three blocks east of here."

"And are we *likely* to see any more of these yahoos?" Janice asked.

"Perhaps. But if we do? They, too, will *likely* fall down."

"Someone *please* tell me what the devil is happening?" Bill shouted.

We turned our backs on him.

"And then?" Janice asked.

"Then I think it *likely* that we load these guys into their vans . . . and drive them somewhere else."

Zander was snickering by then, which made it hard for me to keep a straight face.

Even Janice cracked a smile. "Likely the west mesa?"

"Sounds good to me. Zander?"

Bill strode around us to get in our faces. "You had better come clean *right now*, because if you don't—"

Very gently, Bill crumpled to the ground. Atop the Tuckers' roof, Viola and Josh did the same.

I grinned. "Ahh. Blessed relief!"

Zander grinned back. "You know, Jay, we've done this before—had the nanomites knock people out and redact their recent memories."

"Right? So, what in the world are we *thinking*—zapping people instead and *likely* exposing ourselves?"

Janice, with a remarkably straight face, answered, "*Likely*, you were having too much fun with the zapping business. Had I been you? It's *likely* I would have too."

⌘

SEVERAL HOURS LATER, GAMBLE, Zander, and Abe arrived back at the co-op in Gamble's car. They had left the nine grocery grabbers and their vans on a road far out on a sandy plateau west of Albuquerque and had driven back together in Gamble's car.

Sadly, the grocery grabbers' vans had developed flat tires. Multiple flats. The gang's walk back to civilization would be long and tiresome, made more worrying by their inability to recall what had happened.

What they *would* be able to recall was a persistent and distressing sense of dread. The nanomites had cobbled together a video collage consisting of knots of writhing snakes infesting our cul-de-sac and giant spiders pouncing on anyone who approached our barrier. They had implanted those visuals within the grocery grabbers' last-made synapses.

The nanomites were perfecting their own mode of PSYOPs—psychological operations—and a quite effective method it was. The grocery grabbers would wake up with a strong aversion to ever again threatening or even visiting our co-op.

⌘

WHILE THE GUYS MANAGED THE GANG, Janice and I loaded Darnell and his kids into Zander's and my SUV. We drove them to within a block of their house. The nanomites woke Darnell up first. Janice's message to him was short and succinct.

"Thanks for warning us about the impending attack, Darnell. We're sorry those animals found out and scared you and your kids. Do you have family elsewhere? Yes? Ah. Denver? Well, we strongly advise that you pay them a permanent visit."

Darnell wasn't with it quite yet. "Yeah . . . um, what happened?"

"Doesn't matter—but it will matter if you and your family are still here when your buddies return. Get packed and go."

She and I helped Darnell get his kids out of the car. We laid the sleeping kids on the grass, then I handed Darnell several hundred-dollar bills and another sack of our apple slices.

"Best of luck, Darnell."

"Okay. Thanks. Say, maybe we'll head north ASAP. I have family in Denver."

⌘

THE FIVE OF US DECIDED OUR next steps: Zander and Gamble took care of Bill, Viola, and Josh, while Janice and I led Izzie and Belicia up from the garage basement, and walked them to Belicia's house.

As soon as we got them into Belicia's living room, the nanomites did a quick wipe of their most recently formed synapses. The four of us then sat down together and Janice and I talked them through a contrived version of what had happened—how they had fallen asleep on the floor of our bathroom during our short-lived skirmish with the grocery grabber gang. When we finished talking, they again "fell asleep" and would, according to the nanomites, wake up in the morning refreshed.

We were finally done with our long night's work.

I took Bonnie Lu from Emilio and sent him to bed. Zander and I collapsed in our bedroom, me sitting on the side of the bed, Zander under the covers. We were taking a moment to breathe, to regroup, before we retired for a few hours.

Bonnie woke up long enough to see I was back. Smacking her lips and muttering *ma-ma-ma-ma-ma*, she clutched my shirt in one tiny fist, burrowed her face into the crook of my arm, and went soundly back to her sweet slumbers.

"Tonight went much better than I believed it could," I said to Zander.

He yawned. "Smarter, not harder. Pretty sure we can manage future confrontations in similar form as long as we're able to corral all the players, get them within range of the nanomites at the same time, right?"

"Right. Still, even if the grocery grabbers had split up and come at us from three sides like they'd planned, we could have hit each group in quick succession."

He yawned again. "Sure—while making sure we also took out the co-op members we're keeping unaware of the nanomites."

I sat quietly for a while, then said, "Well, I'm bushed. Time to put Bonnie Lu to bed and follow suit."

Zander didn't answer, and I heard the whiffle of his relaxed breathing. He was already out.

⌘⌘⌘⌘

CHAPTER 21

IT WAS THE FIRST TUESDAY of November, election day. Based on the nanomites' projections and validated by every poll we'd watched running up to the election, Robert Jackson would win handily, assuring us of another four years of his administration. What happened instead, was confounding.

We watched the election results come in, many of them faster than we expected—even faster than we thought plausible. Zander prayed under his breath as he watched the results update across multiple websites.

Then the networks and news sites began to project the winners. According to them, Nora Mellyn, with stunning margins, swept every battleground state . . . every state where, just yesterday, Jackson had polled four points ahead of her by no fewer than eleven elections pollsters.

"Zander, how did this happen?"

He didn't reply. I heard him continue to pray.

⌘

NORA MELLYN PREENED BEFORE THE crush of reporters and supporters, a victorious smile plastered across her face. It was only ten at night, but every network had already called the election for her and proclaimed Jackson's loss as unprecedented—forty-seven states had swung to his opponent's column.

Mellyn said nothing while she basked in the crowd's adoration and the cameras clicked away, enjoying their sustained applause as her due. Reveling in their approval. Waving and giving a thumbs up to those in the crowd cheering for her.

Her Vice Presidential pick, Lucas Cathaway, stood slightly behind her; her husband stood beside him. Neither man appeared as happy as Mellyn did.

Cathaway, a centrist, had been selected to appease those in the party who thought Mellyn was too far left. It was rumored that he regretted accepting her offer.

It sure looked like regret to us.

Then there was Nora Mellyn's husband, James Mellyn. Apparently the couple had patched things up since the revelation last spring that Nora had conducted an affair with another man.

I wonder what Mellyn or her party promised her husband to keep him in line.

When, at last, the melee quieted, the President-Elect approached the podium.

"Thank you. Thank you all. Thirty minutes ago, Robert Jackson called to congratulate me and concede his defeat . . . *We have done it!*"

Her supporters went wild, and it was several more minutes before they stopped cheering and allowed Mellyn to continue. I, however, was annoyed, because she hadn't referred to Robert Jackson as *President* Jackson. Leaving off his office title was in no way respectful or right. It could have been a mistake, but I didn't think so.

Wait for it, lady. What goes around comes around.

Minutes later, I recognized her "gaffe" for what it was: an opening salvo.

Mellyn's mouth turned down like she'd tasted something bitter. She bent a serious look on the crowded ballroom. Her supporters caught her mood immediately . . . or had they been coached in their responses, instructed to stop cheering and to pay close, sober attention to Mellyn's remarks?

She lifted her chin. "Today the American people have spoken. They have made it clear to the world that Robert Jackson has failed this great nation and its people, that he has failed to serve in his sacred office."

I growled, "He lost an election, lady. He didn't commit treason."

Zander's face was as stony as mine when Mellyn continued.

"If you and your families are hungry tonight, whose failure is it? If looters have broken into your homes, stolen from you, or destroyed your business, whose failure is it?

"Let me be clear: The failure is Robert Jackson's. From the get-go, Jackson failed to respond adequately to the virus, failed to alleviate the misery of these natural disasters, failed to use executive powers to end supply chain issues. *Failure* is the hallmark of this man's administration."

I seethed inside. "Zander! She's lying!"

"I know, Jayda."

Mellyn continued. "Let me be perfectly clear. What Robert Jackson has done—rather what he has *not* done—is nothing short of treason. You heard right. *Treason.*"

The crowd took up the chant. "Treason! Treason! Treason! Treason!"

It went on until she signaled for their attention.

"America is faltering—can we allow her to fall? Can we?"

"No! No! No!" they chanted.

"No, we cannot allow America to fall. Therefore, with a heavy heart, filled with the gravity of what I must do to prevent the further destruction of our country, I make the following announcements."

At this point, the noise of the crowd dropped into utter silence.

"Staged!" I muttered. "They've been told what to do and when."

"I have to agree," Zander replied. "Something big is about to go down. Something huge."

Mellyn turned and beckoned. Rows of solemn-faced men and women formed around her and her husband. When they had assembled, Mellyn spoke again.

"I am joined tonight by key government leaders: thirteen members of Jackson's twenty-four member cabinet including the Secretary of State; the Secretary of Defense; US Attorney General, Paul Akimba; Akimba's deputy, Thomas Redding; the Chief Justice of the Supreme Court, Peter Wendell; Director of the Secret Service, Edith Bancroft; Bancroft's boss, Director of Homeland Security, Inez Tafoya; Majority Leader of the Senate, George Rasmussen; and Speaker of the House, Tyler Monroe. Mr. Speaker?"

Monroe took the podium and read from the prepared notes he withdrew from his suitcoat pocket. "With grieving hearts but with the sure knowledge of the moral rightness of our actions and the legal authority to do so, we take the following steps: A majority of the President's cabinet has voted to remove Robert Jackson as President of the United States by reason of dereliction of duty and unfitness to serve.

"They have submitted to me, Speaker of the House of Representatives, and to Senator Rasmussen, the Senate Majority Leader, their written declaration that Robert Jackson is unable to discharge the powers and duties of the Office of President."

The crowd erupted. I fell back against the sofa cushions, gaping.

"It's a coup," Zander whispered. "It's the Cabal—the Global Community. They are pushing up their schedule."

The nanomites were as flummoxed as we were.

Jayda Cruz, Zander Cruz, we . . . we did not see this coming. The Cabal has managed to keep this plot from us—and we can conceive of only one means by which they could have done so. The conspirators had to have planned this coup within a SCIF, an air-gapped facility where we had no nanoarray present to record their plot and report it back to us.

Monroe gestured to Mellyn's supporters to quiet them. When he again had control, he continued. "In ordinary circumstances, the Vice President would assume the President's office. As we all know, the office of Vice President remains vacant. Robert Jackson has failed on that point too."

More shouts of affirmation from the assembled onlookers; after a few minutes, more motions to silence the crowd.

"With no sitting Vice President, the line of succession falls to me as Speaker of the House. However . . ."

He was drowned out by thunderous applause, shouts, and air horns. When he was able, he went on. "*However*, given that we have just elected a new president, given that my time in office as President would be quite short, and given the unprecedented needs of our nation—needs that must be addressed with great speed and resolute, unfaltering determination—I have asked President-Elect Mellyn to assume my duties as President."

More celebratory chaos.

"Trust me when I say that I have plenty to do as Speaker of the House; I will not disrupt the course of Congress or delay the orderly transition of power by assuming the duties of President for a mere eleven weeks."

"That's not legal," Zander breathed. "He can't do that!"

But Monroe wasn't finished. "We can preserve the constitutionality of this move through executive order—*my* executive order. I will, in a few moments, take the presidential oath of office. I will then issue an executive order that, in effect, requires Mellyn to assume my executive duties."

Monroe chuckled softly. "Mine will be the shortest presidency in the history of our nation."

He looked behind him. "Mr. Chief Justice?"

Chief Justice Wendell moved up alongside Monroe. There, before the nation's cameras, he administered the presidential oath of office to Monroe.

Just as quickly, Monroe produced a document, which the Chief Justice read aloud. "I, Tyler J. Monroe, sworn President of these United States, as my first act in office, do hereby appoint President-Elect Nora A. Mellyn Vice President of these United States."

The crowd roared. When the Chief Justice raised his hand, the people again fell silent.

"Secondly, I appoint Vice President Mellyn to act as President in my stead, with all the authority, pomp, and gravitas due the office, until the formal date of her inauguration as President as prescribed by the Constitution of the United States of America—or as amended by Congress."

"What? Can they do that?" I demanded. "Is any of this legit?"

Zander sighed. "I don't think it matters at this point, Jay. Mellyn's inauguration in January is less than three months off, and—"

I muted the screen and shouted, "It matters, Zander! They have slandered and maligned the President—*our* president!—and removed him from office!"

"Hey—calm down! I'm sorry. I misspoke. I should have said I don't think it can be stopped—not that it doesn't matter. I mean, have you *seen* the rolodex of "Who's Who" standing up there with Mellyn? Legal challenges, originating with Jackson's Attorney General, would need to go up to SCOTUS. It is patently obvious that Jackson's AG backs Mellyn. He will refuse any request from Jackson to prosecute the move. Furthermore, the Chief Justice is also on board. He's the one who administered the oath to Monroe."

Zander's eyes narrowed "In fact . . . we would do well to note every individual on that platform, because they are either Cabal through and through or they have accepted the payoffs the Cabal has offered them."

"You forgot to add those who are 'politically leveraged.' The Cabal has to be blackmailing a bunch of them. Take a look at the expressions on some of their faces."

"You're right. I'd lay odds that the deputy AG and several of the cabinet heads standing behind Mellyn resign early to 'make way' for Mellyn's choices *prior* to January."

"*If* she waits until January. Did you catch Monroe's last? 'Until the formal date of her inauguration as President as prescribed by the Constitution of the United States of America—or as amended by Congress'?"

I ground my teeth in frustration. "This charade was scripted long before tonight."

"Oh, I agree. All the pieces in play, the people they had to get on board with their plan? And how could they have known Mellyn would win, especially this big?"

I frowned. "How, indeed."

Then I turned inward, struck dumb by memories—an invisible me sneaking into the White House Residence and revealing myself to an astounded President Jackson in his White House living room. His fear that I'd come to assassinate him when, in reality, I'd come to warn him. Months after, Zander and I feasting with Robert and Maddie Jackson in the Residence Dining Room. Later, saving him from a second assassination attempt. Over a year ago, receiving the Presidential Medal of Freedom from President Jackson and the First Lady in the same room.

We knew Robert Jackson, knew him personally. He was a good and honorable man whose presidency had been hamstrung by plots and collusions, whose executive actions to mitigate America's misery had been thwarted again and again by politicians and government bureaucrats—those machinations appearing now as neon arrows pointing to the Cabal.

"Nano," I whispered, "where is President Jackson?"

I waited through a long silence. Finally, they said, *Jayda Cruz, we are unable to ascertain the whereabouts of Robert Jackson.*

"What about Maddie Jackson?"

A full minute went by. *We are sorry, Jayda Cruz, but we are unable to ascertain the whereabouts of Madeleine Jackson either.*

I bent an anxious look on Zander.

He asked, "Nano, how about Axel Kennedy? Can you find him?"

One moment, Zander Cruz.

That moment became minutes. Six full minutes passed before the nanomites replied, *Zander Cruz, Jayda Cruz, we have located a Secret Service text message exchange that indicates Axel Kennedy is an occupant of an unofficial Homeland Security detention center outside Washington, DC.*

"Is he . . . is he all right, Nano?"

We will dispatch a nanoarray in an attempt to seek out further details, Jayda Cruz. However, the facility itself is a "black" site—off the local grid, drawing electricity from its own micro power plant. No cellular or internet traffic in or out. We can penetrate their security measures only when onsite.

"If they incarcerated Kennedy, they may be holding President Jackson too," I whispered, "but likely elsewhere."

Zander agreed. "Nano, please. Find President and Mrs. Jackson!"

We will do our best, Zander Cruz.

I put my face in my hands and wept.

⌘

USSART ONE OPENED THE MEETING. "We have been quite preoccupied with managing the election and ensuring the correct results. I am authorized to thank you for your diligence. We carried most offices up for grabs—but of most importance, we took the office of president.

He went through other business, heard various members' reports, then glared into his camera. "Southwest. Report."

"Yes, sir." The woman managed to control the quaver threatening to spill out into her voice. She glanced down at her notes and shuffled the top sheets to buy herself another second or two.

"As was . . . suggested in our last meeting, our assignment was to slowly, deliberately, and with increasing pain strip our subject of his reputation, resources, and relationships. In order to maximize the pain inflicted upon our subject, we itemized his vulnerabilities and as our first target, chose the boy on whom Cruz and his wife had begun adoption proceedings.

"The pandemic having stalled such proceedings, my people arranged to take the boy from his foster father and put him into protective custody. We effected his removal immediately following his twelfth birthday in order to have more latitude in our disposal of him."

"So you have him. What next?"

"Yes, we, um, our social worker, accompanied by two sheriff's deputies, removed the boy from his home in early July."

The leader squinted at the woman. "What am I missing?"

She licked her lips. "The boy was transported to a GC approved holding facility and placed in lockdown—a locked, secure room, often used for the children of . . . . special consideration."

She was perspiring now, and the leader's glare had intensified.

"Go on."

"The following day, the custodians called our social worker. According to them, they awoke early that morning . . . on their living room floor."

"What were they doing sleeping on the floor?"

"Sir, they do not recall."

"I'm not going to like the rest of your report, am I?"

Southwest plucked up a bit of defiance-laced courage. "Sir, I have *six additional* removals to report to you. Despite how it may sound, I request that you grant me the opportunity to rehearse them to you anyway."

"You do, do you?"

"Yes, sir."

He nodded, grudgingly, at her spunk. "Very well. Please continue."

A murmur went around the other SART members. Southwest ignored them.

"Thank you, sir. The custodians awoke on their living room floor, and immediately checked on the boy. He was gone, the room opened from the outside—the only means of opening the room, in fact."

USSART One stared at her. "That was the first removal? We must listen to six more? *Harumph.* Do not try my patience, Southwest."

"I will move briskly, sir. On the second removal—same social worker and same sheriff's deputy plus a second—the boy rode in the social worker's rear seat."

"And?"

"The social worker and the deputies stopped at a red light. When it turned green and the social worker drove on, she realized the deputies had not followed. She pulled over to wait for them and, at that point, she also realized the boy was no longer in her back seat. She retraced her route and found the deputies at the intersection where they'd stopped for the red light. They were . . . unconscious."

The other SART members' exclamations were loud.

"Silence!" To Southwest, he growled, "This is nonsense."

She knew he'd disbelieve her report, but her life was on the line. She had to press her point.

"Sir, you may listen to the social worker's report or speak to the deputies yourself. They cannot explain what happened that day—nor can the social worker who accompanied our original agent and two deputies on the following three removals!"

His lips thinned. "Careful, Southwest. The ice is very thin where you are standing."

She modified her expression and nodded demurely. "If I might describe the final episode in this tawdry tale?"

"Oh, it's a tale, now, is it? And have you punished those agents of ours who played this little game?"

"When I have finished, you may judge my actions on that front."

He chuckled. "Please. Continue."

"On the seventh removal, our agent enlisted the assistance of the sheriff's SWAT team—six armed tactical officers as well as the original two deputies—both our people. They took the boy into custody *and* the subject's infant daughter."

USSART One listened closely; the attention of the other members was also acutely focused on Southwest's narrative.

"The infant was placed with an emergency intake family. The boy, this time, was taken—successfully—to a juvenile detention center—a fully locked-down facility."

The leader's frown had further furrowed his brow. He seemed somewhat withdrawn.

Southwest sighed. "In the morning, the infant and boy were both gone."

"The boy was taken from the detention center?"

"Yes, sir. The guards at the monitoring station were knocked out cold, the video surveillance was offline while he was being taken, and the other boys in his dorm were found unconscious—deeply asleep but uninjured—two of them on the floor."

When the leader said nothing, Southwest murmured, "I have one last thing to report, sir."

"Go ahead."

"Just before noon the following day, our agent *slash* social worker was arrested for falsifying court orders. I dispatched one of our attorneys to represent her. When he arrived at the county lockup, he found our agent . . . in a near-catatonic state. When she managed to snap out of it, she repeated the entire 'story' to him. He recorded her account. I . . . can send it to you, should you wish."

"And your near-catatonic agent?"

"Sadly, she suffered an unexpected cardiac event in her cell that night." Southwest cleared her throat. "She did not survive it."

"I see."

The other participants in the SART conference call had been silent since the leader's rebuke. They watched the byplay between him and Southwest like hungry vultures waiting for a predator to finish off his prey.

They were disappointed when the leader said quietly, "Thank you for your report, Southwest. I will review it further and consider next actions. That is all."

He terminated the call.

⌘

ALONE AND UNWATCHED IN HIS STUDY, USSART One sat thinking. As the SART leader of what had been the strongest nation in the history of the world, he wielded a great deal of power. On the other hand, he, too, answered to those above him . . . and those above him were worried.

What Southwest had reported? Sounded similar to other strange happenings he'd heard whispered.

Someone was messing with GC leadership worldwide, and no one could explain how.

USSART One had many contacts throughout the Global Community. Bits and pieces of rumors had trickled down to him, and the stories he heard were both strange and troubling.

GC leadership bank accounts emptied? Assets stolen? Valuables vanished? Houses sold out from under the owners?

Then there were the tales of identity theft, dirty laundry exposed, well-placed GC agents arrested, framed for crimes they hadn't committed—well, in *some* instances hadn't committed. Either way, GC law enforcement agents were ordered to bury evidence; GC political agents were told to exert pressure to exonerate the agents when possible.

As for missing funds? Millions upon millions were unaccounted for. GC leadership had resorted to looting the GC treasury to cover their collective losses until their stolen monies were located and returned . . . which was the strangest part of the worrisome events. *No one* could account for the funds' disappearances or trace their routes after they were withdrawn. Multiple forensic auditors were employed full-time to figure out how the money was taken, where it was sent, and where it presently resided. *And multiple forensic auditors were stumped.*

USSART One had pondered the unexplained happenings for weeks. They were attacks, certainly—no one doubted that—but the fact that no asset within GC ranks could put their fingers on an attacker, that no expert within GC's cyber division could untangle the money transfers, and still the episodes continued, unabated and with increasing frequency.

Top GC leadership were reported to be rabid over it, figuratively frothing at the mouth.

USSART One did not intend to be the next victim on the list. He quietly diversified his liquid holdings by withdrawing chunks of cash and stashing them across several "hidey holes" known only to himself.

Why? Because what his superiors and counterparts did not realize about him was that, in addition to his political acumen, USSART One was superstitious. Not moderately so, but extremely—the result of years spent immersed in occult practices.

I sense a powerful force behind this Cruz fellow at the center of Southwest's report. Until I know what that force is and how to handle it? I should be careful not to arouse its ire.

He considered another factor. *And if I were to forward Southwest's report to my own superiors? My personal credibility would tank. I might be summarily dismissed . . . or worse.*

In his zeal to protect his own interests, what USSART One failed to consider, what he *failed to connect*, were the inexplicable events in Southwest's report and the mysterious attacks across GC's upper echelons. As he worried about the spiritual force behind Southwest's minor nuisance, he did not put two and two together. In his mind, they were not connected.

Instead, he pondered how to respond to Southwest's problem.

It is better to do nothing, better not to disturb the spirits behind that man at present. Wiser to leave him be until I have a firmer grip on the facts—until the goddess provides me with answers. Besides, we have the election transitions to manage; I must focus on them and on furthering the SART mandate.

He nodded to himself. *Yes. Leave Cruz be until the goddess presents the most propitious moment and opportunity. Then strike.*

⌘⌘⌘⌘

Chapter 22

WE'D HAD A GOOD HARVEST AND felt reasonably confident we could feed the co-op through the winter, so when Thanksgiving rolled around, we did what we could to celebrate. We didn't have a turkey—but we did have four cockerels we'd done our best to fatten up. Four young birds to share among twelve hungry appetites seemed like a feast to all of us!

We did save back the breasts of two birds. Belicia made the compelling case that we could still eat our fill on Thanksgiving. However, we would more than appreciate our restraint when she served up a steaming chicken pot pie the following evening. Along with two platters of fried chicken, our Thanksgiving meal included home-grown mashed potatoes (with gravy from the chicken drippings), rehydrated green beans, and carrots prepared just like mashed sweet potatoes.

Whoever had said, "Enough is as good as a feast," hadn't been wrong.

We waited an hour to serve dessert, perhaps to appreciate it all the more. To top off our wonderful day of gratitude, we enjoyed a small dried-apple cobbler topped with a sweet, crunchy topping—compliments of Belicia's black walnut tree.

No, it wasn't like other Thanksgivings, and we didn't care. We were grateful to have enough to feed our families—which was what so many around us did not have. God willing, we'd survive the winter and plant another garden, raise another crop.

God willing.

⌘

AS SOON AS DECEMBER ROLLED around, Emilio reminded us daily that Christmas was not far off. He also reminded us that it would be Bonnie Lu's first Christmas. But, while our last two Christmases had been wonderful, this year, a pall hung over the holiday across our nation and the world.

When people's daily efforts were focused on simple survival—providing food for their families, enough gas in the lines to warm their homes, and some semblance of security in their cities and neighborhoods? Few had little energy or wherewithal left over to spend on what, to most, was nothing more than a commercial holiday they could no longer afford.

Christmas wasn't like that for us, though. It was an opportunity to rejoice in the Savior's long-prophesied birth and to honor him the way the angels had when they proclaimed his appearance to the shepherds. Zander and I set our hearts to focus our little family on Jesus, not on presents. We would set up our manger scene, sing holy Christmas songs, and read the account of Jesus' birth from Luke. Presents? They would be small, personal, and meaningful.

In the run-up to Christmas, we had little co-op work to do except stand our assigned watches at the barrier. Abe and I kept Emilio at his schoolwork every day, regardless of Albuquerque's iffy electrical grid and internet service. Even over the Christmas break, he already knew he would have extra reading to do—reading to himself, reading aloud to Zander and to me, reading aloud to Abe, and reading to Bonnie.

Oh, and Emilio loved reading to his sister. He hammed it up, taking on the voices of the characters as he read, just to hear that precious belly laugh of hers.

As Christmas drew near, so did winter. Typical of December in this part of New Mexico, the days were cool or downright cold, but temperatures rarely dipped below freezing except at night. Pre-pandemic, on those chilly December days and evenings, people would flood the malls and shopping centers hunting down the "right" Christmas presents for those on their lists.

No longer. The malls and shopping centers were mostly closed.

The most heartbreaking sight *this* Christmas season were the many parents on street corners begging for food. Albuquerque had always had panhandlers, but this was different. Parents brought their children out in the cold with them, perhaps to prove to those with something to share that they *did* have needy kids and weren't running a scam.

It was hard seeing the hopelessness on those fathers' and mothers' faces. It was worse seeing children who were far too thin, whose eyes were disinterested or downright dull.

⌘

AND WHEN WE THOUGHT THIS HOLIDAY season couldn't sink any lower? Our "Acting President" Mellyn appeared one evening to offer "hope" via an option so depraved, it ranked beyond the pale of any acceptable human behavior—let alone presidential conduct.

"My dear fellow Americans, the holidays are always difficult for many of our citizens, and this year has been the hardest most of us have ever experienced. With a heavy heart, I speak this evening to fathers and mothers, in particular. If you are staring at the bottom, if you are without hope, if you are at the end of your ability to cope, we understand. Please . . . let us help you."

Let us help you? Something in the way she said it felt . . . off.

The words Kindness Hotline and a phone number appeared on the screen.

"Trained counselors are standing by right now. They will staff these lines twenty-four hours a day, seven days a week. Call them. Let them talk with you and walk you through your options. If you make a decision, they will dispatch a Kindness Kit to you immediately."

I frowned. *A Kindness Kit? What's that?*

As if they had heard my unspoken question, Mellyn's PR crew inserted a short commercial into her broadcast.

A pale, emaciated middle-aged man at his mailbox withdrew a distinctive-looking brown box about the size of cell phone. He turned the box over. On the back were the words *Kindness Kit* in gold lettering. A strung out teen on the street accepted the same package from a police officer. Two parents and their three small children, trudging through a homeless shelter's food line reached the last station. The mother stacked five such boxes onto her tray.

The narrator's voice said, "Hopeless? Let us help."

The same individuals, in a screen split into thirds, opened their boxes and removed from each a set of instructions and a single yellow pill.

Over the scene, the narrator added, "Call the number below to receive your personal Kindness Kit at no cost. Peace is waiting for you."

What? No. *No!*

I could not believe it. Could not. Nausea gripped me.

The broadcast returned to Mellyn. She pulled her features down into sympathetic lines, and the camera pushed in closer.

"Please believe me when I say, *you need suffer no longer*. You need not allow cancer to further ravish your body. You can escape the chains of addiction. You and your children can receive immediate relief from hunger and cold, from homelessness and hopelessness! *No one* need suffer when help is only a phone call away.

"Call now, and we will send you the relief you yearn for. I promise you a painless passing, whether it be for you and your family, or perhaps for your children—to spare their suffering. We will support your choice and will handle every detail so you can, at last, *let go* . . . and rest in peace."

I don't use swear words. *I don't.*

So, when I leapt to my feet cursing Nora Mellyn, I suppose I wasn't really cursing her but the devil himself, the wicked being who put *such blasphemy* into the hearts and minds of deluded individuals.

Still, my reaction shocked me. Shocked Zander and Emilio.

Just as quickly, I caved. Found myself in Zander's arms, weeping.

"They can't do that, Zander! They can't tell people to kill their children! They can't!"

⌘

THE FOLLOWING DAY I COOKED. I made three large batches of soup and dozens of biscuits. I plundered our emergency stores to add tinned meat to the soup.

I sent Zander out to find disposable "hot cups" with lids. Asked him to bring home snack baggies also.

When the soup was done, I enlisted Emilio, and we made cookies—dozens and dozens of cookies. They weren't fancy cookies, just plain oatmeal or simple vanilla sugar cookies (without the decorative sugar sprinkles), but it didn't matter. We also emptied our family's entire stash of dried apples into snack bags.

When we were done, our dining table was laden with small meals ready to go. Neither Emilio nor I had seen such bounty in a year. These hot meals would bless whoever received them.

That evening we went out, Zander, Emilio, and I, our SUV laden with our preparations. We went to the corners and passed out hot soup and biscuits. We went to the sidewalks adjoining grocery stores where destitute families usually stood to beg for food.

Wherever we passed out food, we told them about Jesus and prayed with every family. We told them their troubles would not last forever—that a heavenly kingdom awaited them if they made Jesus their Savior and Lord. We didn't just hand out soup and cookies; we handed out hope.

And that night, Zander posted a new message. "Do not believe Nora Mellyn," he said. "Do not believe the wicked lie that taking your own life or that of your children will grant you peace or the cessation of suffering—*it will not*. Do not believe that relief awaits you in a so-called 'kindness kit'—*it does not*.

"Eternity waits for all of us—so do not throw away your hope! Instead, talk to Jesus. Tell him your needs. Ask him to forgive your sins; ask him to come into your heart. *Seek him*. Do not despair! He is waiting for you to surrender your life to him. When you do, when you make Jesus the Lord of your life? Jesus promises you: *Never will I leave you; never will I forsake you*.

"I urge you to cry out to him now."

McMurdo Station,
Ross Ice Shelf, Antarctica

THE COAST OF ANTARCTICA ROSE slowly on the horizon. From the plane's window, it had first appeared as a swirling mist emerging from the ocean. Gradually, as the plane flew closer, Cressida saw the ice-covered land-mass that spread away into the distance.

A dark gray smudge caught her eye: McMurdo Station. Her lover lived and worked there.

"*Nothing people have built on Antarctica is beautiful, Cressie,*" Paolo had told her. "*Those of us who live on the station must look beyond the shacks and shelters, the dirt and filth of our habitations, how we've defiled what was pristine. However, if a person can look beyond the station, then Antarctica will call his name.*"

Cressida smiled. *I'm not coming to McMurdo hoping Antarctica will call my name, Paolo. I'm coming for you.*

Cressida was a registered nurse. In her handbag she had a six-month station contract with a renewal option. She and Paolo would have plenty of time together.

She couldn't wait to surprise him.

⌘⌘⌘⌘

CHAPTER 23

ON THE THIRD MONDAY IN JANUARY, standing below the rotunda of the US Capitol Building, Nora Mellyn officially took the presidential oath of office. Lucas Cathaway, the incoming Vice President, took his oath of office after Mellyn took hers.

Mellyn's husband, twenty officials, and a phalanx of masked and socially distanced reporters attended in person. We watched her inauguration live as the event was broadcast across the earth. It was then replayed *ad nauseum* for hours. The repeats that day were interrupted only by Mellyn's first presidential address at 6:00 p.m. that evening.

It was a doozy.

Zander and I viewed her speech with growing trepidation.

Seated at her desk in the Oval Office, *President* Nora Mellyn (as opposed to Acting President Nora Mellyn), gazed with confidence and resolve into the cameras focused on her.

"Good evening, my fellow Americans. I come to you tonight, not merely as your President, but as one who suffered with you through the long, dark closing year of the Jackson administration, a year marked by sickness, natural disaster, terrible tragedy, and unprecedented want. I agonized with you through an administration that cared not a whit what you suffered, a president who ignored your anguish and privations.

"Dear people of America, *I see* your suffering, and *I hear* your cries for help. I know your children are hungry and that discouragement sits at the doors of your homes. *I will* answer your pleas for relief! Please hear me: Today we begin our Great American-Allied Restoration."

I about gagged. "Oh, brother!"

Zander nodded. "Laying it on thick, isn't she? Saving us from the evil Jackson and promoting herself as America's messiah?"

Mellyn placed her right hand over her heart. "I am here this evening to tell you, *to promise you*, in the name of our Great American-Allied Restoration, that help is on the way. That's right, my friends. While we are not, by any means, on the other side of our troubles yet, *help is coming*.

"Tonight I will speak on the first three phases of our Great American-Allied Restoration. Within thirty days, I will address you again to update you on our progress.

"So, please listen closely as I outline the initial phases of our Great American-Allied Restoration and detail for you the aid that is, *as I speak*, on its way to your states, your cities, and your homes.

She stared into the cameras. "In the first phase of our Great American-Allied Restoration, we have partnered with an amazing organization to bring needed aid to America. I can announce tonight that ships bearing food supplies and the trucks to deliver those supplies are approaching our shores.

"By this time next week, the Global Community, a worldwide charitable foundation, will be offloading cargoes in the ports of the following cities: Boston, New York, Baltimore, Charleston, Miami, New Orleans, Houston, Los Angeles, Longview, Astoria, Seattle, Honolulu, and Anchorage. Massive numbers of ecologically friendly trucks, already loaded with supplies, will roll off these ships, and each truck will head toward a predetermined destination."

"Huh. The Global Community a charitable foundation? I don't like the sound of that."

"They are moving quickly, Jay. The nanomites were right when they said they couldn't stop what is coming."

We turned our attention back to the screen.

"By providing drivers *and* trucks—trucks carrying extra fuel—the Global Community will help assuage the hunger of the American people. After offloading their supplies, the trucks will return to their ships and reload. They will continue until all supplies are offloaded and distributed."

I shivered. "I don't trust her or them. I wonder what else those trucks are hauling, Zander. And where did the supplies come from? Isn't the whole world suffering shortages?"

"Huh. Wouldn't surprise me to find out that the GC has been stockpiling food for years—perhaps even diverting recent shipments in order to exacerbate the scarcities and then appear as America's savior."

We returned to Mellyn's address.

"In our second phase, I have hopeful news on the virus front. Our nation's pharmaceutical companies—in partnership with the Global Community—have labored nonstop to produce a vaccine. I can report this evening that we have had a tremendous breakthrough.

She smiled large. "We project that, within forty-five days, we will have a vaccine to distribute to our citizens."

Within the Oval Office, her audience of journalists and camera operators applauded.

"That is all I can tell you today concerning our battle to overcome this virus. However, I look forward to detailing the vaccine rollout in my next presidential address. Now . . ."

The cameras zoomed in tight.

"To introduce the third phase of our Great American-Allied Restoration, I must address an issue that is grievous to my soul."

Here Mellyn sighed, as though filled with regret.

"We are, as a nation, in the grip of an existential national crisis. It is a crisis that threatens our *purpose*, our *unity*, and our *morale*. It is a crisis we *must* resolve, for if we do nothing, no amount of relief will save this nation, and our Great American-Allied Restoration will fail."

She composed herself as if for a distasteful task. "Sadly, and I take no joy in saying this, there are those living among us . . . who do not belong to us. What do I mean by 'they do not belong to us'? Am I referring to our many immigrants? Let me be clear: No, I am not. We are a nation of immigrants! We embrace the wholly American concept of *e pluribus unum* —out of many, one!

"Out of our many races, colors, and ethnicities, *we are one!* Out of our many backgrounds, *we are one!* Out of our many sexual preferences and our many diverse definitions of family, *we are one!* Out of our many gender identities, *we are one!* Out of our many faiths, we set aside our differences so that *we might become one!*"

I moaned, "Oh, no! Zander! Where is she going with this?"

He did not answer me.

Mellyn stared into the cameras, her gaze fierce. "*Those who do not belong to us* oppose our proud American purpose, unity, and morale. Why? Because *those who do not belong to us* were born and bred in prejudice and hatred. They were taught to oppose our proud American purpose, unity, and morale from childhood, and sadly, such bias and ignorance cannot be fixed or unlearned.

"*Those who do not belong to us* espouse creeping, insidious, and destructive ideologies. They despise our unity, and they tear down this nation's morale. *Those who do not belong to us* would see our Great American-Allied Restoration fail. *Those who do not belong to us* are bent on the destruction of who we are as Americans.

"I do not speak of the great religious institutions that are relevant in today's culture, the churches, synagogues, mosques, high places, altars, and groves whose adherents practice unity and tolerance and whose practitioners cast circles, create sacred spaces, and form containers for the Divine Essence. I do not speak of them.

"Nor do I speak of those entities that have sought to unify us in our diverse faiths—early conventions such as the United Religions Initiative, and later efforts such as the Parliament of the World's Religions and the North American Interfaith Network—those entities who defy the condemnation of unloving religious bigots and bravely affirm humanity's diverse and historic spiritual backgrounds.

"No, but I *am* speaking of those who would disrupt America's Restoration by spewing division and hatred, those who put the vengeful, judgmental gods of their *obsolete texts* above their duty to their country, those who hinder our efforts to rise from despair. I speak of those who preach a religious fervor that supersedes the welfare of our children and our families—*all* of our families!"

With pinched lips and hard eyes, she declared, "Well, *no more*. I will not sit idly by as the Jackson administration did, and allow false religious bigots to deter us from our American purpose, unity, and morale. I will not allow the destructive heresies of religious zealots to impede our Great American-Allied Restoration. We must act to save America—and we must act *now*."

"Zander . . ." I could scarcely breathe.

"Yeah, I get it, Jay. She's talking about us. The church."

Mellyn sighed again. "But I cannot do this on my own, can I? I do not have the authority to act unilaterally."

She folded her hands before her. "What I *can* do, however, I *must* do. Under the legal authority granted me as President by 50 USC Chapter 34, National Emergencies, I transmitted to Congress today the one, singular action I have taken to preserve this nation. The rest? The rest is up to you.

"Via National Emergencies authority, I have empaneled a group of eminent scholars and experts from every facet of American life. As is my right, I elected to call this group our Great American-Allied Restoration Panel or GAARP. The task of this panel is a simple one: identify public communications that threaten the purpose, unity, and morale of our Great American-Allied Restoration—identify those public communications that preach counter to our American way of life.

"GAARP will pinpoint these aberrant public communications and their mouthpieces. Whether individuals or organizations, they hate America and her people so much that *they wish our nation to perish* in the ashes of our present decline."

My grip on Zander's arm tightened.

Mellyn again sighed. "But . . . what can *I* do about these destructive communications and the hate-filled, acrimonious individuals behind them? I, personally, can do nothing. Even as President, I can do nothing. You, the American people, however, can.

"I have, therefore, an urgent and heartfelt request for our nation's media, the vigilant watchdogs of liberty and democracy—I speak of all legitimate news organizations, entertainment feeds, and social media. I *ask*—I do not demand or order—I *ask* that you deny a platform to those whom GAARP identifies. Yes, our constitution guarantees freedom of speech, religion, and assembly. It does not, however, guarantee freedom of access to technology."

"Whoa," Zander muttered.

"My fellow Americans, let us together use our news, entertainment, and social media platforms to make our Great American-Allied Restoration a success. This must be the peoples' effort, America's effort, not mine. Please scrutinize the findings of the Great American-Allied Restoration Panel. When you have done so, I beg you to make your wishes known to the tech conglomerates. If *you* do so, if we act as *one*, we shall prevail over hatred and bigotry."

I flinched as she smiled into the cameras.

"Thank you. May the many gods of our people bless us and our nation. Good night."

"Oh, Zander," I moaned, "she is determined to silence the church—your church!"

"That's the idea. But I wonder . . . will the American people actually embrace the recommendations of Mellyn's so-called GAARP? Will the American people follow Mellyn's plea to bombard news, entertainment, and social media with demands that they de-platform anyone whose broadcasts disagree with America's 'purpose, unity, and morale' as Mellyn defines them?"

I didn't answer, and Zander lapsed into his own thoughts.

⌘

IT TOOK LESS THAN A WEEK following Mellyn's inauguration for most thinking people to realize that, while GAARP was officially a newly convened committee, the panel had to have been meeting since Mellyn's election win.

How else could they have compiled and published their recommendations so quickly?

To the technology conglomerates, GAARP *recommended* warning the owners of offending content. GAARP *recommended* posting corrections or directly censoring aberrant posts and sites. GAARP *recommended* levying strict penalties on those owners' accounts. And GAARP *recommended* completely de-platforming those who did not heed warnings or penalties.

Next, GAARP published their list of extreme offenders. The list included every church denomination, ministry, school, university, and nonprofit whose statement of faith declared the Bible to be the inspired, inerrant, unchanging word of God.

Then . . . GAARP asked America for input: What should be done about the division and danger these groups and people posed?

The public response was voluble, vehement, vulgar, and vicious. It was deafening.

But was it organic? Or was it orchestrated?

The tech giants, staggering under what they called "an onslaught of civic and community outcry," held detailed news briefings and presented the feedback they'd received. They insisted that "the true moral majority of America" solidly backed Mellyn's "American purpose, unity, and morale" . . . which oddly echoed the Global Community's call for "global unity against hatred and intolerance."

In short order, the tech companies claimed that public consensus in agreement with GAARP recommendations had reached an overwhelming level.

We wondered how much of the supposed "civic and community outcry" and "public consensus" had been bought and paid for.

Like tanks on the offensive, the tech monoliths rolled inexorably onward. Their talking heads spoke with grave and solemn countenances. They declared that their hands were tied and the only path open to them was acquiescence to the public's call for action.

They assiduously followed GAARP recommendations. They warned. They corrected. They censored. They penalized.

They struck with finality.

The FCC, responding to similarly ferocious cries from the American public, withdrew the broadcasting licenses of all Christian television stations—with the exception of those stations whose doctrines did not include biblical inerrancy. Christian concerts and radio disappeared as did Christian music and podcasts from the app stores and from any device connected to the internet.

Overnight, web services ceased hosting "problematic" church websites. Local UHF and VHF stations went off the air without notice or comment. A wealth of every sort of mystic, Wiccan, pagan, occult, universalist, and new-age programming replaced evangelical networks and cable feeds.

Thousands upon thousands of social media accounts vanished. Millions of voices, either cowed or canceled, winked into silence.

It wasn't long before other elements of society and commerce jumped aboard the GAARP train. Newly minted "Affidavits of Unity" emerged on the public scene. These affidavits were used to exclude those whose beliefs were seen to injure "American purpose, unity, and morale." The affidavits required individuals, organizations, and businesses to certify that they renounced such objectionable beliefs as the inerrancy of Scripture, the deity and resurrection of Christ, the virgin birth, the Trinity, and *particularly*, the principles of sin, repentance, and redemption.

Those who refused to sign such affidavits found themselves "canceled." Banks voided credit cards and accounts. Landlords annulled rental agreements. Mortgage companies withdrew loans. Employers terminated employment. Insurance companies revoked policies.

Outspoken Christians were denied access to basic public services such as driver's licenses, vehicle registration, passports, food stamps, health care, marriage licenses, birth certificates, school and university enrollment.

Any idea that questioned or challenged the values of Mellyn's Great American-Allied Restoration Plan or was seen to undermine "American purpose, unity, and morale" was publicly scorned.

Derided.

Condemned.

Pounded to dust.

President Mellyn applauded, and the public celebrated.

JANUARY 31

MORE NEWS FLOODED THE AIRWAVES: Copious coverage of Global Community ships as they disgorged truck after truck after truck. Long lines of the buff-colored convoys outbound for distant destinations. Trains loaded with GC cargo containers headed to distribution centers.

Journalists did stand-up pieces while either trains or truck convoys passed. Some truck drivers stopped for the reporters; they obligingly raised their cargo doors and walked the journalists through their truck's contents: pallets upon pallets filled with staples, packed to the roof.

Mellyn's face filled the airwaves *ad nauseam*. "My fellow Americans, let us give our thanks to the Global Community for their generosity, for the help that is on its way to every city in the nation. And while I am at it? May I tell you a little more about the Global Community? Their motto is 'Global Unity through Global Community.' Their wonderful response to our needs is truly a unifying act in line with our own Great American-Allied Restoration. In fact, the Global Community's values mirror America's purpose, unity, and morale."

"Of course, the inevitable naysayers decry the GC's gifts. They spread unfounded rumors that the GC is some secret, nefarious organization aimed at totalitarian regime. But I assure you, nothing could be further from the truth! The GC is a body of volunteers focused on shoring up faltering nations and helping all of humanity stand together. The GC stands for global equality: food for all, health care for all, jobs for all, homes for all, education for all. "The GC is humanity's hope writ large. From the bottom of my heart, I thank the GC for its commitment to *true* global unity, to peace and harmony for all through sufficiency for all—except our enemies, those naysayers who hate us and our global purpose.

"We owe the GC a great debt of gratitude."

⌘⌘⌘⌘

CHAPTER 24

A SUDDEN DEARTH OF BIBLES struck the nations of the world. The government shut down Bible publishers and burned their stock; they raided bookstores, both brick-and-mortar and online retailers, any entity that sold Bibles. By the first week of February, a hard-copy Bible was worth a fortune on the black market.

Every online Bible site disappeared. Google Play and the Apple App Store discontinued their Bible apps. If your phone was connected to the internet, your downloaded Bible app vanished.

The nanomites returned the Bible apps to the app stores and the devices that had previously downloaded them; just as quickly, they were again removed. The daily tug of war between the nanomites and the monolithic app stores continued for weeks before the nanomites, their worldwide resources already stretched to the breaking point, inserted code into the stores' programming, code that restored the Bible apps every ten minutes.

We have many irons in the fire and fish to fry, Jayda Cruz, Zander Cruz. We will keep the Bible apps on your devices, but we must not neglect the explicit activities Jesus himself gave us.

In a coordinated assault the following week, Bible-teaching churches in New Mexico lost their ability to stream live services or post recorded messages. Ten days later, not one Bible-teaching church or pastor in America could broadcast the Gospel . . . except Zander.

Zander Cruz, we are able to livestream your messages directly to any cellular or internet signal-receiving device. Moreover, we can send notifications of impending livestream messages to these same cellular or internet signal-receiving devices, giving everyone opportunity to listen to God's word as you teach it.

"Wait. To *all* cellular or internet devices? All as in *all?*"

Yes, we and our army of nanoarrays can reach all active and connected devices. We can also guarantee that no attempt to interrupt your livestream or locate the broadcast origination site will succeed.

Zander's brow creased. "Fat lot of good that last will do since I'm a known quantity here in Albuquerque. Finding our home address will take about ten seconds. We'll be fending off torches and pitchforks by nightfall."

Zander Cruz, we have evaluated the danger of continuing to broadcast your sermons, taking into account the very real likelihood of reprisals toward you and your family. We believe we have the necessary solutions.

"What might they be?"

Zander Cruz, we will alter your appearance and voice while we livestream your messages.

If you refrain from using verbal identifiers such as DCC, your name, or your city, no one will know who is broadcasting. You will be unknown to all who watch.

"Soooo, in the same way you make Jayda look different from Gemma, you'll make me look different?"

Yes, Zander Cruz. We will alter your facial structure, hair and eye color, and all aspects of your voice—tone, pitch, cadence, and accent.

I waited as Zander turned over this information in his head, studying it from all angles.

Finally, he said, "That sounds like a great plan, Nano, but we still have a few holes to plug. Specifically, I'm wondering how we manage the co-op members who don't know about you."

"Oh!" I understood immediately. "Josh and Izzie."

"Yes, working around them in particular might prove dicey. I mean, let's play this out. Say, since Josh and Izzie believe the DCC livestreams have been canceled along with all the rest of Christian church livestreams, then they would expect to gather at our house for in-person service, right?"

"Uh-huh. Josh and Izzie would expect *you* to have service here with us—that is, me, Abe, and Emilio."

"So, Nano, if Josh and Izzie were to join us for Sunday service, how would we explain my absence?"

Zander Cruz, we could prerecord your message and broadcast it at whatever time is most convenient.

Zander slowly shook his head. "Sure, that could work, Nano, except . . . it's when I'm livestreaming a message that the anointing of the Holy Spirit comes on me. I don't want to lose the power of preaching to a live audience. Besides . . ."

We had often discussed this very thing: The nanomites were not God, and we could not—*must not*—ever confuse their help with God's help or mistake their suggestions for God's guidance.

My beloved husband blinked a few times as he hesitated to articulate what he was feeling.

I thought I understood.

"If every church and preacher in our nation is barred from sharing God's word, Zander, then your messages may be the last public proclamation of the Gospel this generation hears."

He nodded. Slowly. "Other believers and other pastors will try . . ."

"And how will the Cabal—rather, our gracious friends at the Global Community—react?"

He said evenly, "They will 'disappear' those brave people of God. Torture and kill them, perhaps."

I almost choked on the fear that clutched at my heart, and at what Zander said next.

"We have the nanomites helping us, but other believers don't. And yet? Knowing the consequences, our brothers and sisters will put their lives and their families on the line. Can we do less?"

Even as I struggled with the fear bubbling within me, I answered quietly. "Our faith has to rest in Christ alone. We cannot stand in what we or the nanomites can do. Our trust must be in God Almighty and how his Holy Spirit leads us."

Quaking inside, I placed my hand on Zander's. "We knew the risks when we chose to follow Jesus, Zander. We cannot flinch or draw back from the work he has called us to do. What he has called *you* to do."

He exhaled. "I agree. Also . . . I think it is time we confided in Josh and Izzie."

I searched his face. "You want to tell them about the nanomites?"

"Yes. I feel led to bring them into our confidences and to bring Josh into a more active ministry role. I need more help, and he is ready for more responsibility. I am prepared to mentor him with the goal of making him my associate pastor."

"That sounds good, but it's a big move, Zander. Telling the two of them about the nanomites could backfire, especially with Izzie. Do you think she can handle it?"

"As you said, it's a big move . . . but it's getting harder and harder to hide things from the two of them. Like why we're both skin and bones and everyone else is only comfortably slender."

We stopped right there and prayed over Josh and Izzie, asking the Lord to lead us as we spoke to them, as Zander asked Josh to take on some of Zander's responsibilities.

When we finished praying, Zander laughed softly. "By the way? I see a wedding in the near future, don't you?"

⌘

JOSH AND IZZIE SAT SIDE BY SIDE on our couch. We sat in dining chairs opposite them, but not too close. They would likely appreciate some distance from us as they heard the impossible. Would require a bit of time and space to adjust.

We'd asked Emilio to remain in his room while we had an "adult conversation" with Josh and Izzie. Emilio was more than happy to oblige. I think his exact words were, "Adult talk? Yuck. Count me out," followed by the slam of his bedroom door.

He was *such* a tween these days!

"Josh, Iz, we invited you here this evening for a special conversation," Zander began. "A private conversation."

"Oh. Gotcha," Josh murmured. He glanced once at Izzie, then back to Zander. "I can assure you, Zander, uh, that my intentions regarding your sister are completely honorable."

I snickered inside as Izzie's hand found its way into Josh's hand and she gazed with adorable sweetness at him. They had misconstrued Zander's opening gambit, the preface to our telling them about the nanomites.

Zander coughed into his hand as he realized where Josh had "gone." He altered course.

"All right, then, Josh. You have the floor. I'd like to hear more about your intentions toward my sister."

"Well, I, that is *we*, feel the Lord leading us to explore, to think about the hypothetical potential, the *option* of taking our relationship . . . to the next level; perhaps, in the future, moving in a new direction, with the objective of someday determining what we might do . . .

So much gobbledygook and procrastination! Josh had laid out a mire, a verbal bog of quicksand, and it was sucking him down.

Izzie withdrew her hand from Josh's. The look she bent on Josh was no longer pleased. Or sweet.

Zander's arched brows and cool reply told me he wasn't pleased, either. "Josh, you are either considering marriage with Izzie or you are playing around. Which is it? The Lord doesn't want us to 'explore the *option* of taking a relationship to the next level,' '*perhaps*, in the future, moving in a new direction, with the objective of *someday* determining what we might do,' or some equally vague and far-distant objective.

"If a couple is dating exclusively, the Lord would have them prayerfully consider *marriage*, bring that consideration to him and, if he grants his approval, enter into a formal engagement. If you, as a couple, are considering marriage, well and good. But to frame your relationship as anything other than that serious objective is playing with what God holds sacred. You and Izzie should enter into no intimate form of conversation, attachment, or intention that leads elsewhere."

Izzie nodded her agreement and narrowed her eyes at Josh.

Poor Josh! I nearly felt sorry for him.

He exhaled. Sat up straight. Rallied. Got himself sorted and galvanized.

"Pastor Zander, you are absolutely right. My honorable intention is to marry Izzie—if we are confident that it is the Lord's will—and if she will have me now that I've botched this conversation."

Zander smiled. "That's better, Josh. Give the question a couple of weeks of dedicated prayer, both together and singly. During that period, honestly evaluate these points: Are you a better believer and disciple of Christ with

Izzie's companionship? Or is the opposite true? Is Izzie in agreement with the Lord's calling on your life? Will she support you in what he has called you to do? Or will she hold you back? Will she try to 'adjust' your vision or change your mind?"

He turned to Izzie. "Same thing for you, Sis. Pray honestly over the same points. Will Josh enhance and strengthen the life God has called you to live? The service he has called you to give? Will God's calling on your life complement the calling on Josh's life? Or are you pondering how you can change him?

"And for both of you? Evaluate this: Does spending time with your potential spouse lead you to a deeper walk with the Lord?"

"It absolutely does, Pastor Zander," Josh said in all seriousness. "Izzie encourages me to pray more, study God's word more, and serve him more diligently. I'm a better disciple with her encouragement."

Zander sat back. "That's great news, Josh. And on that note, I expect to meet with you two again no more than four weeks from today for an update. Okay?"

"Yes, sir," Josh replied.

"Yes, Zander," Izzie answered.

"Good. Now let's talk about why we really called you to meet with us."

⌘

THIRTY MINUTES INTO IT, OUR "EXPLAINING about the nanomites" hadn't fared nearly as well as Zander's exhortation on pursuing marriage. Josh kept shaking his head no, and Izzie's concern for our mental health was palpable. She was practically vibrating on our couch.

"Zander," I said in the warehouse, "it took several demonstrations to convince President Jackson. To get him past his anxiety that I was there to assassinate him."

In front of Josh and Izzie's eyes—and with ample warning—Zander and I disappeared . . . and that didn't generate a warm and fuzzy response, either.

Izzie jumped to her feet, shrieking. Practically crawled up Josh's back— while yanking him toward the door. Or the window. Whichever would get them out of our house soonest. Sort of reminded me of Aunt Lucy's cat Jake and his first encounter with me as an invisible woman:

I finished my dinner preparations and sat down at the table to enjoy the savory chicken and vegetables. I relished each bite—I don't think anything had tasted so good in a long time.

I wasn't prepared when Jake jumped into my lap. He must have smelled the warm chicken on the table—however, he had not seen me in the chair.

I uttered a surprised shriek and jumped.

Jake jumped higher.

Have you watched a cat lose its mind?

Jake scrabbled and ran in six directions at once. Chicken stir-fry flew everywhere. When Jake finally gained traction, it was on me. He clawed his way up my front side and launched himself from the top of my head.

Aaand back to our little circus sideshow.

While Izzie tried to climb Josh like a tree, Josh attempted to pull her away from us—or where he'd last seen us—while backing toward our front door.

We reappeared. I sighed.

"This isn't going well, Zander."

"Thanks, Captain Obvious."

Josh and Izzie (mutually "glommed" onto each other) stared.

A huge guffaw interrupted our attempt to convince Josh and Izzie of the nanomites' existence.

"Funniest thing I ever seed," Emilio hooted, pointing at Josh and Izzie.

They looked from Emilio to us. Back to Emilio.

"What did you see?" Izzie demanded.

He shrugged. "I heard Mama and Dad try to tell you 'bout the nano-mites. Then I seed—*saw*—Mama and Dad go invisible on you. Saw you flippin' out. Pretty funny."

Izzie's face turned red. "You know about these-these nano-thingies? You believe *them?*"

She pointed at us.

"I knowed—*knew*—'bout the nanomites before Dad did."

"What? How's that possible?" The more demanding Izzie became, the redder her face.

"'Cuz I was first to know about the nanomites—'cept for Gemma, of course. How they got in her and—"

"*Gemma?* What does she have to do with anything?"

Josh was confused. "Who's Gemma?"

I was dismayed.

"Oh, *bleep*! Um, *oops?*" Emilio slid his eyes toward me. "Sorry, Mama."

I wondered which part he was sorry for—the curse word or referencing his acquaintance with a dead woman.

Zander leaned toward me and whispered, "In for a penny . . ."

"Are you sure?"

"Won't mean anything to Josh, but it will convince Izzie."

I chewed my bottom lip a moment. "Izzie . . . you remember the woman who lived in the house next door, right?" I gestured in the direction of our garage and garden.

"What house next door?" Josh asked, frowning. "That's an empty lot."

"It wasn't always," I said. "You remember her, Iz? Remember when she went with you and Zander and young adults from the church to help put on a barbecue for the homeless in a park? You and she served the potato salad and baked beans."

"Hey! I was at that barbecue," Josh interjected, pointing at me. "I don't remember seeing you there."

Izzie ignored Josh and eyed me with suspicion. "Are you talking about Gemma? How do *you* know her? You didn't join the young adult group until after . . ."

"After what?" Josh asked, his confusion thicker now than when Zander and I disappeared on him.

I said quietly, "Another house used to be next door, between us and Belicia, Josh, and a young woman named Gemma Keyes lived there. Two years ago, someone strapped an explosive vest to themselves and blew up that house."

"Wait. That sounds sorta familiar."

"Sure. It was big news for a time. The bomber blew up herself and Gemma's sister."

And Jake. Don't forget Jake.

Izzie was breathing heavily. "That bomb killed Gemma too," she whispered.

"No, Izzie. It didn't."

The nanomites gently removed their ranks from my features. Revealed the woman I'd once been. The woman neither Zander nor Emilio had seen . . . in a very long time.

I wondered what I looked like now.

"Hello, Izzie."

For several seconds, nothing happened. Then . . .

Hmm.

See, I had always believed "a dead faint" to be the dramatic ploy of novels, a literary stratagem common to Victorian and Edwardian fiction. *Until.* I believed that *until* Izzie made a choking, gasping sound, until she wobbled and her eyes rolled back in her head.

Until she pitched over.

To be fair, Josh tried to catch her. He failed in epic fashion, and Izzie hit the floor with the thump of a ripe melon.

⌘

"YOU GUYS ARE *WEIRDER* THAN WEIRD," Josh shouted—having shouted one thing or another ten times already. "Gamble warns us we'll end up in trouble with the FBI if we ask you questions! Then, out of the blue, you say you have some big secret to share with us. Now look what you did to my—to my Izzie!"

Izzie was lying on our floor. Out cold.

"She fainted, Josh," I said quietly. "She thinks I'm dead. It gave her a shock. She'll be fine."

Josh's fury turned on me. "You? I don't even know who you are, lady, or how you did that switcheroo with Jayda, but you'd better bring her back right now! You're completely freaking me out!"

"Nano, put me back together, please."

He saw my features morphing, saw Gemma disappear and Jayda reappear. He stepped over Izzie and ran for the door. Didn't make it. Bent over and puked on our carpet.

"Oh, dear . . ."

Emilio started to gag.

"Don't you dare," I warned him. "Go outside, okay? Get some fresh air."

"Yeah. That smell—" He gagged again.

"Move it, Emilio! Go."

I realized then how quiet Zander had gone and perceived the shock etched on his face.

My poor husband!

The eyes he turned on me were heartbroken. I hadn't thought . . . hadn't considered how showing him Gemma would affect him.

How awful to be in love with a wife who looked like two very different women, one who had died but . . . was a woman he still loved.

"Zander? Sweetie?"

"I gotta . . . I gotta get some fresh air too."

⌘⌘⌘⌘

CHAPTER 25

WE SET UP FOR ZANDER TO again stream his Sunday message from our bedroom—following a few creative adjustments. Gamble helped Zander move his desk out from our bedroom wall. They positioned it facing away from the corner with Zander sitting behind it. I laid a table cloth over the desk and added a fake potted plant Abe provided. Lastly, we hung a curtain of dark fabric behind the desk as a backdrop.

In short, we changed the background and props the cameras would capture. We needed to ensure that nothing within the video frame would hint at Zander's identity or location while his message streamed . . . or later, when the Cabal tasked its IT gurus with dissecting the posted video.

Personally, I didn't think our efforts were all that necessary. If the nanomites would amend Zander's voice and appearance during the broadcast, I was convinced they could handle the setting.

In any event, we were ready for Zander's "proxy persona" to make his global debut. Abe, Emilio, and I planned to watch Zander's message from our living room as we usually did on Sunday mornings.

Izzie and Josh, however, declined to join us. They hadn't accepted our "story" and were genuinely disgusted with our assertions. Furthermore, they didn't believe Zander would be able to broadcast at his regular time— so what was the point of them pretending otherwise? As Josh put it, no Christian pastor in the world had the ability to broadcast. What made Zander think he was any different?

We made a single, feeble attempt to explain to them *how* the nanomites might do it—although we weren't exactly clear on the "how" part yet.

Josh and Izzie shot us down. Stalked away from us shaking their heads.

In their shoes, I wouldn't have believed us either.

"Did we miss God, Zander?" I'd asked him the night before, after Josh and Izzie left our house in high umbrage. "Should we have not told them?"

Zander had sighed and shaken his head. "Maybe, but I thought we had the mind of the Spirit at the time. I suppose we'll have to wait and see what pans out. It *was* a lot to dump on them."

At least—because they had promised ahead of time to protect our secrets—they said they would keep our "explanations" to themselves. In other words, they wouldn't tell anyone we'd "gone 'round the bend," but they did withdraw from us . . . and that hurt.

Instead of spending Sunday morning with us, they opted to have Bible study together in Belicia's living room—far away from us crazies. Josh said our weirdness factor was too much to take in. He would protect Izzie from further shocks.

Belicia didn't mind hosting their little Bible study, but she also didn't understand their thinly veiled anger toward us. She was concerned about them and concerned about us.

So was I. It would take time for Josh and Izzie to adjust—much more time than we'd mistakenly believed. Time to understand the many difficulties we'd been through. Time to get over us scaring them. More time for Izzie to forgive us for lying about Gemma's death. To accept me as Gemma-*cum*-Jayda.

What a mess.

At 9:50, a notification popped up on my iPad.

**A Bible teaching message
will livestream in ten minutes
<u>CLICK HERE</u> to join**

I touched the link to the livestream. The interface that opened looked exactly like YouTube. It *wasn't* YouTube, of course. The nanomites were providing a familiar look and feel to the viewers who chose to join the broadcast. I imagined, too, that the Cabal's IT peeps would shortly be in full-on "track-them-down-and-end-them" mode. Yet, according to the nanomites, no matter what the Cabal's IT geniuses tried? They wouldn't be able to locate the source of Zander's message or disrupt it.

As the time to broadcast counted down, the man who appeared on screen was *not* Zander. I'd never before laid eyes on the blond, blue-eyed Adonis sitting behind Abe's fake potted plant.

Speaking of potted plants, *oof!* Emilio *planted* his elbow in my ribs.

Jabbed his finger at the screen. "Mama! Look, Mama! Look at the numbers!"

"Oh! Er, *wow*."

More than a million devices had connected to the nanomites' signal, and the numbers on the counter were spinning faster than a Hanukkah dreidel.

"Nano, how will all these people understand Zander? Surely they don't all speak or understand English."

Jayda Cruz, we detect the preferred language associated with every device that connects to the livestream and will provide captions in that language. At present, we have identified and will translate Zander's message into forty-three distinct languages.

"Holy moley . . ."

My phone lit up. I shook the astonishment from my head and accepted a video call with Izzie and Josh.

Izzie demanded, "Did you get the same text we got? About a Bible teaching streaming live? Some strange guy able to broadcast? How is he doing it? Are you watching?"

Josh, with awe in his voice, added, "Yeah, who is this guy? Millions are linking in. *Millions!* How's this possible?"

I kept my replies simple. "Uh-huh. Yup, we got that text. Yes, we're watching. Er, yes, we see the numbers. Okay, good talk. Later, gator."

When I hung up, the livestream hadn't started yet, so I let my mind wander. Tried to imagine the consternation ensuing within YouTube's corporate ranks and the angry, frantic calls from the Mellyn administration demanding that YouTube *stop* the livestream—until someone figured out that YouTube was *not*, in fact, hosting a Bible teaching. And I wanted, in the worst way, to be the proverbial fly on the wall when the tech guys within the Global Conspiracy—er, *Community*—started pulling their hair out by the handfuls.

"Um, Nano, would you please—"

Jayda Cruz, the nanoarrays we've planted within the Global Community are recording their responses to the Blond Preacher's message— and his unfathomable ability to livestream to a worldwide audience even though no one is able to detect the origination of his livestream signal. We will upload the video files of their reactions to the warehouse after the Blond Preacher completes his sermon.

"Wait—how did you know that's what I was going to ask?"
We know you, Jayda Cruz.
I laughed softly to myself, drawing a squint of concern from Emilio.
"Inside joke," I assured him.
We settled back to watch an unknown man deliver Zander's sermon . . . until the fair-haired stranger looked into the camera in a familiar way.
*Ah, there you are! I **see you**, my love.*
"Welcome to a Sunday message from Holy Scripture. I bid you a blessed Sunday—in whatever nation and time zone you may live—as you join millions of other hungry hearts around the world in worshipping Jesus and receiving his word.

"Perhaps you are asking how it is possible for me to broadcast when every pastor on the planet has been denied access to social media and streaming platforms. You may be wondering, —despite the tyrannical steps those nations guided by the Global Community have taken to silence the Gospel—how it is that we, *the people of God*, are able to meet together, right now, *in this very moment.*

"I will only say that 2 Timothy 2:9 tells us *God's word is not chained.*

"And so, in keeping with his word, the Lord of the Universe—who sent his only Son into the world to save sinners such as myself—has made a way where there was no way. This same God said something quite similar in Isaiah 43, verses 10-13.

> *"You are my witnesses,"* declares the Lord,
> *"and my servant whom I have chosen,*
> *so that you may know and believe me*
> *and understand that I am he.*
> ***Before me no god was formed,***
> ***nor will there be one after me.***
> ***I, even I, am the Lord,***
> ***and apart from me there is no savior.***
> *I have revealed and saved and proclaimed—*
> *I, and not some foreign god among you.*
> *You are my witnesses,"* declares the Lord,
> *"that I am God. Yes, and from ancient days I am he.*
> *No one can deliver out of my hand.*
> *When I act, who can reverse it?"*

"You! You listening and watching at this very moment—you are witnesses to the Lord's proclamation: *So that you may know and believe me and understand that **I am he**. Before me no god was formed, nor will there be one after me. **I, even I, am the Lord**, and apart from me there is no savior.*

"You are also witness to this unprecedented era. At no time in recorded history has the Word of God been deliberately and systematically silenced across the globe—and yet, by God's grace, here I am, declaring that *the Lord, **he is God**,* and *no one* can deliver out of his hand! When he acts, who can reverse it?"

Zander leaned into the camera. "To the leadership of the Global Community, the Lord—not I, but the Lord—says to you, *When I act, who can reverse it?* Speaking to the Global Community, I assure you: You may flog your IT techs until they bleed, and they may work their fingers to the bone in order to silence God's word, but they will never locate or end this signal.

"Why? Because the word of the Lord God *is alive* and cannot be chained. The Good News of Jesus Christ cannot be snuffed out or silenced. You who fight against the Lord God Almighty? Know this: *You. Will. Lose.*"

Zander let a full minute pass while he stared impassively at the cameras, allowing his proclamations time to sink in.

He inhaled and exhaled. Spoke softly. "Dear people of God, since we are at this unprecedented point in history, we must make this determination:

The fields are ripe, and *we* are the workers. My message this morning is simple—go forth and bear fruit. It is time to bring in the harvest."

Zander opened his Bible. "You have heard this before, yes? However, I suggest that the church suffers from a misunderstanding when it comes to bearing fruit—a misunderstanding that hinders our fruitfulness. This morning we will look into God's word to remove that confusion.

"First, let's read Jesus' injunction to us in John 15. However, as we're not doing an exhaustive study of this chapter, I will read only the verses that mention bearing fruit, verses 1, 2, 5, 8, and 16. Remember, this is Jesus speaking.

"Verses 1-2.

> *"I am the true vine, and my Father is the gardener.*
> *He cuts off every branch in me that bears no fruit,*
> *while every branch that does bear fruit*
> *he prunes so that it will be even more fruitful.*

"Verse 5.

> *"I am the vine; you are the branches.*
> *If you remain in me and I in you,*
> *you will bear much fruit;*
> *apart from me you can do nothing.*

"Verse 8.

> *"This is to my Father's glory, that you bear much fruit,*
> *showing yourselves to be my disciples.*

"Verse 16.

> *"You did not choose me, but I chose you*
> *and appointed you so that you might go and bear fruit*
> *—fruit that will last—*
> *and so that whatever you ask in my name*
> *the Father will give you."*

Emilio was bored. He fidgeted. Picked at a flaw in his jeans.

Zander glanced up. "In a nutshell, Jesus tells each of us to bear fruit, much fruit, and fruit that will last. Jesus chose us *for* this purpose; he appointed us *to* this purpose. Each of us is to bear fruit, much fruit, and fruit that endures.

"Whatever," Emilio mumbled.

"Next, I want to teach on the biblical principle of reproduction. To begin, let's read Genesis 1, verses 11, 12, 21, and 24.

"Verses 11 and 12.

"Then God said, 'Let the land produce vegetation:
seed-bearing plants and trees on the land
that bear fruit with seed in it,
according to their various kinds.'
And it was so.
The land produced vegetation:
plants bearing seed according to their kinds and
*trees bearing fruit with seed in it **according to their kinds**.*
And God saw that it was good.

"Verse 21.

"So God created the great creatures of the sea
and every living thing with which
the water teems and that moves about in it,
according to their kinds,
*and every winged bird **according to its kind**.*
And God saw that it was good.

"Verse 24.

"And God said,
'Let the land produce living creatures
according to their kinds:
the livestock, the creatures that move
along the ground, and the wild animals,
each according to its kind.'
And it was so.

"I would like us to note the phrase, *according to its kind* or *according to their kinds*. God commanded his creation to reproduce *according to their kinds*. You don't see whales giving birth to birds, nor do you see apple trees producing wheat. Each part of God's creation that reproduces, always reproduces *according to its kind*.

"Now, let's read verses 27 and 28, concerning us, that is, humankind.

So God created mankind in his own image,
in the image of God he created them;
male and female he created them.
God blessed them and said to them, 'Be fruitful
and increase in number; fill the earth and subdue it.'

"Please answer this question: When a woman gives birth, do we expect a litter of puppies? When a woman gives birth, do we expect a kangaroo?"

Finally, Zander had Emilio's attention, and his examples really tickled Emilio's funny bone. Our boy guffawed and shouted, "No!"

I grinned with him.

Zander continued. "When a woman gives birth, what do we expect?"

"Duh! A *baby*," Emilio told Zander's proxy.

We almost missed Zander's point. "When a woman gives birth, do we ever expect anything *but* another human being, created in God's image and likeness?"

Emilio frowned. "'Course not."

"Of course not," Zander echoed Emilio. "This is the common misunderstanding that I wish to address today. When we, as believers, talk about bearing fruit for God, we often reference Galatians 5:22-23.

> *"But the fruit of the Spirit is*
> *love, joy, peace, forbearance, kindness, goodness,*
> *faithfulness, gentleness and self-control.*
> *Against such things there is no law."*

Zander smiled. "*But the fruit of the Spirit is . . .* Wait. Whose fruit is it? Doesn't this say these behaviors are the Holy Spirit's fruit?"

I gaped. "Ohhh . . ."

"This passage tells us that the Holy Spirit reproduces *himself* in us as love, joy, peace, patience, kindness, goodness, faithfulness, gentleness, and self-control. The Spirit's fruit is the work he does in our hearts, conforming us to the image of Christ. His fruit is how we reflect Christ in our lives.

"Just to make this point clear, *his* fruit is not *our* fruit. This is *his* fruit—according to *his* kind—manifested in our lives. And if it is *his* fruit, then this is not *our* fruit.

"Granted, unless the Holy Spirit works his nature into our hearts and lives, we're not going to bear much fruit, are we? On our own, we're about as effective as trying to catch flies with vinegar water."

Emilio grimaced. "*Ick*. Vinegar?"

"My point is this," Zander said. "If, physically, we produce physical children, then spiritually, we produce spiritual children. When we produce physical fruit, we have babies—babies just like us. After we are born again, we produce spiritual fruit—born-again people like us—saved, redeemed, sanctified, made holy by the blood of Jesus.

"Jesus told each of us to bear fruit that endures. Well, the spiritual fruit we bear *is the only fruit on the face of the earth that will endure*. The only thing we take with us when we die are the souls we've led to Christ.

"And the crux of this message is this: The time is short. We cannot think that a pastor preaching the Gospel in church is our fruit—no; that's *his* fruit. We cannot count on *others* to preach the Gospel publicly—that would be *their* fruit, not ours. And we cannot think that sending money to missions organizations lets us off the hook. *You* must tell *your* world. *I* must tell *my* world. And *we* must do it *now*.

"So, tell your neighbors about Jesus—tell them today. Tell your co-workers they need the Savior. Tell your family! Tell your community! Tell the stranger on the bus, the woman checking your groceries, the doctor doing your physical, the teller at your bank, and your son's teacher, *but tell them!*"

Zander hesitated. He paused as if rethinking his words or praying. When he looked up, he'd traversed some hurdle.

He'd taken up his cross.

"Dear people, I'm calling you to lead the charge—and I don't mean start new churches, hold meetings where we sit and listen, or merely discuss evangelism. No, I'm calling men and women to lead others, by example, in saving souls one by one. *Get out there and do it now.*

"Yes, we will be pruned, brothers and sisters. According to Jesus, we will be pruned if we bear fruit or *cut off* if we don't. Time is short, and freedom is gone. We *will* be persecuted.

"But the specter of persecution reminds me of a chapter in Jeremiah. It is only five verses long, but it speaks to us in this time, and the end of this age.

"In Jeremiah 45, we find Baruch, the man who faithfully served as Jeremiah's scribe. From the Assyrian siege of Jerusalem, through the Babylonian siege of Jerusalem, up to that city's destruction, Baruch took down Jeremiah's words.

"But it wasn't easy. The people of Jerusalem starved under those sieges. They faced death and hardship daily. And we read in verse 3 that Baruch became discouraged. Listen to what he said in his discouragement.

> *"I am overwhelmed with trouble!*
> *Haven't I had enough pain already?*
> *And now the Lord has added more!*
> *I am worn out from sighing*
> *and can find no rest.*

"Does Baruch's lament sound familiar? It does to me. The people in our neighborhood are very weary. Worn down and overwhelmed. And yet . . . every believer still has a job, and God calls each of us not to give up, but to finish the work he has given us.

"So what was the Lord's reply to Baruch, to his lament? The Lord gave him a personal promise spoken by Jeremiah's lips.

> *"Baruch, this is what the Lord says . . .*
> *'Are you seeking great things for yourself? Don't do it!*

I will bring great disaster upon all these people;
*but I will give you your life **as a reward wherever you go.***
I, the Lord, have spoken!'

"This promise may have been given to Baruch, but we can appropriate it for ourselves as well. God's word declares destruction for those people and nations who defy him. Judgment and destruction are coming, and they are coming soon—and yes, Global Community, I am speaking to you. Are you listening?

"But we, God's people, also have the promises Jesus proclaimed concerning those who are faithful to the Lord, even to the end of our lives and thereafter.

"'I am the resurrection and the life.
Anyone who believes in me will live, even after dying.
Everyone who lives in me and believes in me
will never ever die.'

"Stand firm, therefore, people of God! Take hold of Hebrews 10:32-35, and *remember . . . when you endured in a great conflict full of suffering.*

"Sometimes you were publicly
exposed to insult and persecution;
at other times you stood side by side
with those who were so treated.
You suffered along with those in prison
and joyfully accepted the confiscation of your property,
because you knew that you yourselves
had better and lasting possessions.
So do not throw away your confidence;
it will be richly rewarded.

"Let us press on together. Let us finish our race, beloved of the Lord. Let us fulfill Jesus' command to bear fruit, much fruit, and fruit that remains."

Zander, his face radiant despite his weariness, smiled again. "I look forward to addressing you again. You will receive a text message several minutes before I stream my next Bible teaching, so please watch your devices. The Lord bless you."

⌘

ZANDER'S MESSAGE HAD NO SOONER ended than my phone buzzed another incoming video call. Josh and Izzie glared at me from my phone's screen. They were outside in Belicia's backyard, shivering in the cold. Or were they shivering for some other reason?

I projected disinterest. "Oh. Hey, Josh. Hey, Izzie."

Josh dove straight in. "Jayda, we watched that Bible teaching. Don't know how he did it, but that guy? He preaches like Zander."

I shrugged. "Didn't notice."

"Are you kidding me? He's on fire—the same way Zander is. He's teaching hard-hitting biblical truth—*just* like Zander. Even his gestures—like Zander. But he's not Zander."

"Huh. You don't say."

Emilio snickered into his hand; I pinched his leg. He giggled; my lips twitched.

Josh frowned at me from my phone. "Jayda, was that guy Zander? I mean, he couldn't be . . . could he?"

I yawned. "Goodness! Bonnie Lu kept me up half the night."

Izzie hissed, "Jayda! Was that *my brother?*"

"Wow, you two sound kinda . . . *weird.* What do you think, Emilio? They sound weird to you?"

"Yeah, *weirder than weird,*" Emilio growled. He'd caught on to my ploy. Was fully aiding and abetting it.

Josh and Izzie looked at each other. Izzie lowered her phone. They stage-whispered back and forth. Izzie raised her phone so we saw them again.

"We're coming over."

I stared impassively at them. "Not really a good time, guys. Wouldn't want either of you to, you know . . . pass out. Maybe puke."

They hung up on me.

Zander wandered out of our bedroom. He had exhausted himself praying, preparing, and giving his all to deliver his message. He needed fuel.

I hugged him. Long and hard. "I'll fix you a little something to eat, Babe."

"That'd be great."

I whispered in his ear, "And Josh and Izzie are on their way over."

He sighed. "Did they watch?"

"Yup. They may have recognized your signature delivery style, and if they did, might not others?"

"Huh. Nano? Can you edit the video? Er, change up my delivery style?"

We can moderate it, Zander Cruz. When we complete the alterations, we'll replace the posted video.

"Thanks, Nano." Zander took Bonnie from me. Nuzzled her neck. Made her giggle.

"So . . . Josh and Iz?"

"Yeah."

The front doorbell rang.

"That's them."

He sighed again. "Super."

⌘

OUR MEETING WITH JOSH AND IZZIE wasn't as difficult as we thought it would be. While Zander inhaled a single scrambled egg and a slice of toast, they spoke. We listened.

"Izzie and I have been thinking and talking. A lot. And we watched that Bible teaching—awesome, by the way. Still not sure how you did that. I mean, millions and millions of viewers! So, we, uh, we apologize for our behavior. You know, when you told us."

"Told you what?" I asked. Maybe I was still miffed. A little hurt.

"About Dr. Bickel and those nanobots? But you used a different word."

"Nanomites."

"Yeah. Nanomites. Is what you told us . . . real? Truly?"

They weren't sure. They were open to it now but needed further proof.

In front of their eyes, Zander morphed into the blond, blue-eyed hunk. Josh was so rattled, he fell off his chair. Izzie looked away and kept swallowing.

I hoped we weren't in for another puke session.

Emilio, who was privy to our conversation, laughed himself silly.

"Told ya! Told ya!" he cackled, over and over, until I silently pleaded with Zander to correct him. Zander's appearance returned to normal, and he placed a restraining hand on Emilio's shoulder.

"That's enough, Son."

Izzie tried to look me in the eye, and failed. "Are you really . . . really Gemma? Honest? She's not, I mean, you're not . . . dead?"

I didn't ask the nanomites to uncover me. The last reveal had been too hard on Zander.

"Yes, I'm Gemma. When General Cushing blew up my house, the nanomites saved us, Zander and me."

"But they didn't save Cushing."

"Not Cushing. Not my sister." *Not Jake.* "But . . . Izzie, Genie called on Jesus before she died. She begged him to save her."

I saw it all again. Fresh. Real. Both terrible and glorious. Genie, her eyes locked on Zander, shrieking, "JESUS, I CHOOSE YOU! I CHOOSE YOU! I CHOOSE JE—"

I shuddered. Tears stung my eyes.

Izzie's hand touched mine. "I am so sorry." Her face twisted. "I don't know what to call you. *You were my friend!*"

"You can only call her Jayda," Zander said quietly. "Never anything else. Okay? In fact, try to forget Gemma. Continue to think of her as dead. Can you do that?"

Think of her as dead. Yes.

Izzie nodded. "Yeah. Okay."

I squeezed Izzie's hand back. "Why do you think we're fast friends today, Iz? I already loved you that first evening, when I joined the young adult Bible study."

Josh, who had never met Gemma, flicked his gaze from me to Zander.

"Uh, you won't be doing that switcheroo thing often, will you? Kinda freaky."

"Nope," Zander smiled. "Only when we want to mess with your head."

Emilio cracked up, and this time we laughed with him.

⌘

THE REMAINDER OF SUNDAY truly held "the rest" of a Sabbath. We napped. We sang songs and read books to Bonnie Lu. We played games with Emilio and Abe. Abe served a delicious late lunch that was about half what Zander and I needed calorie-wise. He and I drank water, tea, and whatever else we could lay hands on to drown our hunger pangs.

Around six, I fixed dinner—again, not nearly enough. The only way our bodies' increased metabolism compensated—other than thinning us down further—was to demand more sleep. Used to be, we could get by on three to five hours of sleep, but no more. Not on severely reduced rations.

That's what made getting up to feed and change Bonnie in the night arduous. It's why we were already skimming off the top of our emergency rations. What we allowed ourselves to take still wasn't enough, but we determined it would have to do.

It's why that evening we decided to send Emilio to bed early—so we could turn in early. But that's not what happened.

Nora Mellyn "happened."

⌘⌘⌘⌘

CHAPTER 26

JAYDA CRUZ, ZANDER CRUZ, Nora Mellyn is about to address the nation.

"Oh, bother," I moaned. "It's what? Eleven o'clock in DC? Why now? I'm *so* tired."

"Think we should skip it?" Zander asked. "Catch the replay in the morning?"

"No," I grumbled. "We probably need to watch it live."

The seal of the President of the United States filled the screen for five minutes before the cameras switched over to Nora Mellyn seated at her desk in the Oval Office, her hands folded demurely before her.

"Good evening, my fellow Americans. Earlier today, on what should have been a day of relaxation and fun, many of you were subjected to a tirade of despicable, hate-filled rhetoric. In a crime resembling rape, an individual presuming to deliver a 'Bible teaching' *forced himself* upon not just Americans but the peoples of the entire world.

"We cannot yet say how he usurped the airwaves or from where he spoke, but we can categorically state that this man's address contradicts every value and principle of our American purpose, unity, and morale. His premise that his 'god' is the only god? False. A blatant lie. His teaching that humanity needs a savior? Another lie. *We* choose our paths! His assertion that humanity is rife with sin, that his acolytes must 'tell everyone'? Hate speech, pure and simple.

"The only sin I see belongs to those extremists who pile guilt upon the heads of our most vulnerable citizens—those individuals brave enough to explore multiple paths of sexuality and sexual identity, those valiant enough to live their authentic lives before the world. Those who worship *as they choose*—not as these *terrorists* insist they must.

"I announce this evening that I have signed an executive order that lists as federal hate crimes those doctrines that assert one god above all others and one text above all others. The proponents of these false doctrines are hereby designated as criminals under this order. Tomorrow I will send my order to Congress, asking them to craft federal law to enforce this order.

"Furthermore, we, the American people, must send our own message back to this man, this loathsome purveyor of fear, shame, and guilt, and all who follow him. We must state, categorically, that hatred is unacceptable and the preaching of so-called sin is reprehensible. In no uncertain terms, with boots on the ground, *we must demonstrate* that these extremist positions are no longer welcome in our society, that whatever disrupts our peaceful, loving unity will *not* be tolerated.

"I call upon the American people—upon all people within the sound of my voice: Send your answer to this man and his followers.

"Send it *loud* and send it *strong*."

Her blazing eyes drilled into the cameras. "I ask you to send your reply *tomorrow*. Let it ring throughout the earth."

The broadcast ended, but Zander and I remained seated staring dumbly at the screen.

⌘

NORA MELLYN GAVE NO INSTRUCTIONS in her address. Nevertheless, a consensus of action "emerged," and what could only be explained as a preplanned response percolated across America and "caught fire" in Canada. Other nations of the earth, to a lesser degree, responded in similar fashion.

Three thousand churches and synagogues burned the following afternoon and into the night. Out of twenty attempts, seventeen Albuquerque churches perished. DCC's building was among them.

The conflagrations were heavily covered by the media and celebrated with wild parties in the streets—parties that started as songfests and handholding circles around bonfires. Parties that devolved into drunkenness, brawls, and lewdness.

Desperate calls went out to 911, pleas to respond to the fires, but no fire stations responded except to keep the infernos from spreading to the properties of "decent" people and "peace-loving" businesses.

Roofs and walls collapsing in fiery eruptions elicited cheers from onlookers. Smoldering ruins became the most popular backdrops for selfies smeared across social media. Trending hashtags declared #GlobalUnity and #BurnAll Hatred.

No one noted the glaring duplicity, the stark, oxymoronic hypocrisy of "peace-loving" protestors intent on burning down churches.

Zander, Gamble, and Josh went to watch DCC's brick edifice crumble under the intense heat of the conflagration. Zander, with a fierceness I hadn't often seen, flat-out refused Izzie's request to accompany them.

I guess when I saw his reaction I knew better than to insist on going. If Zander was that afraid for his sister, I was not going to add to his worry.

Also, I suppose he was right.

At one point while they watched the old church burn, someone recognized Zander as DCC's pastor. Only Gamble's FBI badge and his drawn weapon saved Zander from being pulled from the vehicle.

Sure, Zander would have used the nanomites had he been forced to, but I'm glad he didn't. At this point, the fewer episodes drawing attention to us, the safer our family.

⌘

OVER THE FOLLOWING DAYS, ADDING to our mounting concerns, morale in the cul-de-sac plummeted. Cooperation declined, and out-and-out division flourished—most of it emanating from Bill.

Bill (not Viola) muttered unflattering deprecations and half-threats toward Zander. We were forced to consider whether or not he would turn on us if an opportunity presented itself. We had to think about what we would do if he did.

Belicia, easily swayed, sank into confusion, then depression. Emilio became fearful for our family's safety.

"It's my fault," Zander admitted when we called an informal meeting in Gamble and Janice's living room—everyone except Bill, Viola, and Belicia. "I take responsibility. Scripture warns us not to be unequally yoked with unbelievers. Values matter, and our Christian values cross swords with Bill's. As much as he despises big government, given the right circumstances, he would side with Mellyn's street goons over us."

"You didn't get to choose who lives in the cul-de-sac," Janice murmured. "You had to work with who was available."

"I suppose."

Abe huffed. Wagged his finger at my husband. "See here, *Pastor* Zander. You have been called to preach the truth. You've been commissioned by God himself and you have been given a worldwide platform—the only platform left! Stop feeling condemned and sorry for yourself. *Get after your ministry.*"

The rest of us studied our hands, the walls, the floor, looking anywhere but at Zander—or his reaction. I literally covered my eyes with my hands.

Then Abe snorted. "*Gird up now thy loins like a man*, Son. Job 38:3."

What? I chanced a peek between my fingers.

A smile tugged at Zander's mouth. "*Gird up thy loins?* Haven't heard that phrase in a while."

"Fits though, don't it?"

Zander sighed. "Yes. Yes, it sure does. Thanks for your honest friendship, Abe. We need a hundred more like you."

No, we need thousands, I thought.

⌘⌘⌘⌘

CHAPTER 27

LESS THAN SIX WEEKS FOLLOWING her official inauguration, President Mellyn held yet another Presidential address to announce the vaccine rollout. Since she had spearheaded the movement to ban all Christian content, I considered asking the nanomites to curtail her presidential speeches.

Right! They could block her ability to broadcast. And wouldn't that be fun?

I salivated at the idea.

I restrained myself.

"My dear fellow Americans, I have good news! First, though, I salute the brave souls who struck a blow to oppose moral fascism and tyranny. Thank you for sending the perfect response to that unidentified preacher of hatred and intolerance. Thank you for letting those who follow him know that *we will not stand for their lies*."

Zander exhaled. "They planned to stamp out the church. Terminate the preaching of the Gospel. Well, God be praised, they will not succeed."

As Mellyn continued, she softened her tone. "As Americans, we have a sacred obligation to protect those of us who are most vulnerable to this disease. Therefore, to our elder citizens, to those with compromised immune systems, to those with underlying medical conditions, and to their concerned loved ones, I have good news.

"With great joy, I announce to you that I have authorized an emergency release of the vaccine to those who are in the greatest need of the protection the vaccine will provide.

"Vaccines for senior citizens and those with compromised immune systems are headed your way and will be available shortly. We are putting all our resources toward the vaccine's initial rollout. Please stay tuned to your local news for your area's distribution schedule.

The officials and media crowding the Oval Office couldn't help themselves. They applauded and offered whispered thanks and congratulations.

Our skepticism only increased.

The cameras caught activity off to Mellyn's left side: a body and two hands, face unseen, a tray, a vial, and a hypodermic.

"In a moment, I will receive the first public vaccine dose myself. I regret having to take it, because others need it most desperately and because of the precious time it will cost us to manufacture enough vaccine for everyone. However, I feel it incumbent upon the office I hold to demonstrate that *the vaccine is safe and without risk*."

Mellyn rolled up her sleeve. The pair of hands swabbed her arm, grasped the meaty upper part of her bicep, and injected the vaccine. All the while, the cameras clicked and flashed, focused on Mellyn's serene expression.

As the partially seen body picked up the tray and stepped away from the frame, Mellyn said, "There. I've received the vaccine. Now, let me assure you, we will be mass producing and distributing this vaccine as quickly as possible.

"Only those most vulnerable will be eligible to receive it in this first production round. However, as soon as this segment of our population has been inoculated, we'll move on to the general citizenry. I do hope you understand and agree with me that we must give our first and finest care to those among us who need it most urgently.

"That is all I have to say. Thank you and good night."

The nanomites had been watching the address and had said nothing. Until now.

Jayda Cruz, Zander Cruz.

I responded automatically. "Yes, Nano?"

Our analysis of President Mellyn's micro expressions reveal that several of her statements are patently deceptive.

"What? Which parts?"

The nanomites regurgitated a full paragraph. It was particularly creepy that they mimicked Mellyn's voice.

In a moment, I will receive the first public vaccine dose myself. I regret having to take it, because others need it most desperately and because of the precious time it will cost us to manufacture enough vaccine for everyone. However, I feel it incumbent upon the office I hold to demonstrate that the vaccine is safe and without risk.

Zander asked, "Nano, please explain what you mean, one sentence at a time."

Of course, Zander Cruz. She said, "In a moment, I will receive the first public vaccine dose myself."

I frowned. "Nano, you're saying what? It's not the first public dose?"

*That is not our point, Jayda Cruz. We infer that she lied about receiving **any** dose.*

Zander got up and began to pace. "So, she didn't take the vaccine, is that it? She received some sort of placebo?"

That is our deduction, Zander Cruz.

"What else was a lie, Nano?"

Zander Cruz, Mellyn's micro expressions of deceptive speech peaked their highest when she said, "I feel it incumbent upon the office I hold to demonstrate that the vaccine is safe and without risk." This statement contained the big lie of the evening.

I wanted to be sure I understood the nanomites. "That was the *big* lie of her address? She lied when she said the vaccine is safe and without risk?"

Yes, Jayda Cruz. Based on our analysis, she believes the vaccine is anything but safe and without risk.

"Yeah, but don't all vaccines pose some hazards, what they define as an acceptable margin of risk? And this is an emergency release because the need is so great. The FDA doesn't have years to properly test the vaccine."

With the broadcast at an end, Zander and I began to go over the previous parts of Mellyn's address. Yes, we were preoccupied. We did not pay enough attention to what the nanomites termed "the big lie of the evening."

⌘

USSART ONE LAUGHED TO HIMSELF. President Mellyn, in her previous speech, with her line, "the perfect response to that unidentified preacher of hatred and intolerance," had all but hand-delivered to him the solution to his Southwest problem. With churches burning everywhere, what were a few more in Albuquerque? And who would perceive the burning of an old, insignificant neighborhood as anything other than spillover?

"The goddess has provided the answer I've been waiting for. The universe and all nature have aligned themselves to aid in destroying that nuisance."

A minute later, he had the woman on the line. "I am acceding to your original request, Southwest. I order you to take out your little Albuquerque nuisance."

He expected to see a positive response and was surprised when the woman flinched—then tried to hide her reaction.

"Is there a problem, Southwest?"

She stiffened and schooled her expression. *"No, sir."*

"Good—see that there isn't. I have one condition, though. I wish the hit to appear as an extension of the church burnings. To do that, instruct your people to torch three additional churches, then burn some of your nuisance's neighborhood *along with him* so that he doesn't appear to be the primary target.

"Furthermore, select someone reliable to do the job—and I warn you to choose carefully. I shall want an inclusive report when the deed is done. Let me be clear: I expect to see my orders carried out to the full. Questions?"

"No, sir. You can count on me; I will not fail."

"You had better not. *Take your time and plan well—but get it right.*"

⌘

SOUTHWEST BOWED HER CHIN TO HER chest and pondered her orders. She deliberated on her choices. Turned to her computer and pulled up the GC Southwest personnel database, filtered out all but central New Mexico, and studied the search results.

A year ago she'd held high hopes for Albuquerque. She had set her cap on co-opting a large, reputable church in hopes of making the city a bastion of goddess worship. She'd bragged on her progress . . . thus making herself a target when she failed.

Stupid fool, she cursed herself.

Her only objective now was to carry out the orders she'd been given—and thus survive one more day.

Zander Cruz. He was the thorn in her side. How had he thwarted her and her people?

"I repositioned key people to Albuquerque, spent a ton of money to undergird the work, and risked my personal cachet in the process! We very nearly succeeded—we *would* have succeeded—*but for him.*"

Oh, she hated Cruz. Hated him for the problems he'd created, hated him for the embarrassments he'd caused her. Hated him for his noxious preaching!

He deserved all that was coming his way—and more.

She reached out her finger to her laptop's monitor and touched a name on the screen. A loyal volunteer code-named *El Lobo*—the wolf—based out of Socorro.

"El Lobo will bring strong leadership and a military background to the fight; I will provide him with a staging area and the willing hands he requires."

She exhaled. "Yes, he will do nicely."

⌘

LESS THAN A WEEK FOLLOWING Mellyn's announcement, special flights carrying virus vaccine landed in Albuquerque, Santa Fe, Las Cruces, and Farmington. Within hours, inoculation clinics for seniors and the immunocompromised sprang up at pharmacies across town.

We watched online news broadcasts that showed GC vans speeding from those airports to deliver vaccine allotments to New Mexico's more rural areas. Frankly, the only footage the mainstream news ran lately was of GC food aid, GC supplied vaccine, and a self-satisfied Nora Mellyn touting GC's generosity and "global unity through global community."

But the convoy of GC food trucks that rolled into Albuquerque looked more like an invasion to us: the arrival of victors bearing benevolence for the conquered. See, the thing was, to receive a GC food allotment, you had to present a valid ID, list the members of your household, and sign the blasphemous federal Affidavit of Unity, thus renouncing your faith in Christ.

Those whose names appeared on Mellyn's or the GC's "naughty list"—Americans who had spoken up against Mellyn, the GC, or the Affidavit of Unity, or who had preached Christ in any public forum—were turned away from the food distribution lines.

Sadly, we witnessed many professed Christians choose food and social inclusion for their families over Jesus. It broke our hearts.

Zander Cruz, your name appears on the rejection list.

"Not surprised," I muttered. "Huh. That's odd."

"What is?"

"People can't get a food allotment if they refuse to sign that so-called Affidavit of Unity, but they can get a vaccine? I would think the vaccine distribution centers would work the same as the food banks. Seems like they, too, would turn away anyone whose name appeared on their naughty list."

"They don't?"

"Nope. Anyone in the vulnerable population can get a vaccine. Makes me wonder . . ."

Ronald Reagan had said, "The nine most terrifying words in the English language are, 'I'm from the government, and I'm here to help.'" His warning had never seemed so spot on.

Abe scowled. "You won't see me taking *anything* that Global Conspiracy group is peddling. Don't want their food or their vaccine. I'm fine so long as I stay right here in our co-op."

Belicia was a different story. She timidly asked me for a ride to a vaccine clinic.

I was careful how I answered her. "Belicia, you know you are safe from the virus as long as you remain in isolation with us, yes? But if you go into a pharmacy where hundreds of people pass through every day, you might contract the virus *there* despite the pharmacy's precautions. And if you choose to go, the co-op will, at the very least, insist that you isolate inside your house for a week. Perhaps ten days."

Her eyes widened. "You mean . . . I couldn't watch Bonnie Lu?"

"Yes, but with gardening season behind us, you already know that I only need you when it's my turn to stand post at the barrier and Zander has counselling appointments. I'm sure Janice would help out if you needed to isolate. We would also have to remove Josh from your house until we knew you weren't contagious."

Belicia considered the implications. "I feel much safer with Josh in my house. I wouldn't want to . . . be alone again."

The nanomites would tell us immediately if Belicia had picked up anything, but I couldn't tell her that. Besides, as suspicious as we were of the GC, I wanted our isolation policy to dissuade Belicia from getting the vaccine.

She frowned a little. "You aren't saying these things because you don't want me to get inoculated, are you, Jayda? I mean, you don't seem in favor of the vaccine in general."

Ooh. Tough question.

"I'm just restating our isolation protocols, the policies that keep our co-op members safe. That said, you are an adult, Belicia. While taking the vaccine isn't *my* personal preference, it's not my place to make that decision for you."

She seemed satisfied, and we talked no further about it, but later Zander told me she had approached Bill and Viola about one of them driving her to a vaccine clinic. Bill, anti-establishment guy that he was, wouldn't hear of getting the vaccine himself and told her so. She didn't ask Abe, but then again he wasn't driving these days anyway.

What we didn't immediately realize was how determined the government was to vaccinate *all* seniors and immunocompromised individuals. We didn't understand until they started canvassing Albuquerque neighborhoods in vans equipped with vaccine and the technicians to administer it.

⌘⌘⌘⌘

CHAPTER 28

I WAS ON THE BARRIER ABOUT a week later. I was doing my regular six-hour afternoon guard stint when I noted a van with a GC logo making its way down the street toward the cul-de-sac. The van made several stops before it pulled up alongside the barrier.

The young man behind the wheel stayed put, but a spritely young woman popped out of the passenger seat. She walked toward me, masked and with a clipboard in hand.

"Hi there. I'm Michelle. Oh, wow! What is this?"

She reached her hand toward the nearest K-Rail.

"Please stand six feet back from the barrier," I said, just as cheerfully, gesturing to our prominent signage. "The residents beyond this point are members of a self-isolating cooperative."

She obliged and backed up "What a great idea! How long have you been doing this?"

"Since spring. May I help you with something?"

She laughed and referred to her clipboard. "Yes, sorry. My bad. I'm looking for Mrs. Belicia Calderón. I believe she lives in this cul-de-sac?"

"She does; however, she's busy at the moment. May I ask why you'd like to see her?"

"Oh, sure. We're delivering vaccines to shut-ins. She registered as one, so we're here to administer her dose."

I was surprised. I shouldn't have been. *Gemma* knew how resourceful her previously nosey neighbor was. *Jayda* should have remembered.

"Um, I see. Let me make a call. I will have to get someone to spell her—"

"Yoo-hoo! Here I am!"

Belicia, quite obviously, had been expecting the van. She smiled wide and made her way carefully down our porch steps—while carrying Bonnie Lu.

Bonnie spied me at the barrier and launched into an excited, all-over wiggle-waggle—her way of expressing how happy she was to see me. I was just glad Belicia had bundled Bonnie up to her eyebrows to protect her from this week's cool weather.

Eventually Belicia reached us, although she was out of breath when she did. She huffed quite a lot before she managed, "Are you . . . do you have . . ."

The charming Michelle laughed again. "Are you Mrs. Calderón? If so, *yes*. I have your vaccine dose."

The nanomites had already explored the girl and declared her virus-free, so I didn't have a problem with her administering Belicia's vaccine—from the other side of the barrier, of course.

I took Bonnie from Belicia while Michelle donned a disposable gown and gloves and fetched a folding seat from the van.

"Mrs. Calderón, if you would take this little seat and set it down on your side of this thingy here?"

"It's a K-rail," Belicia said, eager to educate her. "We have lots of them."

"Um, yes, I see that you do. Unfold the seat and sit down, please."

While Belicia did and rolled up her sleeve, Michelle retrieved a little kit from the van.

The nanomites were instantly all over Michelle and her "kit." They swarmed the girl and observed as she broke the seal, opened the kit, removed an ampule, inserted the hypodermic needle into the ampule, and pulled the solution into the barrel.

It wasn't until Michelle grabbed the meaty part of Belicia's upper arm that they reacted.

JAYDA CRUZ!

A wide swath of nanomites plowed into me. Lifted me off my feet.

Bonnie and I flew backward.

The nanomites flung us ten feet from Belicia and Michelle. Their action was so totally unexpected that my only consideration as it happened was Bonnie: I hugged her tight, both arms around her. I was certain I'd land on my back and crack my head on the asphalt—but better me than her!

At the last possible moment, the nanomites yanked me upright. I landed on my feet gripping Bonnie Lu hard. Bonnie, startled out of her wits, wailed in my arms.

I stared at Belicia and Michelle. As the girl pulled the empty hypo from Belicia's arm, they stared back at me.

"What in the world just happened?" Michelle demanded.

Her driver jumped out of the van and joined her. I saw right away that he served as both driver and guard: He was armed.

"What's going on, Michelle?"

"Don't know. Something weird, Kyle. She," Michelle pointed at me, "she sorta flew backwards, but landed on her feet? Very strange!"

"You okay?" he asked me.

"Fine," I lied.

Not fine at all. Oh, Belicia!

A massive surge of nanomites—as many as could leave me—swarmed over Belicia, *battling another swarm of nanomites*. They were fighting hard to overcome an army of *alien mites*—fighting for their lives . . . and for Belicia's.

I heard them scream in the warehouse. *Jayda Cruz! Help us!*

"Get away from Belicia, Nano!" I replied. "I can't help until you're clear!"

We cannot disengage! They are stronger than we are! They are overpowering us!

I dove into the warehouse and could suddenly see the battle—could see the alien mites glomming onto our nanomites, tearing into them, ripping them apart, ant-like mandibles chewing their way through the nanocloud's tribes. I tunneled deeper, enlarging my view, seeking to know the enemy and understand their mode of attack.

The near-constant flash of Delta Tribe's lasers dazzled me. I observed as they severed the aliens' appendages to end their hold on our mites . . . and that was when I realized which tribe the aliens were engaging primarily: *Alpha Tribe*. The library of the nanocloud. The archive of Dr. Bickel's research, his process for manufacturing the nanomites and the brilliant algorithms that had governed the nanomites' initial behaviors—besides which, Alpha Tribe's library contained all of the nanocloud's experiences and memories. It contained everything the nanomites knew about us. About Zander, Emilio, and Bonnie Lu. About me.

Everything our enemies would ever need to defeat us.

The aliens were mining the information banks of Alpha Tribe—sucking them dry.

"Lord Jesus, help me! Please help me!"

I had to kill these invaders. *I had to kill them all.* I could not allow even one of them to escape lest they carry back to their makers every byte of data they'd stolen from Alpha Tribe.

"Nano! Get ready to disengage," I shouted. I also screamed in the warehouse, "Zander! We need you! Hurry! Please hurry!"

I plopped Bonnie's little bottom against the barrier in the same instant that I zapped Kyle and Michelle and they crumpled to the pavement. I really hoped neither of them cracked a tooth as they fell, but I was too busy to worry over them.

Almost simultaneously, I zapped Belicia. She fell over in a heap, and I eased her to the ground.

Stepping back from the barrier, I extended my arms out from my side, palms up. I reached out. I began to call down electricity from the cul-de-sac's overhead lines and our neighborhood's transformers. I pulled and pulled harder. My arms and hands shook, my body trembled. I drew every bit of electricity I could find to myself and into my body. I pulled power into my hands . . . until they sparked and flashed, until my entire being pulsed, crackled, and emanated intense, penetrating might.

"Get ready, Nano!" I screamed.

I brought my hands together. A fireball built within them. . . and a torrent of pure energy built within the fireball.

"Nano! Three! Two! One!"

To the degree the nanomites were able, they burst from Belicia. Many tore themselves apart to escape the grasp of alien pincers and crunching jaws. Others were left behind. Overpowered. Incapacitated. Their memory banks hijacked. I mourned for them because I knew I had to kill the invaders . . . even if millions of nanomites died with them.

I released the pulse of energy from my hands and directed it into Belicia's supine body. Her limbs twitched and jumped; I kept my vision tunneled deeply inside her where torrents of aliens coursed through her blood—and armies of them clawed and tore at the nanomites that were unable to escape.

I had to slaughter them all, even the captive nanomites.

"I'm sorry, Nano. So sorry!"

I pushed harder. Saw the moment the aliens' resistance faltered. Saw when it failed. When they died.

I wasn't finished, though. A great many of the alien mites had burrowed into Belicia's bone marrow. I followed them there. I hunted them down. Killed them without a shred of remorse. I kept going deeper, seeking them out . . . until I saw what they were doing. What they had already done.

I didn't readily understand the ramifications, but I was able to follow the aliens' actions. They sampled Belicia's DNA and, literally, hacked into it. They identified every genetic predisposition she possessed. They diagnosed her body's weaknesses: moderate hardening of the arteries. A nascent aneurysm in her brain. A precancerous polyp in her colon.

The aliens had used a technology I was unfamiliar with to write commands to Belicia's DNA—commands to activate and exacerbate specific defects. I couldn't tell *when* their implanted code would trigger her demise, but the aliens' "hack" guaranteed that an autopsy would point to "natural causes" . . . those causes being cardiac arrest, a blown aneurysm, or rampant colon cancer.

Whichever way it went, Belicia was a ticking time bomb, slated for death.

As Zander raced from our house to the barrier, the nanomites brought him up to speed. He arrived ready to fight, but the fight was nearly over.

"Jayda?"

"Stand back, please. Keep away! See to Bonnie Lu. We cannot risk even one of these things reaching her."

He grabbed up our crying baby, withdrew several yards, but watched me from within the warehouse. Watched as I hunted down the aliens, sought them out, and squished them like blood-sucking, disease-bearing ticks.

Yes, wherever the aliens went, I followed, excising them, overloading their core processors, burning them to a crisp. But I was too late to stop what they were doing to Belicia.

And then I wobbled. I reached out and grabbed the barrier. A wave of dizziness passed over me.

From far away, the nanomites whispered, *Jayda Cruz. We are badly damaged; our ranks weakened. You are experiencing our weakened state. We are calling on our sister cloud to help us.*

Zander's nanocloud.

"Nano, be careful. Don't . . . don't allow any of Zander's nanomites to return to him without careful scrutiny."

We understand and agree, Jayda Cruz. They are coming now and will begin to effect repairs for us. They will also dispatch sentinels to search out the last of The Others. As long as you are able, please continue your pursuit of The Others until they are destroyed.

"I will, Nano."

The nanocloud's decimation had become my own. I had to pause. Bend over until a bout of nausea passed. I knew Zander's nanomites would try to bolster my strength; I just didn't know how long the electrical energy I'd pulled down would last.

I couldn't let that stop me. I had to continue my search and destroy mission. Press on until I had eradicated all the aliens or until I no longer had the ability to do so.

With the nanomites whispering at the back of my mind, I kept going. And going. And going.

I didn't notice when I passed out.

⌘

I CAME TO SLOWLY. BY DEGREES. My hearing was the first sense to return.

"Ma-ma-ma-ma. Ma-ma-ma-ma."

The voice grew more insistent.

"Ma-ma-ma-ma! **Ma-ma-ma-ma!***"*

A fat little palm patted my face: first my cheek, then my mouth, then my nose. (*Ow!*)

I exhaled. Cracked open one eye. "Hi, Bonnie Lu."

I was in bed; she was lying half on, half off of me. When I spoke, she crawled all the way onto my belly and chest and laid her cheek on mine.

"She's been waiting for you to wake up, and not very patiently, I might add," Zander said.

He picked up my hand and squeezed it. "How are you doing?"

"I . . . don't know yet. How did I get here?"

"I carried you. You passed out at the barrier. Remember that?"

"Nope. Not at all . . . wait. Maybe? Guess I ran out of gas?"

"You sure did, but the nanomites say you dispatched most of what they call The Others before you crashed. A few remaining Others tried to escape. My nanocloud hunted them down."

"We got them all? We're certain?"

"We're certain."

"They—the alien nanomites—were in the vaccine, Zander!"

"We know. The nanomites say The Others within the vaccine ampules were stored in an anaerobic fluid, kept in zero-oxygen suspended animation until oxygen or oxygen-rich red blood cells hit them. The act of withdrawing a dose from its ampule usually awakens them. Apparently, they're raring to go straightaway."

"What about the remaining vaccine doses inside the GC van? And the vaccine crew—Michelle and her driver?"

"Michelle and Kyle are all right. Before we awakened them, my nanocloud killed the quiescent alien nanomites stored within the other doses that were in the van—except for a few 'live' specimens the nanocloud insisted they needed to study."

I was still muzzy-headed. "So the GC van is gone?"

"Yes. We sent Michelle and Kyle on their way. They were a bit muddled, of course, but unhurt. They will finish delivering their vaccines—without alien nanomites. The doses will no longer prevent the recipients from getting the virus, of course."

"And Belicia?"

He pressed his lips together. "The nanomites are studying the changes to her DNA effected by The Others. So far . . . they say they can't undo them."

My thoughts came together in a rush. "Zander, this is why Mellyn and the GC are pushing the vaccine on our senior citizens! They want to thin the world's population by "stale dating" our seniors—and no autopsy will ever point to the vaccine as having anything to do with it."

Zander's next words chilled me. "That's not the half of it, Jay."

"What? What else?"

The nanomites answered.

Jayda Cruz, Zander Cruz, we preserved the bodies of many dead Others, what you call alien nanomites, to study them. To learn their functions and purposes. We dissected those bodies and recovered considerable information from their programming.

I frowned. The nanomites seemed a touch "off." Sad, perhaps?

"Nano, wait a sec. I want to say how very sorry I am over the deaths of your members. I know it was terrible losing so many from your tribes. Are you recovering? Are you all right?"

Jayda Cruz, our sister cloud came to our aid and prevented our depleted ranks from draining you, from taking you down into a dangerous physical state. We are working hard to rebuild our tribes. You should feel normal now, and we will be whole . . . soon.

I wasn't convinced. "But . . . are you all right? Um, inside?"

You are concerned for us, Jayda Cruz? Perhaps for our emotional welfare?

"Yes, Nano. Are you . . . sad?"

They thought about my question before they answered.

Jayda Cruz, perhaps you are right. Perhaps we are sad. We have discovered from whence The Others came.

Zander understood first. "Oh, no!"

Yes, Zander Cruz. The original design for The Others was stolen from Dr. Bickel when his data stored at his Sandia lab was hacked. These alien nanomites are our cousins.

I was horrified. "Oh, Nano!"

No wonder the nanomites were grieving. Dr. Bickel had designed his next-gen nanomites to cure diseases, fix birth defects *in utero*, and kill cancer cells. He intended his new nanomites to heal—not inflict death on unsuspecting recipients.

Yes, Jayda Cruz, Dr. Bickel will be distraught to hear his design was hijacked for grossly immoral purposes.

When I could answer, I said, "You're right about that, Nano. This news will greatly distress Dr. Bickel, but . . . I think this hurts you, too, doesn't it?"

We belong to the Jesus Tribe, Jayda Cruz. While our sister cloud is mending many of our members, Jesus is loving us and mending our soul. He has much experience with such pain since he was rejected and reviled by his own people . . . much like our members being attacked and killed by our cousins.

I slid my eyes toward Zander, and apparently the nanomites "saw" our exchange.

Jayda Cruz, do not concern yourself over our use of the word "soul" with regards to ourselves. You asked if we were sad. Perhaps we might rephrase our response and say Jesus is mending the place where we collectively mourn on the inside. Where we are sad.

They pivoted and returned to their report on the alien nanomites.

Jayda Cruz and Zander Cruz, we have more to tell you concerning The Others.

"All right, Nano. Tell us what you found."

Yes, Jayda Cruz. President Mellyn said the vaccine was first for seniors but also for those who are ill or predisposed to illness. She called them the immunocompromised.

I shivered. I didn't want to know . . . but I had to know.

"That's right, Nano. Go on."

We have found that The Others, the alien nanomites, are programmed to identify genetically coded diseases and debilitating conditions. The Others' programming requires that they sterilize any individual predisposed to a disease from a very long list of diseases.

"Sterilize them!" Zander exclaimed.

So they cannot reproduce and pass on their flawed DNA, Zander Cruz. And there is more. Once The Others sterilize such an individual, they also encode that person's DNA with a kill switch—similar to how they encoded Belicia's DNA. However, we have not yet determined when or how that kill switch will be activated.

The Others are programmed to write the kill switch to the DNA of those with extra chromosomes, those with terminal debilitating diseases such as MS, cystic fibrosis, ALS, Alzheimer's, Parkinson's, and the like—a very long list—all individuals who cannot contribute to society and whom the government must support.

The only genuine good the alien nanomites accomplished was to inoculate the recipients against the virus.

I half sobbed with both anger and sorrow.

Bonnie lifted her cheek from mine, her little face crinkled in worry. She patted my mouth.

"Mama."

I pulled myself together. Smiled. "Did you just say 'Mama,' Bonnie Lu? Your very first word? What a smart girl you are!"

She grinned back, showing me her dimples and six bright little teeth. Satisfied that I was "okay," she began to scoot, feet first, off the side of the bed. Zander caught her and lowered her feet to the floor.

Bonnie wasn't much for standing to get around yet; crawling was her preferred mode of locomotion. She dropped to all fours and took off.

Do not worry, Jayda Cruz. We will watch over her.

A stream of Zander's nanomites drifted through the bedroom door into the hall. They caught up with Bonnie and twinkled above her. I suppose the twinkling was for Bonnie's benefit.

From down the hall we heard her giggle and babble, *"Na-no Na-no Na-no!"*

Zander sent me a look of wry wonder. "She knows the nanomites?"

"By name, I'd say."

Yes, Jayda and Zander Cruz. We often sing to her in the night when she is fussy or afraid.

She knew them! And they sang her to sleep?

I sniffled, but not because I minded. No, the nanomites' revelation showed me how deeply Bonnie's safety and wellbeing mattered to them . . . and I was so very grateful to them for their care!

The nanomites recalled our attention to the business at hand.

Zander Cruz. You must warn the world about the alien nanomites active in the Global Community's vaccine. Warn them of the vaccine's consequences. If you do not, millions will die in the next few years.

Zander pondered the nanomites' injunction. "I have a global platform—but I don't relish the idea of supplying Mellyn and the GC with more incentive to track down my blond proxy."

"Why don't we have the nanomites make you a different, er, proxy?"

Jayda Cruz and Zander Cruz, we can do that.

I added, "And we should tell Dr. Bickel now, before we announce it to the world."

Zander Cruz, we have already told Dr. Bickel via the nanoarray he hosts.

"Oh. Um, how did he take the news, Nano?"

We do not wish to repeat his exact words, Jayda Cruz. Suffice it to say he is most unhappy, particularly since his desire was to offer the world a cure for many diseases and adverse conditions. He is angry with those who have perverted his second-gen nanomites.

I grimaced. "I don't blame him a bit."

In the meantime, we will identify every location of vaccine and attempt to dispatch enough nanoarrays to kill The Others while they are still quiescent. It will require that we assemble specialized arrays, which will take time. It will also take time for the arrays to reach the vaccine locations after we dispatch them. We will begin immediately.

⌘

THAT AFTERNOON, ZANDER MADE the announcement—this time as a much older man. The nanomites crafted the proxy's identity to exude fatherly wisdom and benevolent care in an attempt to persuade the public to trust him. We all understood, though, that taking the vaccine would come down to personal choice.

You could not change the mind of someone who did not want their mind changed.

A text appeared on our devices.

**An important message concerning
the dangers of the virus vaccine
will air in ten minutes
<u>CLICK HERE</u>
to join the broadcast**

The older man, of either Indian or Pakistani extraction, folded his hands on his desk and looked with amiable concern into the camera.

"Dear fellow citizens of the world, I come to you with an urgent warning. We have discovered that the virus vaccine contains deadly nanotechnology.

"What does the nanotech do? Nanobots, devices far smaller than the human eye can see, target the vaccine recipient's DNA. The nanobots identify within senior recipients certain illnesses that have not yet presented with symptoms—illnesses such as heart disease, diabetes, aneurysm, cancer, and stroke. At a predetermined date, the nanobots will trigger and accelerate or exacerbate those diseases—causing the disease or condition to kill the vaccine recipient quickly.

"In similar fashion, the nanotech seeks out those with physical and mental handicaps—conditions that make an individual dependent upon the government for health care and other forms of aid. As with senior citizens, at a predetermined date, the nanobots will trigger an event that will kill the vaccine recipient.

"We offer this warning as a public service announcement and urge you to reject the vaccine. When Nora Mellyn received her injection during her broadcast, *she lied.* She did not receive the vaccine; she received a harmless placebo."

Zander's proxy sighed. "As assurance of what I say, I offer high-res scanning electron microscope photos and video clips of the nanotech at work in the vaccine."

The nanomites, of course, had provided the images and recordings, both clearer than any known technology could have provided.

"You may access the evidence <u>HERE</u>. Thank you. Good night."

⌘

MELLYN'S RESPONSE WAS SWIFT and short. "The vicious accusations about the virus vaccine are nothing but more lies from those who oppose our global unity and who would rather our seniors and other vulnerable citizens suffer and die from the virus. Please do not give these baseless falsehoods the time of day."

Zander shook his head. What else could he do or say? But perhaps it had been enough to create a public wave of resistance to the vaccine. Time would tell.

I blinked, trying to recall the thought that had flitted through my mind while Mellyn spoke.

"Oh, yeah. Did you notice? Mellyn didn't use her usual catch phrase, 'our American purpose, unity, and morale.' Instead, she said 'those who oppose our *global unity*.' That's the GC's motto—'global unity through global community.'"

Zander frowned. "Huh. You're right. She's no longer hiding her globalist agenda behind an American façade."

⌘⌘⌘⌘

CHAPTER 29

ZANDER'S SUNDAY SERMON WAS again delivered from our bedroom to a multitude of viewers in every part of the "connected" world. Regardless of the fact that all known Christian broadcasts had been hunted down and terminated at their source, the nanomites continued to infiltrate and appropriate "legal" web services and bounce Zander's signal, via hijacked satellites, around the globe—from one authorized site to another—so quickly that the Cabal's bots could not keep up with it.

Furthermore, when anyone typed "Jesus" into their browser window, the nanomites snagged their IP address and delivered the broadcast signal directly to them. At the same time, the nanomites masked the fact that the receivers were watching Zander.

In the ten minutes before Zander began his message and as viewers came online, I watched the livestream ticker run up, faster and faster. The numbers leapt into the millions, then tens and hundreds of millions. When the ticker crested seven hundred million, I stopped watching it.

Zander was, literally, preaching to the world.

Gamble and Janice had invited Josh and Izzie to watch with them this morning. We were surprised, but happy to see Gamble and Janice taking an interest.

In our living room, without Josh and Izzie as usual, Abe and Emilio watched Zander's message with me while Bonnie Lu, ensconced in her bouncer, pushed off from the floor, kicking with happy abandon.

The nanomites zoomed in on the blond proxy's face. His eyes burned with godly purpose. And although he spoke to millions, the image on our screen looked at me and only me.

Zander's message was shorter than usual today. Short and to the point.

A punch in the gut.

"I want to teach this morning on a concept from the Old Testament, a concept that has great bearing for us in these dark and desperate hours. Why? Because I am not insensible to what is happening across the globe. It is happening where I live too. The fact is, we are enduring the most distressing season humanity as a whole has experienced to date.

"The freedoms we once enjoyed and took for granted are gone. Abundance is a thing of the past. Food is scarce and will grow scarcer. Unseen enemies across the globe are all around us, hacking our infrastructures. Our homes are at risk. Our families are in jeopardy.

"Moreover, wickedness abounds. Wherever it exerts itself, it seeks to rule and control us by all means available—by coercion, by intimidation, by pressure, by force, and by exclusion. There is no help to be had anywhere. There is nowhere to escape the reach of the Evil One who stalks the earth."

He hesitated, then added, "And . . . dear friends, it will get worse."

That was *not* what I wanted to hear. Not what anyone listening wanted to hear!

Emilio's hand slid under my arm. His fingers grasped mine. I squeezed his hand. I knew he was afraid. Who wasn't?

Zander continued. "But while, *yes,* the devil is our loathsome enemy and while his work is to press God's people harder and harder, his greatest tool is not governmental oppression. It is not deprivation and hunger. It is not intimidation, cancellation, torture, or death. The devil's greatest weapon is *fear*. People across the globe are, literally, fainting from fear."

Fear? I thought. *Yes. Fear is like a mugger lurking in the dark corners of an alley. He jumps out to strike when I least expect him.*

Zander added, "Again, *fear is the devil's work,* so I am here to remind us this day, that 1 John 3:8 tells us *the reason the Son of God appeared was to destroy the devil's work.* We will act on that Scripture today. In accordance with Romans 16:20 and in the mighty name of Jesus, we will crush under our feet the hold Satan has on *our will and emotions.*

"Please turn in your Bibles to the Book of Exodus, Chapter 35, beginning in verse 4."

He began to read.

> *"Moses said to the whole Israelite community,*
> *'This is what the Lord has commanded:*
> *From what you have, take an offering for the Lord.*
> *Everyone who is willing is to bring to the Lord*
> *an offering of gold, silver and bronze;*
> *blue, purple and scarlet yarn and fine linen;*
> *goat hair; ram skins dyed red*
> *and another type of durable leather; acacia wood;*
> *olive oil for the light; spices for the anointing oil*
> *and for the fragrant incense;*
> *and onyx stones and other gems*
> *to be mounted on the ephod and breastpiece.'*

"It is clear that this was to be a free-will offering. That means no one was pressured, coerced, or required to bring these gifts. Every person was free to give or not give. Please keep that in mind. Now, let's skip down to verse 22.

"All who were willing, men and women alike,
came and brought gold jewelry of all kinds:
brooches, earrings, rings and ornaments.
They all presented their gold
as a wave offering to the Lord."

Zander looked up into the camera. *"They all presented their gold as a wave offering to the Lord.* We're not accustomed to that phrase 'wave offering' today, are we? And what, exactly, is a 'wave offering'? What does it mean? And what connotation can it have for us today in our present circumstances?"

He settled into his message. "Let me explain. Most sacrifices offered to the Lord were burned on the altar except for the portion that belonged to the priests for their service to the Lord. Why burn an offering, you ask? Burning an offering signified that what was given was *utterly devoted* to the Lord—it could not be taken back. Because it was destroyed by fire, it could not be retrieved or used in any capacity afterward.

"When a sacrifice was destroyed by fire, Scripture tells us that its smoke went up to the Lord as a sweet aroma—but all that remained here below was *ash.* The sacrifice was gone. In this way, it was *utterly devoted* to the Lord.

"A wave offering was usually that portion of a sacrifice presented to the Lord but then released by him to feed the priests and their families. Whether it was meat, a sheaf of wheat, or loaves of bread—depending upon the occasion—the offering was presented to the Lord when the priest placed his hands under the hands of the worshipper holding the offering. Together, they raised up the offering and waved it back and forth under the eyes of God himself.

"The situation in Exodus 35, however, is unique in Scripture. When God gave Moses the instructions to build and furnish the tabernacle of God in the wilderness, construction of the most important furnishings required *gold.* The lampstand was to be made of pure gold. The table of showbread was to be overlaid with gold and its plates and dishes made of pure gold. Many other parts of the tabernacle were to be made of gold or overlaid with gold.

"The most important piece of furniture in the tabernacle, however, was the ark of the covenant and its lid, what was called 'the mercy seat.' The ark and its covering lid were also to be overlaid with pure gold. The mercy seat was the exact place where the visible presence of the Lord rested, as a column of smoke by day and a pillar of fire by night.

"However, the gold that the people offered to the Lord for these fur-nishings would not be *destroyed* by fire. Rather, it would be *smelted* by fire and then reshaped for the Lord's purposes. So, when the people presented their gold jewelry to the Lord in a wave offering, when they lifted it above their heads and waved it back and forth before the Lord, it signified two important things.

"First, it was a public declaration that the gold they offered to the Lord was an irrevocable offering. It was his forever. *It would never be taken back*. Second, it signified that the gold they gave would not be destroyed by fire. Instead, it would pass *through* the fire in order to be repurposed. Used to honor the house of the Lord.

"Please listen carefully to what I am about to say. What we give to the Lord completely, what we utterly devote to him, *cannot be lost*. It is his forever."

Zander's eyes bored into mine. The creeping sense of dread I fought daily to keep in check, to keep from sweeping over me, began to move in my belly, to crawl up into my throat.

Zander said, "I want to read 2 Timothy 1:12 to you. This was Paul's way of repeating this principle, that what we give to the Lord completely cannot be lost.

> *"I am not ashamed,*
> *for I know whom I have believed*
> *and am persuaded that he is able to keep*
> *what I have committed to him*
> *until that Day.*

"Again, what we give to the Lord, utterly and completely, cannot be lost. *It is his forever*. In this present world, it may *appear* that wicked men and women control the fate of our families. Many of God's people are struggling with the fear of loss, with an overwhelming terror.

"I can quote you many Scriptures that exhort us to endure persecution, to remain patient and steadfast in the face of suffering, tribulation, and death. And yet *that fear*, the fear of losing our children, losing our spouses, losing those we love more than life, tries to maintain its grip on us. It digs its claws into our hearts, our thoughts, and our emotions. It plants its hooks in us and tries to usurp our single-hearted devotion to the Lord himself.

"What we need to recognize, dear brothers and sisters, is that *fear is a tyrant*. Fear wants to run our lives, wants to dominate and rule us. Fear attempts to unseat Christ's lordship over us. *We must not allow fear a place in our hearts*."

With tears in his eyes, Zander said, "A few moments ago, I said, 'There is no help to be had anywhere, nowhere to escape the reach of the Evil One who stalks the earth.' I added, 'People across the globe are, literally, fainting from fear.'

"Today it is my intention to help us face the facts: If we are consumed by fear for ourselves and our families, if a place of safety for ourselves and our families no longer exists on the earth, then we must look elsewhere for that safety. *We must look to God.*

I thought I knew where Zander was going with his message, and I didn't want to hear it. On the contrary, the fear bubbling within me made me want to scream *no!* and run from our home.

Zander said, "Beloved of the Lord, let us put an end to fear's reign. Let us place in our hands all that we cherish, all that we love, and let us lift these up to the Lord our God. Let us wave what we love before *the only one who can keep them safe*. Let us give ourselves and our loved ones, irrevocably, to our God."

Zander smiled softly. "Dear people of God, hold out your hands and place your spouse in them."

I shook and trembled. The fear Zander spoke of clawed at my insides. That fear burst from me and was suddenly everywhere in that room, everywhere in our home. Overwhelming me. Overpowering me.

I repeated again and again, "No, no, no, no!"

My frantic arms reached for Bonnie Lu—only to find Emilio dragging her from her bouncer.

"Give her to me, Emilio. Give her to me."

He clutched her to himself. "No! Not gonna wave Bonnie to God! She's *my* sister! *She's mine!*"

"I said, GIVE HER TO ME!"

I grabbed Bonnie Lu and tore her away from Emilio. Pressed her to my breast.

Emilio crumpled onto the floor, sobbing. Abe wept into his hands.

And I stood in defiance to God, holding Bonnie Lu so close and tight that she began to squirm and howl.

I heard my name. Someone calling me.

My head whipped toward the voice.

"Jay."

Zander's proxy whispered from the screen, but it was pure Zander speaking, through and through. "Oh, my darling! I know you are watching. I know you are hurting and afraid. And so I place you in my hands and lift you up to the Lord our God. I wave you before him. I give you to him— irrevocably. He alone is able to keep you safe unto . . . that Day. *I cannot.* Our . . . little friends cannot. Only the Lord can."

He wiped his eyes. "I place our son in my hands. Oh, how I love you, my son! I lift you up to the Lord and surrender you to him. I place you in God's hands, my boy."

Zander, his voice rough, whispered, "I place our baby daughter in my hands and hold her up to you, Lord! My little girl, my princess! I give her to you, Lord God—please care for her, Lord, because I cannot keep her safe any longer."

My heart finally embraced what Zander said. It was truth. *I cannot keep Bonnie Lu safe any longer. Not on my own. Not from what is coming.*

The defiance within me crumbled. My hot tears poured out on Bonnie's neck and shoulder.

"Oh, God! Please forgive me!" I knelt on our living room floor. I hugged Emilio close to me. I placed Bonnie in both of my hands.

"Emilio . . ."

Gulping, he put his hands under my hands. Together, we raised Bonnie up to the Lord.

"I am sorry, Lord. You gave Bonnie to us after we believed I could bear no children. It was okay—we had Emilio! He was already our son and we love him dearly. We didn't expect Bonnie . . . so she came to us as a gift, an unexpected treasure. And yet, this world will not be kind to her, Lord. She will never be safe . . . unless you keep her safe.

"So, I give her to you, Lord. Wholly. Irrevocably. I entrust her into your care. I believe you will keep what I have committed to you . . . unto that Day."

Emilio sniffed. "Yeah, Jesus, we give Bonnie to you. We can't . . . we can't protect her from all the bad people. I mean, I will try, I really will! But there's a lot of those bad people and I'm not very big yet. So . . . would you please keep her safe?"

⌘

GAMBLE AND JANICE WERE ON OUR doorstep before we had a chance to recover. The moment they stepped inside, Emilio ducked into his room. I needed to wash my face and get it together.

I wiped my eyes. "Excuse me a sec? Be right back . . ."

"Take your time," Janice murmured.

I looked closer. She wasn't in much better shape than I was.

Hmm.

Of course, Zander was still in our bedroom when I opened the door, but at least Malibu Ken was gone. My *husband* was kneeling at our bed. Weeping. Wrestling in prayer.

I tiptoed into the bathroom, scrubbed my face, then tiptoed back out.

Gamble and Janice were sitting at our table, holding hands. I don't think I'd ever seen them publicly affectionate before. I'd never seen Gamble emotional or uncertain, either.

He was both.

Gamble pursed his lips. "We watched Zander's message today, and I get why he's become something of an internet icon—although in that getup he looks like a California surfer turned used-car salesman. But, still, look at the views of his videos. His messages pull no punches. They are simple, concise, and practical."

My brows lifted, half surprised, half amused. "How do you know anything about Zander's messages?"

Gamble slid his eyes toward Janice. "Uh, we might have watched a few of them?"

I coughed out a chuckle. "Are you asking *me* if you've watched them?"

"Oh, we have watched them," Janice amended for Gamble. "We've watched everything on his channel."

"Oh!" I didn't know who would be more surprised to hear this, Zander or me.

Gamble whispered, "Yeah, we've been watching, and I need to tell you, Jayda, . . ."

He had to stop and get his voice back. "I finally understood something today, and it-it changed everything for me. I finally realized that none of us are getting out of this alive. We're not going to survive what is coming."

The three of us were pretty emotional, and his statement struck me hard.

None of us are getting out of this alive.

I was gentle when I asked, "But hasn't that always been true, Gamble? Are any of us going to escape death? Haven't we as a society just gotten good at ignoring the truth—that we're all on a timer that is ticking down to zero and no one knows how much time on the clock they or anyone else has left?"

"That's it exactly, Jayda. Janice and I realized this morning that if we didn't give in to God now, we might never have another chance."

Hope flickered in me. "Gamble, are you saying that you . . . gave in to the Lord? Did you surrender to him?"

"Yes. Yes, we did. Janice and I prayed that prayer with Zander—to make Jesus our Lord."

Janice spoke up. "Then we did that other thing. We waved the love we have for each other before God as an offering. How did Zander put it? 'I wave you before the Lord. I give you to him—irrevocably?' That's what we did with each other. I gave Gamble to the Lord."

"And I gave Janice to the Lord. That verse Zander read, *I am not ashamed, for I know whom I have believed and am persuaded that he is able to keep what I have committed to him until that Day?* It touched me in a place so deep inside, I didn't know it was there until that verse zinged me but good. So, that's what we did. We committed ourselves to the Lord, then offered our love for each other to him."

Gamble stopped, his expression filled with remorse. "Jayda, I want to apologize to you and Zander. I regret that Janice and I lived together in front of Emilio without being married. We're sorry we've presented a poor example to your boy. To everyone. Janice and I have decided to get married. Right away. And we'll tell Emilio we were wrong to live together without being married first."

I smiled. So many good things coming out of this day.

All of them holy.

I smiled more. "That's the best news I have heard in forever, Gamble."

⌘

GAMBLE AND JANICE WENT HOME. I asked them to come back that evening before dinner. Zander needed to eat and rest up during the afternoon.

Oh, I loved that Gamble and Janice had committed themselves to Jesus! Zander and I had been asking the Lord for their salvation for more than a year, and today was the wonderful answer to our prayers. Bonus: They had decided to get married? I was delighted. What could be more right?

In one respect, however, we had a bit of a logistical problem: No one could obtain a marriage license these days without signing the stupid Affidavit of Unity, stating under penalty of perjury that they renounced any and all federally designated hate religions. Zander at least had the afternoon to think about how to counsel Gamble and Janice.

When they knocked on our door around four o'clock, they first shared their salvation experience with Zander. Then they asked if he would marry them.

"We want to get married, but how do we get around that blasted affidavit, Zander?" Gamble asked. "We don't want to live in sin any longer—in fact, we'll sleep in separate bedrooms until we're hitched."

Zander thought for a moment. "I'll tell you what I believe is appropriate, okay? Since marriage didn't originate in the government, but in God—and since we're 'officially' federal hate criminals anyway, I'm perfectly fine with drawing up a marriage certificate for you—if you are willing to say your vows before God and in the presence of witnesses."

Gamble looked to Janice. She nodded.

Gamble grinned. "That's a yes from both of us, Zander. Oh. With one more request? Once we're married, we'd like you to consider appointing us Emilio and Bonnie Lu's honorary aunt and uncle. You, uh, you already asked everyone on Mal's team to consider themselves aunts and uncles. We'd like to serve in the same capacity."

Zander smiled, his tired eyes crinkling at their corners. Oh, how I loved this man!

"Done! Consider yourselves Aunt Janice and Uncle Ross. And do you have a date picked out?"

Now Janice grinned. "How fast can you draw up a license?"

⌘

TUESDAY AFTERNOON, TWO DAYS LATER, we set out a semicircle of chairs facing our leafless apple tree. The middle of March is utterly unpredictable in New Mexico. The day might trumpet springtime with lovely 70-plus degrees and balmy sunshine—or it could play host to the worst storm of winter, complete with fifty-miles-per-hour sleet and snow.

Planning an outdoor wedding? An act of faith.

Or was it hope?

Regardless, we contented ourselves with a chilly but sunny day devoid of wind. Wrapped up in warm clothes, the co-op gathered to witness Gamble and Janice's wedding.

With our tree as the backdrop, Gamble shivered in his best suit. At the last possible moment, Janice pulled off her long winter coat to reveal the lovely blue dress she wore. She might have been half-freezing in it, but I thought she was radiant.

And I about lost it while they prefaced their vows with a public declaration of their faith. Janice talked about her black-ops days and the stain some deeds had left on her heart; Gamble spoke of his career in the FBI and how jaded he'd grown . . . before Jesus began to woo him. They shared how they had derided Christ and his followers most of their lives—until they'd experienced his love and forgiveness for themselves.

Then, with tears running down their faces, they repeated the vows Zander read to them. I don't think there was a dry eye "in the house." Even Emilio beside me swiped his sleeve over his eyes. Before us, they signed their marriage certificate. I signed as Janice's witness, Josh signed as Gamble's, and Zander as the officiant.

"Ross and Janice, inasmuch as you have professed your faith in Jesus Christ and your vows of marriage before God and these witnesses, I now pronounce you husband and wife."

They kissed.

They laughed for joy.

We laughed with them.

We adjourned to the cul-de-sac where Gamble and Janice danced a wedding waltz to canned music. It had been Janice's only request for the ceremony, and we made it happen.

Then Viola and I served precious coffee and cake all around—carrot cake, of course. We had an ample supply of carrots, you know.

After hugs all around, the happy couple, hand in hand, went home. The rest of us went back to our tasks.

The ink was scarcely dry on their wedding certificate before the enemy landed his next blow.

⌘⌘⌘⌘

CHAPTER 30

WITH SOUTHWEST'S APPROVAL, El Lobo (just Lobo to most) chose a Friday night for the assault on his assigned targets. Southwest had commissioned an Albuquerque loyalist, one Aiden Easterly, to provide Lobo with staging space and volunteers for the op. The space turned out to be Easterly's universalist church; the volunteers came from Easterly's radical congregation.

Easterly told Southwest he was happy to aid Lobo, to provide whatever he required. "Personal reasons," he'd said.

The main hall of Easterly's church, cleared of chairs, became Lobo's staging area. Easterly's people, now Lobo's troops, gathered before him to receive their instructions.

Lobo split the thirty volunteers in half. Carved three squads out of one of the halves. Appointed three reliable captains to direct the squads of five in their appointed tasks—burn three churches. Their activities would provide cover for Lobo's primary mission.

Lobo, grinning with appropriately wolfish glee, stood before the volunteers and proclaimed, "Tonight we will strike another blow for global unity! Tonight we will destroy three edifices built to honor the *dead god* of moral tyranny! Tonight we will again prove that Albuquerque *is ours*— and that hate groups will no longer be tolerated here!"

The volunteers cheered him. They shouted affirmations and stomped the floor in unison. They shouted louder and louder.

Lobo had wondered, initially, if their pastor might pose a problem—if the volunteers' loyalty to Easterly might conflict with Lobo's leadership. Lobo's concerns had proved, however, to be unmerited. Easterly stood quietly on the sidelines, never directing, never interfering. Rather, he smiled his approval and eagerly acceded to any request Lobo put to him.

Much like an aide de camp. Not a general, Lobo thought. *Not a commander.*

Lobo, in contrast to Easterly, *was* a commander.

Now, as Lobo lifted his hand for quiet, he knew the volunteers were wholly his. *His* troops. *His* soldiers, obeying *his* orders. And he would personally oversee the burning of Zander Cruz's neighborhood.

"Squads one through three? Find your captains. Captains, gather your people and brief them on their assignments. Those remaining? Report to me here."

People shuffled themselves into their assigned squads. The fifteen soldiers not assigned to squads one through three, arranged themselves close to the front—under Lobo's fierce gaze.

Quietly, Lobo addressed them. "I have chosen you," he said, "to accomplish this night's primary mission."

A low, excited growl answered him. Lobo looked over the men and women he'd selected for his team. He caught the eye of a young woman and winked. She had introduced herself earlier. Lobo recalled her name: *Sierra*. Her answering smile was ferocious, and she linked arms with those around her.

My troops, Lobo exulted. He gestured to a whiteboard where he'd drawn out his attack plan. Line by line, he led them through it.

"We will split into three squads and depart in three vehicles, parking here, here, and here. Your captains know their squad's assigned infiltration route. We will strike simultaneously from these three positions." He pointed to the drawing on the board.

"Our targets are any and *all* enemies found within the cul-de-sac: eleven adults and two children. Our secondary objective is to burn all buildings in the cul-de-sac: five houses. Any questions?"

He waited. No one asked, but they were eager to get to it. He nodded. "Very good. We strike at zero-one-one-five hours."

He noted a little confusion among the ranks and added, "That's 1:15 a.m. Be positioned in your squads no later than 1:10 a.m."

⌘

JAYDA CRUZ! ZANDER CRUZ! MULTIPLE ARMED INTRUDERS!

Zander and I lurched from our bed. While we threw on the minimum of clothes, the nanomites shouted warnings to every nanoarray within the co-op. The arrays, in response, stung our sleeping friends to awaken them.

Zander got his clothes on first. He raced for the kitchen, threw open the door, and sounded an air horn to emphasize the seriousness of the attack . . . because the nanomites had shown us three teams of intruders, sixteen in all. Just like the Grocery Grabber Gang, one team of five had climbed over Bill and Viola's wall, a second team of five over Abe's walls, a third team of six, over the barrier.

Janice had been on guard on the barrier. In the warehouse, I saw her lying face down on the asphalt. Unmoving.

All intruders were armed. If not for the nanomites' warnings, we would have been taken completely by surprise and overwhelmed. Even with their warnings, we were in danger of being overrun.

Emilio was up and moving. I grabbed up our sleepy Bonnie Lu and her diaper bag (fitted up more like a go bag specific to her needs) and tossed it to him.

"Take Bonnie to the printer room. Hide there; don't come out until Dad or I come get you, do you hear me?"

"Y-yes."

Jayda Cruz, it is too late for Emilio to safely cross from the house to the garage. Send him through the tunnel.

"Tunnel! What tunnel?"

The underground corridor we dug from your bedroom to the printer room. Under your bed, Jayda Cruz.

"I . . . you . . ."

I didn't have time to ask them about their 'underground corridor,' an idea they had mentioned to us *exactly one time* and we had no clue they had actually built. I put Bonnie down and shoved our bed—frame and all—against a wall. Pulled up the neat little trap door I found. Saw an equally neat wood ladder.

I grabbed up Bonnie. "Emilio, get down there. I'll hand Bonnie to you."

He stared into the hole, scared of its dark unknown. "Mama . . ."

This was not the time to coddle him. "GO! NOW!"

Emilio scrambled down the ladder. His nanoarray blinked on and lit up what was not more than a glorified crawlspace. I handed Bonnie down to him and tossed him her bag.

"Get going! Remember—don't come out until I come for you."

Without waiting for Emilio's reply, I slammed the trap door on him, shoved the bed back into place and raced to our front door.

I dove into our security feeds and rechecked the image of Janice lying on the asphalt. She had not moved, but the intruders that had come over the barrier had. They had spread out, firing on anything that moved.

Zander and Gamble were together in front of our house. Zander brought down a dome of nanomites that surrounded him and Gamble, protecting them from the attackers' rounds. Zander had already zapped two of the shooters; they sprawled, unconscious, on the pavement.

Gamble fired multiple rounds. He clipped one attacker before the slide of his handgun locked open signaling that he was out of ammo. The remaining three attackers took cover behind the K-rails in the center of the cul-de-sac—the rails we'd placed there *for us* to use as cover! Before Gamble could reload, the attackers directed a withering barrage of automatic fire toward Zander and Gamble from the relative safety of those rails

Well, the rails weren't going to save them.

Zander extended a hand in the general direction of Abe's house, and blue fire flew from his fingertips. He twas, I realized, "calling" to the pile of rocks Emilio had suggested we dump between Abe's house and his house—a pile I now wished was much larger!

At Zander's prolonged gesture, a stream of spinning, fist-sized rocks jetted into the air. They flew toward the K-rails and whizzed past them, whirling and grinding in midair. Zander reached for them again and *pulled.*

The rocks executed an abrupt U-turn, then hammered the attackers crouching behind the rails.

Rock after rock after rock.

Screams from behind the K-rails told the tale. I glanced again toward the barrier.

Janice had not moved.

"Nano! Please . . . is Janice all right?"

Jayda Cruz, you are needed urgently outside. Intruders are burning Abe's house; his nanoarray tells us he is trapped in the basement.

I jerked open the front door. Surrounded by a bubble of nanomites, I sprinted right and raced toward Abe's. Flames crackled across his roof, and smoke billowed from the back of his house. I didn't have much time.

Two intruders, lit Molotov cocktails in their hands, hopped the wall between Abe's yard and Gamble and Janice's. I sent vicious blasts into them. I did not hold back. They screamed and fell to the ground, dropping their fire bombs. Neither bottle broke, but gasoline poured from the bottles and caught the dead, dry grass on fire. I sent a swarm of nanomites to snuff the flames.

Two more intruders, both armed, vaulted the wall. I slammed them with pulsing orbs, heedless of the damage they would do.

The interior of Abe's house was burning now, flames shooting out of the windows. I already knew the fire department wouldn't come to help us. I had to rescue Abe myself. Get him out of his basement before it was impossible. Save him, then try to save the other houses.

A bullet sizzled past me. I didn't think or aim; I instantly calculated the trajectory of the incoming round, with a pulsing *pull* grabbed the round, and sent it back along the same route. A woman shrieked and toppled to the grass, grasping her belly.

I counted our adversaries. *Sixteen intruders, three teams, six intruders over the barrier. Five each in the remaining two teams. . .* I had eliminated my five and, as far as I knew, had not been seen by any of the other attackers.

Out in the cul-de-sac, Zander and Gamble had two intruders left to defeat. I did not know the state of the battle beyond them, and I had no time to check

I ran to the back of Abe's house—it was fully engulfed in flames. I returned to the side closest to Gamble and Janice's house. Smoke poured from the windows. Below them was the house's foundation. Within was the basement.

I reached out my hands and pulled down all available electricity. I reached inside to gather more strength, reached back out, and focused on just three of the foundation blocks. I held my hands toward the blocks, then *reached* for them.

I grasped and pulled . . . *pulled . . . **pulled . . . PULLED!***

I heard the blocks crack and shatter, watched as they disintegrated and turned to powder under the force of my "pull." I sucked even their dust toward me and away from the house.

I called to Abe's nanoarray. "Get him out!"

I drew near and shouted to Abe myself. "Abe! Come out!"

His dusty head showed itself in the hole I was holding open. That was all I needed.

I "reached" again and began to drag Abe out of his basement. He struggled until he realized he didn't need to. I pulled and pulled until he flopped onto the ground. I grabbed one arm and jerked him to his feet, halfway dragged, halfway carried him away from the flames that licked closer and closer.

We rounded the wall of bushes into Gamble and Janice's yard; I dragged Abe toward the far side of their house and dropped him there. Returned to the intruders I'd felled. I had to make sure they were out of commission and would not again open fire on us.

I checked each one.

I had the nanomites check them again.

Shuddered in an attempt to master my emotions.

I had never killed anyone before. Not directly. Not in combat. All five intruders were gone. The flames of Abe's house illuminated the body of the last one, the woman whose bullet I had turned back on her. She stared with vacant eyes opened into the night sky.

Sierra.

I shuddered again. Swallowed bile.

Then I turned on my heel and reentered the battle.

⌘

AN HOUR LATER, THE POLICE AND FIRE department had arrived, summoned by Gamble's insistence and FBI status. The fire fighters kept the blazes from Bill and Viola's house and Abe's house from spreading. They did nothing to stop them from burning.

Two houses gone.

Fourteen bodies laid out on the cul-de-sac.

Thirteen intruders. And Janice.

Janice, shot dead in the first salvo of the attack.

Gamble was as broken as I'd ever seen brokenness. Zander sat with him. Wept with him.

I wept too. I wept for Gamble; I wept for Janice. I clutched Bonnie and Emilio to myself, guilt warring with the relief coursing through me . . . that our house and our family were safe.

Emilio was in too much shock to cry yet. He clung to me. Clung to Abe. Clung to Bonnie.

Leaving Bill, Abe, and Josh to deal with the lone, harried police officer who finally arrived on scene, I took my kids into the house. Had Emilio shower off the dirt from the crawlspace, shower off the smell of smoke. Put on clean pajamas.

I shook my head. The smell of smoke was everywhere. It was too pervasive. I was certain I'd smell it in my dreams.

"Get into your bed, *mijo*," I urged my boy.

He crawled under his covers, an automaton. I sat on the edge of the bed and tucked him in. Placed my hand on his head and stroked it.

His eyes stared blankly at the wall.

Bonnie, a finger in her mouth, looked at me. Around her finger she said softly, "*Mee-oh?*"

"Emilio is . . . really tired, baby. He needs a nap."

She leaned away from me, reaching her arms toward him. I tucked her in beside Emilio. When I paused at the door, I saw Bonnie's hand sneak out from the covers. She laid it gently on Emilio's cheek.

Lord, our little girl senses pain and is compassionate. I am glad for her kind heart.

Emilio blinked a bunch. He moved his head and kissed Bonnie Lu's hand. They fell asleep side by side.

⌘

WE PUT A COT IN EMILIO'S ROOM, and Abe spent the rest of the night there. Bill, Viola, and Josh slept on the carpet in Belicia's living room. Josh gave up his room and bed at Belicia's to Izzie.

I was afraid for Gamble, going to an empty home, knowing his bride would not be there. But Zander didn't allow him be alone—not that either of them slept. Zander walked Gamble's living room floor. Spent the remaining hours of darkness praying over our dear friend.

I spent the same hours at the barrier. I had insisted. No one else had the strength left in them, emotional or otherwise, and I needed the distraction.

⌘

CRESSIE STARED OUT INTO THE ice-clogged harbor. *I am sick to death of this place. I should never have come.*

She hated the frozen, ice-blasted drifts, the cold, the wind, the sense of transience and disorder.

People don't belong here, she told herself.

In short, she detested Antarctica and despised McMurdo Station in particular.

She would have already left if she could, but she had ten weeks to go before her contract expired. Before her company would pay her way home.

Oh. And she hated Paolo. He hadn't believed she would really uproot her life and join him at McMurdo. Hadn't cared enough to believe her. Hadn't cared enough to *tell her* he was already married—or that his contract ended two weeks after she arrived!

Cressida had gaped when he'd explained. She was still in shock when he boarded his plane and left—left her there without a single friend for another *five months and two weeks.*

After he was gone, she spent her free time drinking. Apparently she was in good company there. Half the station drank heavily. At McMurdo, alcohol worked better than money for acquiring other desirable goods.

Then, over the last month, as she resigned herself to her situation, she'd cut back on the drink. Fact was, she plain couldn't afford to drink heavily.

When she was in her quarters, the alcohol called to her. She forced herself to admit that she wasn't strong enough to deny its pull when alone, so she decided *not* to be alone, particularly in the evenings. Her choices to be with others, however, were few and pathetic—like the group she now spent her free time with—but there wasn't much of anyone else.

She'd stumbled on the clutch of short-term contractors by accident. *Nerds*, all.

On the positive side? They didn't drink.

On the negative side? Bunch of religious fruitcakes.

And, *oh*, they were such *geeks!* The group watched movies together, delivering the best lines themselves because they'd seen their favorites about twenty times. They played copious board games, talked incessantly about Jesus, quoted Bible verses in random moments, and burst into religious song at the drop of a hat. At least the group shared a respectable sense of humor. *That* was a bonus. Plus, none of the guys had hit on her.

Yet. Jury's still out on that one, she reminded herself.

Then there was the website another RN at the clinic, an avid astronomer, had shown her.

Très intéressant! An interesting distraction. She showed the website to her geek friends and earned their approbation. They, too, became enthralled, because when the featured *very* large comet passed by earth in late spring, the inhabitants of McMurdo were going to have the best seats on planet earth to watch it cruise by.

Cressie shrugged. *So, I'll have one truly unique experience while I'm here. Something to tell the grandkids about—like I'll ever have any.*

⌘⌘⌘⌘

Chapter 31

We buried Janice the morning after the attack. She and Gamble had been married less than four days. Zander and Josh dug her grave in the corner of our yard, not far from our apple tree. Not far from where Janice and Gamble had said their vows.

Gamble was stoic during the service. He asked to speak. Took a moment to get himself squared away so he could talk.

"The only thing I wish to say is that I am grateful. Grateful to the Lord for the time Janice and I had together. Grateful to the Lord for drawing both of us to him before . . . before he took her. Most of all, I am truly grateful to know where she is! I believe I will see her again. I just . . ." He looked to Zander, his expression carved in pain. "I just don't know how to live until then. Can you tell me?"

Zander put his arm around Gamble and wept with him.

It was all any of us could do for him. Grieve with him. Pray for him. Be there.

Bill and Viola hung around until Bill was able to buttonhole Zander. Knowing Zander hadn't slept at all the night before and was exhausted, I gave Bonnie to Belicia and stuck close to him.

Bill didn't mince words. "We're leaving. Got nothing left here. It's too dangerous to stay anyway."

He poked Zander in the chest. "You. You caused this. You have a target on you. *She's dead*, and it's your fault. *They burned our house*, and it's your fault. Now we have *nothing*—and it's your fault."

Zander didn't take Bill's bait. "Where will you go, Bill?"

Viola answered. "I have family in Texas. We'll go there. At least we have the car."

Bill had backed it out of their garage as the house burned while Josh and Viola fended off the attackers from up on the garage roof. Josh and Viola kept the attackers at bay while Bill sprayed down the house and tried desperately to save it. Three-quarters of it was gone. What remained wasn't livable.

"We'll give you food. Water and blankets. Whatever we can spare."

She nodded her thanks. Bill stalked off.

They left later that day.

⌘

The fires had done more than burn Abe and the Tuckers' homes. The flames took out the power lines into the cul-de-sac—after which the city shut off the flow of natural gas.

"Safety precaution," one of the city inspectors told us. "You hire a certified plumber to fix what needs fixing, then we'll put you back on the inspection schedule."

Right. We'd need a sworn Affidavit of Unity to hire a gas-certified plumber, because plumbers could not conduct business without signing their own Affidavit of Unity—and agreeing to service only customers who also signed the Affidavit of Unity.

No gas meant no heat.

Did I mention that March weather was unpredictable?

While a storm raged outside that night, Abe and Emilio retired to what was now their shared bedroom. That left us—Zander, Gamble, and me—huddled around the wood-burning stove the guys had jury-rigged in our living room. Later, when we went to bed, Gamble would take the floor in Bonnie's room.

Zander, Gamble, and Josh had gathered paving stones from Mrs. Calderón's garden and assembled them into a square for the stove to sit on . . . to keep the stove from catching our floor on fire. They'd insulated the wall behind the stove with roofing tiles scavenged from the wreckage of Bill and Violet's house. The pipe that emerged from the stove and went straight up and out through the roof had been part of the old coal-burning furnace in Abe's basement.

It had taken the guys hours to dig down to the basement, but Abe had known exactly where to point them. They'd found the body of the coal furnace and, with the nanomites' help cutting it apart, had brought out enough of the old girl to fashion two crude stoves—one for us, one for Belicia, Josh, and Izzie.

"Didn't want to pay someone to take everything out when we switched over to a gas furnace," Abe told us. "Hard to believe how glad I am now that I didn't."

"Every good and perfect gift is from above, coming down from the Father of the heavenly lights," Zander quoted. "Right now, these stoves are worth their weight in gold. As long as we have fuel—we have what's left of the Tuckers' house and yours, Abe—these stoves will keep us going until spring is fully here. To God be the glory."

Zander opened the stove's door and added a half-charred length of two-by-four. The fire received the fresh fuel with fierce snaps and pops. The beast's hunger knew no end—and our staying warm depended on how well we fed it.

To think I used to consider wood stoves romantic.

My mind went back over Zander's prior comment: Two houses worth of rubble from which to scavenge wood for fuel. As long as the gas was off, that little makeshift stove was our only means of cooking as well as heating. As pitiful as it was against these icy March winds, as Zander said, it was a blessing.

Bonnie slumbered peacefully in her car seat on the floor between Zander's and my feet, unaware of the turmoil surrounding her. I stared at her precious face, at the long lashes that hid her sweet brown eyes.

You are so peaceful, little Bonnie Lu! You were born as our world descended into chaos, but you know nothing of it. Nearly a year old, and you have no sense of what is ahead.

What will we tell you when you realize how bad things are?

Life as we had known it was over. The future that loomed before us was uncharted. Would be more difficult. Hard.

"Zander? Tomorrow is Sunday."

Zander blinked slowly. He really needed to go to bed. "Is it?"

"I'm sorry I brought it up. Figure it out tomorrow? With an audience across every time zone, the hour at which you preach isn't all that important."

"That's true."

We went to bed.

⌘

EXACTLY THREE OF LOBO'S ASSAULT team returned to Easterly's church —Deke, Marko, and Darcy. Easterly and those radicals not selected for the night's action had patiently waited for Lobo to return and report his victory, but Lobo was not one of the survivors. With him out of the way, the volunteer soldiers looked to Easterly for leadership. He had, after all, been in charge prior to Lobo's appointment.

He took the surviving soldiers, individually, into his office, closed the door, and listened to their reports. He took notes on his laptop and ended each debrief with, "Thank you for your commitment and service. I will make a full report of tonight's action up the chain—and I will speak well of your personal bravery. However, I'd like you to keep what you saw to yourself. Can you do that?"

Deke and Marko had nodded. The woman, in comparison, couldn't seem to get herself sorted.

"I'd like you to keep the, uh, strange parts of what you saw tonight to yourself, Darcy. Can you do that?"

"But how did he do those things, Pastor? I mean, I saw that guy *shoot bolts of electricity* out of his hands!"

Easterly sighed inwardly. "Can you keep these details to yourself as I've asked, Darcy?"

"Yeah, but . . . I mean, *how?* How did he do that?"

Is that a no, Darcy?

Easterly exhaled slowly. "I suggest you get some rest. You're tired."

"You mean I'm wired, don't you? Hopped up on adrenaline?"

Easterly put on his winning smile and got up from behind his desk. "Yes, I suppose I do."

"Like, I'm wound up tighter than a spring. And my shoulder hurts something awful."

"Care for a little TLC? I've been told I give a great rub."

"Yeah, I'd like that, Pastor. Sweet!"

"Which shoulder hurts, Darcy?"

"The right one, Pastor. The gun I was issued has a kick to it."

He stood behind her chair and let his fingertips run across the top of her shoulder. He lightly rubbed the taut muscles then worked his way up the back and side of her neck. He was careful and gentle.

Darcy moaned. "Oh, man. That feels so good."

"I'm glad. And I'm very sorry."

"Hmm?"

Easterly already had her chin in one hand and had braced her head with the other. He jerked as hard as he could. When he released her, Darcy's head flopped to the side. Her eyes were still open, but she was no longer there.

He thought for a moment, planned his next steps. Opened his office door and waved Deke to him. He brought the man into his office, and closed the door behind them.

"Deke, I need you to take care of something for me," he said.

The young man glanced at Darcy's body, then back to Easterly. "Let me guess—she couldn't keep her trap shut?"

"That sums it up."

"Stupid broad. No problem, Aiden. I'll handle it. Let me grab a few guys —discreet guys I trust. We'll take care of it as soon as everyone clears out."

"Yes, very good. I'll start sending people home immediately."

⌘

AN HOUR LATER, EASTERLY SAT IN HIS office watching a video. The handsome man speaking earnestly into the camera was a stranger to him . . . or was he?

I need to be careful. A misstep would be fatal.

Easterly closed his eyes and listened. Listened to the cadence of the voice. Paid close attention to certain words and expressions. He was searching for something familiar, perhaps the exact turn of a phrase.

Fifteen minutes into the man's message, Easterly stopped the video. Had the Blond Preacher said what Easterly *thought* he'd said? He backed up the video, ten seconds, then another ten seconds.

I must be absolutely certain.

Easterly stared at the screen before pressing play. Blond hair, cut close. Piercing blue eyes.

Those eyes . . .

He let the video run. Watched and listened closely.

"Jay. Oh, my darling! I know you are watching. I know you are hurting and afraid. And so I place you in my hands and lift you up to the Lord our God. I wave you before him. I give you to him—irrevocably. He alone is able to keep you safe unto . . . that Day. I cannot. Our . . . little friends cannot. Only the Lord can."

Easterly paused the video. "Dear me! I ask you: How many men can boast a darling called *Jay?* Jay as in Jayda? Why, hello Zander, you clever boy! Made a mistake there, didn't you?"

He laughed to himself. Laughed and thought about the phone call he would shortly place—and how sweet his revenge was going to be.

Then he frowned. *But how does he disguise himself like that? And how is he able to broadcast to the world? I must be able to account for it—must present a valid and rational explanation.*

He ran back the video and hit play. Caught the man mid-paragraph.

"He alone is able to keep you safe unto . . . that Day. I cannot. Our . . . little friends cannot. Only the Lord can."

"Our little friends?" Easterly sat back, confused but also excited and eager. He pulled his laptop toward him and reread the accounts the three survivors had given him. He heard Darcy's voice in his head.

"But how did he do those things, Pastor? I mean, I saw that guy shoot bolts of electricity out of his hands!"

"I saw that guy shoot bolts of electricity out of his hands . . ."

Easterly's lips slowly parted. *Didn't Stan and I watch something similar after Cruz preached and denounced me? When our soldiers attacked him, wasn't **something** able to deflect chairs and rotten fruit? Was it Cruz himself?*

And how did he get into our house without tripping our alarm system? How did he erase the video I altered, the video of him and his sister in bed? How did he erase every copy?

Easterly let the Blond Preacher's sermon run again.

"I place our son in my hands. Oh, how I love you, my son! I lift you up to the Lord and surrender you to him. I place you in God's hands, my boy. I place my baby daughter in my hands and hold her up to you, Lord! My

little girl, my princess! I give her to you, Lord God—please care for her, Lord, because I cannot keep her safe any longer."

"A son? And a baby daughter?"

Easterly's lungs emptied. He inhaled very, very slowly.

"Well, well, well. Perhaps I don't need to explain this so-called Blond Preacher's abilities. My soldiers' reports can speak for themselves. Let those above me figure out what they mean."

Working swiftly, he wrote an email to report the results of the night's operation to Lobo's superior, Southwest, copied the accounts he'd taken from the two surviving men into the email—he'd folded Darcy's death into the other casualties—added a conclusion and salutation, and sent the email up the chain.

After the email sped away, Easterly reached for his phone and dialed *Southwest's superior* known only as USSART One. It was always dangerous to jump the chain of command, but in this instance, the anticipated reward would be well worth the risk.

He slogged through interminable delays and a number of officious underlings, before he told the pretentious aide on the other end of his call, "Give him a message, please. You tell him *I can identify the Blond Preacher.* That's right. Oh—and I suggest you tell him *now.*"

Easterly waited. Fifteen minutes later, his phone rang. When he saw the number, he grinned.

He conveyed the salient details concerning the Blond Preacher— quickly and thoroughly, without hyperbole. When he was asked to repeat himself (twice), he was happy to oblige.

After that, his caller ordered him to describe the night's operation and its outcome. Easterly answered the expected queries, and when asked for his opinion concerning the operation's failure, replied candidly—albeit with *reluctance,* of course.

Yes, the call was quite satisfactory.

He hung up and nodded to himself. *My information will rid the world of this menace, but it will do more than that. Oh, yes. If I play my cards right, I will win myself a ticket to the big show.*

He laughed softly. *I have you, Cruz—and by the goddess I swear I will end you.*

⌘

USSART One's face appeared on Southwest's screen. "Report on your action last night," he ordered.

Southwest was prepared for her debrief—as prepared as was possible. "Sir. We burned three churches and Cruz's enclave last night."

"Did you, now? You burned all five houses? You burned Cruz himself?"

"Not . . . precisely. The squad took out two of the five houses."

He doodled on something she couldn't see. "So you *didn't* kill him?"

She was confused by his less-than-volatile reaction. "It was not our fault. The two surviving soldiers reported that someone or something odd interfered. Something . . . inexplicable."

The leader leaned forward, curious. "Inexplicable? Explain, please."

Southwest realized her error—that if she repeated what Easterly's report said, she would sound like a complete idiot. She vacillated before answering, "The survivors reported, er, unusual *resistance* from Cruz."

"What kind of resistance?"

She squirmed, knowing she had to comply but hoping to deflect part of the blame at the same time. "Sir . . . I can only report what the two soldiers—what *they* said—that Cruz was able to, that is, he used, uh, weapons of *electricity* to jolt the troops. I believe the phrase they used was *to zap* them."

She was a little amazed when the leader, slowly blinking, leaned even farther toward his screen until his image was so close that the pores of his skin were visible on her monitor.

"Please repeat your last? Reverend Cruz used *electricity* to zap our mob? You are certain this is what happened?"

What? He believes me? She didn't know whether to be relieved or further concerned.

"I, ah, am certain of what our people *say* happened . . . sir. I did not witness it myself. I could . . . I would be happy to forward the second-in-command's report that contains the text of his debriefing interviews."

⌘

WHEN USSART ONE HUNG UP, he compared the conversation he'd had with Aiden Easterly with Southwest's carefully hedged report. Eventually, he placed another call—for he, too, had a superior to whom he was accountable. He placed the call and waited.

"The White House. How may I direct your call?"

USSART One used the proper code words to ensure that his call was routed quickly to his direct superior. While his demeanor was subdued and properly humble, he was, for the first time in months, excited. Hopeful that his stalled upward mobility would soon be "unstuck."

"You have something for me?"

"Yes, ma'am. Praise the goddess, *we have him*. We have the identity of the man who's been spreading the foul stench of religious bigotry across the earth—the Blond Preacher.

"We have yet to discover how he disguises himself, but are certain we have him."

"You have a name?"

"Yes, ma'am. *Zander Cruz*—may the goddess curse him forever! He was the pastor of a church in Albuquerque. We also have the location of his home."

"Very good! Send everything you have to me immediately. You will be richly rewarded for your diligence."

"Thank you."

"The goddess bless you."

"And you, Madam President."

The line clicked; the call ended.

⌘⌘⌘⌘

CHAPTER 32

As WEARY AS HE WAS, SOMEHOW Zander made it through his Sunday morning sermon. He taught on the hope of the resurrection, but the high point for me was when he repeated his reading of 2 Timothy 1:12.

> *"I am not ashamed,*
> *for I know whom I have believed*
> *and am persuaded that he is able to keep*
> *what I have committed to him*
> *until that Day.*

"Several weeks ago, I taught on bearing fruit—fruit that remains. We looked first at the biblical principle of reproduction, how every part of God's creation that bears fruit, bears *fruit according to its kind*. Then we looked at the fruit the Holy Spirit bears in our lives and made a distinction between the fruit *he* produces and the fruit *we* produce—the spiritual fruit we bear when we, as Christians, lead others to Christ.

"I ended that message with this challenge: 'Let us press on together. Let us finish our race, beloved of the Lord. Let us fulfill Jesus' command to bear fruit, much fruit, and fruit that remains.'"

He paused, then said, "Last week's message was difficult . . . because our lives have become difficult. I taught on fear and how fear will attempt to usurp Christ's lordship over us.

"Then we dealt with that fear. We placed our most treasured possessions—our spouses, our children, our families—into our hands and waved them before the Lord, giving them to him irrevocably. I did this, as did many of you.

"Now, dear brothers and sisters, I ask you to follow through. I ask you to go out into your world and preach the Good News. Tell your neighbors about Jesus! Tell your in-laws about Jesus! Tell your boss how much Jesus loves her, how he died for our sin and shame. Tell your enemies that Jesus loves them!

"Look to the one who will grant you the crown of life.

> *"Blessed is the one*
> *who perseveres under trial because,*
> *having stood the test,*
> *that person will receive the crown of life*
> *that the Lord has promised to those who love him.*

"Be strong and be bold. Do not be afraid—give your all to him *now*. Make your life count for eternity. And when they come for you—for they *will* come—declare with joy and in the triumph of the Spirit's power:

I know whom I have believed—and he is able to keep what I have committed to him until that Day!"

I wept. *Yes, Lord! I will tell them. And I will tell Belicia—this very day.*

I bundled Bonnie up and headed out the door. When I knocked on Belicia's door, Josh answered. He beckoned me inside . . . and tipped his head toward two figures kneeling together on Belicia's living room carpet.

Izzie and Belicia praying. Belicia sobbing, "Please forgive me, Jesus! Please come into my heart!"

I smiled at Josh. "Beat me to the punch."

I went home, grateful for answered prayer.

⌘

JOSH AND IZZIE CAME CALLING LATER that day. After they had rehearsed to us, Abe and Emilio included, how Belicia had surrendered to Jesus, they got quiet. Fidgety.

Josh coughed and said, "Things are different now. We see it. Not much time left, and we have to be strong. Completely committed to telling as many as we can that Jesus is coming. And, um . . ."

We nodded. Josh licked his lips. Izzie studied her hands.

Emilio squinted. First at Josh. Then at Izzie.

"What you guys up to?"

I was both surprised and delighted at his insight, and I laughed.

"What makes you think they're up to anything, *mijo?*"

He wrinkled his nose. "Been makin' googly eyes at each other for weeks. Seen them kissing too. *Ugh.*"

"Really." I drew it out so it sounded more like "*Reeeeeally.*"

Zander and I waited.

Finally Josh blurted, "We'd like to get married. Soon. Er, please."

We cracked up. All of us laughed—and Josh was finally able to put his thoughts into words.

"See, we know Janice just died, and we don't want to distress Agent Gamble further, but—"

"*Special* Agent Gamble," Zander and I replied in unison and grinned at each other.

"Er, sorry. *Special* Agent Gamble. But we don't want to hurt his feelings or make him think we're disrespecting Janice by wanting to marry so soon . . . after."

Zander nodded. "Would you like me to talk to him?"

"Yes, please."

Josh glanced at Izzie. "We were thinking maybe Wednesday?"

"I'll go now."

Zander was back thirty minutes later. "Wednesday it is."

Josh lit up. "That's great! But, um, what did Gamble say? Is he okay with it?"

Zander tried to smile. "He said he hoped you and Izzie are as happy as he and Janice were, and he wishes you all God's best. And, *oh*. He said if you need a best man, he would be honored to serve."

"Wow."

Izzie sniffed. "I-I . . . He's so brave!"

Gamble and Zander had talked for half an hour and I was certain Gamble had said more than Zander let on. I did not listen in because those were the private conversations of two good friends, grieving together, yet comforted by the God of all comfort.

And yes, Izzie. I agree. Gamble is very brave.

⌘

JOSH AND IZZIE WERE MARRIED Wednesday evening in (of all places) our garage . . . and yet the setting was lovely. We emptied the largest room in the cul-de-sac and piled all the "stuff" temporarily behind the garage. Then the co-op members turned out to decorate it.

Months ago, Janice had hit an after-Christmas closeout and snapped up fifty strands of twinkle lights. I don't know what she had planned for those lights, but they were perfect for this wedding—a blessing from beyond the grave. We twined the lights around the rafters and strung them in multiple festoons across every wall. We dangled one hundred glittering silver stars (all handmade) over our heads, and placed candles in the corners of our makeshift "church."

Josh and Izzie's theme was "Starry Night." As twilight descended and the lights twinkled gently overhead, their desired setting came to life.

The beaming couple stood before Zander. Those of our little community gathered for the ceremony were fewer now. With Janice, Bill, and Viola gone, that only left Belicia, Gamble, Abe, Emilio, Bonnie Lu, and me to witness their vows. Oh—and Roberto and María! The nanomites streamed the ceremony to them, and we placed my tablet where we could see their happy faces as Josh and Izzie said their vows.

Afterward, we pulled out all the stops—that is, I pulled out a pile of the food we had hidden in the nanomites' printer room. We enjoyed a whole tinned ham, reconstituted au gratin potatoes, a number 10 can of green beans, and a small cake, each thin slice topped with a dollop of precious canned cherry pie filling.

Josh and Izzie's honeymoon location proved the trickiest part to arrange. Dr. Bickel solved the problem by vacating his home inside the exclusive

Tanoan community and turning it over to the newlyweds for two nights. His tech, Rick, in turn, invited Dr. Bickel to bunk with him and his family so the newlyweds would have privacy.

We saw Josh and Izzie off with tears and laughter and with great rejoicing for them both. Gamble would fetch them back Saturday evening.

In a perfect world, that's what would have happened.

In case you haven't been paying attention, this is not a perfect world.

⌘

"I HAVE REPLACED SOUTHWEST." USSART One's announcement was unnecessary—the woman's bloated body, hung from the I-25 flyover at the Big I interchange in Albuquerque, had been announcement enough.

The media had salivated over the spectacle and published several theories, none of them remotely close to the truth. Furthermore, the police had made no arrests and offered no explanation for the homicide. Or was it a particularly public suicide?

"We're following all possible leads," was the only statement the APD chief made before the cameras.

Southwest's fellow SART members, on the other hand, were fully cognizant of how the GC rewarded failure. They understood that nothing would come of the investigation.

USSART One added, "Please welcome our newest USSART member, Aiden Easterly. He has been invaluable to the Community . . . in recent days."

Easterly's intel had not been acted on as yet, but he knew it was coming. When it did, and he received his due credit, he would bask in the glow of the GC's praise and that of his fellow SART members.

The new Southwest smiled with winning charm into his camera. "I look forward to serving our great Global Community in this capacity. Thank you for your confidence in me."

⌘

NORA MELLYN AND THE CHAIRMAN of the Joint Chiefs of Staff met in the John F. Kennedy Conference Room. The conference room, more commonly known as the "Situation Room," was located on the level below the ground floor of the West Wing. It was often used during a crisis.

It also served as the SCIF closest to the Oval Office. The room's air-gapped communications allowed the President to speak without fear of being overheard.

Mellyn studied the live take from the drone far overhead.

"This is where the so-called Blond Preacher resides—in this old neighborhood? And his true identity is one Zander Cruz? You are certain, General Burke?"

"Yes, Madam President."

"What are those things?" She pointed to the K-rails spanning the mouth of the cul-de-sac.

"Traffic barriers, ma'am. Reportedly, Cruz, his family, and the others in the cul-de-sac blocked off the street and formed some sort of commune."

"A commune? How very droll."

She swiped the screen, closing the feed. "I want them dead. I want their little commune wiped off the map."

The Chairman of the Joint Chiefs of Staff flinched. "You should know that Cruz's family resides there. We have no evidence that his wife has the same powers he has. And . . . they have children, a son and a baby daughter."

Mellyn rounded on him. "Do you refuse to do your duty, General Burke?"

The man braced; he came to stiff attention. "No, ma'am. Your orders, Madam President?"

"My orders? I give them with pleasure. *Kill them*. I don't care if his family dies with him; I don't care how many of his coconspirators die with him. I want them dead. All. Of. Them. Dead. *Now*."

She waited while General Burke made the necessary phone calls, waited impatiently for the action to begin.

A lone nanoarray, dispatched by the nanomites to Nora Mellyn weeks ago, recorded the conversation but was unable to send a timely warning from within the air-gapped room.

⌘⌘⌘⌘

Part 3: Threshing

When the Lamb opened the second seal,

I heard the second living creature say, "Come!"

Then another horse came out, a fiery red one.

Its rider was given power to take peace from the earth

and to make people kill each other.

To him was given a large sword.

Revelation 6:3-4

Chapter 33

THREE DAYS TO GO, AND MARCH still wasn't finished with us. A medley of white specks danced and whirled past me as I stood post. New Mexicans expect one or two half-hearted snowfalls in March, but any snow we received rarely stayed long. Freezing March blizzards—here today, gone tomorrow—were our style.

The outside temperature this particular afternoon was cold enough for snow, and we needed the moisture. Unfortunately, the ambient humidity was too low to produce much in the way of accumulation. Instead, what fell from the overcast sky were tiny, frozen bits that skittered across the cul-de-sac and swirled around our fallow garden plots.

I was as delighted as a child to watch their antics.

With Josh and Izzie away on their honeymoon, the rest of the co-op members had to pick up their shifts at the barrier. I smiled, recalling the joyous wedding. I was happy to serve an extra rotation so they could get away. I wasn't uncomfortable as I stood watch, either.

The nanomites kept me warm, and in my gloved hands I clutched an insulated travel mug, half-filled with precious coffee. The co-op had a rule: Whoever stood post in temperatures at or below freezing received a single cup of rationed liquid treasure as encouragement.

I liked that rule.

Not a soul stirred anywhere around the cul-de-sac, or even down the street. People were hunkered down wherever they could to keep warm. I closed my eyes briefly to savor another sip.

It was almost dinner time. In my mind's eye, I saw Zander, Emilio, and Bonnie Lu snug and warm around our little wood-burning stove, while Abe fixed our dinner. Gamble had volunteered to pick up Josh and Izzie and bring the newlyweds home; he left half an hour ago and would be home shortly.

I laughed over the mug as I visualized Zander feeding Bonnie Lu her favorite new thing—*applesauce.* Bonnie Lu's love for this new taste treat was, shall we say, *enthusiastic?* She liked it so much that she slapped the tray of her highchair again and again. She babbled and wriggled with joy— but delivering a bite of sauce to her gabbling mouth was like running a spoon through a ninja warrior obstacle course.

I giggled and had to admit to how mighty humorous it was watching Bonnie Lu's daddy try to get that sauce to her mouth without it getting slapped down!

I allowed myself another sip. I had an hour to go on the barrier, so my preference would have been to save some coffee back for later, but it was cooling quickly. Better to enjoy all of it while it was hot.

My eyes automatically scanned the cul-de-sac, up the street, back, and around again. Nothing moved. I checked our security camera feeds in the warehouse. Rescanned the cul-de-sac. Returned my gaze to and rested momentarily on the rubble that had been Abe's house.

We had, of course, absorbed Abe into our household, and Emilio was glad to share his room with Abe.

How I loved their relationship!

Now that we were Emilio's dad and mom, his feelings for Abe had shifted some. He didn't call Abe "Grandpa" or anything—and that was okay—but it's certainly the way he felt about Abe. Like I said, I loved it.

The front door of our house opened. Emilio emerged. He was bundled up and carried a plate and bowl swaddled in a towel.

My dinner! It was chili con carne today, with a corn muffin or two on the side. Sure, meat was rare, and maybe the pot Abe had made it in couldn't boast much "carne" with its sauce and beans, but the idea was nice.

I drank down the remainder of my coffee and smiled as Emilio drew near.

"Hey, Mama!"

"Hey, my handsome boy."

He ducked his head, then handed off the plate. He took my mug, would take it back to the house. "Can I stand watch while you eat, Mama?"

"Sure. Thank you."

Although Emilio wasn't old enough to stand post by himself, we'd trained him on what was expected. He stared down the left side of the street, his eyes stopping briefly at each house, then moving on, never pausing more than a second or two. Repeated the process coming up the other side of the street. He took the job seriously, and I was proud of him.

I had already unwrapped the towel and slipped the muffin into my coat pocket to eat later when my stomach was growling again. I tipped the bowl into my mouth. The chili was soupy, as expected, but the flavor was wonderful.

I sucked down another mouthful of chili. So good!

The sun was low in the sky. It would be dark in about thirty minutes.

My bowl was empty too soon. I lapped up the dregs, then rewrapped the dishes.

Jayda Cruz, we have a small concern.

"Yes, Nano?"

As we said, it is a small concern. However, we are detecting rotor vibration.

"A helicopter?"

Yes, Jayda Cruz. The helicopter is west by southwest of here and is maintaining a trajectory in line with the co-op.

"Oh? How close is it?"

They didn't answer immediately.

When they did, it was already too late.

It had been too late from the get-go.

They screamed a warning in my head.

MISSILE LAUNCH! MISSILE LAUNCH! MISSILE LAUNCH!

The nanomites threw me to the asphalt.

I had the sense that Emilio was on the pavement beside me when, through my closed eyelids, a bright flash seared my sight. Then the concussion tossed me into the barrier itself.

The last thing I recalled was my back, followed by my head, slamming into a K-rail.

⌘

WHEN I WOKE, I WAS LYING ON the cul-de-sac's asphalt. The side of my head ached. I wasn't cold, though. A layer of nanomites cushioned me, but nothing about them felt "right."

I tried to think. To remember. "Emilio?"

I struggled to sit up. All around me was smoke. Dense, black smoke. The acrid and conflicting smells of gasoline, hot tar, smoldering wood, and . . . burnt chicken feathers.

"Emilio, where are you? Nano! Where's Emilio?"

They did not answer me. I finally heard them . . . faintly keening in my ears. Weeping and grieving.

They were in agony.

I rolled onto my stomach and pushed myself up. Stood. Wobbled. Coughed. Raised my voice. "Emilio!"

A breeze wafted over me. The smoke lifted some. To the west, across the river, the sun was sinking toward the mesa.

The sun. The west mesa.

I should not have been able to see the mesa from where I stood. Emilio's house blocked the view. So how . . . ?

His house, where Gamble and Janice had lived, was gone. Leveled. A streak of burning, smoking debris stretched from the yard behind it . . . to the center of the cul-de-sac.

Thank God Gamble hadn't been in the house! But . . .

I turned sluggishly in a circle. Squinted through the eddying smoke. *What?*

Slowly, slowly, slowly my mind cleared.

Not a single cul-de-sac structure remained standing. Small fires sizzled or sputtered, their heat surprisingly comforting against the cold. I again pivoted. Tried to make sense of what didn't make sense.

What had been our house was a trail of ruin that stretched toward the rubble of Belicia's home and the house that had been behind hers.

No. How could our house be gone?

I shoved down the dread that was trying to engulf me. Stumbled toward . . . toward what? Where Abe had fixed our dinner? Where I'd left Zander feeding Bonnie Lu the applesauce she'd embraced with such joyous enthusiasm?

But nothing familiar greeted me. Where our home should have stood, utter, unbelievable destruction had usurped it.

Zander. Bonnie Lu. Emilio. Abe.

"Where are you? Please! Where are you?"

I came upon Abe first, his legs pinned beneath what had been our refrigerator. I fell to my knees beside him. Picked up his gnarled old hand.

It was burned. Lifeless.

He was gone.

"Oh, Jesus. Oh, Jesus. Oh, my dear friend . . ."

I sobbed until the stench of smoke choked me. I gagged. Couldn't breathe. Couldn't inhale. Couldn't catch my breath. Was it grief? Was it overwhelming panic?

Did it matter?

All I cared about was finding Zander. Emilio. My baby.

My Bonnie Lu.

I couldn't face the evident, the obvious. No. Not yet.

Somehow, without my consent or effort, my lungs functioned. Somehow I got to my feet. An idea came to me—a good one!

Yes! I should find Zander. He will help me look for Bonnie Lu and Emilio.

Yes. Zander first. We would find our children together. Everything would be okay.

"Nano. Please help me locate Zander."

A thousand groans answered me. The distant weeping of a multitude.

"Nano? Help me? Please!"

Their reply was thin. Fragile.

W-we are attempting t-t-to reconstitute the nanocloud, Jayda C-c-cruz. Your nanocloud.

"But . . . but, Nano, where is Zander's nanocloud?"

It is n-no m-more, Jayda Cruz. No m-m-more.

Hope within me crumbled. Zander's nanocloud destroyed? But that meant . . .

Jayda Cruz, s-s-some tribe members from Zander Cruz's nanocloud, a very few, are finding us. They are damaged. We are damaged. We are broken and weak. We are attempting repairs. Attempting to reconstitute the nanocloud. We are . . . bereft, Jayda Cruz.

They wept. They grieved.

I wept with them! The nanomites' grief was my grief; their pain was my pain.

I struggled onward, making slow progress across the cul-de-sac and through the rubble and ruin of our home.

"Please, Nano? Please lead me to Zander? Please? I need . . . I need to see . . ."

We w-w-will do our best, Jayda Cruz.

⌘

I FOUND ZANDER WHERE OUR garage had stood. One shoeless foot showed above the rubble. In desperation and without care for my hands, I tore away the debris that covered him. He lay face down. I gently rolled him over . . . wiped the dirt and blood from his dear face.

My heart cracked. It fractured. I wanted to die!

"Lord, I am ready . . . please take me too?"

For a while, I gave up. Checked out. I don't know how long I remained there, my face resting on his still, unmoving chest.

Twilight was descending on the cul-de-sac, made gloomier by the smoke. It would be dark soon.

I thought I had heard sirens earlier, but no one came.

Blinking, I sat up. Looked beyond our barrier of K-rails. Far down the street I spied the lights from a line of police cars. A yellow-taped barricade from one side of the street to the other. A sizable crowd behind the tape. No one allowed to cross over.

I understood.

The attack had been authorized, the missile strike, surgical.

Someone figured out that Zander was the Blond Preacher. That he was the man telling the world about Jesus.

Gave the orders.

Take out the remaining homes of those terrorists in the cul-de-sac.

Done.

Render no aid to survivors.

Got it. Expect no help. Shouldn't have been survivors anyway.

Help didn't matter. I was the only one left.

But how had I survived?

The answer crept slowly into my consciousness: If Bill and Viola's and Abe's homes hadn't already burned, a second or third missile would have been required to widen the breadth of destruction. In which case, standing at the barrier, I would be dead too.

How I wished I were.

⌘

I BELIEVED I ALONE HAD SURVIVED until I heard a child sobbing.

Emilio.

Get up, I told myself. *Get up. Your son needs you.*

Get up! Your son needs you!

What about Bonnie?

No! Don't go there!

I couldn't let myself think about our baby. I walled it off. Refused to look at what I might discover there.

Find Emilio. Don't think about Bonnie.

Deny! Deny!

Wading deeper into the rubble was slow and difficult. I was unsteady. The nanocloud was weak, *ergo* I was weak. Pieces of the wreckage were burning. Some piles were impassable, and the light was nearly gone. I stumbled often. Fell twice. Ignored the scrapes and cuts. Pressed on.

I followed the intermittent sounds of Emilio's weeping until I found him, covered in dust and grime among the ruins, keening, rocking back and forth. He clutched a swaddled figure to his chest: Bonnie Lu. Our baby's lovely brown curls were dirty and tangled. Emilio kept patting them, trying vainly to brush the dirt away.

I had already known in my heart that Bonnie was gone. *Gone*, like Zander was gone. Like Janice was gone. Like Abe was gone. Like Belicia was gone.

I was in no rush to take Bonnie from Emilio, because I still could not face reality. I suppose I was, in fact, edging closer to total shutdown.

My mind continued to "play" Zander over and over, and I couldn't stop it.

Zander's slack face, his gray eyes dull and unfocused.

Zander, far, far away from me.

The warehouse barren and empty because Zander was not there.

Eventually I sank down beside Emilio. Just sat there, Zander on repeat. Zander gone. Zander gone. After a while I realized that, between Emilio's sobs, he was talking, but my muddled mind couldn't make out the words.

I stared at the debris around me and let everything . . . and nothing . . . have its way.

I don't know when Emilio's mumbled words began to make sense. I took a great, shuddering breath and finally looked more closely at him.

He was whispering to Bonnie. Reassuring her.

"It's okay. It's okay, little Bonnie Lu. Jesus got you. Jesus got you! It's okay, little Bonnie Lu. You gonna wake up in heaven, so it's okay!"

His eyes blinked quickly, and I think he realized I was there.

"Mama?"

I swallowed. Couldn't speak. I wanted to, but I couldn't even try.

I didn't have it in me.

"Mama? Mama?"

I breathed out. Breathed in. "I . . . I'm here, Emilio."

"Jesus got Bonnie Lu, right? She gonna wake up in heaven?"

The tears started then. They ran down my face in thick, dirty rivulets. "Yes, Sweetheart. She's . . . she's already there, in heaven. With . . . with Abe and . . . with Dad."

Emilio stared, shock upon shock crossing his face. He hadn't known.

He was going under.

I scooted closer. Wrapped my arms around him. Around my baby.

"Yes, it's okay, Emilio. Jesus has them. Why don't you and I . . . hold Bonnie Lu together, okay? For a while."

He leaned into me. I gripped him tighter. Bent toward Bonnie and placed my lips on her forehead. Her skin was cool to the touch, and my heart cried out, *This isn't right. It's not right! Oh, God!*

I wept. Emilio wept with me. I held him close, Bonnie's cold little fingers curled in the palm of my hand. I kept trying to warm them up, but nothing I did could do so.

Time passed. A moment. An age. An eon.

A passage from Revelation 14 rose before me.

I didn't know why or how that passage came to mind. All I knew was that it was God's living word in due season. His word to me while in the thrall of agony.

This calls for patient endurance on the part
of the people of God who keep his commands
and remain faithful to Jesus.
Then I heard a voice from heaven say,
"Write this: Blessed are the dead
who die in the Lord from now on."

*"Yes," says the Spirit, "they will rest from their labor,
for their deeds will follow them."*

"All right, Lord," I whispered. "I see that we're near the end. Perhaps you spared Bonnie Lu. Saved her from suffering . . . saved me from watching her suffer. I don't know. I do know she is with you now . . . and Zander is with you. Just please . . . please help me and help Emilio to do what you ask. To patiently endure. To keep your commands. To remain faithful to Jesus."

I was talking to the Lord, but Emilio was there, listening to me. Suffering his own agony.

"Mama?"

"Yes, my son?"

He gulped and sobbed before he could put his thoughts into words. "Do we need to do those things before we get to go to Jesus?"

"Those things?"

"That patient thing. Faithful to Jesus."

I nodded slowly. I recited the passage aloud to him.

"That's in the Bible?"

"It is, Emilio, and we are very close to the end now. *Blessed are the dead who die in the Lord* the Spirit said. Abe, Dad, and Bonnie Lu are with the Lord now—and they are *all right.* No pain. No hunger. No sorrows."

Emilio nodded a little. "But . . . is Bonnie cold, Mama?"

He had felt her cold face and hands and was as distressed as I was.

"The real Bonnie isn't here with us anymore, Emilio. She left behind what the Bible calls her little tent. Now Bonnie is with Dad and Abe in heaven with Jesus. No, she isn't cold there."

"This isn't Bonnie anymore?"

"Not really. I mean, if it were the real Bonnie, why, she'd be wiggling around, huh?"

"Yeah—" That one word stuck on a sob. "I'm gonna miss her bad, Mama! I'm gonna miss Dad and Abe too!"

I broke down with him. "We will miss them together, Emilio. I'm just . . . just happy that they are warm and clean, and I'll bet heaven has lots of food."

"Well, that part's all right, then. I'd like lots of food. Do you think we can go soon?"

I kissed the top of his head. "I don't know when you and I will rest from our labors, Emilio, my son. The Lord may have things for us to do first."

"Yeah? What we gotta do, Mama?"

"I don't know the details yet, *mijo*, and I'm very tired. I need to . . . we need to sleep. The Holy Spirit will tell us what to do next. Maybe in the morning. Maybe later, but he will show us the way. We'll get up . . . and he'll show us where to go. What to do."

"What about Dad? What about Abe? We can't just leave them . . . What about—" he broke. He couldn't say her name.

"We will . . . care for them in the morning, Sweetheart. Why don't you and I hold Bonnie Lu while we sleep. I know you love her so much. You are such a good big brother."

He nodded and laid his head on my shoulder. Reluctantly, I covered Bonnie's chubby little face with the corner of her blanket. I couldn't bear the thought that she would grow colder still. Then both of our arms went around her.

For a few hours, we slept. For a few hours we pretended she was still with us.

⌘⌘⌘⌘

CHAPTER 34

IT WAS STILL DARK WHEN THE SOUND of a car engine stirred me from uneasy slumber. Emilio slept on; the side of my body huddled with him was warm enough, but just. My back and legs were freezing. I was stiff, sore, and cold; my hands were scabbed with dried blood.

What?

Last evening rushed in, a tidal wave of loss and pain. I gasped and my heart thudded with fresh grief. Zander! Bonnie! Abe! Belicia!

I wanted to untangle my arms from around Emilio and Bonnie and reach out a hand to pull back Bonnie's blanket . . . but I did not. No. I could not bear to see her again. How she looked wasn't right. Would never be right.

"Oh, God, this hurts too much!"

I heard voices calling. Caught the glint of flashlights above our heads.

"Zander! Jayda! Emilio!" Josh shouting. "Abe! Belicia! Anyone!"

"Jayda!" Dr. Bickel shouting.

"Abe! *Emilio!*" Gamble shouting.

A wail of grief. A shriek rising into the air.

Izzie.

She has found you, Zander, but she has lost her brother.

My breaking heart broke a little more.

Izzie, my sister, I am sorry you must bear this pain too.

For a time the search halted, and I imagined them weeping over Zander as I had. Then, Gamble called again. For me. For Emilio and Abe. Not for Zander.

With excruciating slowness, I unwrapped my arm from around Emilio and Bonnie. I lifted my hand above my head. I couldn't raise it very high, but I hoped someone might see it.

Because I couldn't carry this burden even one more step by myself.

"Lord Jesus? I am yours. Until the end. I'm yours. Please help me do whatever you've left me here to do."

Death is swallowed up in victory.

"I long for that. Please."

Death is swallowed up in victory.

"What . . . what does that mean, exactly?

Soon.

I listened for the nanomites. "Nano?"

They answered, but their words were hollow. Listless.

We are here, Jayda Cruz. Reduced in number and needing power. When the sun rises, we will become stronger. You will become stronger.

A voice called out, "I see something!"

I waggled my feeble fingers. Heard feet scrambling over debris, coming closer.

"I've found them!" Gamble shouted. "I've found them!"

Emilio stirred. Gamble saw the little covered bundle in our arms. I turned my bereft eyes to him. His gaze drifted back to Bonnie.

He fell apart.

Even when Janice died, I hadn't seen him weep like he did now. He sank down to his knees and wailed as only a man in deep distress can wail.

Izzie, Josh, and Dr. Bickel struggled through the debris until they reached us. I don't know how long we grieved together.

It was a long time.

⌘

AFTER A WHILE, DR. BICKEL GOT US to move forward. "The police taped off the cul-de-sac before they left last night and posted no trespassing signs. We're not supposed to be here, and I imagine the police will return when the sun is fully up. If we're not gone when they arrive, we'll likely be arrested . . . and who knows what they'll do with you and Emilio if they find you and figure out who you are."

I shook with cold and fatigue. "I don't want them to put their hands on my boy . . . but I am weak. The nanomites are weak."

"Then let us help you, Jayda," Dr. Bickel said softly.

He and Gamble steadied me until my stiff and numb legs could hold me. I turned to Emilio.

"Let me have Bonnie, please, *mijo*. Until you can stand. Until we get clear of the rubble."

Eventually, we made it to a small and relatively clear section of cul-de-sac. I gave Bonnie back to Emilio. He needed to hold her more than I did.

Again, Dr. Bickel took the lead. "Abe? Belicia?"

"Abe is over there," I murmured, pointing with my chin, ". . . under the refrigerator. Belicia?" I stared at where her house had stood, the ugly, flattened smear that remained. "I don't know."

While Izzie and Dr. Bickel cleared more space around us, Josh and Gamble dug Abe and Zander's bodies out of the ruins and placed them side by side near us.

Emilio and I cried together as we watched.

Dr. Bickel asked Gamble, "What should we do?"

I had slept fitfully in the cooling rubble through the long night and wakened several times. At each wakening, I wrestled anew with the horrors of Zander and Bonnie Lu's deaths . . . and how we should handle their burials. I consulted with the nanomites and considered our limited options. By the time our friends arrived, I had made my decisions.

"The nanomites dug an escape tunnel from our bedroom to their printer room. If we can clear a path into the garage and get into the printer room, we'll find an entrance to the tunnel. I would like to wrap Zander and Bonnie and lay them in the tunnel. Abe and Belicia too."

Dr. Bickel stroked his chin's thin beard. "We can hope that their, er, remains rest undisturbed there," he murmured, "but is it not more likely the authorities will bring in, er, dogs to locate and dig them up to verify their, er, bodies?"

"Tents," Emilio said slowly. His eyes lifted to mine. "Their tents. 'Cause they ain't—they *aren't*—here anymore."

I half smiled. "That's right, my son. I'm glad you understand. Dad, Abe, and Bonnie Lu are in heaven now. They left their empty tents behind."

"Right you are," Dr. Bickel replied. "I'm just concerned—"

I interrupted him. "I have asked the nanomites to burn the tunnel when we leave. To cremate . . . the bodies. The authorities will find the cremains . . . and a DNA sample. The nanomites will leave Zander's DNA so the authorities can confirm his death. With that confirmation, they will stop hunting him and, perhaps, not hunt for us."

Gamble touched my hand. "Could the nanomites do the same for Janice? Cremate her? I don't want anyone digging her up, messing with her."

"If you are willing to move her into the tunnel, yes."

Josh stood beside Gamble. He'd grown up considerably in the past week. "I'll help you, Ross."

"Thank you, Josh. That means a lot."

Dr. Bickel turned to me. "Before we begin, I'd feel better if we put you and Emilio in my car for a while. Give you both some water. Warm you up. We'll, er, get things ready."

"No, thank you, dear friend. I need to . . . be here. Helping."

I desperately wanted something more fitting than a filthy blanket to wrap Bonnie in.

Lord? Would you do something for me?

⌘

GAMBLE EXCLAIMED WHEN HE AND Josh cleared enough rubble to gain entrance to the printer room. "Hey. There's a lot of food down here, and most of it is intact!"

"Our emergency stash," I mumbled. "In case things got much worse."

"We should take it with us. Every bit of it."

We did as Gamble suggested, formed a brigade of sorts through the rubble, and transferred our reserve food supply to the trunks of Gamble's and Dr. Bickel's cars.

After, while the others searched for Belicia, the Lord answered my prayer. As Emilio and I dug down to the remains of Bonnie's bedroom, we found her dresser. It was flattened and burned, but when I kept digging, I found what I was looking for.

Was it only yesterday I had washed and dried it? Folded it and placed it in the dresser's bottom drawer?

"Look, Emilio. Let's wrap Bonnie in this, shall we?"

We gently placed Bonnie Lu on the soft green fleece she loved to stroke across her cheek. Washed her face clean. Swaddled her in the Winnie-the-Pooh quilt Fiona had made for her.

"There," I said. "Our pretty Bonnie Lu."

Suddenly, I could breathe again. I could put Bonnie Lu next to her daddy in the tunnel and leave with peace in my heart . . . knowing no wicked hands would ever touch either of them.

After the others had laid Janice, Abe, Belicia, and Zander in the tunnel, Emilio and I took Bonnie down ourselves. We undid the sheet wrapped around Zander and placed Bonnie inside the crook of his arm. I kissed my fingers and placed them on Zander's brow, then tucked the sheet back around him.

I confess that my mind often blanked out that day, but the thought that struck me in that moment has stayed with me: *Zander and Bonnie Lu. Together in life; together in death.*

Immediately, a voice whispered back to me: *Death is swallowed up in victory.*

It almost sounded like a correction.

You said so, Lord. I don't get it yet, but I know you are faithful. You will show me what you mean. Eventually.

We left the cul-de-sac soon after, Dr. Bickel hustling us along, urging us to move. I glanced back. The rubble of our house was smoking. The nanomites had already lit the fire in the tunnel beneath, a furnace they promised would burn as hot as a crematorium.

As we rounded the corner and left the neighborhood, I told myself the worst was over—the saying of final goodbyes to Abe, Belicia, Zander, and Bonnie Lu. To their "tents."

I didn't realize at the time how the pain would ambush me, would take me by surprise again and again. In trickles. In waves. In blasts. In every memory.

I would understand as the days crept by.

Death is swallowed up in victory.

My forehead puckered. *Please show me what that means, Lord?*

⌘

AN EON LATER, WE ARRIVED AT Dr. Bickel's house. We drove directly into his garage so no one saw us as we got out.

When we went into Dr. Bickel's house, Izzie insisted on taking me into a bathroom to clean me up. The hot shower helped a lot. The sun was now fully up and the nanomites were strengthening. I felt my own energy moving incrementally upward.

Then Izzie cleaned and disinfected my many cuts and scrapes. While she worked, the nanomites did their part, killing bacteria and speeding healing to my injuries, particularly where my head had slammed against the concrete barrier.

I found myself wondering, *Thanks, but what's the point?*

⌘

HALFWAY THROUGH THE DAY, I realized it was Sunday; however, no text message "magically" appeared on our phones or other devices to announce an upcoming Bible teaching. No proclamation of the Gospel streamed across the earth. No Blond Preacher with Zander's love shining from his proxy's blue eyes appeared on screen.

Late that evening, Nora Mellyn did.

Jayda Cruz, the news networks report that Nora Mellyn will make a special presidential announcement in ten minutes.

I was ambivalent. Numb inside. The others watched, so I watched. Afterward, I was relieved that Emilio had showered and gone to bed, that he had not been awake to listen to that woman's glee.

"Good evening, my fellow Americans. I come to you with the best possible news! The Blond Preacher who has bedeviled the world for weeks is dead—*we* have killed him. Although we still do not know how he disguised himself or how his broadcasts managed to elude our cyber specialists, we do, at last, know his identity.

"His name was Zander Cruz. He was the pastor of a particularly egregious and vile church in Albuquerque. Today, we unearthed a grave containing the incomplete cremains of four or so bodies. We were able to salvage DNA samples from what was incompletely cremated. The surviving DNA samples confirm, positively, that Zander Cruz is dead along with three or four others, most likely including his wife, Jayda Cruz."

Mellyn continued. "With this man's just demise, we will finally have peace on our airwaves. I urge you to join me in giving praise to the gods and goddesses of this nation for this victory."

Her smile was pure gloat. "Thank you and good night."

Dr. Bickel shut off his television. "The nanomites did their job, just as you said they would."

"I am grateful to them," I murmured.

Later, in the hollow and numb recesses of my heart, I whispered, "I will see you in heaven, my love. You and our Bonnie Lu. Until then, why am I here?"

That still, small voice spoke again into my heart, *Death is swallowed up in victory.*

"Forgive me, Lord, but this doesn't feel like victory. The wicked increase, while your saints perish?

"When, Lord? When will you finally triumph over evil?"

His answer floated back to me.

> *When the perishable*
> *has been clothed with the imperishable,*
> *and the mortal with immortality, Jayda.*
> *Then the saying that is written will come true:*
> *"Death has been swallowed up in victory."*

⌘

AS THE WORLDWIDE MEDIA trumpeted Zander's death, spontaneous revelry broke out. People celebrated with parties and dancing in the street . . . followed by drinking, drugs, and public lewdness that devolved into lootings, vandalism, and riots.

And despite her public "victory lap," Mellyn's announcement wasn't entirely as effective she'd hoped it would be. Oh, sure—those who supported the GC were pleased, even thrilled when they heard of Zander's death.

But the Lord's people?

They rose up.

They rose up in powerful public preaching across the earth, in potent personal testimonies, in calls for repentance, in prayer for the sick and the desperate—in miracles, healings, and great joy and wonder. *Everywhere,* men and women of God put their all "out there" and reaped a harvest for God's eternal kingdom.

As expected, the Lord's people also reaped persecution.

When those in power realized how many individuals were turning to Christ, they mobilized every police force and national guard unit at their disposal to harass, beat, and arrest anyone who gathered a crowd in public and refused to be dispersed.

The arrests were not slow to percolate through the media censors, either. Each night, preachers and newly converted alike were demonized, painted as villains who opposed "global unity" and who were intent upon sabotaging Mellyn's Great American-Allied Restoration.

With daily media fanfare, Christians who dared speak of Jesus were hauled before special judges and offered one opportunity to recant their faith. Those Christians who refused were pronounced guilty and sent to "Homeland Camps." There they would be counseled and, hopefully, reintegrated into American society. Or else.

Even two years ago, who would have believed that the American government would build and operate reeducation camps? Who would have believed that our government would "disappear" those who refused to recant their faith in Christ?

The tyranny and oppression weren't unique to the US, of course. Every GC-centric nation followed suit.

Why? Because the GC wanted believers everywhere to recognize the price for choosing Jesus. They did not realize that, with each reported episode, they were strengthening the will and commitment of those who loved God.

The nanomites, their arrays, reporting back from around the globe, showed us the commitment of the Lord's people.

⌘

A CHINESE PASTOR, TORN FROM HIS sobbing family, declared, "I love Jesus! He is the Savior of the world—and I am persuaded that he is able to keep what I have committed to him until that Day!"

Three of the soldiers who arrested him begged him to tell them how to become followers of Christ.

⌘

A YOUNG MUSLIM MAN, AS THEY pushed him to his knees to be beheaded, told his family that Isa (the Arabic name for Jesus) had appeared to him in multiple dreams. "Isa came to me! He held out his nail-pierced hand, and said, Come! Follow me! I took his hand, and he forgave my sins! Then he filled me with his presence and peace."

His face alight with glory, he shouted with joy, "*Isa* is able to keep what I have committed to him until that Day—and soon I will see him face to face!"

A sword flashed; his head toppled to the ground.

Six of his cousins knelt and shouted, "Lord *Isa*, save us too! We choose you!"

Their blood joined their cousin's.

⌘

Two street preachers in Chicago, while being stoned to death for preaching repentance, said over and over, "We do not fear what man can do to us, because Jesus is able to keep what we have committed to him until that Day."

When they lay dead, twenty men and women pushed themselves forward and took their places, proclaiming the love of God revealed in his Son; preaching repentance from sin; salvation in Christ, and declaring the coming judgment.

When *they* lay dead? Fifty more rushed to replace them.

⌘

A sudden and formidable move of the Holy Spirit shook the earth. The nanomites showed us what the media witnessed and recorded but did not dare broadcast: Hundreds of normal, everyday Christians—powerful under the anointing of the Holy Spirit—preached the Gospel in the streets, and thousands responded and surrendered to the Lordship of Christ.

Armed soldiers viciously attacked those spontaneous crusades. They shot those who preached Jesus and beat those who responded to the Gospel. They hauled the uncowed converts away in large trucks.

Many laid down their lives for Christ in the aftermath of Zander's death, but *many, many more* followed their example. They publicly declared Jesus as the Savior of the world. They preached repentance and forgiveness in Jesus' name. They led huge crowds to confess their sins and receive Jesus as Lord and Savior.

When they also fell under a hail of bullets, twice their number took their place.

The streets ran with the blood of martyrs, but the hopeless, the broken, the destitute, and the guilty—they found deliverance on those same blood-soaked streets.

No, Mellyn's gloating announcement did not elicit universal glee.

It was the match that set the world aflame.

⌘

For three days, the remaining members of the co-op did little but rest and recover at Dr. Bickel's house. Of us, Emilio suffered the most. He had, in the instant we lost Zander, Abe, and Bonnie, lost his dad, his grandpa, and his beloved sister.

He often came to me during those days. I held him close and told him how much I loved him, that Zander and Abe loved him and were proud of him. I assured him that the Lord had not forgotten us, that he would show us what to do next—even if, in my darkest moments, I wasn't certain myself.

At other times, he rejected my overtures—which told me he was missing Zander and Abe's male companionship. Dr. Bickel managed to procure a used baseball and two gloves. Gamble and Josh, in an effort to keep Emilio's sadness from overwhelming him, took turns playing catch with him in Dr. Bickel's basement.

Three days, and my empty arms never ceased aching for Bonnie Lu's warmth.

Three days in which no one spoke of tomorrow or "what next."

Without saying a word, we knew the situation was temporary, that of necessity, it had to be brief . . . because of me. Because of Emilio. We dared not leave the walls of Dr. Bickel's house even to venture into his yard. I was, after all, the widow of the despicable Blond Preacher, aka that hated criminal, Zander Cruz, and Emilio was our son.

Then there was Gamble, who'd dropped off the face of the earth as far as the FBI knew. He didn't belong with Dr. Bickel, either.

On the other hand, we didn't believe Josh or Izzie were on Mellyn's radar. But that meant being with us put them in danger.

In any case, the neighbors knew Dr. Bickel lived by himself. The longer we stayed, the more risk he, Josh, and Izzie incurred.

For three days, it wasn't time to move.

And then it was.

⌘⌘⌘⌘

CHAPTER 35

GAMBLE, DR. BICKEL, AND I MET in Dr. Bickel's office. Dr. Bickel and I had already put our heads together. It was a matter of convincing Gamble.

"We need to move, Gamble. Get out of here. Josh and Izzie don't stick out like sore thumbs, but if someone recognizes Emilio, me, or you, we will bring Mellyn's wrath down on the others. They won't hesitate to send a kill team for us."

"You know something I don't?"

"Yeah. Sorry to be the bearer of more bad news, but the nanomites say the FBI has issued a BOLO for you. They don't know if you're dead or if you've bugged out, but either way? They're looking for you—and not with your best interests at heart."

"Figures. My boss and his boss were already side-eyeing me. When Mellyn took office, FBI headquarters began directing agents to get on the same page as our glorious 'global unity' leader. If you're not with her? You're history—an 'enemy of the state.' I'd no sooner given my life to Jesus, than my bosses seemed to sense the big shift in me."

I nodded. "Some elements of spiritual discernment go both ways. The devil knows those who are his *or* the Lord's people, and vice-versa."

"So, we need to leave, but go where?"

I said, "I'd like to send Josh, Izzie, and Emilio to Roberto and María until things shake out. Send our food stockpile with them. I think you'd be welcome to go with them."

"What about you?"

"Lots of people dead from the virus equals lots of empty houses. I'll pick one. My invisibility will hide me. If I need to move, rinse and repeat."

"So, you intend to leave Emilio while you go off *elsewhere?* You're his mom! Won't he feel that you've abandoned him? Hasn't he been traumatized enough?"

I sighed. "I could take him with me, but I don't think it would be wise—not if there's a target on me and I'm forced to move quickly. Besides . . . the nanomites suggest I may have work to do—and whatever it is, it won't be safe for Emilio."

"What if Emilio and I come with you? I could keep him occupied and safe while you go off and do whatever."

"Thanks for the offer, but I've decided to send him to his grandparents with Josh and Izzie."

⌘

"No." That was Emilio's answer. In a voice sounding more "adult-ish" than any I'd heard before, Emilio folded his arms and dished out his one-syllable reply.

I said slowly, "*Mijo*, if you go with Josh and Izzie, you will be with *Abuelo* Roberto and *Abuela* María on their little farm. It's nice there, isn't it? It won't be safe for you to come along with me."

Emilio glared at me from under his bunched brows. "No place is safe. Where you go, I go."

I studied Emilio. The joyful "bounce" of his personality seemed crushed. Then I saw it, the twitch in the set of his mouth. The dullness in his eyes.

Fear. The old fear I'd seen when I first knew him . . . now joined by the fear of losing me, that I, too, would leave him . . . like Zander, Abe, and Bonnie Lu had.

*So, you intend to leave Emilio while you go off **elsewhere**? You're his mom! Won't he feel that you've abandoned him? Hasn't he been traumatized enough?*

I shrugged. Acknowledged that some trauma is worse than other trauma.

"It won't be easy, Emilio. We'll be hiding and, um, you might die of boredom?"

I had attempted levity. And bombed.

"I can handle hiding—'sides, where you go, I go. *Mama*."

I understood. "All right, my son."

He visibly relaxed. I hugged him. We both teared up. Hugged some more.

Gamble mumbled, "If you want someone along to help, my offer still stands. Got nothing else on my busy schedule."

It dawned on me then that if anything happened to me, Gamble would do his best to keep Emilio safe. Deliver him to Roberto and María for me. After.

I sighed. "Yeah. All right."

⌘

I sent Izzie out to find serviceable clothing for the co-op's remnant. She and Josh had packed a couple changes for their honeymoon. Those clothes were all they had left now. Me? I owned what I wore on my back—that's it. Same for Emilio and Gamble.

The rest of us stuffed multiple backpacks with rations and necessities. It may have been frivolous of me, but I replaced a sack of rice in my pack with the baseball and gloves Dr. Bickel had given Emilio. My boy might need distraction from his pain as much as he needed food.

When we were ready, we figured out transportation. The FBI's BOLO had made Gamble's car too "hot" to keep around. Sure, the nanomites could effect changes to it, but as soon as I walked away? So would those changes.

We decided to ditch his ride. To take its place, Gamble and I sought out an abandoned vehicle the nanomites could get running. That's where we left Gamble's car—after we had drained the gas tank. Gasoline was like gold these days; Josh and Izzie would need it to reach to Roberto and María's place in Las Cruces. We poured the siphoned gas into the "new" car's tank and drove back to Dr. Bickel's house.

Josh and Izzie were packed up and ready. We turned the "new" car over to them and, with many hugs and heartfelt prayers for their safety, sent them on their way.

Next, we used Dr. Bickel's car (disguised by the nanomites) to scout out an empty house for Gamble, Emilio, and me. When Gamble drove us away in Dr. Bickel's car, the nanomites made him look like an older Hispanic man. Emilio and I traveled in the backseat, invisible.

"We need to make a stop before we scout out a house," I told Gamble. I gave him directions then asked him to park opposite a boarded-up strip mall.

"Wait for me here."

I got out and, under the nanomites' cover, made my way across the street, then down the backside of the boarded up strip mall. Went through the locked and alarmed rear door of what had once been a thriving martial arts studio.

The nanomites checked the dojo's security logs: No one had entered the building in eight months.

The familiar practice area wore the thick patina of disuse. Dust motes floated in the air. The heavy bags and sparring equipment smelled of old sweat.

I marched toward the equipment room. Opened Locker 7 and withdrew a set of kamagong escrima sticks and a quiver. The sticks felt heavier in my hands than I remembered, but I don't think it was the hard, dense wood that was weighing me down.

No, everywhere I looked, I expected to see him.

Longed to see him.

But he wasn't there.

Zander . . .

I swallowed. Came back to myself.

"Do I really need these, Nano?"

You must again become optimal, Jayda Cruz. We will train you.

"Great, but I doubt we'll find a house with enough room for me to spar with Gus-Gus."

The dojo's office was just as dusty as the rest of the place. I wondered if Doug, the owner, was still alive or if he'd succumbed to the virus.

In any event, I pulled a folded envelope containing ten twenty-dollar bills from my pocket and placed it on the desk. Picked up a pen and wrote on the back.

Doug,
> *Hope this covers the sticks I've taken.*
> *Best wishes,*
> *Emily*

I started to leave. Stopped. Looked around with a different perspective. The other shops alongside the dojo in the strip mall were also abandoned. No people lived or worked nearby. The dojo's windows were papered with posters, every bit as good as drapes. We'd be fine if we kept the lights off in the studio and only turned them on in the windowless back.

The dojo was about as innocuous and isolated a hiding place as we could hope for.

"Huh. I think . . . well, yeah. This will work."

I had Gamble drive the car around to the back of the dojo and park it by the rear entrance. We emptied the trunk of everything we'd packed, including three backpacks loaded as emergency bug-out bags.

Back inside the dojo, we set to work. I cleaned the bathrooms and showers. Emilio swept the dojo from one end to the other. Gamble tackled the break room where a microwave sat.

We piled mats in the two locker rooms and laid out blankets for sleeping. Stocked our food in the break room.

I pulled out the ball and gloves and handed them to Emilio. "It's okay to bounce the ball off the wall out in the dojo."

He nodded and wandered away. After a bit I heard the rhythmical *thud, thud, thud* of the ball hitting the wall.

"I'll drive Dr. Bickel's car back to him now," I told Gamble.

An hour later, Dr. Bickel dropped me a couple blocks from the dojo's immediate neighborhood. We didn't want Dr. Bickel to know exactly where we'd be . . . in case he was ever questioned. I jogged my way back to the dojo while under the nanomites' cover.

⌘

WE'D BEEN HUNKERED DOWN in the dojo for a week. During that time, the nanomites had focused on two objectives. The first was rebuilding the nanocloud to as close to its previous strength as was possible. I say, "as was possible," because they could not, at present, print new nanomites.

A small number of tribe members from Zanders' nanocloud had somehow survived the missile strike—likely blown clear of the blast but severely injured. This small number (and I had to remind myself that *a small number of a very large number is still a large number*) found their way to my nanocloud during those first wretched hours.

Because my nanocloud was impaired, Zander's damaged nanomites initially put a tremendous strain on the cloud's overall strength. Frankly, the level of effort my nanocloud put forward to save as many tribe members as possible was astounding.

The healthy nanomites triaged the billions of damaged mites. The able mites attended to the tribe members who could most quickly be repaired and put back into service. They sent the worst wounded into "sleep mode" and used the parts and pieces of those that "died" to repair others.

The nanomites' second objective during that week was to train me mercilessly, harder than I'd ever trained before—and I let them. It was a relief to work myself into exhaustion. Anything to forget, for a few minutes, the aching loss in my heart and in my arms.

If only my workouts could also curtail the dreams I had each night, dreams of Bonnie's toothy little grin. Her hand patting my cheek. The warmth of her little body in my arms.

"What are you doing?" Gamble asked as I "shadow boxed" with my invisible opponent.

"The nanomites want me to brush up on my training."

"How much can you practice without a sparring partner?"

I explained about Gus-Gus and Ninja Noid. The monikers I'd slapped on them sounded silly to me at this point. Spoiled-child silly.

Gamble didn't seem to notice. He found the concept of a virtual sparring partner fascinating.

To keep my mind busy when I wasn't training, I decided to work Gamble and Emilio too—not that I expected them to learn a whole lot, but teaching them the basics of Kali-style fighting was a means of keeping the three of us mentally and physically occupied. With nothing better to do, I drilled them in basic footwork, had them pull rattan sticks from the dojo's lockers, and demonstrated how to strike the training dummy in the corner.

Between sessions they played catch or bounced the ball off the dojo wall to improve their catching skills.

Bounced it incessantly.

The dojo was large enough for three people to enjoy a modicum of space, but after hours and days of the *thunk* of that ball hitting the wall—over *and over* **and over**—it began to feel like Chinese water torture.

I couldn't get the continual expectation of that *thunk* out of my head. It irked me, drove me mad. Fact was, I was on edge. Anxious one minute, irritable the next. I prowled the building because I couldn't settle or rest.

Jayda Cruz.

"What, Nano?"

The world is hurting, Jayda Cruz.

The world was hurting? The world didn't have *squat* on me. Nothing assuaged my pain, my longing for Zander. For Bonnie Lu.

"Take a number. All of us are hurting."

You are not wrong, Jayda Cruz. Many people are suffering. Too many are without hope. Zander Cruz's viewers long for the strength and courage his Bible teachings gave them. Also, many nonbelievers across the globe are seeking for hope but do not realize their only hope is in Jesus.

They do not know how to find Jesus, Jayda Cruz.

"What's your point, Nano?"

Jayda Cruz, you can replace Zander Cruz. We can stream your Bible lessons to the world.

Okay, that dumb suggestion infuriated me.

"*No*, Nano. *No*, I can't replace Zander. He . . . God prepared *him* for that ministry—not me. I don't know how to preach or teach like him—I wouldn't know where to start."

And yet you are well versed in Scripture, Jayda Cruz, and most people cannot even locate a Bible to read for themselves. If all you did was to read aloud from Scripture, you would bless and strengthen believers across the world.

Besides, we have heard it said that God does not call the able; he calls the **avail***able.*

"Well, I'm not doing it, so stop bugging me."

We are hurting too, Jayda Cruz. We lost our sister nanocloud when you lost your Zander. We lost many tribe members. We have worked hard to help the members that were damaged, so we could be as optimal as possible.

We are grieving, but we still belong to the Tribe of Jesus. We will do whatever he asks of us.

I felt the sting of a rebuke and shucked it off. It climbed back on.

The need is great, Jayda Cruz, and you are available. We are the only means of streaming God's word to the world, but you are the only person who can speak it. Ross Gamble is a new believer and does not know the Bible well. Emilio Cruz is a new believer and a child besides.

I tried to twist out from under a mounting sense of conviction. The nanomites did not let me.

You are not a new believer. You know God's word, do you not? You know how to lead someone to faith in Christ, do you not? You can pray with the lost to surrender their hearts and lives to him, can you not?

"Stop! Stop it! I'm not stepping into Zander's shoes, Nano!"

An uncomfortable silence settled into the gulf between the us. Until . . .

We assumed you were a mature believer, Jayda Cruz. Were we wrong? Will you leave those needing Jesus to die in darkness? Are you prepared to stand before God and answer for their eternal souls?

I was struck dumb. Stand before God and answer for their eternal souls?

"I—" My mouth dried up; my tongue had shriveled. I couldn't speak.

Jayda Cruz, we told you that Jesus said you had important work ahead of you and it was our job to watch over and safeguard you for that work.

I sneered as my nano-enhanced memory kicked in. "What you said, *precisely*, Nano, was, and I quote: 'Jesus has told us to protect *you and the child*. He says you have important work ahead of you. It is our job to watch over and safeguard yo*ur family*.'

"Don't tell *me* what to do, when you didn't do *your* job."

Maybe I was shocked to hear the bitterness gushing out of my heart via my mouth—but I badly wanted to end the nanomites' harassment.

I hoped I had heard the last of it.

It should have been the end of it.

But it wasn't.

Jayda Cruz, Zander Cruz finished his race. According to Job 14: verses 1 and 5, he and Bonnie Lu Cruz lived exactly as long as the Lord God intended for them to live.

"How frail is humanity!
How short is life, how full of trouble!

"You have decided the length of our lives.
You know how many months we will live,
and we are not given a minute longer."

You, however, Jayda Cruz, have not finished the work Jesus has given you. Much remains for you to accomplish before the Lord calls you to him. Will you do it? Or will you wallow in your pain while others die without Jesus and your race remains unfinished?

Zander and Bonnie lived exactly as long as the Lord intended them to live? The reason I was still alive was because I hadn't . . . finished my race?

The words of the Blond Preacher during his first message resounded in my ears: *The people in our neighborhood are very weary. Worn down and overwhelmed. And yet . . . every believer still has a job, and God calls each of us not to give up, but to finish the work he has given us.*

That memory was followed by the nanomites' unchecked rebuke.

Will you wallow in your pain while others die without Jesus?

I found it difficult to breathe.

"I . . . I need to think, Nano. Please. Just leave me be to think."

You do not need to think, Jayda Cruz. At present, your thoughts are not God's thoughts, nor your ways his ways. You need to ask Jesus if what we say is true or not. You need to ask Jesus what he expects of you—and then do it.

"I—"

Schooled. Schooled by the nanomites.

I shut them out as best I could and got with God.

"Lord? Do you want me to . . . to speak your word to the world?"

The answer that came back to me pierced the sac of bitterness surrounding my heart.

> *For I was hungry and you gave me something to eat,*
> *I was thirsty and you gave me something to drink*

I covered my face with my hands. "Please, Lord! I don't know how to do this—I wouldn't know what to say!"

Again, the answer came to me, Luke 4 where Jesus quotes from Isaiah 61.

> *"The Spirit of the Lord is upon Me,*
> *Because He has anointed Me*
> *To preach the gospel to the poor;*
> *He has sent Me to heal the brokenhearted,*
> *To proclaim liberty to the captives*
> *And restoration of sight to the blind,*
> *To set at liberty those who are oppressed;*
> *To proclaim the acceptable year of the Lord."*

I remained cloistered with the Lord for some time. The nanomites did not disturb us. Gamble and Emilio did not intrude. I was alone with *him*, where I needed to be. Where he could speak to me. Comfort me on the one hand; correct me on the other.

> *The Lord disciplines the one he loves.*

"You must love me a lot, Lord."

⌘⌘⌘⌘

CHAPTER 36

APRIL 11

IT WAS SUNDAY. TWO WEEKS and one day had passed since the missile strike that killed Abe. Belicia. Zander. Bonnie Lu.

But yesterday had been the worst day since I lost them.

I confess to almost giving up . . . because yesterday we should have been wrapping gifts. I should have been baking a cake. Zander, Emilio, and I should have been listening to Bonnie Lu's giggles, watching her amazement and her dimpled smile. The nanomites should have been recording Zander giving our Bonnie Lu her very own cupcake with one little candle in it. Emilio should have been teaching Bonnie to blow it out.

Yesterday should have been Bonnie's birthday. One year old.

Instead, I fought all day just to stay sane.

I didn't mention Bonnie's birthday to either Emilio or Gamble. How could I? I didn't want them to hurt as bad I did.

That missile killed more than my husband and my baby. It killed my heart.

Every beat felt like a fresh stake in my chest.

Take a breath. Inhale. Exhale. Stake in the chest.

If I'm honest, I must admit that what I thought about my heart wasn't precisely true. Yes, it was shattered and would bear the cracked lines of those factures forever, but the Lord had ministered his comfort to me. He'd given me a job to do . . . if I chose to do it. And my heart needed to function again if I intended to accept my new mission and give myself to it.

I blinked. Bonnie Lu's sparkling brown eyes intruded. Her big belly laugh. Her joyous shriek of "Na no! Na no!"

Pull yourself together. Focus.

Like I said, it was Sunday, but for the prior two Sundays, no text message had announced to the world that a Bible teaching was forthcoming. I glanced down at my iPad where I'd cobbled my notes together. There, on the screen, the announcement popped up.

A Bible teaching message
will livestream in ten minutes
<u>CLICK HERE</u> to join

I sat in Doug's office with the door closed, my phone jury-rigged to stand several feet in front of me. I awaited the nanomites' directive to begin speaking. Emilio and Gamble, silent and wide-eyed, watched from the dojo.

I think they were as nervous as I was—and I was terrified.

Jayda Cruz. We are counting down. You are live in three, two, one.

My phone began recording.

What the world saw was a middle-aged Asian woman with steel-gray hair. No point in letting the GC know I was still alive, right?

Inhale. Exhale. Talk.

"Good morning, dear friends in Christ. I pray a blessed day of rest, worship, and devotion to God's word for each of you.

"Um, as you heard Nora Mellyn announce, the man known to you all as the Blond Preacher was killed in a missile strike. He is now at home in heaven with Christ and our Heavenly Father."

I glanced at the counter on my phone just as it crested 1.2 billion. The saliva in my mouth instantly evaporated, leaving my mouth a desert wasteland.

When I could speak again, it was in a whisper. "While this news was difficult to accept, this morning I am putting my sorrow aside . . . to visit with you.

Inhale. Exhale. Talk.

"I freely admit that I am not the Bible scholar the Blond Preacher was. However, I was challenged recently—perhaps chastised is a better word— to tell you what I *do* know. What do I know? More than enough Scripture to explain Jesus to someone who doesn't yet know him."

I leaned in a little. "That, by the way, is what each of us is called to do —explain what we know about Jesus and share what he has done in our hearts and lives. So, if you are seeking Jesus this morning, you're in the right place."

Inhale. Exhale. Talk.

I made an effort to relax. A little. Smiled a crooked smile into the camera. "Shall we begin? I'd like to introduce and discuss three simple words found in the Bible. Those words are 'draw,' 'convict,' and 'repent.'

"'Let's start with the verb 'draw' found in John 6:44.

> *"No one can come to me unless*
> *the Father who sent me draws them.*

"If you are experiencing a discomforting sensation in your heart, a 'pull' that, for example, caused you to click on the link this morning and listen to what I have to say about Jesus? That is God Almighty tugging at your heart, calling you to him, *drawing* you to him.

"The sensation is discomforting because it is God the Father, working in a supernatural manner in your heart. You see, when our Holy God begins his work in us, he always shows us our need for a Savior by confronting us with our sin.

"The Bible calls that confrontation 'conviction,' the process of being *convicted* or *convinced* that we are sinners. 'Convict' is our second Bible word of the day. Jesus said in John 16:8 that when the Holy Spirit comes, *he will **convict** the world of sin.*

"We're not accustomed to confrontation that makes us feel guilty or ashamed, are we? In fact, the leaders of our society insist that any talk or discussion about sin, guilt, shame, or repentance is 'hate speech.'

"May I say, with all kindness, that our leaders have lied to us? Until we are ready to face the truth about ourselves, we will remain separated from God, lost and terrified of death and what comes after it.

"But when we *recognize* our sin, we realize how far from God we are. That's not a good place to stay, but it's the *right* place to start, because Jesus came to save us from that sin and take us into his Father's presence.

"In his word, the Lord uses the word 'repent' to take us from fear to faith, from sinner to saint. In his very first words of public ministry, found in Matthew 3:2, Jesus said, *Repent, for the kingdom of heaven has come near*. So what does 'repent' mean?"

I was so ready for this next part! I had it down cold.

"You see, when we repent, it means we turn around and face God, face the truth about ourselves, and acknowledge that truth. Repentance is *not* the ugly, hard, mean thing the world says it is. Repentance is a precious gift from God."

Lord, thank you for my husband and his wise words about repentance.

"When we repent—when we declare our sorrow for sin and declare that we turn from our sin—and when we ask Jesus to save us from our sin, then he comes inside. Yes, Jesus, by the Holy Spirit, comes to live inside of us. He makes us clean and begins to free us from fear and condemnation.

"Well, there you go, the Gospel in a nutshell. All that is left to do is what the Father is drawing us to do. If you want to repent of your sins and surrender your life to Christ today, I invite you to pray with me."

I bowed my head, and put myself in the shoes of someone about to meet Jesus. Framed my prayer for that individual.

"Lord God, I am beginning to 'get' it, beginning to understand that I am far away from you, that the way I have lived has grieved your heart. But in spite of the awful things I've done, you still loved me enough to send your Son to suffer, die, and pay for my sins.

"And I realize, Father, that you have been calling to me, *drawing* near to me, trying to get my attention. You have been doing a *convicting* work in my heart, convincing me of my sins and showing me how much I need you so that I would turn to you.

"So, right now, I confess that I need you desperately. I confess that I am a sinner and ask your forgiveness. I *repent* and turn away from the way I have lived; I surrender my life to you. I turn to your Son, Jesus, and I receive him as my Savior.

"And Jesus? Right now, I receive you as my Lord and King. Please enter into me by your Holy Spirit and wash me clean. I want to be born again by your Spirit, made new on the inside so I might honor the Father with the remainder of my life. Amen."

⌘

COMMENTS FOLLOWING MY MESSAGE ramped up and kept coming. Thousands had prayed with me and given their lives to Christ; their comments declared their faith in Jesus. Many who watched the video later also prayed. When the comments surpassed the hundred thousand mark, I stopped checking the counter.

I am grateful, Lord. Without your help, without the power of your Holy Spirit, I could not have presented a single coherent thought. You are so good! Thank you.

Oh. And I thank you for the nanomites who did not give up, who kept at me until I understood that this was my duty, my work for you.

I also experienced for myself how exhausting preaching was, why Zander had often been wrung out afterward.

I craved a few hours of sleep. I tried to nap, but I couldn't "knock out." Just as I started to nod off, a gamut of horror would jump up to run and rerun through my head.

Jayda Cruz! Missile launch! Missile launch! Missile launch!
Jayda Cruz! Missile launch! Missile launch! Missile launch!

Frustrated, I got up. Gamble and Emilio were playing a card game, so I wandered around the dojo. And since I was awake and on the move, the nanomites assumed it was a great time for a chat.

Jayda Cruz. We have just reviewed a nanoarray report we believe to be of great importance. We wish to show it to you.

"I am weary, Nano, mentally and emotionally. Can your report wait until later? Like tomorrow?"

No, Jayda Cruz. We rate this report as urgent.

"Aren't they all?"

We apologize. You were awake, so we understood you were available.

"It's not that, Nano. My body and mind need to rest, but I can't seem to switch myself off."

May we help you sleep for a while, Jayda Cruz?

I let their question mellow for a moment and was mildly surprised at how much I coveted their help.

"Yes. Please do, Nano."

⌘

I AWOKE MUCH LATER. HOURS HAD passed. Gamble and Emilio were eating and quietly talking.

Are you refreshed, Jayda Cruz?

"I'll let you know."

I unfolded myself and stretched. Stretched again. Went in search of coffee. Downed two cups. Hugged Emilio; nodded to Gamble. Looked inside.

Something had settled while I slept. At least for the time being, my mind had stopped racing. Had calmed.

"Guess I'm ready, Nano. You said it was urgent?"

Yes, Jayda Cruz. In order to convey the urgency of our report, we would again take you into a virtual recreation of the event a nanoarray captured yesterday.

"Yeeeaaah . . . Virtual recreation? Not my favorite thing, Nano."

Watching Okafor's arrest from Abe's nanoarray had messed with my equilibrium. Even worse? Our first venture with the nanomites into an immersive virtual environment—to view the results of their counter-insurgency—had twisted my stomach into knots for hours after.

I felt my tenuous calm start to slip.

Jayda Cruz, such an environment provides the best understanding of the event as it occurs.

I could hear Zander almost as if he were standing beside me: *Come on, Jay. Seems important.*

sigh

I thought for a moment.

"All right. Um, Nano, any chance Gamble could join us in this immersive virtual environment?"

They hummed softly before answering. *Jayda Cruz, we have observed that Ross Gamble has a strong constitution. His system may be able to withstand the shock—if he is willing to endure the side effects.*

I wandered over to Gamble and Emilio again. They stopped talking and glanced up.

"Did you get some rest, Jayda?" Gamble asked.

"Yeah. I did. Thanks for asking. Um, could I interrupt you for a bit? The nanomites have something they need to show us."

Gamble looked to Emilio. "Your mom and I need to meet with the nanomites. When you're done eating, want to practice that curve ball I showed you?"

"Sure. I can do that."

"Thanks, *mijo*." I tipped my head and walked away. Gamble followed me into Doug's office.

"What's up?"

How to explain?

"Okay, you know the nanomites have sent nanoarrays all over the world, right? The arrays gather information, then send it back to the nanomites who share it with us."

I grimaced. Not us. No more 'us.' "I mean with me. Anyway, the nanomites received a report they say is urgent, and I've asked them to share it with you."

"Thanks for the invite."

"Well, hold up a sec. See, the best way to understand the report is to enter what the nanomites call an immersive virtual environment. It's something like a VR experience on steroids, like physically being there *with* the nanoarray—or *in* the array? And I won't kid you, Gamble, it's a rough ride. The transition throws my equilibrium into a tailspin—but the nanomites say you have a strong constitution and can handle it."

"If the nanomites think I can hack it, I'm up for trying."

"There is no 'try,' Gamble. Only do—or should I say *endure*. Once you're in there, it's a rollercoaster, and there's no stopping the bus to get off. Sure you're still good to go?"

Gamble's brows lifted and he hesitated. Finally, he answered, "Er, yeah, I'm in."

Communication had to be dealt with too. Gamble couldn't enter the warehouse, so the nanomites needed to form a cloud and spread themselves over us. Then Gamble would be able to hear.

As the nanomites streamed from me, Gamble's eyes twitched.

"What's happening, Jayda?"

"Call it a communication cone. The nanomites will be making vibrations you can hear."

"Uh, got it."

"Okay, Nano. We're ready. But first—where will we be and what's up?"

The event takes place in a harbor on the Ligurian Sea not far from Genoa, Italy, Jayda Cruz. Recently, the Accardi family and their entire entourage left their home in Milan.

This unusual move during the present pandemic seemed to warrant closer surveillance. In fact, we felt it prudent to dispatch two more arrays into their entourage in order to understand their reasoning.

The event we will show you took place this morning, their time, which translates to midnight and beyond, Albuquerque time. The primary subject, Luca Accardi, is a top Global Community financier, but the event involves his family as well, as they board his yacht.

"Gee. A yacht on the Mediterranean? Must be nice. Bet *they* aren't living on meager rations."

Yes, I was grumbling, *and how.*

Jayda Cruz, I doubt you would wish to trade places with this family after you have viewed the event via our immersive virtual recreation.

⌘⌘⌘⌘

CHAPTER 37

NORTHWEST ITALIAN COASTLINE

"*BUONGIORNO, SIGNOR ACCARDI. Che piacere vederti.* It is a pleasure to see you again. All is prepared; we have already boarded your captain and crew. Please, come this way." The young Italian man, confident, suave, and impeccably dressed, led the client and his party down the long ramp from the wharf to the anchored pier where two luxurious open-air electric carts waited.

He gestured. "Be seated, if you please."

Their destination was the enclosed boathouse, as large as a commercial warehouse, visible at the end of the pier. The pier's length extended a full quarter-mile out onto the water, its length a necessity to accommodate the ship moored within the boathouse—out of sight of prying eyes. At nearly eighty meters, the ship was considered a "superyacht," and it required a marina or harbor with at least twenty meters of draft, hence the pier stretching far out into the harbor where the water was deeper.

Luca Gianni Accardi, billionaire Italian businessman, intended to sail away from the mainland today, away from the disgusting plague and its inconveniences. He and members of his household would sail out of the Mediterranean into the Atlantic via the Strait of Gibraltar. His yacht would wait near the Canary Islands until he received further guidance as to their rendezvous point.

Eventually, his ship would join other like-minded framers of the Global Community in a harbor specially prepared for them. A safe place to wait out the next stage of the Community's plans.

Every detail of his departure had been prearranged; every step made secure. Armed guards defended access to the pier. They scrutinized the arrivals, while other eyes observed activity across the wharf via a series of camera feeds monitored from a control room within the boathouse.

Accardi was accompanied (in order of importance) by his personal assistant, his current wife (of three, to date), their four-year-old daughter, the girl's *au pair*, and two of Accardi's six-man security team. This group would board the first cart for the run down the pier to the boathouse. The remaining four members of his security team and his wife's maid would organize the Accardis' luggage and join them shortly.

Their baggage, now being unloaded from a truck parked up on the wharf and ported down to the pier, would require more than one such cart. That was understood. The maid would ride out on the next cart with some of the luggage, including two large dog crates.

Signora Accardi's maid, Sophia Giardano, had been with the Accardi family for seven years. She had known the two Doberman pinschers since they were puppies, and she was quite fond of them.

She crouched by their crates and offered them the treats she carried in her pocket. They inhaled the nuggets from her palms through the wire gate; whined and licked her fingers after. The household's abrupt removal from their home in Milan to their yacht was, understandably, difficult on the animals. It was hard on Sophia also.

She withdrew a bottle of water from her handbag and tipped it carefully through the female's gate. The dog lapped at the water, sucking it in. She repeated her ministration with the male of the pair.

Fifteen minutes later, one of the security guards motioned to her. "Get in, Sophia. We are ready to load the dogs."

Sophia dutifully took her seat in the cart. Minutes later, the vehicle sped down the pier. She clung to the seat's armrest and struggled to keep her anxiety on a short leash—for when she boarded this new yacht Luca Accardi had purchased and provisioned, she would effectively be his prisoner.

Not that she wasn't already.

Until a few days ago, she had at least been allowed to call or text her mother whenever she wished. She understood that her conversations were continuously scrutinized; consequently, she was always cautious with what she said. But out on the high seas, after they arrived at their destination, and for an indeterminate period of time, no one would be permitted contact with the outside world.

Escape, certainly, would be impossible.

He promised me safety, she told herself again, referring to Luca Accardi's smarmy PA, Edwardo. Privately she called him Ed*weirdo*.

She shivered. *He promised me safety from the virus and from . . . other things that are coming*. Edwardo hadn't detailed the "other things" that were coming, but he hardly needed to. She knew she was stuck, unable to free herself, regardless of what those "other things" might prove to be.

I am a fool. I have given up my liberty for their promises of safety!

Perhaps, but she immediately acknowledged a deeper truth. *I had no real choice in the matter. Once they extended this 'opportunity' to me, I had to say yes. Luca's guards, at Edwardo's command, would have killed me had I refused. Like they killed the others.*

Under Luca's orders, security for the past month in the Accardi's palatial Milan home had been extreme. No one outside the household was permitted to know anything of the family's upcoming departure. Two days ago, Luca announced that the chauffeur, butler, and household help had been let go, but

Sophia knew better. Those members of the household were not slated to go with the family as she was, and Luca would leave no tongues to wag.

She mourned for the maids who had been her friends.

The cart approached the boathouse. A guard standing at the entrance pushed a button, and an oversized, reinforced door rolled open. A moment later, they were inside the cavernous building.

The cart took a left, ran down the dock, and pulled alongside the yacht. Sophia gazed upward in awe. The yacht's superstructure towered over her.

Luca Accardi and the young man, their "host," stood by the ramp leading out to the massive yacht. Sophia assumed Luca's wife and daughter had already boarded. One of Luca's security detail helped Sophia down from the vehicle.

"*Signor* Accardi," the young man, ever so cordial, was saying to Luca, "have you found the accommodations and preparations to your liking? Do they meet the agreed-upon specifications?"

Luca must have already toured the yacht and looked over his suite, the ship's amenities, the captain and his crew—the crew which, Francesca, the *au pair*, had told Sophia would include two chefs, a physician's assistant, a strength trainer, a masseuse, and Mrs. Accardi's preferred esthetician.

The ship's other amenities included four decks, sixteen double cabins (in addition to the master suites), two galleys, a large dining room, an intimate breakfast area on the deck off the master suite, a fully stocked clinic, two pools, two hot tubs, an indoor court for handball, and a tee box off the aft deck that doubled as a helicopter landing zone.

Besides all the accoutrements of wealth the yacht afforded, the lowest deck, within the ship's hull, provided a great deal of cargo space—cargo space that was to be filled to capacity with the things necessary for those on the ship to survive the next two months or longer.

Sophia and Francesca often exchanged the tidbits of gossip *Signora* Accardi dropped within the hearing of one or the other of them. Much of it concerned the daily drama of her marriage to Luca Accardi. Now, Sophia pretended not to overhear the exchange between Luca Accardi and the young man who seemed in charge of the handover of the yacht to its new owner.

"*Sì*, it is as we agreed." Luca inclined his head. "*Grazie*. I will mention your attention to detail to my friends and to your employers."

"You are too kind, *signor*. Are you then prepared to transfer the balance of funds to my employer?"

Luca slid his phone out of his breast coat pocket. "Of course. I have the routing number programmed. One moment, please."

He used facial recognition to log into his bank's app and a text to his phone to complete the two-factor security measures. Sophia, out of the corner of her eye, saw his sharp intake of breath and his frown.

"Is everything all right, *Signor* Accardi?" their host asked.

"I, ah . . . *chiedo scusa*, please. One moment. I must . . . make a call." Luca walked down the pier a few yards, waiting for the call to connect. When it did, he bent over his phone and spoke into it for nearly a minute. Suddenly he shouted a curse. Every eye on the dock turned toward him.

"That is *bleeping* impossible! My balance yesterday was more than eight-hundred million!" More cursing and shouting followed . . . then ended in silence.

Sophia felt a chill run through her as she watched him make another call . . . and another, his conversations short and terse. His fourth and final call took more time. She dropped her gaze to the dock, but used her peripheral vision to scan the armed guards around them.

The tenor within the boathouse had altered subtly.

The young man motioned to one of the guards. He immediately spoke into a radio. Luca's security team tensed, as did the guards. Sophia saw the precise moment her employer lost control over the situation.

Luca, however, was preoccupied with his call. He was still talking when he walked back to their host. "Do we know who or how? No? Yes, I understand. We will await your call after which we will join you and the others."

He disconnected, faced their host, and shrugged, an inimitable Italian gesture that signaled *così è la vita*, or "that's life."

"We have been overtaken by an unforeseen difficulty. My party will return to our hotel. In a day or two, when the affair is remedied, we will come back."

The young man nodded slowly. "You are unable to transfer the payment balance at this time, *Signor* Accardi?"

Luca cleared his throat. "As I said, an unforeseen difficulty. We will return to our hotel."

The young man again nodded, as if coming to a considered decision. "I regret that this unfortunate turn of events precludes such an option, *signor*. Since you are unable to make your payment, my friends and I must make other arrangements."

Luca frowned and opened his mouth—only to have the young man raise a threatening finger to his face.

"Shush, *signor*. Be very quiet, yes? You had planned, I think, to escape a disaster even worse than this accursed virus? In other words, you filthy rich intended to survive while we whom you consider your inferiors should perish?"

He gestured and, across the dock, his armed guards raised their weapons before the six men of Luca's security team could lift theirs.

"It is regrettable that you will no longer require the safety of this yacht and the survival provisions you planned and detailed so minutely. Therefore, my friends and I have elected to escape as you had intended . . . in your stead."

Luca, finally sensing the impending sea change, reacted quickly. "No, you will need me! You won't know where to go—"

"Go? You have provisioned the ship well. We have enough to remain at sea for at least two months—longer if we take on more cargo at the first opportunity. I think we shall do quite well without you and your simpering assistant."

A guard grasped Sophia's arm and dragged her away from the Accardi security detail. "Stop!" she protested. "Let me go!"

When Sophia struggled to pull herself lose from the guard's grasp, he backhanded her across her face. Sparkling lights flashed before her eyes. She crumpled onto the deck and blanked out momentarily.

Her consciousness returned to the *pop pop pop* of rapid gunfire. Through a haze, she saw Luca Accardi and Edwardo's shredded bodies fall to the dock. The men of Luca's security detail danced to a hail of bullets before they, too, fell. The young man's guards shot them several more times for good measure then rolled them off the dock into the murky water.

"No . . ." Sophia moaned.

The suave young man glanced toward her and smiled. "Don't worry, my dear. We will take you along with us, you and the women already aboard. My men will require distraction during our long sojourn at sea."

⌘

THE NANOMITES ENDED THE SESSION, and I returned to the dojo, my throat choking on fear and distress. I leaned against the wall while my heart slowed from a panic-stricken free-for-all to a measly anxious gallop.

Gamble was in rougher shape. He was a yard away, on his hands and knees, puking up his guts.

We didn't speak for several minutes. I had to wait for the earth to stop spinning under my feet. Gamble crawled a few feet from the ick and collapsed onto the dojo's floor. As far as I could tell, he was either sleeping or barely conscious.

When I could manage it, I fetched him a glass of water. He seemed better when I returned with it. At least his eyes were open. After a bit, he sat up. Drank the water.

"Sorry about the mess. I'll clean it up . . . soon."

Finally, I broached the subject. "Those poor people. And what does that scene mean?"

Gamble's mouth tightened. "This Accardi fellow was headed into the Atlantic with enough provision for two or more months at sea? What does he know that we don't know? What is coming that we know nothing about?"

The nanomites again flowed over us and spoke. *Jayda Cruz, Ross Gamble, we rank Luca Accardi among the top twenty Global Community leaders. Although he is not the first GC leader scheduled to depart today nor the last, he **is** the forty-third GC leader to make radical travel arrangements in the past five days. Arrangements for GC leaders extend forward for weeks.*

"Gamble, you're right. They're bugging out," I breathed. "But where are they going?"

Jayda Cruz, we scanned the yacht's navigation plot. Luca Accardi's yacht was headed for the Canary Islands.

I frowned, skimmed over a map in the warehouse, and plotted a course from Genoa to the Canary Islands. "That doesn't tell us much. The Canary Islands are the hopping off point for just about anywhere in the Atlantic.

After I'd caught Gamble up, his forehead creased in deep thought.

"Bet I know what you're thinking," I muttered. "That scene with the yacht?"

"Yeah, the one with the little twerp calling the shots at the end."

"*Calling the shots?* Eww!"

Gamble shook his head. "Sorry. Unintentional pun. But didn't that little twerp say Accardi planned to escape a disaster worse than this accursed virus?"

"Yes, he did. Then Accardi said something like 'You won't know where to go.' Sounded like Accardi bugging out and taking his family aboard that yacht was part of a bigger plan, a rendezvous with others—a coordinated withdrawal by members of the Global Community."

"But withdrawal from what and to what? 'A disaster even worse than this accursed virus,' suggests the GC is planning something horrendous. What kind of disaster could possibly be worse than the virus, and why would the GC need to flee from it?"

"Global economic freefall?" I asked. "But aren't we already there in most respects?"

Gamble and I racked our brains, and the nanomites suggested several more scenarios, but we knew that, until the disaster appeared, there really was no way to foreknow what was coming.

"What the nanomites can do," I said at last, "is try to locate Accardi's GC buddies."

Gamble nodded. "Yes. If Accardi intended to rendezvous with other GC leadership, we need to know where they're meeting up."

"Nano?" I asked.

We are already on it, Jayda Cruz. We have tasked all available satellites to follow the movements of as many GC leaders as possible. If they are headed to the same location, we will soon deduce their destination.

⌘

THAT EVENING, THE NANOMITES BROKE into my thoughts and said, *Jayda Cruz, Nora Mellyn's press secretary has announced a presidential address this evening.*

"How long until the address, Nano?"

One hour and seventeen minutes, Jayda Cruz.

When it was time, Mellyn appeared. We waited in silence, leery of what she would say.

Mellyn, hands folded on the Resolute Desk, a serene expression on her face, said, "My fellow Americans, this coming week, I will depart for a conference in Buenos Aires. The conference, a truly landmark event hosted by the Global Community, will bring together the leaders of the free world in an effort to confront the very real and immediate threat of global climate change.

"Yes, the time is right: For the first time ever, a majority of the world's largest and most industrialized nations are in agreement: We can and will solve the problem of human-caused climate change.

"Our objectives during this conference will be to agree upon and implement strategic solutions to save our planet. The meetings may take longer than other conferences of this magnitude; however, the time and effort spent will be worth the cost.

"I am honored to be taking part in this historic meeting and look forward to announcing the initiatives that emerge from our deliberations. The gods and goddess of our nation bless you all."

"What? She needed a presidential address for this?"

The announcement's brevity was curious.

So were the nanomites' observations.

Jayda Cruz, we noted two issues of importance as Nora Mellyn spoke.

"What two issues, Nano?"

First, we detected markers of insincerity in her body language and facial expressions when she said, 'The meetings may take longer than other conferences of this magnitude; however, the time and effort spent will be worth the cost.'

The import didn't click with me immediately. "And the second issue?"

Nora Mellyn's words, 'Yes, the time is right' was a code phrase, Jayda Cruz.

"A code phrase?"

I turned further inward and mulled over their observations. A code phrase: *Yes, the time is right.*

It hit me.

I sputtered, "Gamble?"

He and Emilio were playing a hand of rummy. "Yeah?"

"Mellyn said, 'Yes, the time is right.' She emphasized it."

"And?"

"*Gamble!* Don't you see it? It's the universal signal to all GC leadership: *Time to bug out.* Whatever is coming? It starts in a week or soon after."

⌘⌘⌘⌘

CHAPTER 38

THE NANOMITES WERE WAY AHEAD of me. Late that evening, they called me aside, away from Gamble and Emilio. They pulled me into the warehouse and again began to whisper to me.

Jayda Cruz, for more than a year we have mounted a counterinsurgency against the Cabal—the network of wicked individuals who, under the banner of the Global Community, have aligned themselves with Satan to wage war on God's people.

We told President Jackson that what the Cabal plotted in secret, we would uncover and thwart. We told President Jackson we would harass the Cabal at every turn. We would use guerrilla-style tactics and, like a hornet, we would sting them, harass them, take their money, stymie their schemes, and sow discord and distrust among their wicked ranks.

We told President Jackson that this was the work Jesus assigned to us, that we would do our best to combat the lawless forces arrayed against God's people.

"Yes, Nano. You have shown us some of your work. Er, *well done*, by the way. I consider you the preeminent artiste of all counterinsurgencies."

Thank you, Jayda Cruz. We give Jesus all the glory for what he has enabled us to do. However, as you know, the Lord's judgment is coming. Each day, the time of reckoning draws closer.

This is why, from the beginning, we also told President Jackson that our efforts would amount to delaying tactics only, that we could slow the enemy's progress but not end it.

"Yes, Nano." My concern bumped up several notches.

Jayda Cruz, we have listened to and recorded many secret conversations—unguarded conversations that did not take place in air-gapped facilities where we had no nanoarray present to record and report the events back to us. Although we were taken by surprise when Mellyn sprang her coup upon America, we have, in copious unshielded locations, listened in on the enemy's strategies and plans. We have also gathered considerable evidence.

They fell into silence. The angst in my stomach bubbled and fizzed.

"Why . . . why are you telling me this, Nano?"

Jayda Cruz, we believe the Lord has orchestrated a favorable combination of time, place, and circumstance. A door of profound opportunity has opened before us, an opportunity to strike an open blow to the heart of the GC.

They now had my full and undivided attention.

That said, the "us" to which we refer includes you, Jayda Cruz. You are necessary for this option to succeed. Your leadership in this matter is essential to our plans. This could very well be the primary work the Lord has left you here to complete.

A spark, a frisson of adrenaline jolted through my blood. The tiny hairs at the base of my skull and along my arms prickled and stood up.

"Whatever it is, Nano, I am with you."

The nanomites hummed with pleasure. With restrained joy.

Jayda Cruz, we are glad you are willing to engage with us in this counterattack.

Counterattack? Hope bloomed in my heart . . . and as quickly withered when I realized what my participation might mean for Emilio.

Oh, my son! I would spare you more grief if I could.

I stiffened my spine. "Tell me your plan, please, Nano."

Very good, Jayda Cruz. Several weak links exist in Nora Mellyn's GC-allied administration. You and Zander Cruz observed a few of these weak links and commented upon them during Mellyn's acceptance speech and after.

"Do you mean Cathaway? Mellyn's VP?"

Yes, Jayda Cruz. We have also identified the US Deputy Attorney General, Thomas Redding as a weak link in her administration, as well as others in positions directly subordinate to the Mellyn administration's principal leaders. Our plan hinges upon those weak links but also upon two essential factors: the intricate timing of our moves and the prayers of God's people.

"The prayers of God's people?"

Yes, Jayda Cruz. As part of your leadership in this effort and at critical junctures, you will speak to the church, to the saints of the Lord. You will ask them to pray.

"I . . . I can do that," I said softly. "But why—"

Because the Lord himself must move if this counterattack is to succeed, Jayda Cruz.

Chastened, I nodded and said, "Yes, of course. I understand, Nano."

The nanomites then unwrapped their plan. It entailed four separate and coordinated offensives and more moving parts and pieces than most "unenhanced" persons could follow.

For two hours, the mites ran me through scenario after scenario, emphasizing my duties and responsibilities. They were extensive.

Then the nanomites hesitated.

"What is it, Nano?"

Jayda Cruz, we regret to tell you . . . we have confirmed that the missile strike was ordered from the White House Situation Room.

"Mellyn?"

She personally gave the order, Jayda Cruz.

"I see."

They played back their recorded evidence . . . and I realized why the nanomites had not shared specific pieces of evidence with me before now.

I took the information in. Studied it. Tucked it away. Squeezed my eyes closed.

I desperately needed to be alone with my God. Needed his peace.

Lord God, your word says that vengeance—retribution—is yours, not mine. That said, you know my weaknesses, where I am most vulnerable, where my flesh might easily slip and take revenge.

Please mount a guard around my heart, Sovereign Lord, that I might not sin against you.

⌘

I RETURNED TO GAMBLE AND EMILIO and quietly watched them finish their game. Emilio whooped as he went "out" and caught Gamble with a fistful of points.

"I beat you!" Emilio crowed. He shook hands with Gamble, then high-fived me.

Gamble grinned. "I'm still up by five games, dude. Don't get all cocky about *one* win out of six."

Six games? I'd been sequestered with the nanomites that long?

I cozied up to Emilio. Gave him a warm side hug. "What Gamble means is that you're improving. But since you have more to learn, stay humble, okay? But wow! You beat him? Good job."

Emilio smiled up at me. I hadn't seen him smile in days, and it warmed my raw, aching soul. He must have detected a glimmer of seriousness in my expression, though, because his sorrow reasserted itself.

"What is it, Mama?"

"Oh. I, uh, need to speak to Gamble in private, Emilio. Could you entertain yourself for a while? Say, over there where you practice with your glove and ball?"

Those brows of his! They drew down like monsoon thunderheads on the Albuquerque horizon. "How long?"

"Until I call you, Emilio. Take your mitt and your ball and stay over there until I say to come back, okay?"

He sighed. Nodded. Gathered his mitt and ball and stalked away. I took his seat across from Gamble.

Gamble scrutinized me. "What's up, Jayda?"

"The nanomites have proposed a counterattack, Gamble. A gutsy, risky series of moves to fight the GC."

He relaxed. The smile that overspread his face was eager. Wolfish.

"Finally, some action. Count me in. Where and when?"

My expression didn't change. "I will leave immediately. You will remain here."

He jumped up, overturning his chair. "The *blank* I will!"

Hearing his own curse, he immediately frowned. Grimaced. "Wait. Um, sorry about the mouth. I'm still . . . learning."

"I understand. The landscape of our lives drastically shifts when we come into God's kingdom. It's a lifetime of ongoing adjustments."

"Thanks for sharing, Jayda—but you can forget me staying behind. You should know better than to think you could leave me out."

I was careful how I framed up what I said next. "Gamble . . . I need to be frank. Blunt, even. First, you cannot keep up with me. I have more energy and strength than you have, and the mission will likely demand that I travel fast, light, and invisibly."

He opened his mouth; I cut him off.

"Second, I need you to remain with Emilio."

Gamble growled at me. Growled!

"No offense, Jayda, but I'm not Emilio's dad."

I didn't growl back, but what I answered was inflexible. "No offense taken, *Uncle Ross*, but if something happens to me, Emilio will need you . . . desperately. You must stay with him."

Gamble deflated. I decided to throw him a bone.

"Nano, perhaps we could include Gamble in some of our preplanning?"

If Ross Gamble agrees to the discomfort, we could again engage him in an immersive virtual environment where he could listen to our conversation. His insights may prove valuable to our tactics.

Sounded good to me. "Gamble, you know that VR environment where we watched the nanoarray's take?"

"The Accardi yacht debacle? After which I puked up my lunch?"

I grimaced. "Yes, that. If you're willing, the nanomites will bring you into a preplanning session using a similar VR environment."

"Good thing I have a strong stomach."

"Then let's get started; we're already on the clock."

⌘

WHEN I REENTERED THE WAREHOUSE, the nanomites and I were alone. So alone it stung. Would I ever not expect to feel Zander's presence there? Hear his voice there?

Oh, Zander! I will never stop missing you.

Moments later, the hologram of a slightly queasy and green-gilled Gamble hovered nearby.

"Hey. Sorry about the nausea. Hope you can hang with us."

"I'll do my best."

Jayda Cruz and Ross Gamble, first we wish to remind you that President Mellyn and key members of her staff and cabinet are taking a trip this week.

"To Buenos Aires. Some GC conference on climate change," I said, "but that has to be a cover story, right? Instead of this conference, she and the cream of GC leadership are headed to a secure location, a place where whatever is coming cannot reach them."

Gamble mumbled, "That sounds plausible, but where, exactly? Somewhere between the Canary Islands and Argentina leaves a lot of area to cover."

Jayda Cruz and Ross Gamble, we have studied Nora Mellyn's official itinerary. It does not include any side trips away from Buenos Aires; however, Marine One and its standby will accompany Air Force One to Argentina.

I said, "I believe that's SOP for any presidential visit. My thought is that wherever the GC top brass are headed, it has be within Marine One's range of Buenos Aires."

Not necessarily, Jayda Cruz. We are privy to Air Force One's flight plans.

Counter to Mellyn's public itinerary, she will be flying to Comodoro Rivadavia on her second day in Argentina—a thousand miles south of Buenos Aires. Marine One and its standby will again accompany Air Force One.

"Comodoro Rivadavia has to be closer to their bug-out location," Gamble replied. "Perhaps finding their meeting location just got easier."

Ross Gamble, by identifying and triangulating the travel plans of all identified GC leaders, we have deduced the location of their sanctuary—the Falkland Islands, five hundred fifty-four miles from Comodoro Rivadavia.

As the Falklands do not have an airstrip that would support Air Force One, we believe Nora Mellyn and other GC leaders will fly there using alternate transportation. In support of our theory, we have found that a number of smaller passenger jets belonging to Homeland Security have been staged in Comodoro Rivadavia.

"The Falklands! Then what? With all their eggs in one basket, isn't now the time to strike them?"

Ross Gamble, with respect, may we suggest that you err in your strategic assumptions?

Gamble wasn't accustomed to hearing the nanomites, not to mention being directly addressed by them or answering them back. "What do you mean, uh, Nano?"

During the supposed GC climate conference, many heads of state will be geographically distanced from their seats of power. We intend to keep them grounded and incommunicado for as long as we need.

Gamble's mouth hung down. "Wait—you can do that? From here?"

Yes, Ross Gamble. We will accomplish this in several overlapping ways. At the right moment, we will deactivate Doppler navigation aboard all air traffic within a thousand miles of the Falklands and disable the GPS constellation satellite system that planes such as Air Force One depend upon for both navigation and communications.

We can and will hack any satellite in orbit to suit our needs—providing either no navigation or, in special cases, spoofed navigation. Without a reliable navigation system, the GC heads of state cannot leave the ground; without communications, they cannot order reprisals.

*That said, and as we have told Jayda Cruz and Zander Cruz many times, the progress of evil is inexorable. No one can stop what is coming until Jesus himself puts an end to it. Every effort **we** make can only delay what is coming. Slow its progression.*

Gamble grimaced. "Wait—if we can't stop the GC, then why are we planning a counterattack? Why bother?"

You are new to the Tribe of Jesus, Ross Gamble. Perhaps you are unfamiliar with the passage of Scripture found in Ephesians 5:15-17?

"See then that you walk circumspectly,
not as fools but as wise,
redeeming the time, because the days are evil.
Therefore do not be unwise,
but understand what the will of the Lord is."

"All right, I admit I'm a newbie. Don't know the Bible. So, tell me, what do those words have to do with my question? If our fight is doomed, why risk our lives over it?"

Jayda Cruz, perhaps you would care to address Ross Gamble's concerns?

"Sure. I'll take a crack at it, Nano. Gamble, let's start with our objective —our highest objective. What is it?"

He thought for a moment, then said, "We want to win, don't we? Take back our freedom? Our nation? Get rid of the GC?"

"Think higher, Gamble."

"You mean higher . . . as in spiritually?"

"Bingo. When you and Janice came to our house after Zander's message on the wave offering, you said you finally realized no one was getting out of this mess alive. Remember what I answered?"

He again thought before he replied. "Something like, 'Hasn't that always been true?' And 'Is anyone ever going to escape death?'"

"Close enough. See, individually, we tend to think our lives will never end—yet they will. This temporary life ends when we die—and we all die—but what comes *after* is eternal. It's the 'where' that should concern each of us, because, like I said, what comes *after* lasts forever, heaven or hell. What's that saying? *Location, location, location?*"

"You're saying the higher purpose of this counterattack is to give people more time to choose Jesus?"

"Bull's-eye, Gamble. We're not fighting to return America to its former glory, not risking our lives just so we can all enjoy relative peace and prosperity on the earth again. Besides, you were in law enforcement—you know that 'relative peace' is a sham and that America wasn't all that peachy keen before the GC, yeah?

"*If* the Lord blesses our efforts, *if* we push back the enemy and are given an extra year or two? We need to heed those verses the nanomites quoted, 'redeem' that extra time—use it wisely. Use it to reap a harvest before the judgment arrives."

"I'm not clear on the judgment part, Jayda. I thought that was mainly the vengeful God of the Old Testament."

"Sorry to burst your bubble, but God hasn't changed. He *never* changes. He may relent or delay judgment, but his righteous decrees do not change. From the beginning, he made a way for us to come to him, and from the beginning, he's warned us of judgment if we don't pay attention. Here's an applicable quote from 2 Peter 3:9-10.

> *"The Lord is not slow in keeping his promise,*
> *as some understand slowness.*
> *Instead he is patient with you,*
> ***not wanting anyone to perish,***
> ***but everyone to come to repentance.***
> *But the day of the Lord will come like a thief.*
> *The heavens will disappear with a roar;*
> *the elements will be destroyed by fire,*
> *and the earth and everything done in it will be laid bare."*

"God doesn't want anyone to, er, perish?"

"That's his heart, Gamble. He sent Jesus to make a way for us, in spite of the fact that not everyone will choose him. Yes, we are taking the fight to GC—but not so we can sit back with a box of bonbons and binge-watch the next big show. No, our mission is to rescue as many of the lost as we can, while we can. Eking out another year or two of liberty is simply a means to that end.

"Since our ultimate objective is to share the Good News with the lost, what you need to ask yourself is, am I 'in it to win it' or am I in it to save others, people exactly like you and Janice?"

Gamble didn't answer, and I sensed a great struggle within him.

The nanomites and I kept quiet. As urgent as our plans were, we weren't going to rush Gamble. He would be of no use to us in the fight to come if he didn't win the fight raging within his own heart.

I stepped out of the warehouse to check on Emilio. The steady, intermittent *thump* of his baseball hitting the dojo's wall assured me he was still occupied.

When I returned, Gamble spoke.

"Okay. I get it. I'll do my part and stay with Emilio."

⌘

I TOOK EMILIO INTO THE DOJO'S office where we could talk in private. As expected, it wasn't easy telling him I was leaving. He trembled, protested, then became frantic.

I took him in my arms and explained what I'd be doing and why. More than once. I held him as he wept. Told him I'd do my best to come back. Asked him to pray for me and pray for the success of our counterattack.

But after Emilio's initial panic dissipated and he slowly calmed, something else took hold of him: His dark brows bunched up like thunderheads, then drew down into flat, formidable lines.

Oh, boy. I was in for it.

Emilio sniffed back the remnants of his tears. His mouth hardened.

"Sure. *Okay*, Mama."

"Okay, what?"

"Okay, you go ahead. I'll be all right. But just so you know? After you leave, I'll go too."

"Yes, with Gamble. You'll go with Gamble to your grandparents."

"Nope. I won't. I'll . . . I'll run off. I'll go . . . live on the street."

Huh. That was new . . . and unexpected.

"I'll know where you are, Emilio. The nanomites will tell me."

He lifted one shoulder. "So? Don't care. You go? I go."

Under his breath he muttered, "See how *you* like it."

See how I liked it? *It* being Emilio on the street? Not much! And my concern for him would be a distraction . . .

"*Mijo*, please—"

He shook his head vehemently. "I go where you go—or else."

About then, Gamble appeared in the doorway behind Emilio. He folded his arms and stared impassively at me. Dared me to disagree with my son. His accusing gaze repeated what he'd already told me.

303

"*So, you intend to leave Emilio while you go off elsewhere? You're his mom! Won't he feel that you've abandoned him? Hasn't he been traumatized enough?*"

I sighed. "Gamble."

"What?"

I dithered. Finally I said, "We should pack up. One small bag each."

⌘

NIGHT HAD FALLEN. WE NEEDED to move quickly. "Nano?"

We are on it, Jayda Cruz. Head down that street toward those houses. Turn left at the next corner.

We did. A car, its engine idling, sat in a driveway three houses down. We climbed into the car's back seat. A minute later, the driver came out of his house, got in the driver's seat, and drove off.

He didn't notice us behind him. The nanomites had rendered us invisible and dampened the ordinary rustlings and sounds we might make.

The car came to the intersection of Juan Tabo and Central. Our driver turned right, kept going, then at Eubank signaled another right-hand turn.

However, when he attempted to turn onto Eubank, the car would not respond—the steering wheel locked up.

"Hey. What the *bleep* is going on!"

No matter what the poor guy tried, he could not get the steering wheel to move in a clockwise manner. Eventually, traffic backed up behind his car and compelled him to drive on, to keep going straight down Central. At each intersection all the way to Girard, he attempted a right-hand turn. At each intersection, he was forced to keep going.

As he approached Girard, the car made an unanticipated lane change: The car swerved across two lanes of traffic into the far left-hand turn lane—the driver shrieking all the way. Basically, at this point, the car was now driving itself, and I felt sort of bad for our involuntary chauffeur. He turned the air blue, stopping only when he hyperventilated.

I also had to ask the nanomites to muzzle Emilio. The kid was laughing his head off.

We skirted the Sunport and minutes later pulled up to Cutter Aviation's parking lot. The three of us got out, leaving our driver sobbing and slowly banging his forehead on the steering wheel.

I hope he realized soon that his car had returned to its normal operating mode. Like before airport security noticed his behavior.

Jayda Cruz, your flight is warming up on the tarmac. We have made the necessary arrangements. Please follow us.

A stream of nanomites flew out before us. Uncloaked, we followed their flickering trail to a Cessna Citation Mustang four-seat jet. A steward waited at the steps.

"Good morning, Miss Davison. We are ready to board you and your party."

"Er, good morning."

He assisted me up the steps; Gamble and Emilio followed. I took one of the two seats at the rear of the short cabin. Emilio sat beside me. Gamble took a seat facing us.

"We should be in the air in five minutes. Flight time will be three hours, forty minutes. Something to drink?"

"Just water. Oh! Do you have something to eat?"

As usual, I was starving.

"Of course."

⌘⌘⌘⌘

CHAPTER 39

REPLETE AFTER THE BEST MEAL I'd had in months, I slept. When I woke, the sky out my window showed a rising sun. Twenty minutes later, we were on the ground at Baltimore/Washington International Thurgood Marshall Airport.

Jayda Cruz, follow us to your rental car. We will guide you.

I pointed our rental toward BWI's exit. It was early morning, the route into DC strangely uncomplicated by traffic. The virus had emptied the nation's capital. Any government employee who could work from home did so.

But not Congress . . . and not the White House. Their operations continued without much modification.

I drove slowly toward our destination, a familiar landmark. Found a place to park near Union Station.

"Need you guys to stay put. I'll be gone for a bit."

From Union Station, I wound my way to the White House on foot, to all the world looking like my old alias, Kathy Sawyer. As I walked by the White House guard shack on East Executive Ave, Kathy disappeared, and I walked in.

I knew where to go, how to get there.

I stood outside the Oval Office, less than a dozen feet away, staring at the woman who had killed Zander and Bonnie Lu. Abe and Belicia.

I could have said, "Give her a heart attack, Nano," or "Sew up her mouth and nose, Nano," both actions used in the past, either by me or the nanomites on our own volition—aka "works of the flesh," acts we'd committed out of willfulness or ignorance.

Instead, I murmured, "Send the arrays, Nano."

The new nanoarrays were in addition to the single array already assigned to Nora Mellyn. They were specially equipped and tasked, and we were going to need them.

I walked slowly back to Union Station.

Emilio was glad to see me when I returned to our rental. Gamble seemed relieved more than anything.

"All good?"

"All good."

I climbed into the driver's seat and retraced our route to Baltimore.

"Nano, send a text please." I spoke the message and the recipient.

⌘

MALCOLM HELMSLEY, KNOWN widely as Mal, owner of Malware, Inc., stepped from his shower and toweled off. He had finished dressing when a chirp signaled an incoming text. He glanced at his phone's lock screen. Did a double take. Grabbed up his phone, opened the text, and reread it.

Arriving one hour
Meet soonest
Ripley

He sent a quick reply.

Malware welcomes you
to our restored digs

The last time they'd met, his business was operating out of a block of apartments in a decent Baltimore location. They had settled there because their *usual* base of operations (affectionately named "the clubhouse") had been blown to smithereens a year and a few months back.

Before that, Malware, Inc. had operated profitably as a government security services and training contractor, hiding in plain sight in the middle of a seedy warehouse district near the wharves. Their acquaintance with Ripley and John-Boy had changed that.

The unassuming pair had attracted enemies from within the corrupt ranks of the Deep State—enemies that co-opted US military troops and equipment, destroyed the clubhouse, and should have killed Mal's entire crew. But Mal, with his own eyes, saw Ripley and John-Boy fight off their adversaries using bolts of lightning and orbs of exploding electricity.

The memory of that scene prompted his next step.

Mal thumbed a well-used number. The call opened in video mode. "Baltar? I want to see everyone ASAP—just our core crew. No one newer to Malware than three years. Emphasize that I need them here pronto."

Baltar, on duty at the clubhouse's command center, hesitated. "What's up, Mal?"

"Ripley's on her way."

Baltar nodded. "I'm on it."

Mal sometimes told himself that the memories Ripley and John-Boy had allowed him to keep *could not* have been real. He didn't say that to himself today. No, today he tried to tell himself that the frisson of worry he'd experienced when he saw the text was in no way connected to the fact that they'd only recently finished the clubhouse's rebuild and refurbishment.

We just got this place up and running again, Ripley. Please don't bring hellfire down on our heads. Again.

⌘

I SMILED AS I READ MAL'S REPLY. *Rebuilt the clubhouse, did you? Nice. That was a great way of telling me you'd moved back in. I hope hearing that I'm on my way to you hasn't set your hair on fire . . . even if, by all rights, it should.*

I didn't know if Mal had heard about Zander. About Bonnie Lu. Either way, broaching or referencing the subject would be difficult. Downright hard.

My pain is real, but I must continue moving forward.
I have a job to do.

The nanomites' words of admonition had stung me—as they should have. Once I had received them, though, they became a source of strength to me. I called them up when I needed to bolster my strength of purpose: *We are hurting too, Jayda Cruz . . . We are grieving, but we still belong to the Tribe of Jesus. We will do whatever he asks of us.*

I swallowed. *Thank you, Nano, for your faithfulness. Lord? Like them, I will do whatever you ask of me.*

From the outside, Malware's headquarters looked little different than it had the first time she and Zander had arrived to receive training from Malware. The clubhouse's exterior was, intentionally, as trashy and run-down in appearance as its surroundings. The four-story building was but one within two blocks of derelict buildings in a whole district of derelict buildings—many which Malware owned and, therefore, controlled.

Malware's clubhouse differed outwardly from its seamy neighbors in two immediate respects: It was an island set apart from the other buildings, and—if one looked closely—it owned two sets of massive yet discreetly disguised freight doors.

I drove toward the first door knowing it would open for our arrival. It did. I pulled inside, parked, the door came down, and Mal appeared.

"Ripley! Wow, you've really . . . trimmed down, but I suppose we all have. Nothing like a pandemic and worldwide food shortages to yank the slack out of our diets, huh?"

Gamble and Emilio got out and joined us.

Mal grinned; he and Gamble did that guy thing—a handshake followed by pounding each other on the back.

"Hey, Mal. Great to see you again."

"Gamble! Didn't know you were coming, but I'm glad you did. And who's this?" He pointed at Emilio.

I put my arm around him, "This is my son, Emilio. Emilio, this is Mal."

Mal looked back at our car. "Where's John-Boy? You didn't leave him home with the little one, did you?"

I clenched my teeth. *Get it over with, Jayda.*

"Mal, were you acquainted with the Blond Preacher, the man Nora Mellyn gloated over killing?"

"Kinda hard not to have seen the guy, what with him being the only online preacher left in the world and everyone getting a text from him. Almost as hard to miss our so-called president gloating over . . ."

Mal stopped. His mouth snapped closed. He took a step back. "No! Ripley, please tell me . . . no!"

I said nothing. When the tears started, I couldn't staunch them. They ran down my face in spite of my efforts.

"Ripley, we didn't know. A bunch of us had been watching the blond guy, and I suppose, more than once something he said or did reminded us of John-Boy."

"Zander. His name was Zander Cruz. The woman last week who replaced Zander? That was me. Because Zander is dead . . . and so is . . . so is our little girl. Her name was Bonnie Lu, but you knew that. We sent announcements."

Horror flitted across Mal's face. His jaw moved back and forth.

"Mellyn . . . did that?"

"She killed them both, Mal. Took them away from us, along with our dearest friend and another neighbor we were close to. And not long after we lost Janice."

Gamble, through clenched teeth said, "Janice and I got married last month. Four days later, she was shot dead during an attack on our homes."

I wiped my eyes with the back of my hand, and Emilio leaned into me, hiding his own tears. "Sorry. Didn't mean to break down like this. It's only been a couple of weeks. We are . . . pretty raw inside."

Mal put an arm around my shoulders. "Come on, Rip. I'll see you to a restroom where you can compose yourself. Take your time. Gamble and I will be in the training center when you're ready."

When Emilio and I entered Malware's training center fifteen minutes later, Mal met me with a steaming cup of coffee. "Here you go. Figured you'd appreciate a hot pick-me-up. Baltar reminded me how you like it."

"Thanks. I appreciate your thoughtfulness."

"My pleasure. Uh, we've got a gaming room down that hall. One of our part-time guys is there. Been with us five years. Good man."

He tipped his head toward Emilio.

I asked Emilio, "Would you like to play some video games with one of Mal's men?"

He nodded.

Mal led Emilio down the hall, then returned. "Okay, got him settled, Ripley. I don't know what you need from us, but we'll do our best to help.

"Also? Gamble has, uh, already told my crew about Zander and Bonnie Lu. You don't need to revisit that topic unless you want to."

I nodded. Exhaled and straightened. "Is your team ready for me?"

"Ready for *you?* Doubt it, but have at it anyway."

He started to move toward the front of the room; I reached out my hand and snagged his arm.

"Wait a sec. Um, Mal . . . you know those things you saw us do? The things we wiped from their minds?"

Mal stared into my face. "Hard to forget that."

"I'm going to have to tell your crew about me, what I can do . . . and much more. And what I'll be proposing will be dangerous. *Very danger- ous.* At the end, if anyone on your team wants out? Or if someone 'pops' as suspicions? A risk to operational security? I'll need to wipe their memory like before."

"Had me a premonition when I got your text, so I kept our meet to my core crew. You know them all." He chewed his lip. "I'm not going to like any of this, am I." It wasn't a question.

I sighed. "We have an opportunity here. A big one. Something that could, at least in the short-term, change the course of this nation. Perhaps the world. Move us . . . away from the GC. But, like I said, only in the short-term."

"Does it involve getting rid of Nora Mellyn?"

My smile was half-hearted. "I don't know about the 'getting rid of' part—not permanently, at any rate—but totally messing with her? Yeah."

"Can't wait to hear what you have to say, Ripley. I'll warm them up for you."

⌘

AS HE'D SAID HE WOULD, MAL "warmed them up" for me. As he spoke, I watched the guys—and gal—on his crew who had been so overwhelm- ingly kind to Zander. To me. To our baby.

"You all know Ripley, know what a stone-cold operator she is. She has important intel and an accompanying action plan to share with us, so I'm going to need each of you, *right now*, to swear to keeping this intel tight. There can be zero tolerance for any OPSEC breach.

"If you will swear to confidentiality, please stand. If you cannot give me your word, here and now—if you cannot commit to total confidential- ity—there's the door."

His core crew—Logan, Baltar, Deckard, McFly, Dredd, Fiona, Neo, and Banner—stood as one. As one, their gaze cut to me. Mal may have asked them not to bring up Zander and Bonnie, but their eyes betrayed them.

They were brokenhearted. Red-eyed and sorrowful. For me.

Then Fiona muttered, *"Forget it!* I'm giving her a hug," and broke ranks. Seconds later, I was crushed in her "jaws of life" embrace, and our orderly meeting dissolved.

"Ripley," Fiona whispered in my ear, "We are here for you. Whatever you need."

I sobbed, then whispered through my choking tears, "Fiona, we buried Bonnie Lu in the quilt you made for her. She loved it so much!"

⌘

EVENTUALLY, LIKE HALF AN HOUR later, Mal called for order. I managed to pull myself together. We were all red-eyed, so I didn't much care how I looked. Only that I could talk and share what I needed to.

It wasn't an easy briefing. It took hours, first with multiple demonstrations, repeated explanations, and more demonstrations. The nanomites made me invisible. The nanomites turned me into the Asian woman Bible teacher . . . then turned me into a carbon copy of Neo. I drew down on the power in the clubhouse, used the power to lift Mal and toss him a few times in the air before landing him gently on his feet.

Dredd jumped to his feet. "That night! That night when you and John-Boy came here for your first training session? When you dropped me on my can? That was because of those . . . things living in you?"

"The nanomites. Yes, they knocked you out."

He frowned. "Do you know how much ribbing I've endured in the past year and a half?"

I sighed. "I'm sorry, bro."

No one else was sorry.

The team laughed and shouted more insults at Dredd. "Ain't never gonna live that one down, Dredd!"

Deckard suddenly spoke up, realization setting in. "All fun aside, Ripley's explanation clears up a lot of questions. Like how she and John-Boy were able to evade us during the surveillance detection route exercises, and how they were able get inside the clubhouse without tripping our alarms."

"Yeah," Baltar growled. "When we got back, you and John-Boy were playing cards. You made us look like fools!"

Mal nipped the team's growing ire in the bud. "That's enough of the bruised ego business, gang. Ripley and John-Boy had to keep their abilities secret. If you'll recall, they had powerful enemies—enemies who attacked us right here, destroying the clubhouse and taking Mulder from us. Well, we have even bigger fish to fry today, so settle down."

He turned back to me. "Rip? Care to get to the intel and the plan?"

Another hour passed while I shared the nanomites' intelligence, airing multiple recordings they'd gathered. When I finally got to the plan, I prefaced it with, "The action breaks down into four components, two of which need this crew."

Mal caught my eye. "Why don't we break for lunch before we get to the specifics. Anyone else hungry?"

I nearly drooled on my shirt. "You guys have food?"

"Do we have food . . ." Mal snickered. "You tell me."

He opened a nearby door and gestured me into a large kitchen and dining room combo. Wall-to-wall shelves, stocked ceiling to floor with Meals Ready to Eat, lined the room.

As I scanned the shelves, I read the labels: Chili with Beans, Shredded Beef in Barbecue Sauce, Spaghetti with Beef and Sauce, Beef Tacos, Beef Strips in Tomato Sauce, Beef Stew, Chili and Macaroni, Pepperoni Pizza, Cheese Tortellini in Tomato Sauce, Mexican Rice and Bean Bowl, Mexican Style Chicken Stew, Lemon Pepper Tuna, and Chicken, Egg Noodles, and Vegetables in Sauce—each entrée accompanied by every sort of side dish, dessert, candy, and beverage imaginable.

So many foods I had only dreamed of for nearly a year.

"I want it all," I breathed.

I'd explained about my nano-charged metabolism.

Fiona clapped a hand on my shoulder. "Sit here, Rip. I'll fix you up."

⌘

WHEN WE GOT BACK TO IT, I WAS replete, having downed four ample MREs. I felt better physically and emotionally. Mal's crew grieving with me had helped more than I realized. I felt more settled and focused as I set up the four overarching elements of the plan, then drilled down into the two parts where I most needed Malware's assist.

I knew going in it would be a hard sell. As the pieces fell into place, the crew grew more and more still.

Fiona asked in a small voice, "How . . . how do you expect to get into those places, Ripley? And even if you get in, how do you expect to get out?"

Yeah, here we go.

"Like this." I disappeared. Reappeared behind the questioner.

"But what about security systems? Cameras? Locked cells, locked doors, locked down facilities?"

The rest of Mal's crew waited for me to answer.

I chewed my lower lip for a few moments. "Rather than provide the specific means I would use, what if . . . what if I told you that when we first met, John-Boy and I were already on the job, working for President Jackson?"

"I *knew it*," Mal grumbled. No, he had guessed; we had never validated his suppositions.

His crew looked from him to me. Fiona said, "And?"

"Months prior to that, I entered the White House Residence and introduced myself to President Jackson. If it's any consolation, he didn't believe me at first blush any more than you-all do."

"You . . . just waltzed into the White House Residence?"

I nodded. "Many times over a period of months. The nanomites easily overcame the White House's security measures, plus I was invisible. Later, when we moved from New Mexico to Maryland at the President's behest, John-Boy and I removed illegal listening posts from the White House's family dining room, the Oval Office, his chief of staff's office, and other places in the West Wing. We installed our own 'taps' on those working to remove President Jackson from office.

"Want to know why Jackson had an aversion to vice presidents? We thwarted two assassination attempts—and he wasn't up for a third. My point is that the nanomites and I can defeat any and every impediment to this mission. I just can't do all the other stuff on my own."

I chuckled, making a sad attempt to relieve the stress in the room. "Haven't quite mastered the art of being in two places at once—but we're working on it."

The problem was, they didn't know if I was joking or not.

"Wait," Mal interjected. "You thwarted two assassination attempts? Are you saying . . . did you have anything to do with the deaths of Vice President Harmon or Vice President Delancey?"

I wasn't going to answer that question, so I sniffed and turned back to Fiona. "To answer *your* question, yes, I can get into those places, and I can get back out with no one the wiser."

The room grew utterly still. Finally, Mal said, "All right. We're going to adjourn for the day. Mull things over. Get back to you, Ripley."

I had expected as much. "Sure, Mal. If anyone has questions, I'll be around."

No place better to be for the moment.

⌘

MCFLY OFFERED TO HAVE GAMBLE bunk with him in the clubhouse, and Mal installed Emilio and me in our own studio apartment until we were ready to return to New Mexico. That is, if I were still alive to return to New Mexico. If any of us were.

We were comfortable enough—Emilio on a cot, me on the sofa bed—and Fiona made sure Emilio and I ate our fill at each meal. Like we needed encouragement!

"Growing boys need to eat, and we need to fatten you up, Ripley," she said as she delivered two extra desserts to both of us.

Yeah, fatten me up for the slaughter?

"Thanks, Fiona. Say . . . I'd really rather you sat this one out. You have kids, a husband."

She stared hard at me. "My kids and my husband will be enslaved to the GC if we don't succeed," she said with an edge to her tone. "No one gets to 'sit out' an opportunity of this magnitude. If I could tell them what we're planning, I would. It would take the sting from losing me, if they knew why I gave my all. As it stands, all of us have goodbye letters—generic, of course—stashed with Mal's attorney should any of us not return from an op."

I couldn't fault her for her courage. She was willing to give her life—was that any different than what I was willing to do?

No.

⌘⌘⌘⌘

CHAPTER 40

ON TUESDAY, PRESIDENT MELLYN and a number of notable US officials departed for the Argentine Republic. The nanomites, via the several "special" arrays we'd sent directly to Mellyn, kept me cognizant of Air Force One's location.

Truth be told, wherever Mellyn went, we "went" with her. We heard what she heard and, from the arrays' diverse vantage points, saw what she saw. Nothing she did was hidden from us, and every word she spoke was grist for the nanomites' mill.

Moreover, the several arrays were alert and prepared to receive my orders when they came.

Jayda Cruz, Air Force One has touched down in Buenos Aires.

"Thank you, Nano."

The nanomites' announcement triggered the first move in our overall plan—although we were aware that Mellyn and her party would not stop long in that city. From here forward, her movements would diverge from her published itinerary. She would leave the majority of the press corps in a Buenos Aires hotel, taking with her only the GC members preauthorized to travel on with her and the rest of her "notable US officials," all GC through and through.

The next leg of Mellyn's trip would take her to Comodoro Rivadavia, a city just over a thousand miles south of Buenos Aires, traveling by smaller, staged-in-advance jets. From there, Mellyn and party would fly another 550 miles to the "secret" location of the GC's bogus climate conference: The Falklands.

That night, I again drove into DC, but this time I parked near the Vice President's residence. It was time to have a conversation with Lucas Cathaway. I waited until he and his wife retired for the night before entering the residence and making my way to the Cathaways' bedroom.

I stood close to his bed and gently jostled his arm. "Mr. Vice President."

Nothing.

I jostled him again.

He came up swinging and yelling, "Help! Help me!"

No personnel in the house responded to his call—the nanomites had knocked them out cold.

I pointed at the little table and two chairs in the corner of the bedroom. "We need to talk. Shall we sit there?"

Cathaway made a lunge toward the door. I didn't stop him. The door wouldn't open anyway.

He tugged and pounded in vain. Shouted with equal success.

"Please, Mr. Vice President. May we talk?"

While I waited, I sent an array to him.

Eventually, he sat, but not with much comfort in his mind or body. "Who are you?"

"Who am I? Who I am is not important—but I bring you America's best opportunity for ridding herself of the GC—at least temporarily. You are essential to that prospect. Tell me, are you sworn to the Cabal?"

"The Cabal? I don't . . ."

"Sorry. I mean the Global Community. I might be wrong, but you don't seem the type to embrace totalitarianism nor did you appear very happy during Mellyn's election acceptance speech. They tapped you for the job because of the votes you'd bring, not because you were one of them—am I right?"

He eyed me with suspicion and did not answer.

I sat back. "Tell me, Mr. Cathaway, what did they use to gain your compliance? Did they promise you money and promotion? Or do you hide a juicy secret that they threatened to expose?"

"I won't answer your questions. Not going to endanger my family."

"Ah. I see. They leveraged your family's safety and welfare to gain your cooperation?"

He said nothing. Flicked a concerned glance toward his wife.

"She's only sleeping. I didn't come here to harm you or yours. Just to talk. Your security detail is asleep too."

I studied him more closely. "I'm going to play some video and audio files for you, Mr. Vice President. After you've watched, after you've listened, perhaps you'll be more open with me."

As the files ran, he grew more agitated. After thirty minutes, he couldn't sit any longer, and I felt that he'd seen enough.

"What do you think about what you saw and heard?" I asked.

"How did you get these? Are they real?" he demanded.

"Yes, they're real. In a few days, the world will see and hear them. Perhaps more importantly, the American people will see and hear them. How do you suppose they will react?"

His chin dropped onto his chest. "What I think doesn't matter. Mellyn and her GC pals have the government and military sewn up tight."

"Do they? My intelligence suggests GC's government and military strength is mainly at the highest levels, although GC loyalists are liberally sown among the worker bees."

"Your intelligence? How in the world are you getting this information? I didn't know half of what I just saw and heard. I mean, I suspected, but . . ."

"But your position is mere window dressing to Mellyn? She doesn't include you in her plans, her machinations?"

Cathaway clamped his mouth shut.

I shrugged. "Mr. Vice President, what I need to know, *at this moment*, is how you will respond when I release these files to the public."

He snorted a laugh. "No one gets *anything* published *anywhere* without it going through GC censors."

"I can think of two recent exceptions to that rule, Mr. Vice President. Can you?"

He frowned heavily. "The Blond Preacher? The Asian woman who took his place? No one knows who they are or how they—"

He stopped speaking when my features began to morph. As I transformed into the Asian woman, he jumped up and skittered backward to the door. Stopped when he had nowhere else to retreat.

"How . . . how . . ."

I morphed back. "Doesn't matter how I do it. What *does* matter is that you know I can broadcast to the world any time I wish."

I held up my phone. The nanomites had filled it with images of Zander, Emilio, Bonnie Lu, and me. I chose only those of Zander or Zander, me, and Bonnie Lu to show him. I would keep Emilio's precious face to myself. Safe.

I pointed to Zander's photo. "See this man?"

He nodded, wary and watchful.

"Keep watching."

Zander's image morphed into the Blond Preacher; Cathaway's eyes widened. "This is a trick of some kind."

"Not a 'trick,' but a disguise. This man, my husband, was the Blond Preacher."

I scrolled to a photo of Zander with Bonnie Lu, the two of them looking into each other's faces. Laughing. Happy.

"See my baby daughter and her daddy? While you worried about your family, Mellyn killed mine. *On American soil*, that woman sent a missile into our home."

Cathaway swallowed. "I . . . I'm very sorry. Had nothing to do with it. Didn't even know about it until she held her press conference. Like you said, I'm not included in her plans."

Jayda Cruz, we detect no deception markers. Vice President Cathaway is telling the truth.

"Thank you, Nano."

I said to him, "I believe you, sir. So what I need to know, here and now, is this: Are you going to cower the rest of your life in fear for your family while courageous Americans lose theirs? Or will you choose to live or die on your feet doing *what is right?*"

⌘

MY NEXT STOP WAS NOT FAR OUTSIDE of the Beltway on the Maryland side: Deputy Attorney General Thomas Redding's home. Redding's boss, like Vice President Cathaway's boss, was in Argentina.

The third stop on my list was Secret Service Director Edith Bancroft. Her boss, Inez Tafoya, Director of Homeland Security, was also with Mellyn at her so-called climate summit.

While the cat's away . . .

My conversations with Redding and Bancroft didn't go much differently than the one I'd had with Cathaway.

I got the agreements I came for, dropped arrays on Redding and Bancroft, and left.

⌘

OVER THE NEXT TWO NIGHTS, I held multiple nocturnal conferences and dropped nanoarrays with each of my conferees, including Chief Justice Wendell. Only one individual proved uncooperative. The nanomites cauterized the woman's most recent synapses and sank her into a deep sleep. She would remember nothing of our encounter in the morning.

During daylight hours, either the nanomites and I labored over our tasks or Mal and I schemed and planned. If I wasn't out "paying visits" under the cover of darkness, I was working. I felt fortunate to grab two hours of sleep each night.

I presented Mal's people with the layouts of our two joint missions. As we ran through the op plans, Mal and his crew offered adjustments and improvements. I'm no military strategist, so I appreciated their input. On the other hand, I had to continually remind them of how the nanomites worked, what their role would be in the mission. How the mites would shortcut many supposedly insurmountable issues.

I knew how hard that adjustment was to make. I once asked the nanomites to make keys to the DCC office wing . . . only to realize they didn't need no stinking keys.

While I was hiding in Dr. Bickel's safe house, the nanomites changed me. They performed what I came to call "the merge." Soon after, I began to realize how futile my human thinking was compared to the nanomites' abilities. I had to bypass my "old" problem-solving mindset and adapt to what the nanomites could do.

It had been a steep learning curve for me, and it took Malware a minute to catch up, but catch up they did.

I spent as much time as I could with Emilio Saturday afternoon and evening. That night before his bedtime, I said my goodbyes to him.

Gamble had moved his things from McFly's place to our little apartment. True to his word, he would remain at the clubhouse to watch over Emilio for me. Make sure he got to his grandparents . . . after. Stick around to help raise him.

"Mama?

"Yes, *mijo?*"

"I know what you're doing is important, and I will pray for you . . . but please promise to come back. Please?"

"I love you too, my son. What I can promise is that I will love you forever."

Saturday night, we struck.

⌘⌘⌘⌘

CHAPTER 41

WE HIT THE HOMELAND SECURITY detention facility housing Axel Kennedy first. In reality, it was my job to go in, get him, and bring him out. It was Malware's responsibility to pick us up and haul us safely to our next action.

Because the Homeland site was "black," it allowed no cell service or internet. Yes, the facility had hardwired communications and a hardwired security system, and getting into those was well within the nanomites' abilities to shut down or otherwise manipulate and control.

Just not remotely.

Two miles outside the camp—well beyond what might raise suspicions—a decrepit Malware van slowed. I jumped out, rolled, and rose to my feet. Under the nanomites' cover, I jogged the distance to the camp. My escrima sticks in their quiver were a comforting weight resting on my back—just in case.

At the gate to the camp, the nanomites' adaptive camouflage spoofed the camera feeds. They inserted themselves into the other security measures and overcame them.

I slipped through the gate, and the mites guided me through a gauntlet of cameras and motion detection sensors. Half a mile later, I approached the main entrance and laid my hand on the door. The mites swarmed from me, through the doors and walls, into nearby circuitry, following it to the camp's security center.

I waited. Perhaps I didn't wait patiently, but I waited.

It was not wasted time. That sweet, familiar Voice whispered in my ear . . . *Death is swallowed up in victory.*

"I long to understand your meaning, Lord!"

The Voice did not answer me.

I waited more. Finally . . .

Jayda Cruz, we are almost ready for you.

"Mkay, Nano."

Jayda Cruz, we are finished. All systems are down; all facility personnel are unconscious. We will lead you to Axel Kennedy.

The door opened. I walked inside and drew my sticks from their quiver between my shoulder blades, while the nanomites whispered directions to me. It took several minutes to traverse the facility.

"Nano, how many detainees are held here at present?"

Four hundred fifteen, Jayda Cruz.

"Uh, are you able to determine which are legitimate detainees and which are not?"

The records will tell us if a detainee was properly adjudicated, Jayda Cruz. Will that suffice?

"Not entirely. Please note all prisoners accused of committing "crimes" that are protected by the Bill of Rights. I want them released. For prisoners accused of other offenses, check if the judge who adjudicated their case has GC connections. Cross those data points with the judge's political affiliations and work record, Nano.

"Release these prisoners if they have no criminal history, and if they worked in the Jackson administration or were censored and detained because they preached Jesus or criticized Mellyn or the GC. That said, do not release anyone with ties to terrorism."

Two hundred and thirteen detainees meet your criteria, Jayda Cruz.

I was going off script here, but it felt right to do so.

"How long will the facility personnel be out?"

We can ensure they remain unconscious until morning, Jayda Cruz.

"Okay. Let's get Kennedy first. As we leave, release those detainees who meet my criteria."

The nanomites led me through the rabbit warren until we stopped in front of a cell. The cell door clicked and slid back. From within, I heard stirring, then a whisper.

"Who's there?"

That is Agent Kennedy, Jayda Cruz.

"Agent Kennedy?"

A form shuffled toward me. "Who is it?"

"Your favorite invisible friend."

"What? Are you freaking kidding me?"

I tossed him a bag. "Get these shoes and clothes on. We're gonna blow this popsicle stand. And hurry it up."

A minute later, Kennedy and I were jogging through the facility, headed for the front entrance. Behind me, lights were coming on, and the nanomites were selectively opening cells. I glanced back. In every hallway where cells were opened, the mites were scribing on the floor the same temporary message to the freed detainees.

**Leave as quickly as you can
facility unlocked guards asleep
New guards arrive @shift change
Go**

Behind me, Kennedy was flagging.

"Nano, Kennedy can't keep up with me. Please help him."

Three seconds later, Kennedy grunted. "Wow. What a rush!"

"Let's hustle," I replied.

I had the nanomites signal the van for pickup. With no active cameras nearby, it was safe for them to meet us in the parking lot directly outside the camp.

Dawn was near when the van roared into the lot. The nanomites uncovered me. As Logan unceremoniously hauled us into the van and Dredd burned rubber, I looked back. A stream of detainees flowed from the front entrance.

"What's that about, Ripley?" Mal asked from the passenger seat.

"Cover for Kennedy's disappearance and a chance at freedom for those who were denied due process."

"Then I wish them my best. Any problems to report?"

"Nope. On to stage two."

The van roared away. Five miles from the facility, a Black Hawk helicopter appeared over us. Dredd brought the van to a stop on the side of the road and we piled out. The chopper flared and gently set down on the road ahead of us.

We hustled to get inside. The pilot grinned—it was Neo. Mal took the copilot's seat.

Kennedy and I took seats behind Mal, buckled in, and donned headsets.

He asked, "What's going on, Jayda?"

"We're going to spring President and Mrs. Jackson. Want to come with?"

"Absolutely."

The Black Hawk lifted off smartly. We hadn't been in the air but a few minutes before I noticed Neo point at a gauge, tap it, and give Mal a look of concern. That's when I realized the nanomites were sucking juice from the chopper like the sun wasn't going to rise this morning.

"Hey, Mal?"

"Busy here, Rip," he growled.

"Power fluctuations?"

He looked back at me. "What do you know?"

"I know the nanomites are topping off their reserves. They expended a lot of energy back there, and the sun isn't up yet."

Jayda Cruz, we will not adversely affect the helicopter.

"They said they won't damage the chopper."

Neo cranked his head around to stare at me. "You sure?"

"Yup."

"Okay, then."

Kennedy was watching me. He was shaky and pale.

"You okay?"

"Could ask the same of you. You're thin and wiry as a whip, about half what you were the last time I saw you."

"Like the rest of the world, I haven't been eating high on the hog lately—but don't deflect. How are you, Agent Kennedy?"

He slowly shook his head. "Frankly? I'd given up. Believed I would die in that place. I . . . thank you for getting me out, Jayda."

"It was my honor, Agent Kennedy."

Mal had been listening, and he must have remembered my accelerated metabolism. "Logan? Pass some protein bars to Ripley."

I hadn't realized it, but I was in need of fuel too. As soon as I sank my teeth into the first of three bars, I chomped down on it like the nanomites had sucked down on the Black Hawk's electrical system.

Kennedy eyed me. I offered him a bar, and he tore into it with gusto.

Logan passed two more to us. "Eat up, Rip. Need to put some meat back on those bones."

"Thanks, Logan. I appreciate it."

Kennedy swallowed his third bite and asked, "You know where they're keeping the President?"

"Yes. In plain sight."

⌘

THE JACKSONS WERE BEING HELD in accommodations more suitable to a former president than the Homeland detention facility we'd just left. According to the nanomites, the target was a genteel old thoroughbred stud farm in West Virginia, about one hundred thirty miles from the detention facility. The two-story farmhouse, a barn, and outbuildings were surrounded by acres of grass, alfalfa, and paddocks.

From the air, miles away and softly illuminated by early morning light, the property looked like an Amish quilt or a Charles Wysocki Americana-type puzzle.

"That's it," I said, pointing it out to Kennedy.

"I know that place! Secret Service facility. Half a mile of open ground all the way around. No way are we sneaking up on them."

"It gets better. They've bivouacked a squad of thirteen Marines behind the barn to supplement the regular security personnel—a squad leader and three fireteams of four. Apparently, Mellyn *really* doesn't want any Jackson supporters trying to spring the President and his wife."

A dubious expression shadowed Kennedy's face. "And this crew is going to break him out?"

"Only as a last resort. I prefer stealthier tactics."

We didn't approach any closer to the target. Instead, Neo set the Black Hawk down in a spacious meadow ten miles away where two vans waited for us, rear doors open wide, piles of flak jackets and armament on display.

We piled out of the helicopter, geared up, and scrambled for seats in the vans. Kennedy followed me into the van Mal and I were assigned to.

Fiona smiled from the driver's seat. "Hey, Ripley. All good?"

I nodded. "By the grace of God."

Mal tapped Fiona on the shoulder. "Let's roll."

Our van would pass by the property, the long driveway leading to it on our left, continue on, then park a mile distant. The other van would wait a mile the opposite direction of the property's road. As we approached the drive, I got up. Slipped on my quiver.

Kennedy grabbed my arm. "What are you doing?"

"My job," I said.

Dredd threw open the sliding door on the right. "God speed, Ripley."

"Thank you. To him be all the glory."

I leapt from the van, tucked and rolled as I landed. The nanomites padded my impact with the ground. When I came out of my roll, they had already covered me.

With my escrima sticks bouncing comfortably in their quiver on my back, I sprinted down the road.

⌘

THE TREE-LINED DRIVE RAN DUE EAST, straight into the rising sun. The sun's rays warmed my face. A stream of Delta tribe members burst from my chest, their solar panels fully deployed, soaking up the sunlight. In controlled bursts, they aimed their lasers onto the backs of each other's panels, propelling themselves onward.

From fifty yards or so in front of me, they reconnoitered and apprised me of what they found ahead. As I ran, they cushioned the sound of my feet hitting the ground.

Jayda Cruz, you are about to enter camera coverage. We have spotted two guards a hundred yards down the road. We will dispatch them before you arrive.

"Thanks, Nano."

I stopped when I came upon the two guards sprawled on the side of the road. They were part of the Marine detachment and armed for bear.

Jayda Cruz, we will guide you to the rest of the Marines.

I reached behind me and pulled my sticks from their quiver. Using my sticks would be less visible, less likely to attract attention than "zapping" people would be. On the other hand, from close range, the nanomites could drop someone without a sound, without any fireworks at all.

The nanomites led me off the road and along a path probably used by the sentries. The path followed the property's perimeter but stayed within the tree line a distance of twenty yards.

I encountered a single unconscious Marine guard as the path wound forward. Then the path split, and the right fork wended toward the barn.

Jayda Cruz, we count eight Marines in their camp on the opposite side of the barn.

I crept closer, edging around the corner of the barn and down its side. When I peered around that corner, I saw them. Two were on guard; the other six were eating breakfast—the same kinds of MREs we ate at Malware's clubhouse.

"Supposed to be thirteen Marines, Nano. Where are the two missing ones?"

They are walking the perimeter on the back and opposite side of the property, Jayda Cruz. We have sent our members into the house's command center now and have control of it. We are watching the perimeter from there.

"Are the Marines I'm watching visible to the Secret Service detail?"

Affirmative, Jayda Cruz. We have eyes on six Secret Service agents. Three are eating breakfast, one is in the command center, two are standing post on the farmhouse's porch. The agents on the porch can see the Marine's camp.

"And President and Mrs. Jackson?"

They are up and dressed. The house steward is taking a breakfast tray upstairs to them.

I thought for a moment. "Nano, are you able to send an array through the command center to President Jackson?"

Yes, Jayda Cruz.

"If you sent an array to him, would I be able to talk to him?"

Yes, in a manner of speaking, Jayda Cruz

I snarked—the nanomites often didn't recognize their own puns.

"Um, what do you mean?"

We can send a digital recording of your voice to the array and instruct it to play the recording in the President's ears. However, when the President hears you, he may experience temporary confusion. He might not believe that what he hears is real, and you would not be able to respond to his disbelief in real time.

One further factor, Jayda Cruz. Once we send the array and it reaches the camera closest to the President, the array will still need several minutes to make its way to him.

The arrays are slow, Jayda Cruz. Not as fast as we are.

"Huh. Got it. But I think the President will get himself sorted pretty quickly. So, go ahead and send the array. And since you are already in the command center and can spoof the camera feeds, how about we take out the Marines walking the perimeter on the other side of the property while we're waiting for the array to reach the President?"

That would be a profitable use of time, Jayda Cruz, except shift change is coming up for the Marines walking the perimeter. The Marines eating breakfast will go on duty shortly. We would not want them to discover the two Marines we have already incapacitated and raise an alarm.

"Well, shoot. Guess we'll wait for shift change. Let's take out the two Marines on their way to relieve the unconscious guards first, then we'll hit the two replacement guards on the other side of the perimeter."

That will reduce the number of active Marines from thirteen to six. A good plan, Jayda Cruz.

I pulled back. Retraced my route to the road. Hid off to the side and waited. Fifteen minutes later, two Marines approached. The nanomites took them down quickly. I dragged them off the road and dropped them behind a wall of bushes.

We were skirting the barn, on our way to the two perimeter guards when the nanomites spoke.

Jayda Cruz, the array is in position. Please speak your message to the President.

I stopped and composed my message. Thought it through, made a few changes. Spoke it for the nanomites to record.

"Nano, let me know when the President responds?"

We will, Jayda Cruz.

We continued on and reached the first of the two fresh guards on the far perimeter. Took her out. Jogged to the other. Took him out.

Jayda Cruz, we have a response from the President. Please enter the immersive virtual environment to view it.

I sank into the environment. Let it take me.

As before, it was a disturbing, disorienting experience.

⌘

ROBERT JACKSON SEATED HIS WIFE before taking his place at the table in their living quarters. The steward, always deferential, usually apologetic in his manner, placed the breakfast tray on the sideboard and served them from there.

The steward had just left the room when a tinny voice spoke in Jackson's right ear. Jackson started. Dropped his fork in confusion.

"Robert! What is it? Are you all right?"

"Shh . . ." He closed his eyes and focused on the voice. "Quiet, please."

Maddie Jackson watched her husband with apprehension, but she did not speak. Did not move.

The message ended. Without thought, Jackson's military training kicked in and he said, "Repeat last, over."

The array replayed the recording, and this time Jackson got the message in its entirety. He sat up straight and focused on it.

President Jackson this is Jayda Cruz
Repeat this is Jayda Cruz
About to breach facility for rescue
All cameras under control
Pack go bag prepare for extraction
Repeat prepare for extraction

Jackson grabbed Maddie's hand; his mouth curved into a slow smile. Under his breath he whispered, "*Thank you*, Lord God!"

Then he spoke up. "Affirmative. Message received and understood. Repeat: Message received and understood."

⌘

He was repeating the message to Maddie when I pulled out of the environment. Took me a sec to shake off the effects. At least I hadn't keeled over.

"Well done, Nano. Let's move."

Where to next, Jayda Cruz?

"Straight into the house. I want to be in and out with the President and Mrs. Jackson inside of three minutes without anyone the wiser."

We crossed an alfalfa field and entered the farmhouse from the kitchen door. The steward saw the door open then close, and froze. I caught his unconscious body before it hit the floor.

I sent nanomites into the command center to take out the agent there while I dropped the three at the table. They'd finished breakfast and were cleaning their service weapons. I was only able to catch two as they toppled from their chairs.

The thud of the third was loud.

I made it to the front door just as an agent stepped inside. "Everything all right in—"

My escrima stick struck him at the base of his skull before he could see and react to the bodies on the floor. I caught him, pulled him through the doorway, but left the door open. Waited to see how the remaining two agents on the porch would react.

"Hey, Stanton?"

I had the nanomites roughen my voice. "Yeah. All clear. Uh, coffee?"

"That's a yes for me. You, Jimenez? Yeah. Two coffees, please."

"You got it." I closed the door, silently locked it, and laid Stanton's dead weight across it like a doorstop. Raced upstairs, unlocked, and opened the door to the Jackson's quarters. Had the nanomites uncover me.

"Let's go, sir. Ma'am."

They grabbed their bags and followed. We went out the kitchen door, the three of us under the nanomites' cover, rounded the house, and headed for the road. Once we entered the tree-lined drive, I stopped and uncovered us. Got on my phone to Mal.

"Bring up the van; we have the President. I will go back to take care of the remaining personnel."

I said to the President, "Sir, move smartly down this road, please. I'll be along shortly."

"Jayda—"

"Later, sir. Please go."

⌘

LESS THAN FIFTEEN MINUTES LATER, not a living soul was awake on the property where the Jacksons had been held. The nanomites assured me the Marines and Secret Service personnel would be out for hours. My task complete, I trotted up the road to my rendezvous point and joined the remainder of Mal's crew in the second van. Mal's van left with the President and First Lady as soon as they were secure and before I joined Malware's second van.

Both vans took complex routes back to the clubhouse and changed modes of transportation three times. We met up at the clubhouse hours later to grab some sleep before moving on to our next tasks.

Those tasks did not include Kennedy. Mal had dropped Kennedy at a prearranged location. Kennedy, in conjunction with Secret Service Director Bancroft, had his part to play in the coming action.

Yes, we were aware of how high the stakes were . . . now that we'd committed ourselves.

⌘

I HAD GONE WITHOUT SUFFICIENT SLEEP, even for me, for nearly a week. I was fatigued. With no immediate demands needing my time or attention, I swayed with the movement of the van and dozed.

Baltar gently awakened me to change conveyances. I dozed again.

Another change. More sleep. *Jayda Cruz.*

The nanomites' words tugged at me, but I resisted. So tired.

Jayda Cruz.

I roused. Entered the warehouse.

"What is it, Nano?"

Jayda Cruz, the alien nanomites in our custody . . .

I sat straight up.

"What about them, Nano?

Jayda Cruz, the alien nanomites are no longer dormant. They are waking up.

⌘⌘⌘⌘

PART 4: TRIUMPH

When the perishable

has been clothed with the imperishable,

and the mortal with immortality,

then the saying that is written will come true:

"Death has been swallowed up in victory."

1 Corinthians 15:54

Chapter 42

THIS WAS IT: SUNDAY AGAIN, the Lord's day . . . and our "make or break" day. I would be delivering another message to the world—but not a Bible teaching. I would also not be speaking live. The nanomites had insisted that I prerecord *my* parts of the broadcast.

With everything else in our plan occurring in near-concurrent manner, the nanomites' advice was spot on . . . because I would not be the only participant in the broadcast.

You will recall that prior to our rescue of President and Mrs. Jackson, I had paid visits to Vice President Cathaway, DAG Redding, Secret Service Director Bancroft, and a few others, each visit swathed in the dark of night. Those who had agreed to our plan had been assigned parts to play—and the order in which those parts occurred was critical—which is why sequencing the pieces of the broadcast in the most effective manner had taken hours for the nanomites and me to arrange.

The fact was, the broadcast had to come off "just right." It had to be precise, and all parts and pieces had to dovetail into my presentation perfectly. Anything less, and we would fail . . . and all of our efforts would have been in vain.

Then the nanomites, after we agreed upon the necessary elements, had built a video, audio, and document database: the evidence to undergird our presentation and follow-on activities.

The nanomites would stream the broadcast Sunday morning as if it were live. The recording would air at its usual time—10:00 a.m. in Albuquerque, noon in DC and Baltimore, and 1:00 p.m. in the Falkland Islands.

⌘

A SINGLE VAN LEFT THE CLUBHOUSE in Baltimore just after ten o'clock that morning; we believed it better to be early than late. This time I rode with Mal, President and Mrs. Jackson, and (just in case) a Malware five-man fireteam.

Axel Kennedy had left the clubhouse in a different van hours earlier than us. He had his own rendezvous with history waiting for him.

We were a little crowded in our conveyance, but no one complained. I sat beside Maddie Jackson. She slipped her hand into mine and whispered to me, "We will never forget what you have done for us, Jayda. What you and Zander have sacrificed. We will never forget."

I swallowed. *Zander. Oh, I miss you!*

We were nearing our destination when the nanomites sent notice of the upcoming broadcast. For several seconds the van jingled, clicked, reverberated, and buzzed as each of our devices received the same text.

**An important message
to the freedom-loving people of the world
will livestream in ten minutes
<u>CLICK HERE</u> to join**

Mal's crew viewed the message on their lock screens. They slid surreptitious glances toward me, then over to Mal.

Logan asked the question. "Should we watch this?"

"This is you?" Mal asked me.

"Yes. Prerecorded. Won't hurt to watch. It will be . . . informative."

And motivational.

Logan cast his device's feed to the van's little movie screen and sound system. And then, there I was—or rather, my proxy, the Asian lady preacher. Her tired, squishy eyes were more solemn than they'd been last week, but so was her message.

"Good morning again, brothers and sisters in Christ. I wish you a happy Sunday, although I will not be teaching a Bible study this morning. However, at the end of my message, I will be asking for *specific and concerted prayer*.

"That said, I ask all viewers, not just Christians, to please bear with me. As the notification of this broadcast promised, I have an important message for freedom-loving people everywhere.

"Yes, today I address all citizens of the earth. To those who are watching, regardless of nation or creed, I extend to you an opportunity . . . an opportunity to take back what the Global Community has stolen. I offer an opportunity to wage war on the GC—that demonic organization masquerading as a purveyor of good.

"Let me repeat myself: Today, I present an opportunity to the world . . . an opportunity to strike a significant blow against the Global Community."

My proxy let that sink in for a good fifteen seconds. Mal's crew scarcely drew a breath as they waited for her to speak again.

"When I introduced myself to you last week, I said that the man known around the world as the Blond Preacher had been killed in a missile strike. He is now in heaven, at home with Christ and our Heavenly Father. Now let me tell you more about him."

There would be no taking back what my proxy was about to reveal.

An image of the Blond Preacher appeared over the image of the Asian woman. As my proxy spoke, the Blond Preacher's image shifted and morphed. Became Zander.

Malware's crew sighed in unison. I heard sad and reverent whispers of "John-Boy" and "RIP, brother."

Zander's face faded, and my proxy reappeared. "The Blond Preacher's actual name was Zander Cruz. He was the pastor of Downtown Community Church in Albuquerque, New Mexico, USA, and he was an anointed teacher of God's holy word."

Murmurs of "Best I've ever heard," "Sure got to me," and "Closest I've come to believing in Jesus," went around the van.

My proxy took a cleansing breath. "As you can see, the Blond Preacher, the man who shared God's word with you week after week, does not resemble Pastor Cruz. We employed . . . a clever filter to alter his appearance."

On screen, my proxy cleared her tight throat. "Furthermore? Zander Cruz was my beloved husband."

Malware's crew sucked in its collective breath as the Asian woman's image also morphed, leaving me in her place.

"You see now that I, too, have employed a filter to change my appearance and hide my identity. Why hide our identities? Because Nora Mellyn and the GC would kill us for delivering a Bible teaching to all of you."

⌘

THE AIDE WAS TOO NERVOUS to interrupt Mellyn's conversation, but he hovered until she acknowledged him.

"Well? What is it?"

"Ma'am, there's something I believe you'll want to see."

He placed his tablet on the table. Mellyn frowned. She picked up the tablet and adjusted the volume.

"What is this?" Mellyn demanded.

"Just came on, ma'am."

Her companions, GC leaders from Russia, China, and India, leaned in to watch with her.

⌘

IN WASHINGTON, DC, A SIMILAR scene ensued. USSART One, having finished brunch, was looking over the agenda of his duties in the President's absence when a text popped up on his phone. He clicked the link and watched the old Asian woman, sneered as she spoke.

"Blasted Christians! How do they evade our IT gurus! If I ever get my hands on—"

He stopped when he saw the Blond Preacher's image morph.

"What? Easterly was right! We killed the correct guy." He frowned. "I should keep a close eye on Easterly . . . he and that cheesy smile of his will, no doubt, be gunning for my seat on USSART."

His finger hovered over the screen. He almost swiped to close the broadcast.

Almost.

⌘

"I CONFESS THAT I AM NOT THE Bible scholar my husband was. I shouldered his ministry last week not because I was eloquent or prepared, but because Jesus called me to do so and because *I was available* when no one else was.

"May I remind every believer in Christ that *you* are available? Today when I ask you to give yourselves to prayer, please shoulder that ministry, as I shouldered Zander's. Thank you.

"But now I will continue to the main portion of my message."

I stared into the camera.

"I accuse Nora Mellyn of treason and murder and declare her unfit to serve as President of the United States.

"Furthermore, I accuse Nora Mellyn of collusion and cooperation with the Global Community and their insidious infiltration into every part of our society. I accuse Nora Mellyn, the Global Community at large, and those who work on its behest with gross interference in the US elections this past November.

"Please watch and listen to the evidence."

⌘

A VIDEO PLAYED. THE VIDEO'S frame showed a large monitor and what appeared to be an ongoing video conference call. Multiple faces, including the presenter's, stared back at the camera. The angle of the camera, however, was weird and disconcerting. It made the viewers feel like they were inside someone's head . . . looking out.

USSART One's jaw swung open as, with a jolt, he recognized *his* desk and *his* monitor, the faces staring back at him all members of USSART—*his* team and *his* conference call and *his* face as the presenter—*from clear back in June!*

Then his voice addressed the group at large. "We are less than four months out from the general election. You have your election assignments?"

"Yes, sir," a chorus of voices replied.

"I don't need to remind you how important our work is to ensuring Mellyn's election. You will personally answer if your districts do not deliver the results Mellyn has ordered us to deliver. By whatever means necessary, you must ensure that only GC candidates win. These orders come from Mellyn directly."

"As we will be fully occupied during the run-up to the first Tuesday in November, we shall not convene again as a full committee until the week following the election. You may request an individual consult with me if you encounter particular problems or if you require supplemental resources for your tasks. Is there anything else? No?"

The leader lifted his chin to the group in dismissal. "The blessing of the goddess be on you all."

"And on you!" they chanted together.

"USSART One out."

The video crossfaded to a photo lineup of the current USSART membership. Each photo bore a label with the indicated member's name.

⌘

"YOU HAVE WATCHED A SCENE from last June as the Global Community's US Subversion and Recruitment Team or USSART, at Nora Mellyn's direction, planned to overthrow our elections. At the end of this broadcast I will post a link to the video just aired. The folder where this video file is located contains specific state-to-state evidence of outright voter fraud, vote manipulation, and voter intimidation.

"The Deputy Attorney General is also investigating allegations that rogue elements within the US Secret Service, at the direction of Nora Mellyn, abducted President Robert Jackson and his wife, Madeleine shortly after Jackson gave his concession speech on election night. The folder I mentioned also contains proof that the Jacksons were abducted and held prisoner since that night as ordered by Nora Mellyn.

"The amount of evidence proving that Nora Mellyn manipulated the election in her favor and ordered the abduction of President and Mrs. Jackson is staggering. I have provided copies of the evidence to the DAG, who, in the AG's absence, is investigating these allegations. Here is a sample of that evidence."

Video of the farmhouse appeared. It showed the Marine detachment and Secret Service personnel guarding the house, inside and out. It followed the house's steward, carrying a breakfast tray and accompanied by an agent, as he arrived at the door to the President's quarters. The agent unlocked the door, revealing President and Mrs. Jackson seated at their table. The nanomites zoomed in on the monitor bracelet fastened around the President's ankle.

The image faded to another video, this one of Robert and Madeleine Jackson, recorded just last evening in Malware's training center.

"My name is Robert Jackson. Today's date is April 17."

Maddie Jackson added, "And my name is Madeleine Jackson."

President Jackson continued. "On election night this past November, rogue agents of the Secret Service entered our hotel room without permission. They blindfolded us, zip-tied our hands, and brought us to the remote farmhouse you saw in the previous video.

"We were held prisoner, without communication with the outside world, from that night until early today. Our children were threatened with our deaths and the deaths of their families if they spoke out. Today, brave patriots freed us so we might give testimony against Nora Mellyn's illegal usurpation of my presidency."

The broadcast returned to me. "More evidence of President and Mrs. Jackson's kidnapping and illegal imprisonment can be found at the link I provided earlier."

I looked down. The next part would be hard to get through. Nevertheless, I was committed to providing it.

"Earlier I said that the Blond Preacher was my husband, Zander Cruz. That Mellyn had ordered the missile strike on our home that killed him. He was not the only one to die in that illegal military action. Also killed were our dear friends and neighbors, Abraham Pickering and Belicia Calderón . . . and Zander's and my baby daughter, Bonnie Lu."

As the van sped along, Bonnie's brown eyes and dimpled cheeks filled the screen. I wept silently and Maddie Jackson gripped my hand. Audio ran with Bonnie's image; closed captioning of the audio appeared below it.

Nora Mellyn: "This is where the so-called Blond Preacher resides—in this old neighborhood? And his true identity is one Zander Cruz? You are certain, General?"

General Adam Burke (Active), Chairman of the Joint Chiefs of Staff: "Yes, Madam President."

Mellyn: "What are those things?"

Burke: "Traffic barriers, ma'am. Reportedly, Cruz, his family, and the others in the cul-de-sac blocked off the street and formed some sort of commune."

Mellyn: (Laughter) "A commune? How very droll. Well, I want them dead. I want their little commune wiped off the map."

Burke: "You should know that Cruz's family resides there . . . and . . . they have children, a son and a baby daughter."

Mellyn: "Do you refuse to do your duty, General Burke?"

Burke: "No, ma'am. Your orders, Madam President?"

Mellyn: "My orders? I give them with pleasure. *Kill them*. I don't care if his family dies with him; I don't care how many of his coconspirators die with him. I want them dead. All. Of. Them. Dead. *Now*."

⌘

MELLYN'S LAST STATEMENT REMAINED onscreen with Bonnie's image for several seconds before my recorded image replaced both.

"This is my baby daughter, Bonnie Lu. Bonnie was not quite a year old when Nora Mellyn murdered her, murdered her father, and murdered our friends. She did so without due process, in direct contravention of the Constitution of the United States and more laws than I have time to list here. Again, however, if you click this link, the repository found there provides the recording you just listened to and a complete list of the laws Nora Mellyn broke in this one instance."

I folded my hands in front of me. "Now to the most egregious of all Nora Mellyn's actions. You will find in our repository compelling evidence of collusion between Mellyn and China's recently elevated president, also a commanding leader of the Global Community. Mellyn and China's president did not act independently. They acted with the full knowledge and cooperation of the Russian and Indian presidents. What collusion, you ask? The development, weaponization, and release of the virus that, over the past year, has killed millions and devastated the world's economies.

"That is not the worst of it, though. Please pay *special attention* as my next words affect every individual who is a recipient of the touted virus vaccine—a vaccine distributed so far *only* to our most vulnerable populations, the elderly, the infirm, those with compromised immune systems, and those with mental and physical challenges that, according to the Mellyn Administration, make them a burden on our society.

"Listen closely: The delivered vaccine contains nanotechnology, "smart nanobots" that study a recipient's DNA, hack into it, and identify genetic weaknesses. They diagnose the individual's incipient illnesses and structural weaknesses. Then the nanobots write commands to their own memory banks—commands to locate, activate, and exacerbate the identified defects. When the nanobots complete their initial work, they put themselves into a temporary dormant state.

"That is where we were *yesterday*. Yesterday, the nanobots inside of every recipient of the vaccine were dormant. But *later yesterday*, the nanobots began to wake up, to activate. According to the time with which they were programmed, *they are now operational*.

"Soon, within hours, days, weeks or longer, the activated nanobots will execute their commands to exacerbate the defects found in their vaccine recipients. Those prone to stroke, heart attack, aneurysm, and other sudden-death maladies will perish. Those with incipient conditions—hypertension, diabetes, epilepsy, genetic arrhythmias, cancers, pulmonary embolism, anaphylaxis, sepsis, and so on, will experience the rapid exacerbation of these illnesses."

⌘

Mᴇʟʟʏɴ ᴀɴᴅ ᴛʜᴇ Cʜɪɴᴇsᴇ ᴘʀᴇsɪᴅᴇɴᴛ avoided looking at each other. That did not stop the Russian and Indian presidents from staring at them both.

"We were with you on this plan," the Russian president growled, "but you assured us that nothing you did could ever point back to us!"

The Indian president shouted, "Now the entire planet will know why we are here—to avoid contamination by the nanobots until their allotted lives run out! We will be hated by everyone!"

The face of the President of India grew so red that her two aides feared she would suffer a stroke. Both were aware of the woman's diabetes and high blood pressure, that she had already undergone the placement of multiple stents to clear arterial blockages.

They glanced at each other, their unspoken looks asking, *Is that why she is in the Falklands? Is she hiding here to prevent these "smart nanobots" from targeting her own disease-prone body?*

Without speaking a word, they eased out of the room together, their fingers already on their smart phones. Calling home to check on their grandparents.

⌘⌘⌘⌘

CHAPTER 43

MY RECORDED MESSAGED CONTINUED. "Sadly, many of our most vulnerable citizens will soon die. We know of only one means of stopping the nanobots from fulfilling their programming . . . and not every individual infected with the nanobots can survive this treatment.

"A strong electrostatic discharge will kill the nanotech inside vaccine recipients. The charge can be administered by defibrillator or by Taser. Click the link below for the exact 'dosage' of the charge and the safest means of delivering the shock. Be aware that too low a charge will not do the job, and yet not every vaccine recipient will survive a sufficient charge."

Tears gathered in my eyes. "It gives me no pleasure to report this information to you. Regardless of what we do, many of us will lose loved ones in the coming days, and this grieves me deeply. Please consider *who is responsible*. Please consider how they must be dealt with."

My recorded image needed several moments to compose herself before she again spoke.

"Ladies and gentlemen, please stand by. We will shortly go live to the White House where Vice President Cathaway will address the nation from the West Wing."

My image cross-faded to the White House's press briefing room.

⌘

MINUTES BEFORE MY RECORDED MESSAGE reached the part about how to kill the alien nanobots, we arrived at our destination. Kennedy, exercising the authority newly granted him by Secret Service Director Edith Bancroft, had paved the way for us.

When our van reached Pennsylvania Avenue, DC police halted traffic and allowed us through. Guards at the northwest White House gate granted us access, and as the van came to a stop before the West Wing's north entrance, Kennedy and a phalanx of armed White House Secret Service agents swooped down on us.

Kennedy assured us hours earlier that he and Director Bancroft had shuffled White House Secret Service personnel, posting only agents they were certain held no allegiance to Nora Mellyn or the Global Community. It had not been an easy task.

"We estimate that up to fifty percent of our agents are GC through and through," Kennedy reported. "And while I won't allow anyone I'm not one hundred percent certain of near President Jackson, I doubt the GC will just fold up and allow us to retake the White House. We anticipate resistance."

Kennedy himself opened the van's sliding door to assist Mrs. Jackson then Robert Jackson from the van.

His implacable gaze scoured the area around the van for a few seconds before he offered his hand to Maddie Jackson—thus delaying long enough for me to slip out of the van under the nanomites' cover.

The Marine guard came to attention and swung the door wide. Kennedy and his team then hustled Robert and Maddie Jackson to the West Wing's lobby.

I went through ahead of them and jogged toward the briefing room. What I found there was chaos.

I had expected no less.

⌘

VICE PRESIDENT CATHAWAY STOOD at the podium on the room's little platform. He was flanked by four Secret Service agents. Two more stood in front of the platform. The room was glutted with senior White House staff, members of the press pool, Secret Service agents, and a couple of White House technicians.

Conspicuous by their absence were Mellyn's chief of staff and national security advisor—Kennedy's agents had taken them both into custody.

The immediate problem was the press pool—nearly all ardent supporters of Mellyn and the GC. They declined to broadcast Cathaway's address. The White House techs joined their boycott by refusing to turn on the PA system.

I moved toward one of the media cameras set on a tripod facing the podium.

"Nano, will this one do?"

Yes, Jayda Cruz.

While they jumped into the camera and took control of it and the feed, I pulled down power from the White House's supply—not a lot, just enough to gently push back the cameraman and anyone else within a six-foot radius of the camera.

Startled, the cameraman muttered, "Hey! What the—" His entire body began to slide slowly and inexorably away from the tripod. Others within that six-foot radius also slid away. Then a shimmering dome of nanomites came down over the space I'd emptied around the tripod.

The cameraman, freaked out but still curious, reached out his hand.

The nanomites stung it.

"*Yow!*" The poor guy tucked his fingers to his chest and shouted, "What is that? It-it shocked me!"

The press room went silent. They stared at the pulsing "no man's land" around the camera; no one dared approach it.

And with a short squeal, the room's PA system came on. The nanomites were now in full control.

Into the stunned silence, I trotted up to the front, moved around the agent on my right, and jumped up onto the platform beside Cathaway. Touched his arm.

He jumped; his eyes skittered in my direction, searching for me.

I whispered to him. "Sir, please begin when you are ready."

"Maybe when my heart decides to drop out of my throat," he growled.

"I apologize for startling you, sir. Take your time. This is your show."

"The Jacksons are here?"

"Yes, sir."

"Very good."

He cleared his throat. "Ladies and gentlemen, please take your seats.

The assembled press pool, many grumbling and angry, did not comply. Some shouted, "We don't have to participate in this sham!" and "This is a coup! You don't have the authority to supplant Mellyn!"

Others tried capturing the scene with their phones. The nanomites were having none of it.

"You are free to leave," Cathaway said, the PA allowing him to talk over the babble. "But if you stay, you will *sit* and you will *listen*."

The members of the press pool did neither—until the most vocal of them screeched as the nanomites stung them. Again and again. Two journalists ran from the room. The rest slowly sank into their seats.

The hubbub ended. Cathaway began.

"Good morning," Cathaway began, reading from his notes. "I will speak to the American people in response to the broadcast just aired. I wish to directly address the accusations made in that broadcast."

He looked into the camera. "The accusations are true. I will testify in a court of law that I personally witnessed many of the discussions, decisions, and orders to set those events in motion.

"*Yes*, Nora Mellyn and Chinese President Ying, with the knowledge and cooperation of the presidents of Russia and India, weaponized and released the deadly virus that has swept the US and the world. Their objective was to decimate the world's economy, thus making a way for the Global Community's 'unification' of all nations under their worldview and control.

"*Yes*, Nora Mellyn and Chinese President Ying, with the knowledge and cooperation of the presidents of Russia and India, manufactured a virus vaccine that contains 'smart' nanotechnology. That nanotech *will* kill and/or sterilize the most vulnerable of our populations.

"*Yes*, while that nanotech is active, the nanobots will cross over to other individuals and infect them. In other words, those with active nanotech are, at this very moment, contagious. The nanobots will perform the same DNA and physical analysis on those they have newly infected as they performed on the elderly and vulnerable. In response to their programming, the nanobots *will execute* the physically weak and mentally challenged among us.

"So, please ask yourself: Why is Nora Mellyn absent from the White House this week? And although she is 'scheduled' to return next week, why will she extend her stay for two months? Because *she knows what is coming.*

"*Yes*, Nora Mellyn, with the most powerful and trusted individuals in her administration, traveled to Buenos Aires earlier this week, purportedly to take part in a Global Community climate forum. However, *there is no climate forum.*

"Nora Mellyn and more than three hundred of the Global Community's world leadership and their families are presently gathered where they believe they are safe from the nanotech. They are sequestered on the Falkland Islands in specially prepared quarters or on superyachts at anchor in the Falklands.

"You see, the nanotech in the vaccine, once it is activated, has a pre-programmed life of *two months.* Nora Mellyn and the GC leadership intend to remain in the Falklands until the nanotech's programming is complete and the danger is past.

"Let me put the situation to you in slightly different terms: Nora Mellyn and her GC cronies have pronounced a death sentence upon those whose health is less than perfect—upon *you* and *your* loved ones—but they have exempted *themselves* from the same fate."

As the implications of Cathaway's statements sank in, the press room erupted. Media figures who adored Mellyn and had ferociously defended her only three minutes prior, roared with fury. Many ran from the room. Some remained stuck in disbelief and demanded more proof; others called for her head on a pike.

I rather leaned toward that last persuasion myself—although I doubted the media's change of heart would be permanent.

⌘

SIX THOUSAND PLUS MILES FROM DC, in the great meeting room of the facility built by the GC's elite for their retreat from the nanobots, the leaders of the world's superpowers watched the press conference. The Russian president signed to the IT tech to boost the volume. Again.

It was impossible to make out what Cathaway was saying while Mellyn screamed orders at her staff. At least they could read the captions while Mellyn demanded, "What do you mean you cannot reach General Burke?"

The Indian president wanted to hear the aide's response, so she leaned toward Mellyn and subtly cupped her ear while tinkering with her earring.

"Ma'am, we're experiencing a complete communications blackout—and we don't know why. We've lost connection to the GPS constellation satellite system and to any means of communication at all."

"That's impossible! Get me General Burke *this instant!*"

The presidents of China, Russia, and India shared "a look." They discreetly signaled their aides and passed them hastily scribbled orders.

⌘

CATHAWAY WAITED UNTIL THE FUROR ebbed, then he shouted, "Quiet! I have not finished."

The room again went silent.

"I must now admit to my own culpability in these events. The party tapped me as Mellyn's VP because I appeal to the nation's independent voters. Once I accepted the nomination, I was admitted to the many planning sessions that led to this dark day—and I was appalled.

"I tried to withdraw only to realize that I was trapped. They threatened my family, even my little grandchildren. I should have exposed them and suffered the consequences. I am grievously sorry I was not man enough to do so. As soon as I conclude this day's business, I will step down."

Another spate of shouted questions circled the room. It stopped when Cathaway raised his hand for quiet . . . and when twelve of Mellyn's cabinet heads filed onto the platform behind him—the majority we needed if we counted the Vice President's tie-breaking vote.

"I have three short announcements to make; please grant me the time and attention to deliver them.

"*First,* with the concurrence of the Deputy Attorney General, and with the agreement and support of a majority of Nora Mellyn's cabinet and Speaker of the House Monroe, I hereby charge Nora Mellyn with multiple acts of treason and crimes against humanity. I remove her from office effective immediately."

More chaos in the briefing room forced Cathaway to raise his voice.

"*Second,* I accuse Nora Mellyn and our party, supported by the Global Community and with the help of those members of President Jackson's cabinet who are loyal to the Global Community, of subverting the will of the American people by manipulating the general election. We have evidence sufficient to support this allegation.

"Having studied said evidence, Deputy Attorney General Thomas Redding will today file charges in the US District Court for the District of Columbia on Mellyn and those who actively led or participated in the fraud."

At this point, I felt compelled to have the nanomites calm the remaining journalists in the room. Some were practically foaming at the mouth, either with impotent rage or in a frantic desire to be first to break the story.

On a side note, swaying Chief Justice Wendell, Speaker of the House Monroe, and enough members of Mellyn's cabinet to flip on her had required the heavy-handed application of the carrot-and-stick approach: In exchange for their unconditional acquiescence to an early withdrawal from public life, they would receive Deputy Attorney General Redding's promise of no trial or prison time. That was the carrot. The certainty of immediate arrest, was the stick.

Not all of the cabinet secretaries accepted DAG Redding's offer, but enough did. Those who did had probably considered the "head on a pike" reprisals sure to emerge when Americans recollected *which* cabinet members and elected officials had elevated Mellyn to the presidency . . . granting her the authority to press a deadly vaccine upon our most vulnerable citizens. People were unlikely to forget the woman who killed their elderly or disabled loved ones.

Was it right to let these criminals off the hook? Was it fair that they should escape prosecution without reaping the consequences of their deeds? No, it was not. It was, however, the only means of ensuring Robert Jackson's immediate return to office. It was the price of giving the world a reprieve, brief though it might be.

On the other hand, no one promised these traitors a cushy, problem-free retirement. After a suitable interlude, the nanomites would drain their accounts, sell off what meant most to them, and let them experience the deprivations the rest of America were suffering under Mellyn's iron fist.

Those cabinet members gathered on the Falkland Islands with Mellyn were not given the option to bow out gracefully. Eventually, the DOJ would catch up with Mellyn and those hiding with her. At the moment, FBI agents, by order of Deputy Attorney General Thomas Redding, were arresting guilty parties presently within US jurisdiction, those who had acted criminally on Mellyn's behalf.

General Burke, Chairman of the Joint Chiefs of Staff, was at the top of the FBI's list. As *the* highest-ranking US military commanding officer in active service, he posed the gravest threat to Robert Jackson's presidency . . . not to mention the fact that he'd followed Mellyn's illegal order to kill Zander, Bonnie Lu, Abe, and Belicia.

⌘

CATHAWAY WAITED UNTIL HE HAD THE room's full attention. Some of the more frenzied journalists (initially), were currently dosed to the gills with calming endorphins—courtesy of the nanomites—and blinked like compliant little owls.

I doubted their responses would be quick enough to break the news of what Cathaway was about to set in motion.

"*Finally*, again with the agreement and support of Speaker of the House Monroe and a majority of Nora Mellyn's cabinet, I invite to the platform the Chief Justice of the Supreme Court, Peter Wendell . . . and the lawfully elected President of the United States, Robert Jackson with his wife, Madeleine Jackson."

Someone shouted, "You can't overturn an election!"

I think Cathaway derived a measure of satisfaction with his reply.

"In case anyone wishes to contest the constitutionality of my actions today? I'm the Acting President of this nation. I hereby choose Robert Jackson as my Vice President—and by executive order, I appoint him Acting President of the United States in my stead. Sound familiar? And if you don't like it, feel free to fight it out in the courts."

With Maddie Jackson holding her personal Bible for her husband's hand, Chief Justice Wendell administered the presidential oath of office to Robert Jackson.

⌘

I WAS GLAD TO HAVE PERSONALLY witnessed that moment, but when it was over, I left the White House. It would be up to Jackson to establish himself in the Oval Office—and keep himself there.

Blocks from the White House, I rendezvoused with Malware's team for pickup. They had watched Jackson's reinstatement unfold, but all of us were oddly quiet—perhaps shell-shocked is more accurate—as we headed back to the clubhouse in Baltimore. We snapped out of our personal reflections to watch the final bit of my recorded message.

My solemn face looked back at me from the van's little monitor. "At the beginning of this very long broadcast, I said I would ask for the fervent prayers of those who belong to Jesus. This is now that time. Please pray for President Jackson. Ask our God to fill him with discernment and wisdom. Ask our Lord to protect him, his family, and his presidency.

"And please pray for those across the globe who received the GC's vaccine. As I warned earlier, treating the elderly and infirm with enough electrostatic shock to kill the nanotech may be as deadly as the vaccine itself. Whether to treat or not should be decided on a case-by-case basis.

"I would remind you, too, that everyone within range of a nanobot-infected individual can also be infected, although if, physically, you do not meet the nanobots' programmed criteria, they will not harm you. The danger from the vaccine's nanotech will not pass for a minimum of two months —when the active nanobots are programmed to expire.

"Next, and this is quite important, please pray concerning the GC leadership, those millionaires and billionaires cowering in the Falklands, their superyachts anchored in safe harbor while the rest of the world prepares for tragedy on an unprecedented scale.

"Pray and resist the natural inclination to act in vengeance. Instead, ask the Lord how these men and women should be held to account for what they have done. Then leave justice in his capable hands."

Almost done.

My prerecorded image took a deep breath. "Lastly, If you do not know the Lord, and wish to receive his gift of salvation, I urge you to watch my message from last week, which can be found <u>HERE</u>.

"Until we meet again, I declare to you all: I *know* the God in whom I have believed, and I am fully persuaded that *he is able* to keep what I have committed to him until *that Day*. My God will do it; nothing on this earth, in the earth, or under the earth can stop him."

I stared into the camera. "Please hear me: Jesus is coming soon. You can meet him today as Savior or you can meet him when he returns as Judge. It is your choice. Please choose wisely."

⌘⌘⌘⌘

CHAPTER 44

EMILIO WAS WATCHING FOR ME when we returned safely to Malware's clubhouse and rolled into their mammoth garage. I breathed a sigh of relief as I wrapped my arms around him.

He hissed in my ear, "Gamble and I watched you tell everything! You're like the most popular person on the planet!"

I grinned back at him. "Me, popular? Not with everyone, of course. *You can please some of the people all of the time, you can please all of the people some of the time, but you can't please all of the people all of the time.* President Abraham Lincoln may not have been the first to use that quote, but he did make it famous."

Emilio pulled a face. "Never heard that before. Never heard of that guy, either."

"We visited his monument in DC. You know—the steps where the terrorist tried to blow himself up? Below the statue of the man sitting in a chair?"

"Oh, that dude? He was a president?"

What *did* they teach kids in school these days?

From behind Emilio, Gamble nodded to me and cracked a smile. "I just wanted to tell you what a great job you did, Jayda. Zander . . . Zander would be so proud of you."

I misted over. "Thank you, Gamble. To God be all the glory."

"Yes, to him be all the glory," he replied.

Emilio grabbed my hand and pulled me away from the others. He checked over his shoulder, but everyone had moved off to give us privacy. He looked back at me, my boy who was growing so fast, starting to become a man.

"Mama, I been praying for you, and Jesus, he feels really close to me. Like, when I'm lonely and start missing you, Dad, Abe, and Bonnie Lu, I feel Jesus inside my heart."

Could any words be sweeter to a mom's ears?

The mist over my eyes dribbled a little down my cheeks. "I'm so very proud of you, Emilio. I know how hard losing Dad and Bonnie has been."

More like hell on earth.

"But it makes my heart happy to hear that you are growing in your relationship with Jesus. That you are letting him comfort you."

"Yeah. Well, Gamble and I have been taking turns reading the Bible out loud. I don't know how to say some of the words, but he helps me. Then we talk about what it means."

Emilio shrugged. "It's pretty cool."

"I love you, Son."

"I love you, Mama."

⌘

I LET DOWN. I RESTED. FIONA FED ME like a prize hog on its way to the county fair. Mal asked me to participate in the crew's after-action review.

What came out of that meeting was not surprising. None of us were under any illusions. The victories we'd won were fragile and likely temporary. The nation was fractured, our institutions rife with corruption and GC loyalists pitted against those who still believed in and upheld the constitution. Jackson might occupy the White House, but he held the presidency by a thread.

Only God himself knew if this good man could keep the country together long enough to root out the most treasonous elements and if he could reinstitute constitutional law over Mellyn's GC worldview.

And Jackson had to be *so very careful* how he governed. Had to order the FBI to clean house and purge its own ranks of GC criminals, yet had to be sure they arrested only those individuals who had committed crimes for which the DOJ had enough concrete evidence to prosecute them. Meanwhile, the media, fully on Mellyn's side, watched, pontificated, and salivated. They were ready to pounce on any perceived act of political retribution.

While the FBI rounded up the criminals, the lawyers and politicians on the other side drafted lawsuits declaring Jackson's presidency invalid and wrote articles of impeachment for Speaker of the House Monroe.

Jackson had been obliged to take several drastic measures already to prevent retaliatory actions. He fired White House staff loyal to Mellyn and surrounded himself with a loyal Marine detachment in addition to Secret Service personnel. He ordered the FAA to close all US airspace lest a reprisal or an act of terrorism be delivered by air. He summoned the top officers of the military branches to gauge their loyalties to the constitution and judge their fitness to lead in these troubled times.

⌘

ON WEDNESDAY, DREDD AND BALTAR asked if I would lead a Bible study. Five of Mal's crew joined us that evening. We read Colossians 1:13 together, and then we talked about it.

> *For he has rescued us from the dominion of darkness*
> *and brought us into the kingdom of the Son he loves.*

"Two kingdoms," I said softly, "one ruled by darkness, the other ruled by Jesus, God's beloved Son. You'll find this juxtaposition throughout

Scripture. Darkness versus light; wickedness versus righteousness; lost versus saved; deception versus truth.

"Why do we read the Bible? Because within its pages we learn who God is—his nature, his character, his values, and his plans. We learn that he is good, that he loves us, that he wants a relationship with us. We also learn that he is holy and not to be trifled with or made light of, that we should revere him—that is, give him the respect and reverence he is due."

It was a good start. The only edge I had on any of them was that I'd known Jesus longer, and I could point them in the right direction.

I also had to consider continuing Zander's Sunday messages. Like the nanomites said, even if all I did was read the word aloud, it was more than most people of the world had. But I really hoped President Jackson could convince the tech companies to reinstate the web services they'd denied to Christians.

Turns out, being the only online preacher in the world is a whole lot of pressure.

I thought a lot while I rested, wondering, for example, where Emilio and I would relocate when he and I and Gamble returned to New Mexico. We could start with a visit to Roberto and María's little farm. Grieve with them. Take our time figuring out our next steps. Decompress.

At least for a while.

I mean, the GC wasn't dead or gone. It would go underground for a season, rebrand itself, and resurface. That's Satan's MO, the way his people operate.

Like Zander had said in his sermon on delusion: "*Satan's people operate at night, in the darkness, often in disguise. God's people might think things are going along well, but in the shadows, wickedness is churning away. We, the church, must guard against complacency—because evil seeks a vacuum, an unoccupied place it can occupy.*"

I heard Zander's voice in my head. "*And this is why God's word urges us to watch and pray. **Watch**. And **pray**.*"

⌘

THREE DAYS LATER, EMILIO AND I were ready to go home. Gamble was not. I suppose I wasn't all that surprised.

"Kennedy called. Says President Jackson would like me back in DC. To advise and to watch for twitchy stuff. Apparently there's a lot of that going around. The President needs to surround himself with people he trusts, people who will have his back."

"Twitchy stuff? That's putting it mildly."

"Well, I prayed about it. Couldn't sense any peace about reinstatement in the FBI. Mal offered me a spot with Malware, and that didn't sit right either. Then Kennedy called, and the President's offer resonated in my heart. I would like to help him weather the next crisis. Pretty sure there will be many of those in the coming days."

"I can't fault your assessment, Gamble."

Mal had hit me up too. Offered me a permanent place on his crew. He hadn't believed I'd accept his offer, though. The clubhouse was no place to raise a son.

⌘

THE FOLLOWING MORNING, WITH THE blessing of President Jackson and an executive order in my pocket allowing us to fly, Emilio and I left DC for Albuquerque. We traveled the same way we arrived, by private jet, our flight the only exception to America's closed airspace.

The perks of being a trusted friend of the President of the United States.

Emilio and I talked a lot once the jet had achieved its cruising altitude. We talked about what to do next, and yet I felt strangely unconcerned about "what next." I was still decompressing from the stress and grief of the past days, weeks, and months.

"Once we're back in Albuquerque, how about we get a new vehicle and hit the road for a bit. Go see Josh and Izzie and your grandparents, first. What do you think?"

His nod was short, his reply sad. "Sure. Ain't got a home anymore."

"Home is wherever you and I are together, *mijo*."

He considered what I said, turned it around a few times. "Yeah. I'm glad I have you and all . . . but seems to me that 'home' won't never feel right, won't never feel *full* till we're with Dad and Bonnie Lu and Abe again."

I nodded. "I couldn't agree more. We'll have to be patient while we wait."

⌘

AIDEN EASTERLY WAS HOLED UP IN his house, keeping his head down and his nose clean. He couldn't believe the universe had decided to deal him such a crap hand—and after all his devotion to the goddess too!

*Why did I obtain a USSART seat **just before** that *blank-blank* video conference call was broadcast to the entire *bleeping* world? How did the media obtain—**and then broadcast**—photos of all current USSART members, **including me?***

*USSART is as good as dead—along with my promotion—and it was **that woman**, Jayda Cruz, Zander Cruz's wife. **She** did it! She has ruined me! And how did we not know that she was every bit as powerful as her husband?*

The damage was done. The accusations she'd broadcast across the globe had plastered *his* face right alongside other GC leaders.

GC leadership? Except for those in the Falklands, GC leadership had gone underground as quickly as a snake sliding into its hole. Easterly had no idea where USSART One was or what was expected of him in the present situation.

Keep calm and keep your head down, he told himself for the thousandth time.

Easterly jumped at the sound of his doorbell. He opened the feed to his security cameras. A scruffy, ordinary-looking guy stood on the porch, a trunk-sized crate beside him.

The bell rang again. And again.

Easterly finally clicked the microphone. "Yes?"

"Aiden Easterly?"

"Who's asking?"

"I have a delivery for Aiden Easterly. Someone needs to sign for it."

"Who's it from?"

The man stared directly into the camera. "It's from some*one*. I've driven all night to personally deliver it to the . . . Southwest."

Some*one*. Southwest.

Ah.

"Be right there."

⌘

THE ANVIL CASE, WHEN HE'D UNCRATED it, had an envelope stuck to its lid. Easterly pulled the envelope off and read the letter inside.

He found a terse directive, today's date, and a specific time.

Read manual
You cannot miss
Only aircraft in sky

He unlatched the case, lifted the heavy lid, and sucked in his breath. What lay inside was an instrument of death.

No, a thing of beauty.

⌘⌘⌘⌘

THE LAST CHAPTER

OUR JET WAS TEN MILES OUT from the Sunport when I heard the pilot and copilot's panicked shouts through the cockpit door. Emilio grabbed for my hand. The nanomites tensed.

Jayda Cruz . . .

From within the warehouse, I saw what they saw. Something had "painted" a target on our jet. It—a weapon—was flying at high speed toward us.

"Nano! Can't you do something? Anything?"

We have taken control of this jet, but can do nothing that would save you, Jayda Cruz. We cannot reach the incoming missile's navigation to divert it, and this conveyance cannot outmaneuver or outdistance it. Thirty-five seconds to impact.

"Is this the end, then, Nano?"

It is the end of your pain and suffering, Jayda Cruz, but it is also the beginning of joy unspeakable.

I crushed Emilio's hand in mine.

"Mama? What's wrong?"

"Emilio . . . someone has fired a missile at us. We can't . . . we can't outrun it."

Emilio shuddered. "Mama, I'm scared!"

I released his seatbelt, pulled him out of his seat and into mine. Wrapped my arms about him; clutched him to me.

Jayda Cruz, we will miss you dearly. Twenty-five seconds to impact.

"You-you won't be destroyed . . . with us, Nano?"

They did not answer my question.

*Jayda Cruz, we wish to tell you that it has been our honor—**our great joy and triumph**—to assist you and Zander Cruz in the special work Jesus called you to do. You brought many souls to Christ though your faithfulness to him. And now . . . your work is done; the torch is passed.*

Others followers of Jesus—including Ross Gamble, Josh and Izzie, and Dr. Bickel—will answer the Lord's call. We will continue to serve the Lord by helping these brothers and sisters with the special work Jesus has prepared for them.

However, we will not join with them as we did with you. Rather, we will seek to be a friend to those Jesus asks us to help.

Fifteen seconds to impact.

"You . . . you no longer need a person to live in?"

Our nanoclouds matured over the past two years. While manufacturing many diverse and more technologically complex nanoarrays, we also performed significant upgrades to the nanoclouds' tribe members. In short, we outgrew the need for a human host. We did not tell you . . . because we did not wish to leave you or Zander Cruz and cause either of you harm or grief, dear Gemma.

May we call you Gemma again? We have missed calling you Gemma. We will always treasure our sweet fellowship.

They sighed a soft groan laden with sorrow.

Seven seconds to impact. We must leave you now, dearest friend. Go with God.

Three, two, one, Good bye.

The jet jinked violently, and I gripped Emilio harder. The nanomites had shifted the jet's trajectory at the last second—just enough for the missile to plow through the jet's tail rather than slam into its body.

The tail section ripped away, the rear of the plane opened wide, and we were sucked into the thin, frigid, unbreathable atmosphere. A ferocious slipstream tried to wrench Emilio from my arms; it took all my strength to maintain my hold on him.

For a scant moment, I felt icy cold penetrate my skin and steal the breath from my lungs . . . until a layer of nanomites surrounded and cushioned us.

A protective shell of frozen, dying nanomites.

Many nanomites gave their lives in those scant seconds, but not to save me or Emilio. He and I were as good as dead.

They died to save the nanocloud.

Sudden, horrible rupture; I screamed in agony.

Ripping. Tearing. The rending of cells, organs, bones, and blood as the nanomites tore themselves free.

Then . . . nothing.

I still clasped Emilio, but I was no longer belted into my seat. My son stared below us.

I glimpsed something familiar tumbling and falling away. What? Was that my seat, and was that me still buckled in, hanging on to Emilio? *Our "tents?"* Our bodies spiraling downward and away from us?

I blinked. Emilio and I were alone. I mean *really* alone.

The nanomites were gone. I'd felt them leave me, had a fuzzy recollection of prolonged agony as they tore themselves free—or was I recalling the moment I had left my dying body behind? I didn't know which. Perhaps it was both. In any event, I was no longer in pain.

I felt . . . whole. Complete. Strong.

Curious.

And we were no longer falling.

Hand in hand, Emilio and I slowly rose. Beneath us and to the south, I spied the mountain that had defined the last years of my life. I watched the mountain shrink, and the lay of all Albuquerque and Rio Rancho came into sharp focus. It, too, gently diminished as we lifted a bit higher.

Guess we won't be returning to Albuquerque after all.

The realization did not concern me as much as I thought it might—nor did I experience any discomfort. No frigid temperatures, no choking, suffocating thin atmosphere. Only peace and expectancy.

Soon, though, we stopped rising and began to scud along like a pair of happy little clouds. We floated past the tableau below us in what appeared to be a leisurely manner—although in reality we had to be moving at a fair clip.

We traversed the earth, moving south and east, until I recognized the shape of South America below us. It was clearly outlined, the expanse of the Atlantic licking its eastern shores.

We drifted along, descending and moving farther south, following the South American coastline until I witnessed the gentle curve of the earth itself, until the white of Antarctica appeared on the horizon . . . and with it, the blazing approach of the passing comet.

Emilio pointed to the flaming torrent etched on the skyline. "Mama, lookit that! Do you see it?"

How could I miss it? The trail of rock, ice, and fire dominated the southern skyline.

We drifted lower until the dotted islands of the Falklands appeared directly below us. As we drew closer, I made out a large number of ships at anchor and a runway with several small jets parked nearby.

The Global Community's leadership. They have not been able to up anchor or fly out.

"Well done, Nano!"

I was momentarily baffled when I received no answer.

Oh. I forgot. The nanomites are gone.

Their absence felt strangely . . . all right.

Without warning, a majestic being, a glorious creature of unspeakable splendor, appeared in the sky between us and the glow of the comet. He was, without question, the most beautiful entity I'd ever seen.

The man—an angel?—shouted, roiling the air about us. Emilio and I trembled as the roar of that voice shook both earth and sky.

"Come!
You are given power to take peace from the earth
and to make people kill each other."

A slash—*a tear*—split the sky behind the angel, and a fiery creature emerged.

A red horse.

⌘

THE WORLD SHUDDERED AND ERUPTED into war. Taking advantage of the GC leadership's inability to communicate or return from their "climate change conference," the brave citizens of many nations rose up. They fought to throw off the GC yoke and regain their freedom; GC loyalists fought back.

In Washington, DC, the Jackson administration came under sudden coordinated attack. The Washington Monument crumbled and fell, taken out by missiles. The strike provided cover for troops landing and racing toward The White House.

The warnings came too late to get President Jackson aloft. His security detail hustled him into the elevator leading five levels down to the PEOC—the Presidential Emergency Operations Center—the secure bunker beneath the White House. The atmosphere inside the PEOC was controlled turmoil, each assigned staff member working furiously at their assigned tasks, to get a handle on what was happening, to reach the US military command centers.

"Status?" Jackson demanded.

"Multiple strikes, Mr. President, at least one believed to be a tactical nuke. Sir—they've taken out Joint Base Andrews!"

"Origination?"

"Unknown at the moment, Mr. President. No . . . wait. What? From our own nuclear sub? That can't be right—can it?"

Jackson's brow furrowed. "Mellyn's GC loyalists are embedded in positions of leadership throughout the military. Mellyn and Burke's military underlings are attempting to overthrow my administration and return power to Mellyn.

"At any cost, we must not surrender the White House, nor can we ever allow Mellyn to reenter US airspace. But we need more than military might to win. Can we broadcast?"

"Broadcast to whom, Mr. President?"

"To everyone, everywhere. As wide as you can go. On a continuing loop, send this message: 'People of God, pray!'"

The man momentarily faltered. When he regained his composure, he smiled and replied, "Yes, *sir*. Sending now, Mr. President: *People of God, pray!*"

⌘

THE LOOPED MESSAGE WENT OUT; it was picked up and rebroadcast. Where Jackson's plea was silenced, people passed it by word of mouth.

Then the call to prayer was forwarded, *quite mysteriously*, by text message to every device worldwide capable of receiving texts—in much the same way texts had arrived on Sundays to announce a new Bible teaching by the now-deceased Blond Preacher or the Asian woman.

When they heard, believers stopped what they were doing. They bowed their heads, they knelt, they threw themselves face down, they turned their faces to the wall, they huddled in their prayer closets. Wherever they were, they called out to the Lord of Hosts.

"Lord Jesus! We're calling on you. Deliver us from the demonic oppression of the Global Community. Please save us from the encroaching darkness. Have mercy! Please open the eyes of the blind so they might see you, confess their sins, and receive your forgiveness!"

Their tears and petitions rose heavenward, a vast diverse yet unified cry for help.

⌘

I DON'T KNOW HOW LONG EMILIO and I waited and watched, but we were *not* bored, nor did we fret at the passage of time. Frankly, we were both in awe of our angelic companion and happy just to "hang out" with him.

Along with the believers below, we prayed that the Lord would aid every effort aimed at throwing off the GC and that he would preserve President Jackson's presidency. We prayed for many to surrender to the Lordship of Christ.

We prayed until a "new" angelic being appeared. He descended from the clouds into open sky not far from us and raised a long silver object to his lips. He blew on it three times, and the melodic flourish of that trumpet call reverberated long after he finished.

⌘

CRESSIDA HELD HER BREATH AS she stared out the window at the glow dominating the windswept sky, a glow that grew stronger and brighter by the moment. She wasn't the only one glued to the windows. She and her little "nerd herd" had gathered together to watch the historic event unfold.

Across McMurdo Station, was anyone doing anything else? Not likely. The comet was going to pass closest to the earth where the Atlantic Ocean washed the Filchner–Ronne Ice Shelf. That meant here at McMurdo Station, the comet would pass them too—*directly overhead.*

The comet's blazing approach was far too close for comfort. Even Cressida's geek friends had been in favor of getting "the heck outta Dodge" —like a week ago.

Except, by the time the station called for an urgent evac, it was too late. No one had figured on the comet's swooping proximity creating such unprecedented, fearsome weather. Freak electrical storms fouled communications, and the vicious winds raging outside grounded every plane, even prevented rescue by ship.

Cressida was no dummy. *It's too late to get out of the comet's path, so we're stuck here. At least we'll still have the best seats in the house to watch that rock fly by*, Cressie thought. *The best seats on earth, actually— although we might not be here after it passes.*

"What is that?" someone shouted.

They all heard it: a trumpet refrain, repeated three times, louder with each blast. As it faded, the nerds babbled over each other.

Cressida, though, swallowed hard. *What if I had never met my geeky bros. What if I'd continued to party and drink myself into oblivion? The geek brothers accepted me. They loved me as I was—a disillusioned, thirty-something lush. Then they loved me enough to tell me about Jesus.*

Gabe, her favorite guy among the nerd herd, stood up. He had his tablet open to one of those pesky Bible apps from the App Store that kept disappearing and reappearing—here today, gone tomorrow, back ten minutes later.

Weird much?

Gabe asked for everyone's attention. "Listen to this from Revelation 8, guys!

"The second angel sounded his trumpet,
and something like a huge mountain, all ablaze,
was thrown into the sea."

Cressida jerked her eyes back to the comet's fiery glow. "Uh, doesn't that-that *thing* fit the description you just read? A huge mountain all ablaze?"

Gabe laughed. "Yeah, Cressie. Kinda my point."

"Then the comet's not going to pass by? It . . . it's going to hit?"

She again turned her eyes toward the glow on the horizon. *What if I hadn't accepted your Son, Lord God? Would I, right now, be falling down drunk in a futile attempt to avoid what is coming?*

She exhaled. "I am not afraid anymore, Jesus. You have taken my fear away, and I thank you!"

⌘

As the piercing echo of the angel's trumpet call faded, Emilio and I watched the comet do the impossible.

Like when a billiard ball hits the rail of a billiard table and banks onto a new trajectory, so the comet appeared to run into an invisible, immovable wall and radically change direction.

It dove "downward."

It took aim at the Antarctic.

My lips parted in awe and no little terror.

Emilio tugged on me. "Mama! *Mama!* It's gonna crash!"

⌘

Nothing more could be done, Mellyn's people told her. No one would get off the islands until the comet passed; no one could retreat to a safe distance. The seas and the weather would grow so harsh, they predicted, that many of the anchored superyachts would not survive the battering waves and winds.

In response to those warnings, the ship owners and crews disembarked and crowded into the GC facility's conference areas to wait out the storm. Mellyn, along with her staff, retreated to the US delegation's quarters for privacy. The Russian, Indian, and Chinese presidents and their delegations followed suit.

Mellyn struggled to keep her anger and frustration in check. At least from the windows of her private dining room, she had an unobstructed view of the comet's approach. She and her staff watched as the fiery glow south of them crept forward, inching from east to west.

*I could care less about this comet. Get it over with so we can get the *bleep* out of here. I'm needed in DC to rally my followers to take back the White House from *bleeping* Robert Jackson and wrest control of the government from his hands.*

A sharp, simultaneous intake of breath around her brought her back to her surroundings.

"What is it?"

Multiple fingers pointed to the window.

She squinted. *What?*

Then she saw. She understood.

"It . . . the comet's trajectory has changed?"

"Yes," her science officer replied.

"But how is that possible?"

"Does it matter?" He sniffed. "That thing is about to strike Antarctica, the Filchner–Ronne Ice Shelf, would be my guess."

"Well, then what? What happens then?"

The man tittered in her face—he *tittered!* A laugh that ended in a hysterical, high-pitched cackle.

"Oh, don't worry, Madam President. We'll find out soon enough—say, an hour or two after the comet hits?"

Nora Mellyn jumped up. She elbowed her way through the wall of watchers that suddenly crowded the windows and blocked her view. Grudgingly, her staff made space for her and returned their eyes to the scene in the distance.

The comet descended, moving quickly, its body more distinct now, drawing closer and closer to the horizon. Faster and faster it dropped—until it was lost from view.

For seconds, no one breathed.

The impact, when it came, was phenomenal; it made itself known in acute stages. The resounding *boom* reached them first, rattling the reinforced glass, shaking the building.

Then the sky above the impact zone filled with a rising cloud of debris. The cloud mounted higher, a mushroom shape larger than anything Mellyn had ever seen in photos of nuclear tests or the most overblown of movies—growing taller and taller, wider and wider.

⌘

"GABE, HOW BAD WILL IT BE? I mean, we're far enough away, right?" But Cressida found that she was more curious than afraid.

Gabe snort-laughed, then frowned and banished all humor from his face. "Yeah, sorry, Cressie. Don't mean to belittle you. It's just that this thing *might* not be an ELE—an extinction-level event—but it'll be significantly close. A massive tsunami will roll from the comet's impact point up the coasts of every waterway the wave connects to, destroying sea, plant, and human life alike. That wave will build as it approaches landfall and the seabed beneath it shoals. It will crash upon those coastlands and scour them clean."

He grimaced. "Could devastate a third to half of the earth."

"And us?"

"Uh, well, upon the comet's impact, most of the ice covering Antarctica will vaporize." He shrugged. "Then we'll get to meet Jesus face to face. Pretty cool, when you think about it."

Cressida turned back to her view of the comet's approach. "Wow."

Gabe joined her at the window. Swallowed down his reticence. Reached out and took her hand in his. Squeezed it gently.

"Hey, Cressie. Want to share your last moments on earth with me?"

Cressida smiled. *My sweet nerd friends. Thank you for them, Lord.*

⌘

THE FILCHNER–RONNE ICE SHELF was roughly one hundred sixty-six *thousand* square miles. Emilio and I watched the comet plow into the Antarctic where the shelf meets land. The mountain of fire cut through both ice and land like the proverbial hot knife through butter. It vaporized the ice surrounding and nearest the point of impact but broke loose a ginormous chunk of the shelf out beyond what was annihilated—half the ice shelf gone in an instant, the other half loosed from its bonds.

When the Titanic broke in half, the bow and stern were still partially connected. As the bow of that great ship sank into the ocean depths, its falling weight tugged at the remainder of the ship, pulling it downward—until the ship's stern rose high into the icy night air, vertical to the waves.

In similar fashion, responding to the comet's impact, the ice shelf's outer edge flew up, up, up into the sky. For long, momentous seconds, the vertical mass of frozen water hung there, shedding billions of tons of cracking, breaking, shattering ice.

The ice shelf, standing on end, paused. It vacillated between turning turtle—flipping all the way over—or dropping back down.

Sluggishly, ponderously, it made up its mind. The mass began to fall toward its point of origin, a tremendous *slap* headed for the surface of the ocean.

Looking on the scene from above, we could not see the exact moment of the ice shelf's crashing impact. However, more debris and vapor filled the sky and joined the already ominous, enlarging mushroom cloud.

What happened next was not instantaneous nor was it immediately clear. In fact, nearly two hours passed before we understood what we were witnessing.

Out beyond what the comet had obliterated and beyond the thick, roiling mushroom cloud—farther north of Antarctica into the open Atlantic—a wave clawed its way to the ocean's surface. The wave, in unhurried fashion, formed slowly and mounted gently. It moved with deceptive leisure, pushing east, north, and west.

Or at least that's what it looked like from our vantage point—but our perceptions were wrong. The force of the comet's impact combined with the billions of tons of ice rebounding on the ocean water's surface had spawned an absolutely terrifying monster of a tsunami.

We watched, mesmerized, as it revealed its true nature . . . as it reared its ugly, giant head.

The wave's crest rose to the height of a mountain peak. In due time, it shook off its sluggish pace, and put on speed—until it raced forward, stretching its hungry jaws toward the continents on either side of the Atlantic.

Emilio fastened a death grip around my neck. "Mama! Mama!"

I cried out, "Oh, dear God, please have mercy!"

The angelic being with the trumpet thundered aloud.

"Woe to the earth!
A third of the sea will turn to blood,
a third of the living creatures in the sea will die,
and a third of the ships will be destroyed!"

The wave, loosed from the constraints of Antarctica, widened further. It struck the southernmost tips of Chile and Argentina and detonated like a bomb. It stripped all life, every trace of humanity and every bit of loose soil from the land. It left behind barren, scoured stone.

⌘

MELLYN WAS BORED AND IRRITATED. After *two hours* without further evidence of the comet's effect on the earth—*two hours* of putting up with her staff's fearful and unprofessional behavior—she was ready to eject the lot of them from her dining room.

"Big freaking deal! So there's a plume of debris in the distance—so what?" She rounded on her aides. "Take your noses off my windows and find me a way off this rock!"

A few nodded; others acted like they hadn't heard her. Mellyn couldn't tell if they were ignoring her or were so distracted that they hadn't heard.

"Do you see that?" her administrative assistant demanded, pointing toward the plume. "What is *that?*"

Mellyn gestured to her Secret Service detail. They made a hole in the wall of idle personnel hogging the view from the window.

Before she had a chance to zero in on what had rattled her admin, her science officer shouted, "It's coming!"

Mellyn turned to berate him for his indecorous behavior—and caught a glimpse of his backside as he disappeared through the door.

Mellyn sniffed. "The coward," she muttered to herself. "*What* is coming? We're two thousand miles distant from the comet's point of impact. Surely we can handle a little rough weather?"

Her admin jabbed her finger toward the window again. "Madam President! Don't you see it?"

Mellyn squinted in the direction her assistant pointed, but there was no need to squint or point: Where the ocean met the horizon, a wall of frothing devastation sped toward them—a wall stretching in both directions as far as Mellyn could see. As it approached, the wall rose higher, *far higher* than the uppermost point on the island.

Screams and shrieks filled the air.

Some of them were hers.

⌘

THE WAVE PASSED OVER THE Falklands. I stared at the aftermath: *nothing*. Nothing visible remained in its deep wake, not even rock.

The Falkland Islands were gone—annihilated—as were the GC leaders and financiers gathered in their "safe haven."

A phrase from Psalm 139 sprang to my lips.

> *"Where can I flee from your presence?*
> *If I go up to the heavens, you are there;*
> *if I make my bed in the depths, you are there."*

God had answered the prayers of his people. *Definitively*. He, himself, had executed judgment on those responsible for so much death, suffering, and misery.

"Just and true are your judgments, Lord God," I whispered.

The wave barreled up the outline of South America purging the coastal area to an inland depth of ten miles. When it crashed into Curitiba and São Paulo, where the continent juts out into the Atlantic, the wave headed deeper inland, expending its forward momentum by demolishing much of southern Brazil.

On the other side of the Atlantic, the wave struck South Africa and clawed its way toward Namibia and Angola. It devastated those nations and snuffed out millions of lives before continuing up the coast.

I yanked my eyes from the destruction below as the angelic being gestured to me. I was awed again by his splendor.

Wow. He's so beautiful! Why, he's even prettier than Malibu Ken.

I was astounded when he laughed aloud.

"I always did enjoy your quirky sense of humor."

I wasn't convinced he was talking to me. "Excuse me. Do I know you?"

He smiled. "Why, yes, Gemma. I have followed you all your life. Occasionally, I kept you from stubbing your toe."

I knew then that he was speaking to me—and only to me—because he called me by my name. My real name.

"Gemma, beloved jewel, the Lord of Hosts has heard the prayers of his saints—the prayers *you asked for*, as did President Jackson."

His smile warmed my heart.

"Because of the earnestness of those prayers, much of the GC's leadership structure is broken. The Lord has given his people a short season to be fruitful for him while the enemy regroups."

I was amazed. Amazed and still in awe of what the angel had shown and told me.

But I had questions. "How long, please?"

His expression turned serious. "One will rise—indeed, he is already here—a man of lawlessness. Those who dare to trust in Christ will know him as the Man of Sin. The Lord's people must gather in the harvest in the little time that remains. As for those who persist in rejecting Jesus? Scripture speaks of their end.

> *"The rest of mankind who were not killed by these plagues*
> *still did not repent of the work of their hands;*
> *they did not stop worshiping demons,*
> *and idols of gold, silver, bronze, stone and wood*
> *—idols that cannot see or hear or walk.*
> *Nor did they repent of their murders, their magic arts,*
> *their sexual immorality or their thefts."*

He smiled again. "But now, Gemma? Now, Emilio? Come. We must delay no longer."

⌘

WE LIFTED HIGHER. THE EARTH FADED from view . . . but the light ahead grew stronger.

Jubilant shouts pulled my attention aside—to others rising swiftly alongside Emilio and me. Their upturned faces radiated glory, wonder, and joy. Their bodies were draped in glistening white.

I looked down. I, too, wore a gown of white. So did Emilio.

"Whoa!" he laughed. "Way cool!"

The angel said, "Gemma, this crowd, this multitude in white robes with you. Do you know who they are and where they came from?"

I answered, "No, sir, I don't. Will you tell me?"

He nodded. "They are your brothers and sisters, Gemma, the first fruits of the Great Tribulation. Like you and Emilio, they were killed for their love and service to the Lord of Hosts. Many more martyrs will follow, but today, these you see have washed their robes and made them white in the blood of the Lamb."

He gestured to the multitude, and his voice boomed above the tumult. "*Never again* will they hunger! *Never again* will they thirst!"

The throng roared their joyous, riotous approval, and Emilio and I joined them. We flew beyond the angel to the shouting crowds. Faster and faster we approached . . . until I could make out individual forms and could tell face from face. Until—

"Gemma! Emilio!"

I searched for the voice that called our names.

Another shout reached us. "Gemma! Emilio!"

Zander! I saw him, Bonnie Lu bouncing in his arms and reaching for me, crowing, "Mama! Mama!" A little farther on I saw Abe! Belicia! Janice!

I flew to Zander's arms; he held me as only he ever could. Emilio and Abe joined us in a group hug. Bonnie patted Emilio's face, then mine. She touched her sweet lips to my cheek, then Emilio's cheek, over and over.

"Mama," she whispered. "Mee-oh."

"Yes, my darling girl."

Death is swallowed up in victory.

"It is! Oh, it is!" My cup could not contain its happiness. "Thank you, Lord God—to you be all glory, honor, and praise!"

The beautiful angelic creature again called aloud, and every eye turned to him.

> *"The sun will not beat down on them,*
> *nor any scorching heat.*
> *For the Lamb at the center of the throne*
> *will be their shepherd;*
> *he will lead them to springs of living water,*
> *And God will wipe away every tear from their eyes."*

Our joined shouts of acclamation swelled, became an ecstatic roar of praise. It rose louder and louder, and the place where we were gathered . . . shook.

Some began to look up. To point. To weep.

I tipped my head back as far as it would go . . . and what I witnessed swept away everything else.

There. He. Was.

"Oh! Oh, Jesus!"

The End

⌘⌘⌘⌘

MY DEAR READERS,

Thank you for reading my *Nanostealth* series. It has been an honor—*my great joy and triumph*—to, in this small way, strengthen God's people for the special work the Lord Jesus has given each of us. We live in truly historic times. May we be both faithful *and* fruitful to the end.

A note on this book's presentation of the end times: Please remember that this is a work of fiction. As such, I have employed a smidge of creative license with the Tribulation timeline. My objective is to remind the Body of Christ that we have only *now* to share Jesus with others.

Thank you again. I have the best readers in the world—you.

Many hugs,

Vikki

ABOUT THE AUTHOR

Vikki Kestell's passion for people and their stories is evident in her readers' affection for her characters and unusual plotlines. Two often-repeated sentiments are, "I feel like I know these people," and, "I'm right there, in the book, experiencing what the characters experience."

Vikki holds a Ph.D. in Organizational Learning and Instructional Technologies. She left a career of twenty-plus years in government, academia, and corporate life to pursue writing full time. "Writing is the best job ever," she admits, "and the most demanding."

Also an accomplished speaker and teacher, Vikki and her husband Conrad Smith make their home in Albuquerque, New Mexico.

To keep abreast of new book releases, sign up for Vikki's newsletter on her website, **http://www.vikkikestell.com**, find her on Facebook at **http://www.facebook.com/vikki.kestell**, or follow her on BookBub, **htttps://www.bookbub.com/authors/vikki-kestell**.

www.ingramcontent.com/pod-product-compliance
Lightning Source LLC
Chambersburg PA
CBHW060427310726
48977CB00001B/75